THE NEXUS SERIES BOOK TWO

THE COSMIC DIVIDE

THE COSMIC DIVIDE

Copyright © 2024 by Abby R. Laughlin

WWW.ABBYRLAUGHLIN.COM

This is a work of fiction. Names, characters, places, and incidents are either the product of the author's imagination or are used fictitiously. Any resemblance to actual persons, living or dead, events, or locales is entirely coincidental.

ISBN: 979-8-9857247-5-2 (e-Book)
ISBN: 979-8-9857247-3-8 (Paperback)
ISBN: 979-8-9857247-4-5 (Hardback)
ISBN: 979-8-9857247-6-9 (Hardcover Special Edition)

Cover Design: Alexandra Purtan, Fenix Cover Designs
Editing: Magic and Moons Press | Enchanted Author Co
Book Design and Typesetting: Enchanted Ink Publishing

Content Warnings Page

Please note that this story contains themes and situations which could be considered triggering. If you aren't concerned with potential triggers, feel free to skip this page.

This book contains the following;

Foul language
Physical violence
Blaster (gun) violence
Death
Death threats
Brief mentions of torture
Mentions of war
Dissociation
Depictions of grief & regret

While many of these themes are only touched upon briefly or shown in one or two chapters, I would never want you to risk your mental wellbeing while you're reading my book. Please be assured that there are no scenes which contain sexual assault of any kind. In addition, none of the LGBTQIA+ characters depicted are deadnamed or misgendered. I want you to feel safe as you escape into the world of *The Cosmic Divide*.

THE NEXUS SERIES BOOK TWO

THE COSMIC DIVIDE

WRITTEN BY

ABBY R. LAUGHLIN

CHAPTER 1

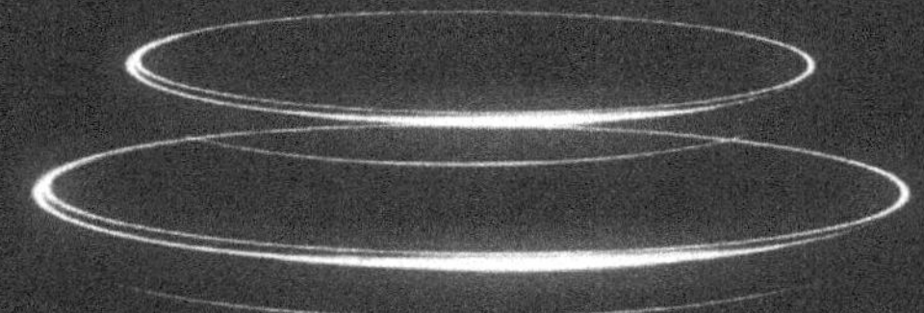

*T*his isn't going to work.

Caldera squeezed her eyes shut, absently rubbing the line of soft scar tissue that trailed down her cheek, attempting to drown out the discontented rabble of the other sector leaders and their political advisors.

The light blue band accentuating her waist and keeping her shirt tucked seemed to tighten with each subsequent breath she sucked in. Matching heels tapped against the floor as she nervously bounced her foot while their voices echoed off the ceiling in the small conference room of Sector Five.

A personal-sized charcuterie plate filled with assorted cured meats, cheeses, crackers, and sector-local fruits sat untouched in front of her, although her champagne flask was completely empty. The strong smell of salt and smoke hit her nose every so often, making it harder and harder not to forcefully push her platter further away as the minutes turned into hours.

It was always the same at the start of the meetings that began after the Council disbanded three months prior. The remaining members had been arrested, and their acts of treason and war-mongering brought out into the light for everyone, including the general public, to see. Five different groups of previously disenfranchised rulers were attempting to band together and effectively run their sectors for the first time in their reign—talking over each other as if they had any idea what they were supposed to be doing in the first place.

It was not going well.

Behind the walls and closed door of the essentialized modern meeting area, the sound of rustling branches from wild trees making up the general structure of the palace hit her ears as animals swung along the branches.

She wasn't fond of Sector Five; while being keenly aware that too much enterprise was bad for the planet, Muléus whipped that notion in the other direction. There was too much wild territory, and not enough developed industry—but due to the weekly rotation, she had no choice but to brave the forests.

"It's the blind leading the blind," Caldera said, leaning over to whisper in Aloriea's ear and trying to ignore the overpowering smell of pine needles. "Nobody knows what we're supposed to do, *especially* me."

"Give yourselves some credit. These are unprecedented times," Aloriea whispered back, popping a red berry into her mouth from the plate in front of her. The shimmery, loose-fitting pastel pink tank top that she wore glittered with the movement. "That's why we're here, to bring you all together. To share your experiences."

"What experiences? We were all oppressed—"

"Excusse me, Queen Caldera, Lady Morin. Iss there ssomething the resst of uss sshould know about?"

Caldera glanced across the table at her political ally, Jasik Okona, the ruler of Sector Three.

Yellow, elliptical eyes blinked back at her, silently encouraging her to share her thoughts as they lifted the champagne glass to their lips, their tailored black suit as crisp as ever. Green-ochre scales rimmed their brow and cheeks, seeming to absorb all the light around them as their snake-like tongue flicked in and out of their mouth between sharp teeth.

"I was just saying," Caldera said, as Aloriea's hand gripped her arm tight, imploring her not to continue—to not, inadvertently, start an argument... again. She shook her off. "I was saying that we need to move on with the proceedings." She glanced around the table, meeting each sector leader and political advisors' eyes. "Do you not agree?"

Aloriea raised her eyebrows, giving an approving nod before turning her attention back to the others and crossing black-slacked legs.

Caldera sighed, the long sleeves of her blouse cinched at her wrists, keeping the light material from sliding down her arms as she leaned heavily on a closed fist. *See? I'm learning.*

"That we should," Eldra Ione, one of the queens of Sector Two, replied with a quick, approving nod in Caldera's direction. Her soft cerulean skin glittered in the fluorescent light of the Sector Five conference hall, external gills clamped tightly closed against her neck.

"What do you suggest we start with?" Mokan Taun, the king of Sector Five, asked. His dark brown skin and black fur blended beautifully together as he sat with his back as erect as possible, ears twitching from side to side beneath his copper crown that was shaped to look like intertwining branches. He was perched at the edge of his seat, like a cat ready to pounce.

"Why would you ask such a ridiculous question?" Desrin Prike, the Queen of Sector Four, replied. Short horns curved backward on the top of her head, as long pale-blonde hair fell down her back. She laced her ash-colored fingers together, red eyes piercing into Caldera. "We've gathered to talk about Earth."

Caldera swallowed hard. *Here we go...*

"Yes... and I stand by what I said at the last meeting. We should make contact. Try to form a treaty of some kind."

Like Quill wanted.

An uproar filled the conference hall, inadvertently scaring the wild animals lingering outside and causing a flurry of branches to smack against the outside walls and roof of the enclosed room. Sector leaders talked over each other as political advisors tried to get their two cents in.

Closing her eyes, Caldera's fingers slid across the smooth wooden table as she balled them into fists. Her resolve hadn't wavered over the course of several meetings, and yet the matter was nowhere close to being resolved. She began to rise, sliding the food in front of her completely aside.

"It's okay," Aloriea said, placing a firm grip on Caldera's shoulder to keep her in her seat and leaning in so she could be heard. "You need to let them get it out."

Caldera gritted her teeth, her shoulders tensing and ears ringing. *No. I'm done playing along.*

"Stop!" she yelled, shaking off Aloriea's grip once again, standing from her seat and causing platinum hair to fall over her shoulders like waterfalls.

The room quieted as all eyes turned to her.

"This is the twelfth meeting we've had about Earth, and we're nowhere close to a resolution—"

"That is because you, along with a few members of your court, are the only ones who have been to the planet," Nari Taun, the queen of Sector Five, interjected.

She donned an identical, smaller crown as her husband and her snow-white fur seemed to shift with an invisible breeze as her bright blue eyes locked onto Caldera.

The black of her pupils tapered in a thin vertical line down her eyes and canines poked out from behind her lips on either side of her mouth as she spoke.

"I—"

"Not to mention you're still harboring two of the inhabitants in your palace," Fenry Ione, the second Queen of Sector Two added.

Eldra tapped her fingers on the table, tilting her head toward her wife, her eyes narrowed.

Fenry shrugged, causing her floor-length white hair to rustle over her indigo shoulders. "I'm simply stating a fact."

"No, you're twisting it," Caldera countered, tucking a strand of hair behind her ear. "I'm not *intentionally* harboring Mei and John Miller. In fact, I'd be more than happy to send them back if that's what's decided. They're the ones being forced to stay on Bersama.

Not even that—they're being forced to stay quarantined in my palace because we can't come to a consensus." She took a deep breath, retaking her seat.

Please don't let this backfire. They need to have a choice... She swallowed hard, knowing full well Mei and John had no intention of returning to Earth.

"They would tell otherss on their planet about our existence," Jasik hissed, their accent on full display.

"They'd come off as crazy if they did."

"So you say," Mokan said. "But as my queen pointed out, no one from this table has been to the planet—"

"Or have even *spoken* with the two inhabitants that currently reside on this planet," Nari interjected.

"Exactly," Mokan continued with a nod. "What are we to do? Simply take you at your word?"

"That would be nice," Caldera mumbled as Aloriea nudged her shoulder.

"It's true," Aloriea said, raising her voice so everyone around the table could hear. "We are the only ones to have direct contact with the Earth inhabitants, but I too vouch for them. If you cannot take Queen Caldera at her word, whether it be because of inexperience or the circumstances of her rise to rule, then take me at mine. Do you not trust me as well?"

You say this every time. And they say—

"Of course we trust you, Lady Morin," Desrin replied, her red eyes gleaming. "You've proven yourself invaluable as a political advisor over the years, but this has nothing to do with personal feelings toward you, Queen Caldera, or anyone else."

Caldera exhaled sharply. *Hmm, Desrin said it this time. It's usually Eldra.*

"It has to do with the very principle of the matter. It is not something that we can take lightly. Our way of life, our very *planet,* could be at stake."

Jasik nodded. "What we decide here will, no doubt, have massive implicationss for Berssama."

"So you think it's best to continue to blindly steal Earth's resources?" Caldera questioned. "The fact of the matter is, what we decide will affect not only Bersama but Earth as well..." She paused. "And I care about the people of both."

"Why?" Desrin asked, flipping her cornsilk hair over her shoulder. "You don't even know them or what they're like."

"I don't need to. They have a right to survive... just like us."

The hall erupted again in a storm of begrudging agreements and counterpoints.

"Quiet!" Caldera snapped, and the roar of multiple voices slowly died. She stood again and took a deep breath, squeezing her eyes closed before opening them and meeting the gaze of each sector leader.

Universe, give me strength.

"The next weekly meeting takes place at the Tellin Palace... I'll formally introduce you to the Earthlings then." She retook her seat to surprising silence, glancing over at Aloriea, whose eyes were wide.

"Umm, well... that would be fantastic," Mokan replied, stroking his long beard.

Nari nodded, standing and snapping her fingers. Palace servants appeared from the shadows, taking the food plates, some of which were completely eaten, most of which were picked at, and one—Caldera's—which was untouched, and drink flasks away in one swift motion.

"We have kept you all too long. The final ruling as of now, on the issue of Earth and the two fugitives, is unchanged. Bersama will stay hidden, and so shall its inhabitants currently residing on Bersama. Meeting adjourned," Mokan said with a bow.

All the sector leaders followed suit.

Caldera stiffly bowed, turning on her heel and rushing out

of the conference room as soon as her hand was scanned by the security guard.

Fugitives? That's a new one, she fumed as she and Aloriea were met by a palace guard and led away.

Outside the sterility and necessitated modernization of the conference hall, the palace of Ozryn—the capital of Muléus—was mostly open, purposefully reclaimed by the surrounding wild jungle. The few walls that held the palace together as a structure were covered in lush green vines, with massive trees forming the hallways—a perfect blend of architecture and nature.

Caldera and Aloriea were guided back to their ship by a palace guard, the calico fur of their catlike legs swishing rhythmically as they padded silently across the combined brick and woodland floor.

This place is insane. This is the third time we've been here and it's no less confusing, Caldera thought, glancing upward and eyeing more palace guards lining the hallway trees, crouching on the thick limbs, completely cornering the market on high ground, cat-like eyes glowing down at them.

"Your ship," the guard said with a fanged smile and bow as the monument of metal came into view.

Caldera glanced up at the bright blue sky through the thick canopy of trees. Transports criss-crossed the sky in droves and, though she couldn't see them through the thicket, she could hear the calls of vendors from the distant markets of the capital trying to entice the patrons to buy their wares.

When did we leave the palace and enter the forest? The sound-muffling tech surrounding the palace is truly incredible.

"Thank you," Caldera said with a nod before sprinting the rest of the way to the already descended ramp and hurrying up it, with Aloriea in hot pursuit.

"Hey, make any progress?" Rennick asked, closing a metal holobook and standing as the two women entered the ship and retracted the ramp.

Caldera didn't answer, settling down hard on the couch and leaning her head back, squeezing her eyes shut.

"I'm guessing not..." he muttered, blowing out a breath. "What happened?" He sat next to her and furrowed his brows, the scar that cut through his eyebrow scrunching from the action. "And for the record, it's kinda hard to do my job as body-guard when I'm not even allowed in the palace."

"Nothing can be done about that," Aloriea replied, detangling curly black hair from her artificial metal horn. "Their palace is a sacred place. Only kings, queens, rulers, and their political advisers are allowed in if they're outsiders."

"Still, I was worried. What if something had happened?"

"They have plenty of palace guards and would take full re-sponsibility—"

"That's not good enough!"

Caldera ran a hand through her hair, ignoring the familiar argument. "I told them that at the next meeting they could meet Mei and John," she blurted, opening her eyes.

Rennick paused his tirade. "What? Last time I checked, Mei and John didn't want to do that. Did you ask them first?"

"No."

"Callie, that was a bad idea—"

"I know what I did."

Aloriea shook her head, pressing the button to indicate that they were ready for takeoff. "Good luck telling them." She smirked. "I'm sure it'll go over well."

CHAPTER 2

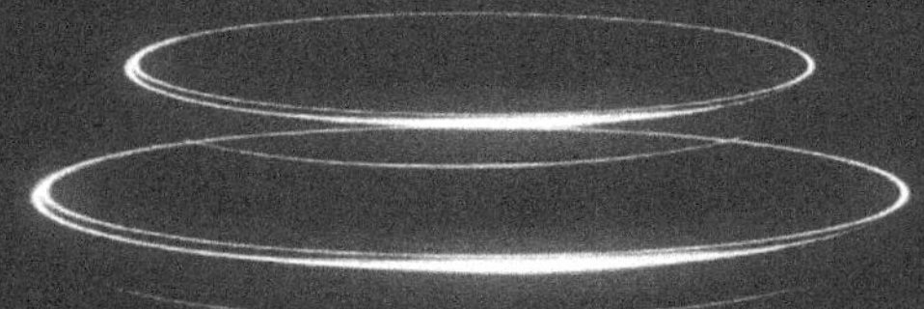

"You what?" Mei crossed her arms and shot a glare in Caldera's direction that could melt steel. Her black hair was pulled into a tight ponytail, and the loose-fitting, hole-filled jeans and dark shirt she wore made her look younger than she really was.

Caldera said nothing, knowing it was better to let her get out her raw emotions right away before interrupting.

Less than seven hours after the meeting in Sector Five, she sat in the desk chair of Mei's quarters, desperately wishing to open the window. The smell of wet paint she had supplied for Mei weeks ago stung her nose.

An easel was set up in the corner, splattered with colors across the spectrum. An unfinished project, waiting to be completed, adorned its tray.

The metal walls were covered with art of various subject matter—flying transports, garden flowers, flyers, Earthen plants and animals that Caldera didn't know—pretty much anything that Mei could see clearly out her window, when she went to the garden, or could remember from her home planet as she desperately tried to make the best out of the living arrangement.

These are good. I wonder if I should let her decorate the entire palace? Caldera mused, taking a deep breath. She knew Mei would never admit to missing Earth, even a little bit, but the subject matter of her artwork told a different, subconscious, story. *It might make her feel a little more at home...*

Rennick leaned against the wall with his arms crossed, staring out the window at the bright sky and wearing an 'I told you so' expression.

Caldera had to resist the urge to roll her eyes in his direction.

John pushed the sleeves of his white sweater up to his elbows and placed a tender hand on his sister's shoulder. "Calm down."

Mei's cheeks flushed red. "No way! This is bullshit. How could you do this to us?"

"Because—" Caldera tried.

"We asked you to do one thing. One!"

"Mei, it was the only way to try and get you both equal rights here—or, as equal as I can manage," Caldera stated, determined to explain herself. "Don't you want to leave the palace?"

Mei stopped angrily pacing and looked from John to Caldera, her angular eyes narrowing. "What if it backfires? What if they demand that we leave?" She lowered her voice. "What if we have to go back to Earth?"

"Would that really be so terrible?" Rennick offered, pushing off the wall and placing a hand in his suit-pant pocket.

"Yes," Mei and John answered at the same time.

"'Course it would be... I can't leave. I can't," Mei said, dramatically pressing her back against the wall.

"And I *won't*," John added with a quick nod, wiping imaginary debris off his khaki-colored jeans. "I'm not leaving Mark... Unless he would want to go back with me to Earth, which... I don't know if he would."

Caldera couldn't help but smile at the nickname that Markarian only let John use. "I don't know either..." she muttered, blowing out a breath.

"Just seeing how the situation sounded out loud," Rennick said, rubbing his forehead, "and it's not good."

"But I can't in good conscience keep you locked up, essentially prisoners, in this palace forever. Even if you say it's what you want." Caldera stood up and glided her hands down the front of her shirt, eliminating the wrinkles as she steadied her voice in resolution. "You're going to have to face the sector leaders at some point. It might as well be at the next meeting."

Mei shook her head, her long black ponytail swishing against her back. "How're we supposed to defend ourselves? Honestly, what 'grounds' do we *really* have to stay here?"

Caldera and Rennick glanced at each other, sharing the same worried expression, but said nothing.

"That's what I thought..." Mei hung her head, voice low.

"Have you told Markarian yet?" John asked, changing the subject and flicking wavy blond hair out of his eyes.

"No, but he's on my side in this."

He rubbed his forehead. "I know..."

Caldera stood, motioning for Rennick to follow her toward the door. "Present your case at the next meeting. I believe you can do it," she said. "We'll support you every step of the way."

With a nod, she and Rennick left the room, letting the door slide shut behind them.

"Your Majesty."

Caldera jumped, readying herself instinctively for combat. Rennick placed a hand on her shoulder, expression calm.

She exhaled sharply, relaxing at the familiar face. "Bruna..."

The newest member of palace security took a few steps forward, no longer standing adjacent to Caldera, but directly in front of her. She stood tall and sharp, her broad shoulders resembling the top of a square and her uniform perfectly tailored—the crisp black suit had not a wrinkle in sight.

The gold encircled crown, embroidered on the right breast pocket, was a bright beacon against the black clothing.

They began walking down the hallway, with Rennick following a few paces behind.

"What is it?" Caldera asked, furrowing her brow after Bruna didn't respond.

"Saro asked me to retrieve you, Your Majesty" she replied shortly.

"What for?"

Bruna shook her head and shrugged.

"All right... fine. And how many times do I have to tell you to drop the 'Your Majesty' crap?"

"Unacceptable," she replied instantly, running a hand over her hairless head before snapping her shoulders back into place, her green eyes gleaming, contrasting brightly against her dark skin. "My father always said, 'titles exist for a reason, so be aware and use them accordingly. That's how you show respect'."

"Why would he say that?"

"He worked as a head of palace security too, as well as his father before him."

Caldera raised an eyebrow. "Wait... your family's worked here in the past?"

"My father was head of palace security for your uncle, King Quill," Bruna replied, with a sharp nod, her gaze never wavering from straight ahead. "And my grandfather worked for your grandparents, or, King Quill's parents—King Rerran and Queen Lila."

Caldera let out a shaky breath. She rarely thought about her grandparents; that part of her ancestry all seemed so disconnected from her life that it hardly mattered. She never knew them. She never even knew Quill.

"Wow... You have a bit of a legacy to protect, then?"

"A legacy to *mend*. I was on a fast-track toward the Tellin militia special forces, figuring that would do the trick... but I changed my mind."

"Okay... but why 'mend'?"

"My father let King Quill get murdered right under his nose," Bruna replied, her voice hard as stone. "He was promptly discharged from service after that by Justle."

Caldera blinked, slowing her pace. Her chest tightened at the sound of Justle's name.

"That was a set-up, though," she said, finding herself whispering and coming to a complete stop in the middle of the hallway. "You know that, right? I released all the information about how the Council puppeteered its leaders to the public—"

Bruna stopped walking after continuing to take a few steps, as if she realized Caldera had halted behind her. "Yes. I know."

"Then you also must realize that he couldn't have prevented it even if he had known... and if he *had* tried, he would've been killed right along with Quill anyway..."

Bruna exhaled sharply, casting a stern glance over her shoulder at Caldera. "Then he'd be in the same place he is now... Six feet under."

Caldera swallowed hard, deciding not to pry more into a stranger's personal life, regretting what she had already learned, and the three quickly continued through the palace in silence, from the top floor, three stories down. The hallways, branching off from the main staircase that had once all looked the same, now clearly differentiated themselves to her eyes.

She looked around as they went down a flight of steps. *The servants' quarters make up the entirety of this level, leading off to the right and left, once you hit the second floor.*

Some of the doors that were visible were decorated with personal items—a sign here, a picture there—anything to let them bring out their individuality. She smiled at the recent policy she implemented once she was officially in charge and not answering to Vandren or the Council anymore.

Breezing down the steps, she waved as her group walked past the newly hired curators, caretakers, and custodians—many of which bowed and placed closed fists over their hearts in a sign of respect.

They eventually stepped onto the main floor. *The hallway that leads to the kitchen is off to the left,* she thought, continuing to quiz herself. Even though the palace was far from unfamiliar at that point, she still sometimes managed to get lost. *It's like Al-oriea said, continual practice is the key.* She sighed. *The entrance to the back courtyard is directly behind me...*

Saro was waiting directly ahead, guarding the palace doors.

As they approached, Bruna silently retook her spot on the other side of the palace entrance.

"What's going on?" Caldera asked Saro, while crossing her arms and raising an eyebrow.

"You have a request for a visitation from *him...* again."

Caldera's throat involuntarily constricted. Reaching for Rennick's hand with one arm, she put a hand on Saro's shoulder with the other, turning him sideways and leaning in close.

"Tell the prison to stop letting him try to contact me," she hissed. "Tell them I'm never going to speak to Vandren again. Never."

"I have told them."

"Well, keep telling them!"

Bruna glanced over before returning her attention to the front courtyard and driveway.

Saro blinked his brown and blue eyes, taking a step back and adjusting his tie, seeming to subconsciously tighten it in an attempt to cover up the large scar leading down his throat to his chest. "Of course."

Caldera bit the inside of her cheek and squeezed Rennick's hand tighter. He squeezed back, anchoring her to reality. "I'm sorry... I know you're doing your job," she said, lowering her voice. "And I know things haven't been easy for you—"

"It's all right, Callie," Saro replied, raising a hand to gently cut her off, a soft smile appearing across his face, which she gladly returned.

She took a deep breath, glancing over her shoulder at Rennick before releasing his hand and leaning in close to Saro again. "Where did you find her?" she whispered, changing the subject and motioning with her head toward Bruna. "She's kinda..."

"Strict?" he offered with a grin.

"Exactly."

"I knew her from the academy. She was friends with my brother." His face fell for a fraction of a second before the smile returned. "After what happened, I couldn't take over as head of security."

"Yes, you could have," Caldera replied sternly.

A splash of crimson blood spattered across her memory as Saro's twin brother Sol was murdered by Vandren in front of her and her friends, and the forced explosion that followed—almost killing, and permanently scarring, everyone she cared about.

The fact that it was her fault for not thinking of a better way to stop him was something she still couldn't fully face.

"You didn't have anything to do with what happened."

Saro shook his head. "It wouldn't have been right... I mean, Aloriea still doesn't trust me..."

"Aloriea's... Aloriea. She's a hard-ass sometimes, but she means well."

"She still thinks I had something to do with Quill's death..."

"She'll come around," Caldera said, solemnly patting his shoulder.

Saro sighed. "Whatever you say."

Caldera offered a supporting smile before turning to leave. She paused, glancing behind her. "Saro."

"Yes?"

"*I* trust you. Okay?"

His eyes lit up, and he nodded sharply. "Okay. Umm, where are you going?"

Caldera grinned, catching his eyes. "To the Vault."

Saro nodded, retaking his post as Caldera and Rennick rushed to the back courtyard entrance, past the hustle and bustle of the kitchen crew preparing for lunch—the smells of cooking bread and simmering vegetable soup hitting her nostrils, making her stomach growl in anticipation.

Moments later, she and Rennick were at the entrance.

Caldera's hand brushed the door handle. Her heart raced. Everytime she went to the back courtyard, the memory of the wormhole ripping into existence and tearing her life apart involuntarily flashed across her mind and the insanity that followed—Rennick's supposed death, the destruction, the emptiness, Earth, the ensuing fallout with the former councilmembers.

"Ready?" Rennick asked, his voice soft.

"How long have I been standing here staring at the door this time?"

"Thirty seconds, maybe."

She blew out a breath. "New record."

"You don't have to force yourself—"

She shook her head and pushed the doors open. A completely restored courtyard greeted her, along with Grey and Sylvie, like it always did when she got the strength to return.

Grey jolted to attention, throwing his still lit cigarette into the recycler beside the door and blowing the smoke out in one quick breath. The gray cloud swirled into the air and disappeared as he placed a closed fist over his heart.

"Smoking on the job isn't exactly permitted," Caldera said, smiling softly and making sure her tone could be construed as playful.

"I'm sorry Your Majesty—uhm—Callie, it's just, switching jobs is—I—it won't happen again—"

"Grey," Caldera said, holding up a hand to effectively quiet his ramblings. "Calm down. You're fine."

Rennick smiled next to her. "Try and remember the importance of what you're doing here, and if you need anything, like an extra break, let us know."

Caldera nodded in agreement and turned her attention back toward the courtyard.

Gardeners had put in fresh flowerbeds and populated them with Tellin's native greenery, blooming bright and vibrant. The fountain at the center had been restored by landscapers, and the red-brick walkways had been relayed. New tree saplings had been planted and fast tracked to grow quicker than what could be considered natural; it had only been thirteen weeks and they were already around ten feet tall.

The sky was bright blue without a cloud, or transport, in the sky. She took a deep breath, finally starting to get used to the "no-fly" order over the sector leader palaces—for increased safety—that had recently been put into effect.

"Sorry about my brother," Sylvie said, her red side-braid bouncing around her shoulder as she leaned in close. "He swears he's trying to quit." She beamed so wide almost all her teeth were on display. "Anyway, it's nice to see you today! I hardly ever see you out here—"

"Headed to the Vault?" Grey asked, all-business after his light scolding, and raising an eyebrow, his freckled face red from sun exposure.

Caldera took a deep breath and nodded, not used to having so much security, and continued to trace the environment with her eyes.

The wall surrounding the palace had been redone so it was no longer a crumbling mess of loose stones and exposed masonry—with proper, built-in, steps so her and her friends could easily walk to the top without having to climb. Her eyes lingered on the repaired wrought-iron bench, the plaque on it reading *'In memory of King Quill'*, before landing on the entrance to the Vault carefully guarded by Markarian.

"You two didn't have to quit the Vanguard to work for me," Caldera said while waving at Markarian and eyeing Grey. She and Rennick began walking toward the Vault entrance with Grey and Sylvie in the lead.

Sylvie giggled, swishing her hands over her black suit, slowing her pace and walking beside her. "You always say that."

Grey nodded, clasping his hands behind his back, making the palace guard uniform stretch across his chest. "You needed support staff, and we *wanted* to help you, so here we are."

Caldera smiled but said nothing, the constant reminder of how young they were smashing into her mind. *I needed allies, people I could trust...* She bit her lip, trying to force herself not to regret hiring two nineteen year olds as part of her main security crew.

The young brother and sister duo led them to the entrance, continuing to make small talk the entire way. Markarian placed his hand on the scanner stone, opening the entrance as the group approached. The walkway sunk into the ground, exposing the stairs that led down into the previously hidden and unknown room below the palace.

Caldera turned to Grey and Sylvie. "I can take it from here."

The two nodded and returned to their posts at the back door.

"Cal, Ren," Markarian said, nodding at them. He raised the black sunglasses he was wearing, revealing his bright green eyes, and rested them on top of his head.

His black hair, which he had grown out on the top, was pulled into a loose bun with the bottom half shaved short, since hair was no longer able to grow where a long scar lined the side of his head above his left ear—running from the back of his head to his eyebrow.

"How's it going today?" Rennick asked, glancing up at the clear blue sky and covering his eyes.

Markarian scratched another scar that ran over the bridge of his nose and halfway across his cheek. "Not too bad," he sniffed. "I have to be at Vanguard headquarters in an hour—overseeing a captains' meeting, so now you two get the pleasure of kicking the brainiacs out of their lab." He smiled and winked before replacing the sunglasses over his eyes.

Caldera laughed. "Have I ever told you how much I appreciate you being my Vanguard liaison and part-time palace security?"

A crash sounded from down below. "You are going to have to drag me out of here, Markarian! I am not at all close to being finished with my calculations!"

Markarian blew out a breath and exaggeratedly motioned for her to head down the steps. "Not nearly enough. Being 'Overseer' of the Vanguard captains and crews is cake compared to,"—he hooked a thumb toward the stairs—"them."

"Oh boy," Caldera muttered.

"I know, and that was through the secondary door too," Markarian said, holding out a secondary scanner pad. "Your handprint, please."

Caldera obliged, the device lighting up green after she retracted her hand, confirming her identity and authorization.

"Have fun," Markarian said, waving sarcastically as Caldera and Rennick headed down.

The steps lit up as she descended, making her way to the bottom. *It wasn't that long ago that we discovered this place... and now the security is so beefed up that even I can't enter without logging it...* Caldera grimaced as she reached the landing at the bottom and scanned her hand causing the floor to rise and the door at the bottom of the steps to whisk open. *It's because of what's down here. This information is going to change Bersama and we need to protect it...* she reminded herself, her thoughts trailing off as she entered the wide area.

Loose-leaf paper was balled up or strewn all over the floor. A 3D model of Earth spun lazily in the middle of the table, with Aloriea sitting next to it, her cheek resting in the palm of her hand. Calculation after calculation was crossed off on the upgraded holoscreen.

The equations floated freely in the air in front of Sear, whose cat-like leg was bouncing up and down so quickly, it was like he was trying to bust a hole in the floor.

The updated computer system that was connected directly to the other sector leaders' science and development departments sat *whirring* in the corner. The handwritten journals had all been alphabetized by title, with the miscellaneous or unreadable ones stacked sideways and crowding the bottom shelf.

"Okay..." Caldera muttered, approaching Sear gingerly. Her eyes fell on Aloriea. "What's going on?"

"Callie!" Aloriea said, her eyes lighting up. "Well—"

"I cannot seem to figure out how to maintain a stable portal—though I am *close*," Sear interrupted, completely ignoring the fact that Caldera was down in the Vault for the first time in weeks, and baring his fanged canines while running a hand through his wild fawn colored hair.

The button-up shirt he wore was rolled up to his fur covered elbows and half untucked, while one extended claw frantically stabbed the air in front him, directing equations away or toward him with each strike.

"How the former councilmembers managed it, it seems I will never know," he snarled, narrowing his golden eyes. "They had a stable portal before it was destroyed..."

Caldera raised her eyebrows. "I can see you're frustrated."

"Rightfully so!" Sear added, taking a breath.

"In other words," Aloriea mumbled, "it's not going well."

"What about the portal bracelet tech?" Rennick asked, taking a seat next to Aloriea. "You got Markarian and Callie to Earth and back, and got Mei and John here."

"It is not the same," Sear breathed, his good ear flicking back and forth while what was left of the other one stood still—a nub on the top of his head. "That was a quick opening and closing of a barely controlled wormhole. A snap of the fingers, so to speak," he said as he performed the motion. "What I am trying to do is make a stable portal that can stay open as long as needed and can be closed on command.

"Much like what the former councilmembers attempted before we stopped them." He turned and padded toward the table, taking a seat. "The portal bracelet hypothesis is too unstable. It is nothing short of a miracle that no one was killed." He sneezed, rubbing his nose and glancing away. "What we really need is to ask, or *find*, someone who already knows the calculations."

"The only people who know are the former councilmembers..." Caldera crossed her arms, her mind wandering to Vandren's summons.

No. I won't ask him. I won't see him—any of them. Sear can do this, he just needs more time...

"Well, you can pick up again tomorrow. Markarian has to go, and you know we can't be down here on unlogged time."

"Which brings me to my next point," Sear stabbed a clawed finger onto the tabletop. "Why? This is your palace and I am a member of your court, as well as Aloriea, Rennick, and Markarian. Any one of us should be able to stay down here for as long as we want if you so approve." He motioned around the area with a flourish. "Uninterrupted. I need to figure this out. The technology could not only be used for interplanetary travel, but intergalactic as well."

Rennick and Aloriea sighed audibly.

"This was the deal we made, Sear," Caldera replied, trying to keep her cool and tired of having the same conversation almost everyday with the stubborn genius. "The other sector leaders agreed not to completely gut this place if we give them access to the computer, keep an extremely detailed log of everything that we do here, everything that's discovered, and everyone that goes in and out of the Vault, and to share with them all daily so they can distribute it to their top scientists."

"We're all working together to find a solution to the portal problem," Aloriea added. "And if they find something, they'll let us know too."

Sear scoffed. "As if their scientists could come up with a solution when I cannot."

Rennick let out a laugh.

"You sound like a narcissist," Caldera muttered.

Sear eyed her skeptically. "You know better than anyone that I am one."

"So self aware," she replied sarcastically. "On that note, time to go. Come on, everyone out."

A low growl escaped Sear's throat. "Very well... but at the next sector leader meeting, ask for extended time... please."

Caldera grinned. "Deal."

CHAPTER 3

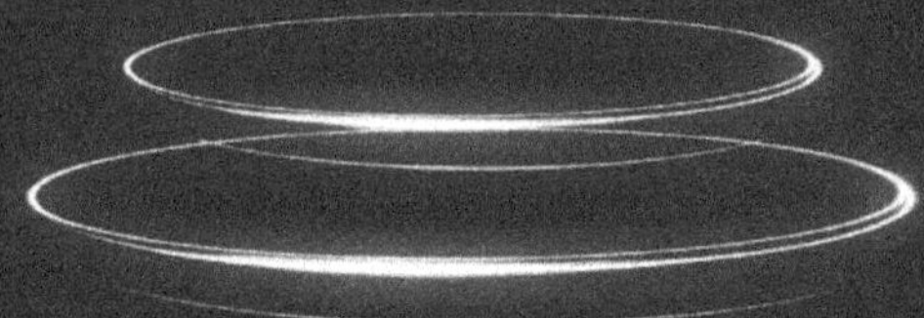

Caldera sighed, spreading her arms and letting herself collapse backward on top of the bed.

Her mind flashed through the events of the past week.

A consultation with Deimi Auris, the CEO of the Vanguard, to check on the upgraded rail-beam tool and planter orb shield had taken up most of a day.

According to their reports, the objects were stable and safe. The R.B. was no longer a weapon, and the planter orb shield, rebranded to 'orb shield', was officially on the market for members of the Vanguard and militia and had no adverse effects.

The next line of business featured a call with the head of the Tellin Environmental Restoration Agency, or T.E.R.A., organization asking when their conservation funds would be released. After checking with Aloriea, it would be at least three more days—plenty of time to reserve the land they had their eyes on for preservation.

There were at least two more meetings she had attended, but they blurred together so much she couldn't recall specifics.

"These sector leader meetings are too frequent. Meetings are all it seems like I'm doing nowadays," she groaned.

Rennick laughed, rubbing a cloth coated in oil over his metal leg. "That's an understatement, but it's only until you can all come to an agreement about Earth and then they'll be pulled back to once a month, right?"

"Right..."

"Okay, then what's wrong?"

"I'm beginning to think that we're *never* going to come to a consensus."

Rennick placed the towel on the tabletop before walking over to where Caldera still lay facing the ceiling and crawled next to her. "Remember what Aloriea said. This is what being a political figure is all about."

Caldera scooted closer to him, shifting so she could rest her head on his shoulder and place her hand on his chest. "I guess she knows better than anyone, but... I don't think I'll ever get used to it."

He kissed the top of her head. "You will. I know it."

"That's just it. What if I *do*?" She paused, balling his shirt in her hands. "What then? Will I lose who I used to be?"

Laughter filled her ears as Rennick sat up, pulling her with him. He turned to face her, his hazel eyes boring into her dark blue ones. "Callie, I know for a fact that no matter how much you get pulled into the political realm, you will not lose sight of who you are."

"You know this for a fact do you?"

"I'd bet my life on it... again."

I don't know. All this political jargon, putting on airs, wearing a damn crown... I think I'm already losing who I am... Nonetheless, she kept her thoughts to herself and smiled, grateful for his belief in her abilities. Leaning forward, she kissed him as the door slid open.

"What are you doing?" Aloriea's voice said. "The sector leaders will be here any second."

Caldera and Rennick separated.

"You have a knack of bursting into my quarters at the worst moments, you know that?" Caldera muttered, getting to her feet.

Aloriea said nothing, only pointed to her watch.

Caldera exhaled sharply. "Okay." She stood up, smoothing the wrinkles out of her navy-blue dress, eyeing Rennick, who nodded, straightening his tie. "Let's go."

"Crown first," Aloriea said, walking over to where the simple silver-pointed circle sat, gathering dust most of the time, on Caldera's dresser. She picked it up and plopped it on top of Caldera's head, adjusting it to fit.

"Is this really necessary?" Caldera asked, clenching her jaw as the crown gripped her head as if it were trying to cut off circulation.

"You ask that every time, and the answer is never going to change. Sector leaders wear their crowns when *hosting* a meeting."

"Okay. Let's get this over with," Caldera snapped, leading them out of her quarters.

"Do you think Mei and John are ready?" Rennick asked, facing Aloriea after a few moments of silence.

"I trained them as much as I could in a week, but..." She paused. "Mei's mouth is almost certainly going to get her into trouble."

"Reminds me of someone," Rennick replied, nudging Caldera's arm.

She forced a smile, unable to make herself speak. *Please don't let this be a disaster.*

The walk to the conference room was quick, the group's shoes clicking off the marble floor and dissipating as they came to a stop in front of the ornate doors.

Taking a deep breath, Caldera stepped into the remodeled room, soon to be full of sector leaders anxious to share their thoughts and opinions. With the previous front-facing dias no longer relevant, it had been removed in favor of a large circular table, so everyone could see each other equally, shaped around an open area in the middle so one could stand and walk around in the center if they really wanted to present their point.

Caldera took her seat on the far side facing the door and Aloriea sat beside her. Rennick took a few steps back, taking his place along the wall behind them, where the other bodyguards were soon to populate.

One by one the sector leaders, their advisors, and their bodyguards came in, escorted by either Saro or Bruna, taking their predetermined places at the table or against the wall and seeming to cram the space.

After everyone was settled, Caldera rose. "Let's begin." She paused, glancing from each leader to the next. "Why don't we start with Vanguard cooperation between sectors?"

A cacophony of objections filled the room.

"We wish to talk about Earth and meet the inhabitants as promised," Mokan said, the black of his catlike eyes a thin line.

A chorus of agreement echoed off the walls.

Caldera didn't flinch, beginning to find her footing. "And we will, but we need to talk about other things first. We absolutely cannot let Bersama's pressing issues fade into the background!"

There was a pause, followed by soft whispering.

Caldera glanced behind her at Rennick, who was beaming, and retook her seat.

"You're doing great!" Aloriea whispered in Caldera's ear, gripping her arm and giving her a quick, excited shake. "I can't believe you're actually doing it."

"Thanks for the support."

"You know what I mean."

"I agree," Jasik said, speaking up in their thick Saurian accent, their forked tongue snaking in and out of their mouth. "Berssama's issuess are getting worsse by the day." They grinned, their yellow elliptical eyes meeting Caldera's. "Pleasse go on, Your Majesty."

She nodded in thanks, leaning forward on her elbows. "It has come to my attention that the sector Vanguard operations are still not quite working together in the way we had initially hoped. This needs to be rectified immediately."

"Where did you get this information?" Eldra asked, her cerulean skin shimmering under the light.

"My Vanguard liaison and former captain, Markarian Ales. He attended a captains' meeting six days ago and their number one complaint was that they were not getting adequate support from other sectors, especially when it comes to sharing airspace." She laced her fingers together. "Threats of attack, unlawful boarding, and even unprovoked scuttling have been reported."

"What would you have us do?" Desrin asked, flipping her shiny hair over her shoulder. "Terminate our entire Vanguard fleet so only yours is operational?"

"Of course not," Caldera grated, "but if there needs to be some restructuring, then it's something that needs to be looked into."

She rose, walking around to the opening that the table surrounded to stand in the middle.

"We are not being *controlled* anymore... I suggest putting laws in place to prevent further misconduct," she continued, moving around the edge of the circle to stop in front of each sector leader, before returning to the middle with a flourish.

"That is a very good idea, Your Majesty," Eldra said, lacing her long, slender fingers together and smiling across the table at her.

Heat rushed to Caldera's face at the unexpected, and immediate, agreement. "Th-thank you," she stammered, walking back to her seat.

Aloriea nudged her arm with a grin on her face.

"Sshall we sstart with airsspace then?" Jasik asked, leaning forward and motioning for their political advisor to start typing out the conversation. "What we own, what we don't, and sso on."

Caldera glanced over at Aloriea to see that she, as well as all the political advisors, were already doing the same thing—keeping a detailed record of everything that was said and potentially passed as the leaders spoke among themselves—only interjecting when asked for advice.

"According to Queen Caldera, that does seem to be the point of most contention." Nari nodded.

Caldera cleared her throat. "It is. I believe we need to enact a law that allows for *open* airspace that will be shared between everyone."

Mumbles from the leaders chatting with their political advisors rose to meet her ears.

"That would be chaos," Desrin said, her voice rising above everyone else's.

Eldra tilted her head to the side. "How so?"

"What if, for example, a Vanguard member from Sector One finds something in Sector Fours area—our current airspace? Who do they report it to?"

Caldera shook her head, trying to remember that the other sector leaders had been indoctrinated with lies from the Council since birth.

"Shouldn't it be obvious? They'd report it to *everyone*," she said, taking a deep breath. "You need to understand that we shouldn't have 'designated sections' of the galaxy anymore. It's everyone's to explore equally, and the Vanguard members' conduct, as well as our laws, must reflect that."

More muffled conversations rose as the leaders got advice from their most trusted allies and partners.

Caldera scanned the area in front of her. "A lot of head nodding," she whispered over to Aloriea.

"That's a good sign."

"I believe we've come to an agreement," Eldra said, standing and looking down at her wife, Fenry, who remained seated; the classic frown that never left the woman's face was ever-present as she leaned on her hand. "Will the representatives for each sector please rise as they reach their decision?"

Aloriea quickly nudged Caldera to her feet. Her face burned again as involuntary heat rushed to it. *Damn it, I should've been the one to say that.*

Mokan rose, keeping his clawed fingers laced together.

Jasik nodded, rising to their feet as well, palms laid flat on the table.

The last to stand was Desrin, her red-eyed glare holding strong on Caldera.

"All right," Caldera said, swallowing hard. "Let's vote. All in favor of open airspace for the Vanguard and restructure as it pertains to misconduct, say aye."

Jasik, representing Sector Three, Eldra, representing Sector Two, and Mokan, representing Sector Five said 'aye' in unison. Only Desrin and the spouses of the other sector leaders that didn't need to stand stayed silent.

Caldera grinned, retaking her seat as a rush of adrenaline coursed through her body. "The motion passes."

We did it! We agreed on something... mostly. She looked around the table at the beaming faces of almost all the other sector leaders and couldn't help letting a sense of pride bloom in her chest. *They're all realizing that they're capable of doing things on their own.*

"Very well then!" Desrin snapped, breaking Caldera out of her revelry, standing, and taking Caldera's place in the center of the circle. "Sector Four will comply, but now I must insist that we are introduced to the Earth inhabitants." She glided around the table, her silver dress haloing around her feet, and coming to a stop in front of Caldera. "If you wouldn't mind."

Caldera took a deep breath, reluctantly breaking eye contact with Desrin. She turned to Rennick and nodded.

He nodded back, lifting his wrap-around watch up to his mouth. "Bring them in."

Desrin smirked and returned to her seat.

After a few minutes, the conference room doors opened and Mei and John stepped forward, ushered in by Saro, who whispered something in their ears and quickly closed the doors behind him.

The room was silent, as if the air had been sucked out of it.

Caldera cleared her throat. "Leaders, this is Mei and John Miller, the inhabitants of Earth."

The siblings slowly stepped into the middle of the circle, dwarfed by the surrounding leaders of Bersama.

Mei wore plain black slacks and a bright blue blouse, something she never would have picked out for herself. Her long black hair was pulled back into a tight ponytail and a permanent scowl adorned her face. Caldera didn't know if it was from the clothes she was forced to wear at Aloriea's insistence to appear presentable, or from the situation, but she couldn't help feeling anxious.

John, on the other hand, seemed cool and collected; his neutral-colored sweater and dark jeans from his own closet fit him perfectly, and his shaggy blond hair bounced over his ears as he was led to the center of sector leaders.

"These are the inhabitants?" Nari asked, speaking for the first time, her white fur bristling.

"I told you, their genetic makeup is similar to tellins," Caldera replied, nervously tapping her fingers on the table.

"We don't need to dwell on the obvious," Fenry said, lacing her fingers together and resting her chin on top of them, her long white hair falling over one of her eyes. "Please,"—her eyes slid from Caldera, over to Mei and John—"tell us about Earth."

"Okay... well," John cleared his throat, "what would you like to know?"

"Are your people trustworthy?"

John blinked, meeting Caldera's eyes.

You can do this. She found she was digging her nails into her palms from balling her hands into fists so tightly and motioned for him to continue with a small nod.

"That... that's kind of an unfair question," he finally replied.

Fenry furrowed her brow. "How so?"

"Because it's wanting us to speak in absolutes." He took a breath. "Of course not everyone on Earth can be trusted, but some can. That's the way life is."

Caldera exhaled sharply, the knot in her chest loosening a little. *Good, keep going.*

"That is a fair assessment." Eldra placed a hand on Fenry's shoulder. "We cannot even speak in absolutes about our own people, and we shouldn't ask it of them either."

"Would you object to going back?" Mokan asked.

"Yes," Mei and John said in unison.

"Why is that?" Desrin said, tilting her head to the side, her red eyes gleaming. "Are the conditions on your homeworld un-livable?"

John ran a hand through his blond hair. "Well, no—"

"Are you fugitives, on the run?"

"No—"

"Homeless?"

"Well, technically—"

"Spies for Earth?"

"No!"

"Then why?"

Caldera slammed her hands down on the table and stood. "Enough. They aren't criminals or freeloaders. They're two peo-ple who helped us out when we were searching for answers," she paused. "And they certainly didn't have to...

"We never would've figured out what the Council was doing if not for their help." She slowly lowered herself back into her seat, closing her eyes. "They deserve your respect, and I won't let you speak about them as if they warrant anything less."

She reopened her eyes to see Mei and John's shocked and smiling faces staring back at her.

Desrin scoffed, waving a nonchalant hand in the air. "Tell us why you object to going home when you have not even been outside this palace." Her eyes whipped to Caldera. "They haven't been outside the palace, right?"

"No, we haven't," Mei said, stepping up to Desrin, their bodies only separated by the table. "And frankly, it's none of your business why we wanna stay," she continued, crossing her arms.

"Oh no..." Aloriea muttered, placing her face in her hand.

"With all do resspect," Jasik interjected. "It iss."

Caldera's chest retightened. *Please. Please leave Markarian out of this.*

"You, the rational one," Desrin said, pointing to John. "Answer the question. Why do you want to stay if you're not an agent sent to spy on us?"

Come on, John, don't mention Markarian. If you say you're in a relationship with him, who knows how they'll react? They think you and your sister might be our enemy right now... They'll most likely think he's a traitor and want him out of my court...

John rubbed his arm. "Well..."

A burst of white light exploded from across the room.

Caldera covered her eyes, instinctively grabbing Aloriea's arm and dragging her down underneath the table. Her ears rang as icy coldness ran down her spine.

This sensation... I know it... Her body went rigid and phantom pain stung her wrists.

She blinked the white spots out of her eyes and saw Rennick was there, crouched beside her. His blaster was drawn but his expression was undoubtedly one of shock.

Red and black smoke tendrils curled around the floor and her feet, making every hair on Caldera's body stand up. "A portal just opened," Caldera muttered, gripping the edge of the counter and pulling herself to her feet.

"Callie, no," Rennick snapped, grabbing her arm and forcing her back down.

"Well, well, well," an unfamiliar male voice said from the other side of the room. "This is an interesting development."

"Holy fucking shit, it actually worked!" another unfamiliar male voice added. "I mean, fuck!"

"Team Bravo, this is Team Alpha reporting," yet another unfamiliar, but female, voice said. "We made it. The coordinates proved accurate and true."

"Freeze! Don't move!" sector leader bodyguards were yelling.

"Stay here," Rennick whispered, before jumping over the table to join them.

Caldera turned her attention to Aloriea. "You all right?"

She nodded, motioning for her to move away.

"What?"

"We both know you're going out there. Please be careful."

Caldera smirked. "Of course." She glanced around. "Find Mei and John and get them out of here."

Aloriea nodded.

Taking a deep breath, Caldera stood and leapt over the table to where the wall of bodyguards had three people surrounded. "Mei, John, where are you?" she whispered, trying not to draw attention to herself and hoping Aloriea had already found them.

"They're fine," Jasik's bodyguard said. "They're with my ruler and advisor, but you sshouldn't be out here."

They placed a hand on Caldera's shoulder, but she pushed it away, finding and locking eyes with Aloriea, who nodded and started ushering out the rest of the political advisors who hadn't already fled.

Caldera made her way next to Rennick.

"You never listen," Rennick muttered, gripping his blaster tighter.

"You expected me to?"

He shook his head and sighed. "Stay behind me..."

Caldera smirked. "I don't think that's going to happen."

"Callie—"

"Someone has to talk to them," she interrupted, walking forward and pushing past the throng of sector leader bodyguards.

Who are you? How did you get here? What do you want? Caldera's mind was racing as she shouldered her way to the front of the group, followed closely by Rennick.

The three strangers stood in a loose clump on the far end of the conference room. They all wore business-casual clothes, as if it were another day at the office—with the men in slacks and plain-colored button ups, and the woman in a long skirt, hitting below her knees, and a brown blouse.

As far as she could tell, none of them had weapons, only identical watches wrapped around their wrists.

The taller man turned to face her, dusting off his gray pants, brown eyes gleaming. "Ahh, Caldera Keane I assume. I was wondering if you'd be here... Nice crown."

Caldera's body froze as a chill ran down her back. She clenched her fists tighter to try and keep them from overtly shaking. "How do you know me?" she managed between the growing lump in her throat.

"How don't we?" the woman said, tucking short red hair behind her ear, revealing a listening device, and placing her manicured hands on her hips. "You caused quite a ruckus on Earth before you left."

"You... You're *from* Earth?"

"Damn straight," the shorter, stocky man added, scratching his head, his thinning black hair unsuccessfully trying to hide a growing bald spot.

Rennick put a hand on Caldera's shoulder. "Callie, you should get out of here—"

"Rennick Silvera," the stocky man interrupted, seeming almost excited. "Anyone else here? Maybe Markar—"

"That's enough," Caldera snapped, taking another step forward. "Who the fuck are you people?" She glared at each of them, assessing her chances of winning in a three on one fight. *I am a little rusty, but they don't have any weapons...* "Answer me. Now!"

"How rude of us," the redheaded woman said with an exasperated sigh, blinking brown eyes. "My name is Evie Wells." She pointed to the tall, lanky man. "That's Barrett Sharpe." She turned her attention to the stocky man. "And that's Dominic Lowe." The woman smiled. "We're from Area 51."

CHAPTER 4

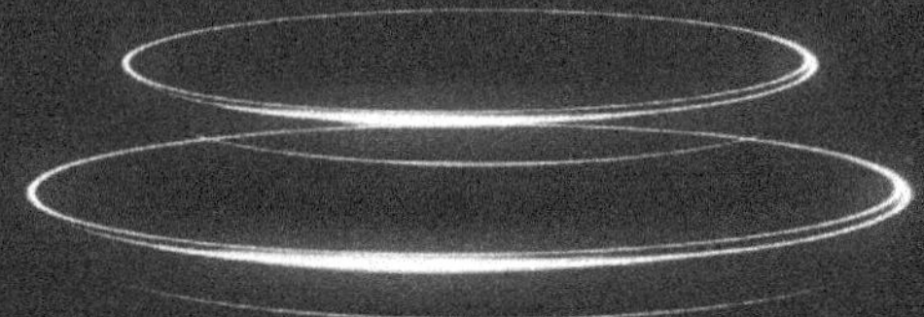

Caldera's heart pounded in her ears, causing her body to grow whitehot and the entire conference room to become muffled. *This can't be happening...*

A voice from her right caused Caldera to jump. "What is an 'Area 51'?"

She looked over to see Mokan standing next to her. His bodyguard's fur was puffed out and standing on end, ready to attack, but Mokan's was smooth, as if he didn't have a worry in the world—a perfectly trained politician.

Evie tilted her head to the side, her gaze never wavering from Caldera. "Keeping secrets, I see."

"I shall not ask again," Mokan said. He raised his hand, a signal to his bodyguard to take aim with his blaster.

"Whoa, there," the man named Dominic said, raising his hands. "You'd shoot unarmed civilians?"

"Unarmed *invaders*," Desrin corrected, appearing on Caldera's left. "And don't be ridiculous." She raised her hand, prompting her bodyguard to do the same action as Mokan's. "You will be stunned and detained. Not killed."

The woman named Evie sighed again. "Area 51 is a... let's say, corporation with vested interests in things such as," she motioned her hand around the area—"this."

"Other worlds, extraterrestrials, unexplained phenomena, etcetera," the man named Barrett explained.

"I'm surprised that Caldera didn't speak of us," Evie continued, glancing from one sector leader to the next. "Especially since we're the ones that are cleaning up her mess on Earth... Actually, that's how we got here."

Rage boiled inside Caldera's chest. *Olivare...* Her throat threatened to close at the thought of him—of his hands around her neck.

She shook her head. "Explain yourself," she muttered, forcing her body to resist the overwhelming urge to pummel them, to beat them until they left Bersama and never came back, her nails continuing to dig firmly into her palms.

Evie raised an eyebrow. "Well, one of the jobs of Area 51 is to cover up unexplained phenomena, as Barrett briefly mentioned, and the events at the Miller cabin have been truly eye opening." She took a few steps to the side, the bodyguard's blasters following her every move. "Tell me, are Mei and John Miller dead?"

Caldera swallowed hard, glancing back at Rennick whose full attention was on the intruders. "They—"

"Are," Desrin interrupted. "They are."

Caldera cast a sidelong glance at the leader of Sector Four, before slowly nodding in agreement. "Yes... We tried to save them but... they didn't survive the trip."

"Hmm, too bad," Evie mused. "We were going to take them with us, but it seems they will continue to be 'missing'. The cold case investigators are going to have a field day," she chuckled.

"Since you're so willing to give out information," Caldera continued, gritting her teeth, "expand on how you got here."

"Willing?" Evie laughed. "Of course we are."

"We'll gladly tell you anything you want to know," Dominic continued. "If you think you can handle it."

Caldera forced herself to stand straight, despite her shaking knees. "Tell us."

Barrett lowered his head. "After you left Olivare's body to rot, we had to pick up the pieces before the citizens of Reville became curious." He raised his gaze to meet Caldera's. "The technology we have is more advanced than you, or even the rest of Earth, knows."

"We dissected his brain, scanning it for information about your planet," Dominic continued, crossing his thick arms over his broad chest.

"And we found the answers we were always looking for," Evie said. "The information we needed to make artificial painite—the catalyst for intergalactic travel." She scoffed. "Neither Olivare, Vandren, or any of the councilmembers would tell us that."

"Took us six months," Barrett added. "I believe that's around three on this planet?"

The room fell silent. Caldera's head spun. "How could you do that?" she asked, breaking the silence.

"It was quite easy," Evie replied, tilting her head. "He wasn't using it anymore."

"No. I mean, *how* did you do it? Scan Olivare's brain?"

Evie sighed. "Ever heard of optography?"

"That is the theory of retrieving and viewing an image from the retina of the eyes," Mokan cut in.

"Exactly," Evie said, snapping her fingers. "We simply took that theory and applied it to the brain instead. After all, what is it? A storage bank powered by electrical impulses." She shrugged. "It wasn't that hard to manipulate."

"The hardest part was actually finding the information we were searching for," Barrett said.

A maniacal grin spread across Dominic's face. "It took weeks of routing around in that guy's dome—triggering random impulses, getting him to speak."

Caldera's stomach flipped, nausea rocketing through her body as the color drained from her face. "You had his body and... made him... speak."

"Yeah, and a lot of nonsense came of it."

"If you have the right tools," Evie interrupted, taking a step in front of Dominic, "death is not the end."

The only thing Caldera could hear was the sound of her own blood rushing to her ears. The memories she'd tried so hard to force to the back of her mind—to push deep down into the darkest areas of her soul so she could continue living—rushed to the forefront of her brain in a blur.

She hated Olivare, truly hated him, and she was glad he was dead, but if the people of the Area 51 organization were willing to desecrate his body to such an extreme... A person they knew and were working with...

Nothing else mattered but getting those people away from her—away from her friends, her fellow leaders, her people.

She ripped the blaster out of Rennick's hand, taking several steps forward, the barrel never wavering from Evie, the one who seemed to be in charge. "That's all very interesting, but I suggest you leave. Now." Her breath came in short, shallow gasps. "Or I *will* kill all of you. Unarmed or not."

Evie shrugged. "That's too bad. Ultimately, we've come to strike a bargain—"

"No! Not from you." Caldera shook her head, now alternating her blaster between the three intruders. They were surrounded, backed into a corner of the conference room by bodyguards with weapons pointed at them, and sector leaders scrutinizing their every move, but it didn't faze them. "Not interested. Leave!"

"I must agree with Queen Caldera, although not with her actions," Mokan said, with a nod. "We have nothing for you here and are not interested in your exploits."

"Hold on jusst a moment," Jasik said, speaking for the first time, their voice hitting harshly against her ears as they stepped out from behind the wall of bodyguards, joining Mokan and Desrin. "I believe we sshould hear them out."

"I concur," Eldra's weary voice replied, stepping out from behind Caldera. "That was the whole point of these meetings, after all."

"Don't you understand?" Caldera faced the other sector leaders, struggling to control the level of her voice. "These people... this organization, they don't speak for Earth—not even a portion of it!" She whirled around, turning to face the congregation that had gathered behind her. "They don't represent anyone but themselves! They actively *helped* The Council—Vandren, Randis, Kex, Thael, and Cleo—the people who actively oppressed us and were willing to sacrifice our lives like they meant nothing! Do you think it'll be any different if we partner with them?"

The leaders aren't listening to me—they won't listen. She turned back toward Evie and other Area 51 invaders. Fire blazed in her chest and her eyes widened. She pointed the blaster at them. *They deserve this...*

Rennick ran up to her, never taking his eyes off the intruders, grabbing the blaster out of her grip with one hand and wrapping his arm around her with the other, pulling her back until she was behind the wall of bodyguards once more.

"Ren—"

"Be quiet, Callie."

She blinked, taking a step backward as if he'd punched her. Unable to speak, she stared at his rigid back.

"All right. Why don't we do this officially?" Evie asked. "It seems we've interrupted... a meeting of some kind?"

"You have," Eldra said. "Please, let us all re-take our seats, with our... 'guests' standing in the middle to present their case."

"Not without proper precautions," Caldera snapped, her voice low.

"Like shooting them?" Desrin quipped.

The fire inside Caldera's chest blazed, extending to every extremity. "No... but chaining them up wouldn't be a bad idea."

A grumble of agreement emerged from the rest of the sector leaders.

Caldera nodded to Rennick, who spoke into his wrist communicator.

The arrivals from Area 51 were herded into the middle of the open area, that the circular table surrounded, and moments later, Bruna appeared with three sets of metal mitts used for transporting criminals to various locations. Every palace had some on retainer in case of a break-in.

Systematically, Bruna clamped them over the intruders' hands and placed the corresponding magnetized circle on the floor at their feet. With a press of a button, the magnetic circle activated, anchoring itself to the floor, connecting with the signal of the restraints, and pulling Evie, Barrett, and Dominic's hands down with enough force so they could still stand, but could no longer lift their arms.

Seemingly satisfied with her work, Bruna stood off to the side of the detainees, her shoulders square, and continued to oversee the proceedings.

Aloriea reappeared beside Caldera. "Mei and John are in their quarters guarded by Grey and Sylvie," she whispered, leading her back to her seat. "The other political advisors are waiting in the great hall with Saro. I'm going back to join them and try to keep everyone calm."

Without another word, Aloriea whisked away.

Evie, Barrett, and Dominic glanced around at the sector leaders, seemingly unimpressed by their restraints. The bodyguards, instead of pressing their backs to the wall, stood next to their corresponding leader, ready for a potential attack.

Caldera couldn't move, her body frozen in the chair with her gaze glued to the tabletop, unwilling to accept what was happening. The air was thick with tension as the sector leaders waited for the strangers to speak. She slid her eyes around the room; if she didn't know better, she'd say there was nothing wrong.

There were no overturned chairs or tables, no signs of a scuffle, no blood had been spilled and no weapons had gone off. There were absolutely no indicators that Bersama had been invaded.

"State your case," Nari said, baring her sharp canines.

"Listen," Evie began, dawning a bright white smile, "I acknowledge that the way we arrived here was... less than ideal, but we really aren't that bad. Certainly not as bad as Queen Caldera there would have you believe." She slid her brown eyes over to Caldera as if challenging her to speak up.

Caldera balled her hands into fists so tight, her nails started cutting into her flesh; but she said nothing. *I already made a fool out of myself once. I almost killed them.* She took in a shaky breath, forcing herself to focus.

"Area 51 is a place of research and development," Evie continued. "We've always been interested in alien races but never really get the chance to speak with them. That's essentially all we want."

The word 'alien' hit Caldera's ears like nails on a chalkboard, making her flinch. It didn't sit right. It sounded wrong. Derogatory.

"What kind of research are you pursuing?" Eldra asked, taking control of the interview in her typical poised and political way.

"To put it simply, advancement of technology for our own planet's sake."

"That does seem interesting," Mokan replied, taping an outstretched claw against his chin in contemplation.

"You don't have to put it ssimply," Jasik said, furrowing their brows, their forehead scales shifting. "We undersstand."

"Are you sure?" Evie asked, locking eyes on Caldera, clearly trying to get another rise out of her.

Caldera gritted her teeth as all eyes fell on her. *She thinks I'm the weak link...* A realization hit her, threatening to steal the air from her lungs. *She's trying to turn them against me because I'm the only one who's been to Earth.* Straightening her shoulders, she leaned forward.

"Are you saying you're interested in pursuing some kind of 'meaningful' relationship with us?"

Evie blinked, a look of surprise briefly flashing across her face before dissipating. "Of course."

"In exchange for what?" *You lying pieces of shit.* "You can't expect us to believe you don't want anything."

"It truly is simple," Evie said. "We want to study you. That's all." She took a deep, satisfied breath, as if finally getting to the point she had been beating around the bush about all along. "In exchange, we'll let you come and go from our planet as you please. You can take whatever you want and we'll cover it up, so the rest of Earth will be none the wiser."

"Study us how?" Eldra asked, her arctic blue eyes glinting in the light.

"After all the years of inhabitants of this planet secretly coming and going, we were never able to. You see, we do not have different species such as you on Earth," Evie replied. "Seeing how you function would benefit our planet greatly."

See how we function? Something's wrong. Goosebumps rocketed up Caldera's arms and she found her voice once again.

"That sounds like a threat."

The three said nothing, as if they were unwilling to respond. Unwilling to tell the truth.

"You... what?" Eldra whispered, her arctic eyes darting between the three Earthlings.

Mokan and Nari exchanged nervous glances but stayed silent.

Caldera caught Desrin's gaze, noticing her clenched jaw and tensed body language. Even Fenry seemed to be stunned silent.

"Yess," Jasik said, nodding in her direction, clearly picking up on the fact that the three were hiding something. "In that case, we appreciate your offer, but we musst decline."

Caldera frantically glanced at each sector leader, silently pleading with them to agree. "Yes, we're declining. Right?"

The other sector leaders stood and nodded in agreement—a complete consensus—their faces a mix between shock and horrific realization.

"If you stay any longer, you'll be arrested," Caldera continued, standing up from her seat.

"How disappointing," Evie said, exasperation coating her every word.

"You may regret it," Barrett added, his cold eyes peeling over Caldera's skin.

Dominic grinned ferociously. "Yes, I do have a feeling we'll be seeing more of you in the future."

Without another word, the three forced their wrists together, successfully pressing the buttons on what looked like watches, opening another portal, and disappeared.

Caldera stood in stunned silence, her head spinning. "What happened..." she whispered.

"Something unprecedented," Eldra replied, a worried look never leaving her face. "We'll be needing upgraded security—"

"Obviously," Desrin chided. "If they can disappear into thin air even after being detained..."

"What elsse can they do?" Jasik said, finishing Desrin's thought.

"We need to add security drones over our palaces for the foreseeable future," Mokan said, his deep voice booming.

Caldera nodded. "And sanction our scientists to try and come up with a security measure to counteract their versions of the portal bracelets."

The room fell silent.

"Well, is this something we can *all* agree on?" Caldera asked.

No one spoke.

Caldera hung her head, her jaw beginning to quiver. "I know your faith in me must be wavering at best, but please, if it's the only thing you can spare at this time, trust me. These people are dangerous, and we need to find a way to protect ourselves.

"Very well, we'll do what you recommend, Your Majesty," Eldra replied, looking around at each of the other sector leaders. "Starting as soon as we return home."

A cacophony of agreements followed suit, all meeting Caldera's ears at once. *They all look to Eldra for guidance—they'll follow her no matter what.* She bit her lip, knowing that they'd never respect her the same way.

"Okay then. We're adjourning."

"I believe that is a good idea," Mokan replied.

The sector leaders and their bodyguards shuffled out of the room one by one.

Desrin turned, her red eyes burning into Caldera. "If you want us to reveal ourselves to Earth—to those... barbarians..." She shook her head. "Then you're an even worse leader than I initially thought."

Without another word, she flipped her long hair over her shoulder and was gone, leaving Caldera and Rennick alone in the conference room.

CHAPTER 5

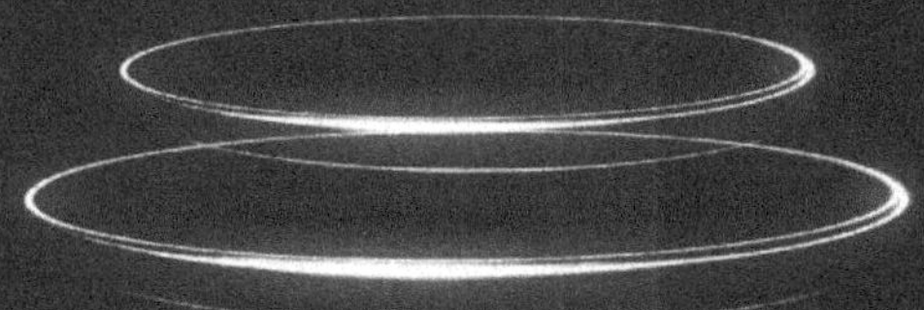

"This can't be happening," Caldera muttered, sitting at the table in her quarters, across from Aloriea and Rennick. Bersama's two moons shone through the balcony doors, shut tight against the growing blackness of night.

The rest of her friends milled around, equally trying to make sense of the earlier events of the day. Markarian leaned against the wall while Sear paced back and forth across the room, his claw tapping constantly against his chin. Mei and John sat in chairs pulled away from the table to face everyone.

"They said they scanned Olivare's brain?" Markarian asked, glancing out the window of the balcony doors and zipping up his black windbreaker jacket over a plain undershirt. "That's some freaky shit."

"It honestly doesn't surprise us," John said, flipping blond hair out of his eyes and crossing his legs while motioning from himself to Mei.

Mei nodded, pulling her jeaned knees up to her chest. "Yeah, Area 51 is known on Earth for freaky shit."

"I still cannot believe that they have that sort of technology at their disposal, though," Sear added, padding back and forth across the room.

"Well, do *you*?" Mei asked.

"Bersama overall... has dabbled in the area..."

"Exactly. So why not Earth? You guys seriously need to stop thinking of us as primitive cavemen."

"Cavemen?" Aloriea tapped her long fingers over the table-top and raised an eyebrow. The light of the moons glittered off her metal horn and white blouse.

"I'm assuming it's a person who lives in a cave," Rennick said, leaning heavily on his elbows and pointedly not making eye contact with Caldera. His suit was wrinkled, and black circles were beginning to form under his eyes.

"Ugh," Mei groaned, dramatically hanging her head.

"The fact remains," Caldera said with a sigh, forcing herself to look into each of her friends' eyes. "They know how to get here now. What are we gonna do about it?"

"What *can* we do?" Rennick asked, directing his question away from her.

"Most likely nothing," Sear replied, his good ear laying flat against his head. He scratched the nub of what was left of his other ear. "The most logical thing to do would be to make a deal—"

"Absolutely not." Caldera jammed a finger onto the tabletop for emphasis. "We should only be making deals with the ruling government."

"How many times do we have to tell ya?" Mei tucked strands of black hair behind her ears. "There is no ruling government."

"At least not in the United States; that's a democracy and a republic," John corrected, picking at a thread from his sweater. "But there are countries with rulers like you... I guess, for lack of a better comparison."

"And that's my point," Caldera said, motioning her hand toward him. "Area 51 isn't one of them."

"But Sear's right," Aloriea protested. "We can't let them have free reign of this planet without restrictions and a deal could essentially rein them in."

"There are ways to monitor when a portal opens," Caldera tried. "We could have the whole planet constantly monitored. We certainly have enough satellites..."

"That is a preposterous suggestion," Sear said, with a wave of his hand and stopping his incessant pacing. "Even if the other sector leaders go for it—"

"What would a security force do when they got there?" Markarian pushed himself away from the wall. A low growl escaped Sear's throat at the interruption. Markarian winked at him, causing John to laugh.

"Exactly," Rennick added with a huff, rubbing his eyes. "It's not like we can shoot them on sight."

Caldera clenched her jaw, narrowing her eyes in his direction. "I know that," she grated, "but I'm still bringing up the option at the next meeting."

"Speaking of that..." Aloriea muttered, nervously clicking her nails across the tabletop, "the sector leaders are postponing in-person meetings effective immediately."

"When were you planning on telling me this? You know I don't like being kept out of the loop," Caldera said, her eyes widening. "And why was I not included in the vote for that motion?"

"Because there *was no* official motion," Aloriea replied, fiddling with the tip of her artificial horn. "Apparently they all had the same thought. I got four separate messages addressed to 'Political Advisor, Lady Aloriea Morin' with special attention to Queen Caldera, requesting a halt on meeting activity due to the unidentified threat of Area 51... They want you to visit each of them at their palaces to discuss potential options."

"Again... When were you planning on telling me?"

"Soon. Maybe when you cooled off a little more—"

"So, they don't want to leave because they're scared of being killed, but they don't care if I am?" Caldera scoffed. "Great."

"The message said it was because you're more trained for combat and you've actually been to Earth—"

"Bullshit," she muttered. "Do you have anything else that could fuck up my day?" Caldera asked, sighing heavily and rubbing her eyes.

Aloriea nodded slowly.

Caldera couldn't hold in a guileless chuckle. "What?"

"I also received a formal request from the heads of Tellis's top organizations—"

"The annual Summit Conference," Caldera muttered, slamming a hand down on the table. "Fuck!"

Mei's eyes widened. "Is that like a ball?"

"More like a glorified meeting," Rennick muttered under his breath.

"Sounds interesting," John chimed in.

"It's not," Caldera replied brusquely.

"Is this something that is really necessary?" Sear asked, coming to Caldera's aid.

Aloriea met his eyes, shooting him a look that said, 'you know it is'. "If we want Tellis to avoid societal collapse, it is."

Markarian blew out a breath. "Don't you think you're exaggerating a little?"

"No."

"But we don't have time—"

"It's something we have to *make* time for," Aloriea pressed. "This is part of being a leader, Callie…" She paused, taking a deep breath as if trying to organize her thoughts. "You can do this."

Caldera bit her lip, flicking her eyes between each of her friends until they landed back on Aloriea. "How many are attending?"

"All of them. There are ten signatures on the request."

"When's the requested date for?"

"Next week…"

The room fell silent, night flyers cawed outside the window as the second moon rose fully into the sky.

"On that note," Markarian said, stretching his arms and yawning. "We should go." He made eye contact with John who nodded and nudged Mei out of her chair and to the door.

"I do agree," Sear said, padding over to Aloriea and extending his hand to her. "Keep us updated," he added, meeting Caldera's gaze, his gold eyes gleaming.

"They're expecting a response as soon as possible," Aloriea said, taking Sear's hand and allowing him to help her up.

"Noted," Caldera muttered, as they all shuffled out of her quarters, leaving her and Rennick alone. The sudden emptiness of the room let her untense her shoulders for the first time in hours.

The two leaned back in their chairs, almost simultaneously, the familiar and repetitive movement reminding Caldera of when they were simply captain and first officer. The memory hit her like a transport, nearly causing her to lose her balance and topple over. It felt like a lifetime ago.

Facing Rennick, she forced herself to speak through the awkward silence. "Are you ready to stop being such a passive aggressive asshole and talk this out?"

Rennick chuckled sarcastically, shaking his head. "Oh yeah, I'm the asshole in this situation. It's all my fault—"

"You haven't so much as looked at me since the meeting."

"I didn't realize it was a crime to be mad."

"What are you even mad about? They attacked us—"

"No, they didn't, Callie!" He rose to his feet. "They came here, and we pointed weapons at them... You threatened to kill them—unarmed, for all we know, civilians." He walked around and knelt in front of her, taking her hands in his. "That isn't like you..."

"They're dangerous..." she whispered, unable to pull her eyes away from his. "I know it."

Rennick lowered his head. "You're probably right, but you're a queen now, Cal. You're going to have to think of another way to deal with threats other than pointing a blaster at them."

Caldera gripped his hands tighter. "All I ever wanted was to change Bersama." Her voice caught in her burning throat as Rennick looked back up at her. "Everything's so fucked up now," she gasped, forcing the tears that threatened to flow down her face to stay in their tear ducts. Her chest was on fire as her body shuddered. "I don't know what to do. I feel like I'm losing my mind."

"We'll get through it," he replied, leaning forward and wrapping his arms around her, rubbing her back.

"I know *we* will... but at what cost? Who am I Ren?"

He cupped her face in his hand, brushing her cheek with his thumb. "How can I help you?"

"I don't know... I think I need to help myself."

"Do you need someone to talk to?" He paused, as if carefully contemplating his next words. "Professionally, I mean?"

She leaned back so she could look into his eyes that were filled with understanding—with the desire to do anything he could to help her. The trauma of the past year that she'd worked so hard to push away threatened to overflow, like the tears still stinging her eyes.

"I think..." She took a deep breath, clenching and unclenching her fists as the resolve to seek help settled throughout her entire being. "I think that's probably a good idea. As long as you go with me."

"Of course."

"This—this recklessness—that I can't seem to shake almost cost me my allies..."

"I... I don't know how true that is, Callie, but listen to me, whether you realize it or not, because of your reckless tenacity, you've already done great things for Bersama. For everyone. I hope one day you'll realize that."

Caldera smiled, her chest filling with warmth. She wrapped her arms around his neck and kissed him like he was the air she needed to breathe. The world fell away as he folded an arm around her back while the fingers of his other hand got tangled in her hair as he pulled her closer to him.

She let her body meld against his until the only thing she could think about was his lips pressed against hers—until nothing else mattered.

CHAPTER 6

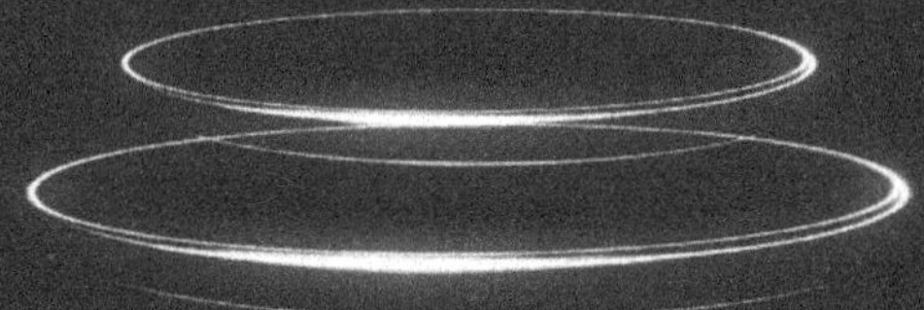

Rose-colored light shone through the balcony door windows of the next morning as Caldera blinked awake to the sound of her communicator chiming. With a groan, she rolled over, grabbing it off the bedside table and answering it with a flick of her finger.

"Hello?"

"Queen Caldera, good morning to you. At least, I believe it's morning there. Here in Penkith, it's already late in the afternoon."

Caldera jolted upright, rustling the covers and waking Rennick. "Queen Desrin?"

"What..." Rennick yawned, "is going on?"

"Ren—"

"Are you sleeping with your bodyguard?" Desrin scoffed.

Caldera furrowed her brows. "He's my partner, so—" She stopped herself from going on. "It's none of your damn business."

"Wow." Desrin replied with a laugh. "You are so... unprofessional."

"What the hell do you want?" Caldera snapped, throwing the covers to the side and getting out of bed. "And why are you calling me on a private line?"

"I want to inform you of a decision that was reached earlier today."

Caldera shook her head, orienting herself to Sector Four's timezone. "And?"

"The other leaders and I have come to a consensus about what should be done with the Earthlings in your possession."

"You had a meeting without me," she said, her breath catching in her throat. "That hardly seems fair."

"It was," Desrin replied without hesitation. "I was the one being reprimanded, after all."

Caldera blinked. "Why?"

"Because I forced everyone's hand by telling the Area 51 representatives that your Earthlings have died. You weren't invited because we all already know your stance on the issue."

"First of all," Caldera said, wrapping her fingers tighter around the communicator, and walking out onto the balcony, resentment rising in her chest, "I still should've been witness to this motion! And secondly, the Earthlings aren't *mine*. They're free."

"Exactly."

"W-what?"

"That was the decision. The Earthlings are free. Free to roam around and no doubt wreak havoc. We can't send them back now."

Caldera sucked in a breath as cool morning air settled on her bare arms and legs making her shiver. "You could if you really wanted to."

"Not in good conscience." Desrin exhaled sharply. "You were right about the councilmembers. We were disposable to them—everyone who didn't further their plans was... But we aren't like them. We care about the lives of others as you do." She paused as if not sure she wanted to continue. "We are your allies, Caldera, and will continue to be. We just... don't understand you. Why didn't you tell us about Area 51?"

Why didn't I? How could I?

"Desrin, I don't—"

"That's all I needed to relay to you. The other sector leaders and I sanction the citizenship of Mei and John Miller on Bersama—with caveats. They must stay within Sector One. It's up to you to put restrictions on them...

"And for the record, I'm actually looking forward to our one on one meeting. Once dates are decided, Aloriea will be informed."

"Wait!" Caldera said as the line went dead. She stared down at the communicator, its dark screen reflecting the bright morning light back into her eyes causing her to squint and look away.

"Who was that?" Rennick asked, walking up behind her.

"Desrin," Caldera replied. "Come on. I don't like how we got here, but we have some good news for Mei and John."

After throwing on clothes and quickly recapping her conversation, Caldera and Rennick hustled down the hall toward Mei and John's quarters.

"They can do whatever they want?" Rennick asked, rolling up the sleeve of his shirt to his elbow as they turned a corner.

"She said it's up to me to put restrictions on them," Caldera replied.

"So, are you?"

Caldera didn't answer, slowing to a stop and pounding her fist on Mei's door, while Rennick went one room down and did the same.

John answered almost immediately. "Ren, Callie? What's going on?"

"Just a minute," Rennick replied, stepping aside and letting the shorter man into the hallway. "We're waiting for your sister."

"Good luck. She sleeps like a brick."

Rennick chuckled, crossing his arms. He paused for a brief moment before continuing. "Have you thought about what you want to do here? I mean, job-wise?"

"I studied environmental sciences on Earth, but—" He shook his head, scratching the back of his blond mop of hair. "Where is this coming from?"

"It's only a question… and one you might want to start figuring out the answer to."

John furrowed his brow.

Caldera continued to pound her fist against the metal door and after a few minutes, she could hear commotion from inside.

"What, what, what!" Mei yelled as the door swished open. "Do you know how early it is?" She blinked, her black hair was a tangled mess and the oversized sleep shirt that fell below her knees had deep wrinkles in it. "Oh, it's you two. What is it?" she asked, rubbing sleep out of her eyes.

"I have something important to tell you. Are you listening?" Caldera said, as Mei yawned.

"Yes, I'm listenin'," Mei said, yawning again and stepping out into the hallway, finally noticing her brother. "What the hell is goin' on?"

Caldera took in a deep, excited breath. "You're officially inhabitants of Bersama! I mean, you'll have to sign some paperwork and get your DNA into the Tellin census system, but…" She trailed off, deciding not to overload them with the details right away.

Their eyes widened. John's jaw dropped as the widest grin Caldera had ever seen spread across Mei's face.

"Seriously?" she screamed, jumping up and down, all traces of sleepiness gone.

Caldera let a soft smile settle on her face. "Seriously."

Mei screamed again, wrapping thin arms around Caldera and squeezing as tightly as she could while continuing to bounce. "Thank you! Thank you! Thank you!"

"How did you do it?" John asked, grabbing his excited sister by the shoulders and prying her off of Caldera.

"I, umm, didn't," she said, smoothing out the newly-made wrinkles from her blouse and shoving her hands into the pockets of her slacks.

The siblings shot her a confused glance.

"She was informed this morning about the decision," Rennick said.

"It was made without me because my stance has been known since the beginning," Caldera continued. "The other sector leaders decided they can't send you back now in lieu of the Area 51 situation."

"I don't care how it happened," Mei said, her brown eyes shining. "Does this mean we get to leave the palace? We can go wherever we want now?"

Caldera nodded, letting out a chuckle. "Kind of. You have to stay within the Tellin borders, but that's better than nothing." She paused, thinking about what Desrin had said. "And I won't put any limitations on you as far as activities or jobs you can, or want, to pursue. Do you have any ideas?"

John shook his head, glancing over at Rennick. "I honestly thought this day would never come..."

"Well, I do," Mei said, interrupting him and nodding vehemently. "I'm going to join the Vanguard."

Caldera raised an eyebrow. "Really? I would've thought you'd do something artsy."

Pink flushed across Mei's cheeks. "I love art, but..." she lowered her voice, "I wanna be like you."

"Mei..." Caldera managed before the words got tangled in her throat. *Does Mei actually look up to me... Does she want to follow in my footsteps?* Caldera forced a smile and took a step forward, placing a hand on the girl's shoulder. "Being me is overrated. You need to be you."

"Yeah, I know. I think I would like it... I've always wanted to go to space."

Caldera let a more genuine smile spread across her face. "Well, it's up to you now. You'll figure it out. I know it."

She turned to John as the first bustling of the morning kitchen staff met her ears and the subsequent smell of cooking breakfast meats began floating down the hallway, making her stomach grumble. "You said you studied environmental science?"

A quick rush of pink speckled his face before dissipating. "Yes, but it was Earth related... I focused on conservation, but I doubt my knowledge about that will be of any help here."

"You need updated information," Caldera said with a wink. "The T.E.R.A. organization is always looking for people to add to their network."

"Not to mention Tellis, and all of Bersama, really need conservationists," Rennick added, leaning against the wall and tucking his hands into his leather jacket.

"I don't know. What's T.E.R.A.?"

"The Tellin Environmental Restoration Agency," Caldera replied, tilting her head to the side, eyeing John's jittery hands and darting eyes. "You know what? It's not something that you have to decide now. Think about it, talk to Markarian about it."

"Seriously, John? Now is not the time for your indecision to take over," Mei said, turning to her brother. "You can stand up to sector leaders, but when it comes to deciding what you want to do with your life, you can't make up your mind?"

His body tensed. "Excuse me for not wanting to rush into anything."

"You did the same thing on Earth, essentially getting us outcasted from that shitty little town, mister unemployment check!"

"There were no substantial options! I didn't go to college for four years to work at a diner on the extraterrestrial highway."

"That's where *I* worked, you asshole!" Mei clenched her fists together and took a step forward, as if she were about to attack her brother.

Rennick stepped in between the two, holding up quieting hands. "How about we all take a breath? This isn't a huge deal."

Caldera's head spun at the siblings' sudden outburst toward each other. "Mei, it's okay," she chided, while attempting to smile over at John. "Honestly, you don't have to do anything you don't want to," she added, meeting his gaze, desperate to try and deescalate the argument while making him feel comfortable with the situation. "Let me know what you decide."

John blew out a breath, his shoulders relaxing. "I definitely will." His eyes flicked from Rennick to Caldera, before he settled a glare on Mei. "Thanks for letting me weigh my options."

"Of course," Caldera replied, turning and motioning for Rennick to follow her back down the hall. "Why don't you both get ready for the day, and we'll see you downstairs at breakfast with everyone else?" She stopped short. "Oh, and don't forget about the Summit Conference in a few days. Now that you're full-fledged citizens, and residents of the Tellin palace, you can come."

Mei's eyes lit up, already seeming to forget about her recent outburst. "It's a ball, isn't it? I know you said it wasn't, but it *is*, isn't it?"

Caldera and Rennick blew out simultaneous breaths while John absently shook his head, pinching the bridge of his nose between a thumb and forefinger, clearly exasperated by his sister's mood swings.

"Sure," Caldera replied, over her shoulder with a chuckle. "It's a ball."

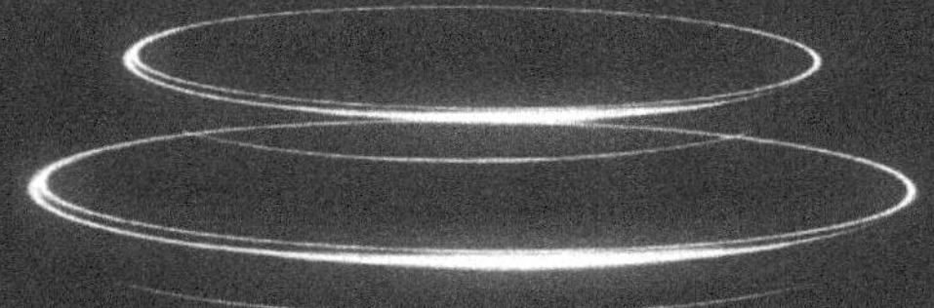

CHAPTER 7

After confirming the date and time of the Summit Conference with the heads of the ten Tellin organizations, Caldera gave the word to start preparing for the event. Over the next five days, the great hall nearly vibrated with excitement as the palace workers decorated for the annual Summit Conference.

Caldera and Aloriea walked through the archway entry a few hours before the event, their heels clicking against the marble floor that had been polished so vigorously, its glossy surface reflected their images. Her simple black tank-top and slacks contrasted with Aloriea's green formal dress that haloed the floor as they came to a stop in the middle of the great hall. Caldera flicked her dark blue eyes around the area, hungry to see how the setup was progressing.

Her gaze was immediately drawn to the thin drapes that were tied open on each side of the ten large picture windows that lined one wall of the great hall, letting in the golden hues of the setting sun.

Grey and Sylvie stood watch over the multitude of palace workers and caterers as they put on finishing touches to the area, making sure everything was progressing smoothly and efficiently.

"Do you remember what you need to do?" Aloriea asked, taking a few quick steps forward and whirling around to face Caldera. The long sleeves of her dress swirled against her thin arms, and her black curly hair caught on her metal prosthetic horn with the movement.

Caldera nodded, taking a deep breath. "Like last time, I'll be speaking to the department heads of Tellis," she replied, her voice echoing off the vaulted ceilings as her attention moved to the outskirts of the room. "Pretty straightforward."

Round dining tables, complete with white tablecloths, perfectly polished and spaced silverware, and gold-edged porcelain plates lined the perimeter of the great hall, with enough open area in the middle to walk around and converse. Only around twenty guests were expected to attend, but the hall was large enough for at least fifty if need-be.

In previous years, entire families, including children, had been allowed at the event, but Caldera decided against it going forward, limiting the representatives to one guest each; kids only caused distractions and worry among the parents.

She thought back to when she was young, running off, getting into trouble, and especially trying to sneak into places she wasn't supposed to be. Her guards weren't babysitters, and she didn't want unsupervised children running around the palace, putting unnecessary pressure on them.

"Straight forward, for the most part," Aloriea agreed with a sharp nod, "but there *is* a difference," she continued, holding up a dark finger. "From this year on, you actually have the power to allocate funds to the organizations of your choice."

The tiered, crystal chandeliers glowed with artificial light, and Caldera could have sworn she heard the soft buzz of the yellow-colored bulbs that continued to emit constant illumination, even as the outside world became gradually darker and darker with each passing minute.

Caldera gripped the bridge of her nose, her head pounding. "I understand," she said, crossing her arms. "My plan is to essentially give funds to every organization... Who gets the most is yet to be decided."

Aloriea shrugged. "That's a good plan. Undoubtedly, someone will leave angry, though."

"At least they're getting something."

Aloriea opened her mouth to respond but quickly snapped it shut as footsteps approached.

Sylvie walked up to Caldera, interrupting their conversation and placing a hand over her heart, before a wide grin took over her face. "What do you think?" she asked, spreading her arms wide, red hair tumbling down her back. "It's coming along great, isn't it?"

Caldera nodded. "It looks beautiful. Thank you for helping oversee the setup since Saro and Bruna have to guard the entryway."

"Of course!" she replied, glancing over her shoulder at her brother Grey. "We won't let anyone here sneak hidden cameras, weapons, or any other unauthorized items into the great hall during this process."

"I don't think they would, but..."

"It's better to be safe rather than sorry," Sylvie cut in, finishing Caldera's sentence and furrowing her brows.

"Exactly. There are a lot of unfamiliar employees, and I honestly haven't met them all yet. Not to mention I've almost been assassinated once already... That was in Sector Two, but still—"

Aloriea cleared her throat. "You're doing great, Sylvie. Continue on."

The girl nodded and turned her attention back to the setup progress, walking toward a group of workers and pointing this way and that.

"Be prepared," Aloriea said, continuing their earlier conversation. "I'll let you know now that the militia isn't used to not getting their regularly scheduled funds."

"Well, they'd better get used to it," Caldrea muttered, turning on her heel and walking out of the hall. "I'm not the Council, and the militia is the least of my worries—and Tellis's. There are other organizations that need money more than the military."

Aloriea let a smile spread across her face. "I'm glad you still feel that way."

"Why wouldn't I?"

"I mean... Area 51—"

"It doesn't matter," Caldera said, cutting Aloriea off and starting up the staircase to her quarters. "We still don't know what their game is yet... and I'm not going to start a war."

"Good," Aloriea replied, her voice stern. They rounded the corner of the second floor and started their ascent to the third. "Get ready and I'll meet you in the great hall in about forty-five minutes. I'm going to freshen up a bit, and then I'll be overseeing each representative's check-in with..." She let her sentence trail off.

Caldera took a deep breath, quickening her pace. "Saro?"

"Yes." Aloriea shook her head, as if to clear her thoughts as the two stepped onto the third floor and started down the hallway.

Caldera placed a hand on Aloriea's arm, bringing them to a stop right before their quarters. "I understand why you're skeptical of him," she whispered, meeting Aloriea's brown eyes, "but he helped save us... Maybe give him some credit?"

The hallway fell silent for a moment. Aloriea pursed her lips. "I don't understand why you're *not* skeptical." Her voice was hard as stone. "He and his brother were complicit in the murder of your uncle, for universe's sake."

"Saro wasn't."

"Are you sure about that?" Aloriea asked, crossing her arms.

Caldera nodded. "I'm sure. I trust him, Aloriea."

Another bout of silence filled the area. The bustling from three levels below in the great hall filtered up the staircase, followed by a crash and quick commotion.

The words, *I'm all right, I'm all right*, from an unfamiliar voice hit Caldera's ears and threatened to draw her attention.

"Regardless," Aloriea scoffed, turning toward her door. "He may have helped us take down the Council in the end, but one good deed doesn't absolve him from past misconduct."

Caldera shook her head, letting out a bitter chuckle before heading to her quarters.

"Once the reps have all been scanned in and are gathered in the great hall, I'll start conversing with everyone until you arrive," Aloriea added over her shoulder as she disappeared into her room.

"See you down there," Caldera muttered to herself as the door to her quarters slid open.

CHAPTER 8

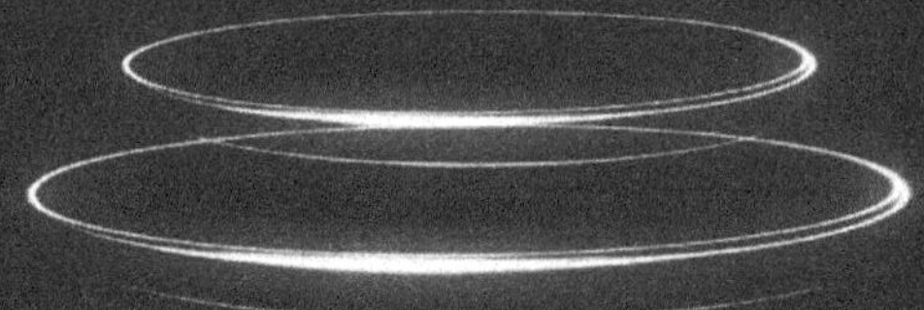

The bright light of her private bathroom successfully illuminated Caldera and the mess of makeup strewn around the sink, the same as it had for the past thirty minutes. She finally finished braiding both sides of her hair, pulling the two thick strands behind her head and fastening the ends together in a small bun. The remainder of her platinum hair hung down loose below her shoulders.

"You still alive in there?" Rennick called from the other side of the door. "We have—" There was a pause. "—exactly fifteen minutes to get to the great hall before we're late... for the second year in a row. That must be a record of some kind."

"Almost done!" she replied, sliding the beige silk choker-shirt over her head and adjusting the sparkly tulle that covered the entire outside of the garment.

The wide sleeves of the top cinched at her elbows and billowed as she moved back and forth, hanging down past her hands when she was at the resting position. The thick waistband of her wide-leg, black slacks accentuated her thin waist and the overlay of sheer, chiffon fabric, breezed freely against her legs, flitting behind her as she stepped out of the bathroom to face Rennick. "Okay, what do you think of this outfit?"

His eyes widened, briefly giving her a once over before standing and meeting her gaze again. "That's the one for sure." He placed his hands in his black slack pockets. "I'm sorry I'm in a normal suit."

She laughed, sliding on short black heels. "You look great."

A loud knock echoed throughout her quarters.

Rennick glanced at her with a look of skepticism on his face, one she was sure she shared.

Pressing her hand against the inside scanner, she let the door slide open.

Mei was standing there, nervously wringing her hands together. Her black hair was wrapped in a bun near the top of her head and she wore a light pink sheath dress that landed at the marble floor, barely grazing it.

"Mei? What're you doing here?" Caldera asked, motioning for her to enter the room.

"Are you okay?" Rennick added, concern flitting across his face.

She nodded. "I'm fine... I..." She glanced from Caldera to Rennick before falling quiet.

Caldera pursed her lips, placing a hand on Rennick's chest. "Why don't you head down to the conference? I'll be there in a minute."

He nodded, squeezing her hand and exiting the room without question.

The door slid shut, leaving the two women in silence.

"Umm, will you help me with this?" Caldera asked Mei, pointing to the back of her neck where the clasp of the choker-style shirt she wore was, realizing it still needed to be fastened.

"Sure thing..." Mei replied, quickly moving Caldera's hair to the side and snapping the clasp closed with nimble fingers.

"All right, what's wrong?"

"Nothing... it's just..."

"Mei, seriously," Caldera said, glancing up at the clock on the wall. Its digital hands read *'21:50'*. The sun had completely set, and the first moon was beginning to rise. *Ten minutes until the conference starts.* "What is it? You never act like this."

"I'm... a little nervous," Mei replied, her eyes darting from side to side.

"You're saying your whole 'bravado' thing is an act?" Caldera asked, trying to keep her tone as light as possible.

"Sometimes," Mei muttered. "Depends on the situation, and this is something I've never, ever, done before..."

Caldera's mind flashed to Mei's journey through the portal, and the events leading up to it. The resolve to save her brother's life, despite not knowing what would happen to him or her. The desperation to not be alone. The constant determination to not let her homesickness show.

She looked into the smaller woman's dark, angular eyes. "You've been through worse. This is nothing."

"Well..."

There was a quick pause.

"All right, first of all," Mei continued, the words beginning to spill out. "I look ridiculous, and second of all, the head of the Vanguard is down there! How am I supposed to talk to them without looking like a total suck-up?"

Caldera couldn't hold in her laugh. "Aloriea forced the same formal wear on me in the beginning. Now, I honestly kinda like it." She turned to face the younger girl, shirt-sleeves swishing around her, and placed a hand on Mei's shoulder, smiling. "I was nervous the first time I met these people, too."

"You were?"

"Absolutely shaking with anxiety... but it's not as scary as it sounds," she said, deciding to leave out the fact that she was *still* nervous about meeting the organization representatives, even though she had spoken to them all over a dozen times now, at least. "I ended up being fine, and so will you. Okay?"

Mei set her jaw and gave Caldera a vigorous nod. "Okay."

Caldera stood up tall, hoping to give Mei all the second-hand courage she could muster. "Ready?"

"Yep!"

"All right," Caldera said, absently placing her silver crown on top of her head and ushering Mei out of her quarters.

They walked quickly to the stairs, past drawn-open curtains, letting in pools of silver moonlight. The clicking of their heels against the marble soon got lost in the muffled conversations filtering up from below.

Caldera picked up her pace, with Mei following quickly behind, descending the three levels to the main floor where the great hall was positively teeming with revelry.

Rennick was waiting for them at the bottom of the staircase outside the entryway. "Right on time." He grinned at Caldera and held out his hand.

She took it, letting him help her down the last two steps.

"I'm going to see if I can find John and Markarian," Mei said, nervously flicking her eyes around the area as her feet reached the bottom of the stairs.

"Grab me if you need anything," Caldera called, as Mei took a deep breath, squared her shoulders, and walked into the fray of people populating the hall. She turned her attention back to Rennick, looping her arm around his. "Let's do this."

They walked through the archway, where Saro was diligently standing guard, and into a revamped great hall. All the guests had arrived, filling the large space and making it look much more cramped than it really was.

A small live orchestra played softly in the far corner, away from the guests, the electric string and bass instruments of the five composers making perfect, subtle background noise. Palace waitstaff, in crisp black uniforms with the golden embroidered crown on their right breast pocket, made their way around the room, weaving in and out of the chattering representatives and their partners, delivering hors d'oeuvres and exchanging empty crystal champagne flutes for full ones to anyone who wanted them.

Every guest was dressed in their best—tuxedos, gowns, iron-pressed slacks, and blouses—accompanied by updos, slicked-back hair, and expensive jewelry.

Caldera made her way through the mingling crowd with Rennick by her side, carefully meeting each guest's gaze as she passed, making sure to nod in acknowledgement that she saw them. Thick clouds of cologne and perfume stung her nose, threatening to make her sneeze and causing her eyes to water when she resisted the urge.

She spotted Markarian, John, and Mei sitting at a currently unoccupied table—Markarian and John in their suits, talking frantically to a clearly jittery Mei. They spotted her and she waved, pointing toward Aloriea and Sear, signaling that she was going to talk to them first before heading their way.

The gold inlays of the white marble wall glittered in the combined light of the chandeliers and moonlight from the windows as she approached Aloriea, who was talking enthusiastically to Sear next to a large, roaring fireplace, a glass of champagne in each of their hands.

"You're here," Aloriea said, turning her attention to Caldera. She wore the same green dress from earlier, but her hair was in a tight bun at the base of her neck with two curly pieces of intentionally left out hair framing her face. Her natural and prosthetic horns were on full display, curling behind her ears.

Sear adjusted his long tie and swished imaginary debris from tailored black slacks that fell to his knees with his free hand. "And on time, no less," he added, taking a small, padding step forward, clawed feet clicking against the floor, and the fur on his legs swishing with the movement. The black tail-coat he wore was buttoned over a white dress shirt.

Caldera chuckled, taking a drink from a passing tray, the golden bubbles rising in the flute.

"That's what I said," Rennick laughed, waving a hand at the worker holding the tray and shaking his head, indicating he'd pass on the alcohol.

"What were you two talking about?" Caldera asked, ignoring the jab at her lack of time-management, and turning her attention to Aloriea's and Sear's conversation.

"Deimi Auris is extremely excited about Sear's progress with the teleportation technology," Aloriea said, her eyes shining. "If appropriate funds are allocated to the Vanguard, Sear's team could receive a huge research grant!"

"So, that's your vote on where I should allocate the most funds?" Caldera asked, arching an eyebrow and sipping her drink.

"Obviously," Sear replied immediately. "But I know you need to weigh your options first."

"Keep that in mind." Aloriea smiled, locking her arm around Caldera's—before she could protest—and pulling her toward the center of the room. She picked up a knife from a passing table and tapped it against her champagne flute to direct everyone's attention toward them.

Caldera's stomach flipped over on itself as every head in the great hall simultaneously turned toward her and the room fell silent. *Damn it, that never gets easier.* She took the opportunity to practice her breathing exercises as Aloriea spoke.

"Hello, everyone, and welcome back to the annual Summit Conference. In case you missed it, the queen has arrived. Please feel free to mingle with her about your respective organizations and, above all, enjoy the night!"

She raised her glass in the air and the crowd followed her action with *'hear, hear'*, and general cheers of agreement.

"Thanks for the intro," Caldera muttered, tightly gripping the stem of her glass as some groups went back to their conversations, while other guests immediately made their way over to her.

Aloriea laughed, squeezing Caldera's arm reassuringly as a tall man approached. "Good luck. You've got this," she said, taking a few steps away and letting Caldera begin the negotiations on her own.

"Your Majesty, it's nice to finally meet you in person," the man said, outstretching his hand as he came to a stop in front of her. His salt and pepper hair was combed back with not a single strand out of place. Round, black rimmed glasses adorned his long nose, and his business suit was perfectly tailored to his large, lithe frame without a wrinkle in sight. "My name is Oron Tyse, and I'm the head of the Tellin Courts and Justice System. Do you mind if we chat right away? Unfortunately, I cannot stay long."

"Of course we can," Caldera said, taking his outstretched hand and shaking it. It was cold, and she quickly released it as the chill threatened to travel up her arm, taking a step back. He towered over her and she took yet another step backward, not wanting to crane her neck in order to look the spindly man in his face. "What can I do for you?"

His light blue eyes blinked down at her, and he hunched over slightly, as if all too aware of his monstrous height. "What I'm requesting is simple," he said, his deep voice steady. "I would like allocated funds for larger wages to be able to pay my employees more."

"Are they not adequate now?" Caldera asked, tilting her head to the side. "I was under the impression that the authorities, especially in Astrum, were more than well-off."

Oron kept his face perfectly neutral, no doubt the result of years of practice. "That's not my point." He leaned in close, hunching his body even more.

Caldera had to force herself to stay put.

The black-rimmed glasses slid down his nose and he quickly pushed them back up as he spoke. "Something... unprecedented is happening. There has been an uptick in disappearances that are being reported as of late, forcing my detectives and officers to put in extra hours." He stood up tall, clasping his hands behind his back in a matter-of-fact way. "They deserve to be compensated for their extended efforts."

"What do you mean an 'uptick' in disappearances?"

"Just that, Your Majesty," Oron replied, adjusting his glasses yet again. "It's not enough at the moment to cause major concern, but it's enough to grab one's attention, if you will, and certainly enough to justify overtime."

Caldera's head spun. *This couldn't be them... could it?*

"Please think on it, Your Majesty," he continued with a small bow, snapping Caldera back to reality. "Now, I must take my leave, back to work and all that. I'll leave my official request with your political advisor." He placed a hand over his heart, the universal sign of respect, and started making his way through the crowd toward Aloriea.

Caldera cleared her throat. "Thank you," she called after him, not sure what else to say. "Umm, please keep me updated on the disappearance reports!"

Oron glanced over his shoulder, a skeptical look in his eye, and nodded as another person stepped into view to introduce themselves, barely giving her a moment to recover.

"Your Majesty—"

She squeezed her eyes shut. The room was getting smaller. She couldn't breathe. "I'm sorry, could you give me a second to catch my breath?"

A familiar voice cut through the chaos. "Please take a step back from the queen. I'll personally come get you when she's ready."

Immediately, a rush of air drew itself into her lungs, and the crowded, trapped atmosphere subsided. Caldera opened her eyes to see Saro standing in front of her.

She blew out a breath, running an absent finger down the scar on her cheek. "Thanks, I thought I was a goner."

"No problem. Rennick's running interference for Sear and Markarian—"

"As usual," Caldera retorted, letting a small smile break across her face.

"I can go get him if you want."

Caldera tilted her head to the side and leaned against the wall, letting the coolness of the marble sink through her clothes and into her skin. "That's okay, I'm sure he'll make his way over in a few minutes."

An awkward beat passed between them.

He cleared his throat, turning to leave. "Well, I'd better—"

"Saro, can I ask you something?" Caldera blurted. She bit her lip, not sure what had overcome her, nor why she wanted to know the answer to this question so suddenly.

His shoulders tensed as he turned back around to face her. "What is it?"

"Are you happy here?"

His multi-colored eyes glinted with curiosity before settling into contemplation. "That's a loaded question, isn't it?" he replied after a few seconds.

"Is it?"

"You're expecting me to respond in a certain way, aren't you?"

"And what way would that be?"

"Well, you're probably thinking, how could I be, right? After all, my brother was murdered after revealing he, himself, was a murderer—using 'protecting' me as an excuse, by the way. Your court, at the very least, distrusts me. Aloriea downright hates me, and to top it off, I gave away the lead guard position to a woman way less qualified than myself."

Caldera nodded, eyes wide. "It sounds like the answer's actually quite simple then..."

"It's not," Saro replied, exhaling slowly while rubbing the back of his neck, drawing her attention to the scar at the base of his chin.

He took a step closer to her, instinctively causing her to back completely against the wall, muscles involuntarily tensing. *Maybe I don't trust him as much as I like to believe I do...*

"Look, Callie," Saro said, his voice low. "All I want to do is prove that I had nothing to do with Sol, Vandren, or Olivare..." He ran a hand through his short, sandy brown hair. "I'm not like them..." He pressed his palm against the wall, next to her head. "And if I have to lay off, and let people come to their own conclusions about that, so be it."

"You don't have to do that from here, if you don't want to," Caldera muttered, placing her palms flat against the wall behind her as if willing a secret door to open. "You were proven innocent in court, you don't have to stay in the palace."

He nodded, lowering his arm and leaning back. "I know, and I'm not gonna lie, it hurts, walking around these halls, but I want to push through that pain. This is how I want to handle things... Can you let me do that?"

"Yes," she whispered as Saro stepped away from her.

"That's all I can ask for," he replied, turning away. "I'm going to go grab the rep that was way too eager to talk to you..." He glanced over his shoulder at her. "They're hovering."

Caldera relaxed, letting a soft chuckle escape her lips.

Saro widened his eyes in an *'oh boy'* kind of way, leaning into the tease, before walking off.

CHAPTER 9

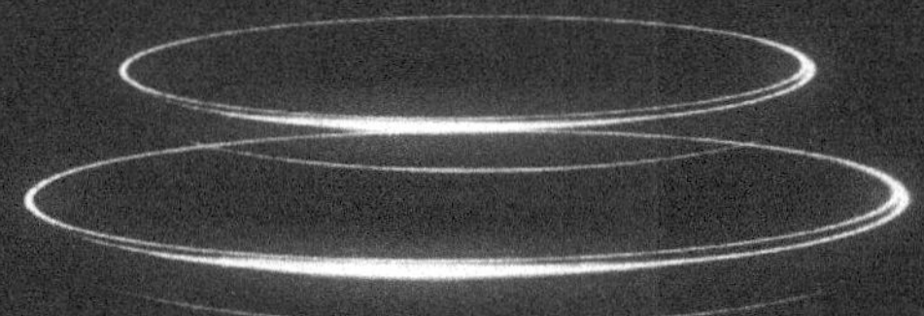

Taking a deep breath, Caldera sat heavily in a chair at one of the few empty tables. It was later in the night and almost all of her guests had already staked their claim to a resting place. She had only been talking to representatives for a little over two hours, but her mind was beginning to jumble the information they were giving her together.

Deimi wants grant money for Vanguard scientists.

The head of Tellin Transports wants allocation for newer, more technologically advanced transport vehicles and larger speedways. She scoffed to herself. *As if the roads aren't big enough already.*

And the Tellin Hospital Organization needs their own grant money to give to their researchers. She groaned out loud, placing her head in the palms of her hands, thinking about all the time she had spent in the hospital over the past year. *I should probably give the T.H.O. what they want... and I can't forget about Oron with the T.C.J. or the other six organizations that all, rightfully, want something!*

"Doing okay?" Rennick asked, appearing in front of her and kneeling. "Tired?"

She shook her head, looking at him through spread fingers before lowering her hands to her lap. "No, I just need a break. It feels like my head's about to explode."

"Well, we can't have that, now can we?" he chuckled, looking over his shoulder. "So, let's go," he said, standing and outstretching his hand toward her.

Caldera raised an eyebrow. "Go where?"

"To the dance floor."

She laughed out loud, placing a hand over her mouth to quiet herself. "You're joking," she replied, glancing behind him at the couples already swirling around to the music.

"Nope. You said you weren't tired, and needed a break from the bombardment."

"Yeah, but I didn't say I wanted to dance."

A sly grin spread across his face. "What's the matter? Don't know how?"

She matched his expression, adjusting her crown and clasping his still outstretched hand. "Oh, I know how to dance, Silvera," she replied, standing and letting him lead her to the middle of the room.

He wrapped a hand around her waist, pulling her close. "Then show me."

Caldera sucked in a breath, wrapping one arm over his and placing a hand on his back while the other continued to grip his free hand. She looked into his hazel eyes, letting him lead as the next song started.

They swayed back and forth to the gentle beat of the music, occasionally swirling around at random intervals as the crowd around them continued on with their own conversations or dances, seeming not to notice them, even though Caldera was sure that wasn't that case.

"I think you're doing great, by the way," Rennick whispered as he led her around the dance floor to the beat amidst the other couples.

"I know how to dance—you know that," she replied with a smirk. "It was something my parents taught me."

"I was talking about the whole queen thing, ruling the sector—you know, political stuff." He paused, a look of distress seeming to cross his face before quickly dissipating. "I don't know if I've ever told you that."

Caldera smiled, her chest swelling with warmth. "Maybe not in so many words... but you didn't need to. I could tell..." It was her turn to pause. She gripped his hand tightly, afraid that if she let up, she'd fall to the floor, her past mistakes all rushing into her brain at once. "Even though I've messed up... quite a few times now?"

Rennick didn't flinch, gazing down at her with unwavering loyalty. If he was uncomfortable with her sudden death-grip, he didn't show it. "This should go without saying," he said, twirling her away from him—their fingertips barely touching at the peak of their arms' extension—before pulling her back in, "but nobody's perfect."

"I'm not talking about being perfect, I'm talking about being competent."

"And you are."

"Then why do I feel like, I don't know, you don't approve of what I'm doing sometimes?"

He smiled. It was an easy, comfortable smile, built on years of friendship, trust, and love. And one she knew all too well. "We can disagree, Callie, but that doesn't mean I'm not proud of you."

Her heart ricocheted against her chest as the music picked up in pace. Knowing the man before her, she had expected some type of reassuring sentiment to leave his mouth, but his words rang so true, and were so *unconditional*, they brought her to the verge of tears.

"Thank you, Ren," she whispered.

He pulled her close, kissing her forehead before spinning her around in tight circles, his metal leg not slowing him down at all.

Caldera never took her eyes off him as the music escalated.

Melancholy gave way to elation, and she let everything else in the immediate vicinity melt away.

Her breath quickened as they danced. Rennick's golden brown features, including the scar that ran vertically through his eyebrow, appeared softer, more lustrous as they passed through puddles of silver moonlight. His hair swayed with constant movement, bouncing over his ears and across his forehead as he locked eyes with her and smiled in a way that always made her heart skip a beat. His eyes were pools of honey, staring down into her soul.

He saw her, really saw her—her true self—all her shortcomings, successes, failures, and strengths, and he never, not once, turned his back. He had been there for her through the best, and very worst of times, and he always would be.

She couldn't put those feelings or what that meant to her into words, and she didn't need to. Loving him was as natural as breathing.

The billowing sleeves of her shirt fluttered around them as they spun, the sewn-in sparkles of the tulle glittering in the light like shooting stars as their bodies moved together in harmony.

A shock of excitement coursed through her as Rennick hooked his hands under her arms, lifting her into the air in a half spin before returning her to the ground as the music began to die down and their perpetual movement came to a slow stop.

She stepped closer to him, pressing herself against him until their foreheads were touching. To her surprise, they were both out of breath. Their chests rose and fell in synchronicity, and Caldera closed her eyes, not wanting the moment to end. The smell of mint hit her nose and she inhaled deeply, taking in every aspect of him.

"Callie," Rennick's voice whispered in her ear.

Her eyes fluttered open, once again locking onto his, their lips only inches apart.

"Feel better?" he asked, his breath caressing her cheek.

"I do," she said, looking up at him with hooded lids, "but I really don't want to go back to work."

CHAPTER 10

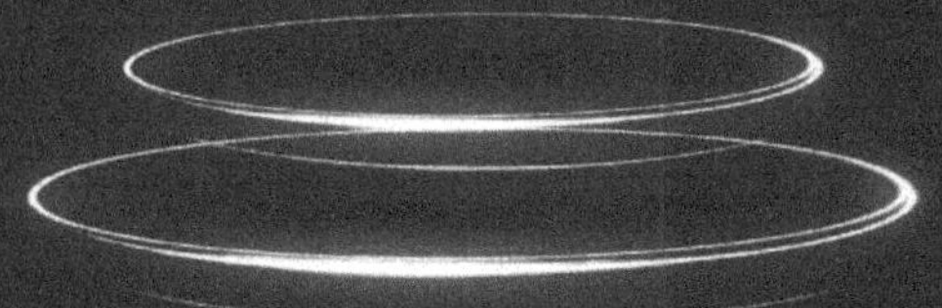

After the success of the Summit Conference, another, more casual, meeting with Oron Tyse came and went, and Caldera ultimately agreed that it was only fair to raise the pay of the overworked officers and detectives of Tellis—focusing within the capital of Astrum.

The remaining funds were allocated throughout the rest of the nine organizations appropriately.

The Vanguard and hospital systems got their grants, T.E.R.A. got approved for further conservation efforts, and the militia and transportation organizations—though initially unhappy with their smaller stipends—were ultimately appreciative of what they did receive. The other organizations such as the schools, social welfare, labor, and treasury systems had all asked for minor, or less planetary invasive requests, which were accepted immediately.

As a busy two weeks came to a close, Aloriea announced that the sector leaders had finally decided on the dates they were expecting Caldera's visit.

"Are you ready?" Caldera asked, turning to Rennick.

"Not really. I can't tie this damn tie, and my leg is killing me."

She smiled, walking across the room to where he sat fiddling with the piece of fabric around his neck.

"Okay, well, I can help with the tie issue," she said, grabbing the cloth, ripping it away from him, and tossing it on the ground. "You don't need one." She glanced down at his metal leg. "You're probably experiencing phantom pain... If I had to guess."

"How long does that last? I've had this thing for almost four months now. You think I'd be used to it."

She shrugged. "I can't remember the Vanguard training manual any better than you can, but I think you're due for a checkup with Doctor Vareis anyway. That thing might need to be calibrated."

"Calibrated?"

"I don't know how it works." Caldera chuckled, kneeling down and helping Rennick adjust the cuff of his tailored pant leg around his knee since it would no longer fit over his metal prosthetic comfortably.

"Knock, knock," Aloriea said as Caldera's door slid open. She fluttered into the room, her emerald-green dress haloing at her feet. "Come on, your ten-day trip across the globe isn't going to start itself." She grinned. "I'll help you grab your things."

Caldera raised an eyebrow. "You seem a little... hyper. Everything okay?"

"Absolutely! I used to love going on these extended trips with Quill. Meeting with the sector leaders, getting to put my knowledge about sector policies to use, everyone agreeing with my proposed solutions..." She sighed longingly. "It's been a while."

Caldera and Rennick glanced at each other before laughing.

"I'm glad you're excited," Caldera said, grabbing her luggage out of Aloriea's grip and fishing her communicator out of her pocket. "But this is seriously cutting into my personal life." She headed toward the door, messaging Sear and Markarian to meet them at the ship on the roof.

"Look, I'm sorry that these meetings coincided with you finally agreeing to get help for your multitude of problems..."

Caldera shot her a glare.

"Not that that's a bad thing!" She held her hands up as they continued walking down the hallway. "All I'm saying is that after these meetings, then you can go to therapy to your heart's content."

"Therapy, huh?" Markarian said, meeting them at the alcove stairs leading up to the roof. "Have you two scheduled your first session yet?"

"No." Rennick took the lead as they ascended. "We were going to but then we got distracted with Mei and John becoming full-fledged citizens, and then the sector leaders decided that this whole meeting thing needed to be done sooner rather than later."

Caldera sighed. "It keeps getting pushed off, is what he's trying to say... but despite that, we're still working through things."

"Well, let me know if you need any doctor suggestions."

"You've been?" Caldera asked, tilting her head to the side.

Markarian nodded. "It was mandatory after my sister died, to stay in the Vanguard." He exhaled sharply. "And after the required sessions were up, I kept going for a while."

"Enough of this talk for now," Aloriea said, flicking through the dossier on her holopad. "Your head needs to be in 'political leader' mode."

"That's easy for you to say," Caldera muttered, blowing out a breath.

"I'm serious, Callie. This log details your meeting with each of the sector leaders, reiterating how you're the only one traveling because they're all too scared, but I can promise you, there's something else going on here."

"I have to agree, Cal," Markarian added, rubbing the back of his head. "This is too weird."

Rennick nodded. "Not to mention the convenient timing of it all."

Caldera's stomach twisted. *They're right... I need to be on my game, but what could the other leaders possibly gain from this?* She shivered, caught between instinctually wanting to trust them, given all they'd gone through, and the urge to scrutinize every move they made from this point on.

Her thoughts were swirling around in her head, a tornado of racing notions and images, as they reached the top of the stairs, pushing the door open and stepping out into the sunlight, where Sear, Mei, and John were waiting next to the palace's personal shuttlecraft.

"It is about time you showed up," Sear said, pressing a button on his holopad to lower the ramp and straightening his black tie with a monogrammed 'S' at the bottom. "You are late."

"We're right on time," Caldera said, looking down at her wrist monitor.

"You would have been on time ten minutes ago," Sear countered, tucking a hand into his shorts pocket and walking up the ramp. "I will be waiting inside until takeoff."

"I'm right behind you," Rennick said, squeezing Caldera's shoulder before following Sear onto the shuttlecraft.

Caldera chuckled and glanced over at Mei and John. "What are you two doing here? Shouldn't you be at VHQ?"

"We came to see you off." Mei grinned. "Sylvie's taking me to Vanguard Headquarters right after! Wish me luck—I'm officially trying out for the entrance exam today."

"That was quick," Caldera said, returning the smile.

"There's no time to waste!" Mei replied. "I want to start contributing to this world right away."

"You're sure you'll be okay by yourself?"

Mei met Caldera's eyes, her voice taking on an unusually serious tone. "I'll be all right."

"I'm going with her," John replied, embracing Markarian. "Maybe I'll figure out what I want to do while I'm there. After talking to Ms. Qin Zhang at the Summit Conference, I'm starting to think T.E.R.A. might actually be my calling, but I want to check possibly working for the Vanguard off my list first."

Caldera smiled. "Promise to look out for each other," she pressed. "I've also told Saro and Bruna explicitly to watch over you."

"We'll be okay, geez," Mei interrupted, placing her hands on her hips. "You don't have to send the whole cavalry."

"I'm only making sure," Caldera countered. "I know if you're with Sylvie, she won't be paying attention to her surroundings, or any potential danger."

Mei shrugged. "She's cute... but so is Grey..." She tapped her chin. "I may have trouble focusing myself."

"You always have trouble focusing," John said, shoving Mei's shoulder.

"Shut up!"

"Listen!" Caldera snapped, shaking her head. "Just know I have two guards who will not let you out of their sights no matter how much you bat your lashes at them."

Mei rolled her eyes and headed to the stairs, exaggeratingly extending her middle finger as she walked away.

"What is that?" Caldera asked, tilting her head to the side and starting up the ramp.

John chuckled, kissing Markarian on the cheek before walking after his sister. "She's playfully saying, 'fuck you'."

CHAPTER 11

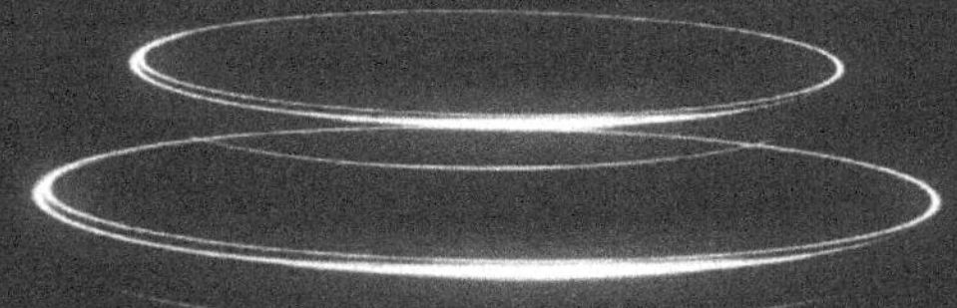

aldera leaned forward on her elbow, watching the endless ocean spread out before her. They had flown over the border into Natioh hours ago and were coming up on the palace of the capital—Mirstone.

Taking a deep breath, she let the rhythmic movement of the waves hypnotize her into letting down her defenses as she stared without blinking into the curling blue, incomprehensible mass of sparkling water below and in front of her, stretching out to the horizon.

Slowly, everything seemed to melt away and she was no longer bothered by the upcoming meeting with the queens of Sector Two. No longer afraid of what they might say, nor how they might try and dictate her actions moving forward. Sheer emptiness spread through her body and, although she was conscious of her friends talking amongst themselves, she could no longer hear their individual voices.

Mirstone... Caldera ran through the schematics of the palace in her mind the way she always did before her visits. She had been there half a dozen times but still found herself wanting to mark the exits and escape routes. Her skin tingled with remembrance of the assassination attempt on her life the very first time she ever stepped foot in Eldra and Fenry's home.

The shuttle shifted as the pilot lowered its metal arms to touch down on the concrete landing pad, jostling her out of the trance.

"We're here. Look alive, people," Aloriea said, getting to her feet and clapping her hands together. "Remember your talking points!"

Rennick, Markarian, and Sear stood, stretching, and walked over to meet Aloriea at the open door as the ramp began to descend.

All eyes fell on Caldera. She didn't move.

Rennick waved them on before walking over to Caldera and kneeling in front of her. He placed a hand on her knee. "What's wrong?"

Swallowing hard, she balled the fabric of her pants into fists. "I have a really bad feeling about this, Ren."

"What kind of feeling?"

"There's something off about this whole thing... Why do they want to meet with me—with *us*—like this?"

"I mean, it clearly has something to do with Area 51..."

Caldera clenched her jaw. "I'm not questioning the guise. I'm questioning the motive behind it."

Rennick inhaled deeply, standing and reaching out his hand. "The only thing we can do is be on guard."

She took his hand and nodded, letting him lead her out of the shuttle and down the ramp where the rest of her friends were waiting.

"Ready?" Aloriea asked, wrapping her arms around herself as a harsh wind blew through the clearing and over the cliffside where the landing pad was located, the current whisking everyone's hair away from their faces and pressing their clothes tight to their bodies.

"I'm ready," Caldera confirmed, releasing Rennick's hand and pushing forward, leading them toward the outcropping of the cliffside on which the palace sat.

After several minutes of walking upwind, they reached the pearly gates.

Waiting for them was Dathan, the head of palace security. His luminescent stone-gray skin glittered in the light of the rapidly setting sun, and his fin-like ears pointed straight up as if standing at attention. "Greetings, Queen Caldera and Court," he said, pressing two fingers over his heart and bowing—the sign of respect from Sector Two's inhabitants.

Caldera and her group nodded in thanks and began scanning their hands on the presented device in front of them.

"Dathan," Aloriea said, stepping forward and placing her hand on the scanner after Caldera, "what should we expect from this meeting?"

What's she trying to do? Caldera flicked her eyes from Aloriea to Dathan. She was aware their friendship and mutual respect for each other had been present long before she had come into the picture, but she also knew that his loyalties to his queens were fierce and unbreakable.

The external gills on the side of his neck vibrated but stayed tightly clamped shut. "I can't say," he replied, lowering his voice and taking a step closer. "But I will warn you, there have been stirrings..."

"Stirrings?" Caldera said, furrowing her brows.

"Of what kind?" Sear added, blinking golden eyes, nose twitching.

Dathan raised a hand to the side of his mouth as if he were sharing a secret. "This sector has been on edge for the past few weeks. It seems like dissent is brewing throughout the capital and major cities."

Caldera's eyes widened. "Ever since the—"

Aloriea jammed her elbow into Caldera's ribs, causing her to cough and effectively stopping her from continuing.

"Shit, Lor," Markarian said, raising his eyebrows.

"Umm," Rennick cleared his throat, stepping forward and drawing the attention to him. "Do you know why?"

Dathan's eyes narrowed, skepticism and curiosity floating behind his green irises. "I'm unaware of anything the queen's have been doing differently that would cause such a shift."

He's deflecting, Caldera thought, standing up straight. The brine-filled air stuck to her arms as another gust of wind blew through her hair and over her skin. "Thank you, Dathan. We'll head inside now, if that's all right."

"Of course," he said, pressing a button and letting the gates and front doors of the palace swing open.

"Thanks for knocking the air out of me," Caldera muttered as they climbed the white marble steps and entered the great hall. "What the hell was that about anyway?"

"I was trying to get information to maybe make you feel a little more at ease... I'm sorry about what I did, but I had to stop you from talking about Area 51."

"Why?"

"Because the general public doesn't know about it yet."

"Dathan is not the general public. Do you really think Eldra and Fenry wouldn't tell their head of security?"

Aloriea blew out a breath. "Honestly, they probably have, but that's not something that we know for sure. And it isn't our place to inform someone of something that the queens should have done themselves."

The group passed through the large inner archway into the multi-tiered great hall, shoes clicking against the blue agate floor. The queens Eldra and Fenry were patiently waiting at the head of the table for them to approach.

"He's your friend. Don't you think he has a right to know if he doesn't already?" Caldera pressed, leaning in close.

"Callie," Aloriea said, stopping short and turning her attention completely on her. "The whole reason we're in this mess is because we haven't been doing things properly." Her brown eyes glanced from the queens—giving them a quick, forced smile— and back to Caldera. "Don't you think we're in enough trouble?"

Caldera's back became increasingly rigid with every word Aloriea spoke. Her actions over the past year had put not only herself, but also her friends under extreme scrutiny. *And withholding information about Area 51 only made it worse for them.* "You're right."

Aloriea's expression softened. "We'll get through this, okay?"

Caldera nodded sharply, walking over to the queens. "Eldra, Fenry," she said, "it's nice to see you again."

Palace workers appeared behind each person, pulling the chairs out for them before quickly disappearing into the shadows along the wall and under the second-floor balcony.

"As it is you," Eldra replied. Her tone was cool, methodical— the warmth that usually accompanied her greetings was nowhere to be found. "I hope your travel here was fair."

The twin white-dotted lines that ran under both her eyes shifted as she talked. Situating herself at the head of the table, she never quite made eye contact with Caldera. A crown of swirling white and blue stone, resembling the action of waves, sat atop her smooth head.

"It was," Caldera said, glancing at Fenry, who hadn't spoken a word. An identical crown adorned her head, and her navy eyes glowered past waves of floor-length white hair.

Within minutes, platters were spread out before them featuring small assortments of shrimp, tuna, and oysters accompanied by sauces, crackers and a blue, bubbly drink.

The acrid smell of fish filled the air, and Caldera wrinkled her nose at the accosting odor. Her stomach turned in jealous circles as she eyed Sear's plate that got exchanged for an arrangement of bright succulent fruit due to his shellfish allergy.

Minutes, that seemed like hours, passed as the group silently picked at their food and sipped at their drinks before Eldra cleared her throat, dabbing at her lips with a cloth napkin. The sun had sunk completely below the horizon, the oranges and pinks turning to navies and indigoes as the first moon of Bersama appeared, twinkling its crescent reflection off the water outside beyond the full-length windows.

"I know that you all must be weary from your travels, so let us begin the meeting, shall we?"

Caldera laced her fingers together under the table. "Where would you like to begin?" she asked, knowing full-well what the answer would be.

"With the arrival of the curious Earth agency, Area 51, of course."

"Yes..." Caldera said, her voice brittle. "It was quite a shock."

"Was it?" Fenry replied, speaking for the first time since their arrival.

"If you're implying that I knew they would show up, you're mistaken."

"I'm not *implying* anything."

To Caldera's surprise, Eldra stayed silent, not acting to quiet her wife with a sharp intonation or gentle hand like she normally would have. *Have I seriously lost that much trust?...*

Her stomach wrenched, twisting tightly with the realization. "I'm only going to say this once," she said, squaring her shoulders and making sure to catch each of the queen's eyes. "I have nothing to do with Area 51 or its people." She leaned forward, resting an arm on the tabletop as she did so. "And I'm not asking you to believe me... I'm demanding it."

Eldra looked slightly amused. "You sound confident."

"It's the truth."

Fenry said nothing.

Another uncomfortable difference, Caldera noted. *She never misses an opportunity to take a jab at me...*

"Regardless," Eldra finally said. "We should leave speculation alone for now."

She doesn't believe me.

"What are your suggestions on how we handle them?"

"I'm not sure," Caldera said, wringing her hands together. "There are ways to track and trace the openings of portals..."

She flicked her gaze from each of her friends, already knowing how they felt on the subject.

"That would take every satellite we have," Eldra replied with a sigh. "Although, it is something we have considered."

"It's something that should take top priority," Caldera continued, pushing through the opening Eldra gave. "At least consider allocating a few. If every sector were to do that, and work together, then we could stop them!"

Eldra and Fenry exchanged a glance that Caldera couldn't quite read. *Are they... scared?*

"Stop them from doing what exactly?" Eldra asked, her voice uncharacteristically harsh.

"I don't—" Caldera stammered, unsure of where to go from there. "I don't know what they're planning to do, but I know it's nothing good."

She bit her tongue, forcefully stopping herself from bringing up what Dathan had mentioned earlier. The last thing she needed was to be the reason that they stopped trusting him, or worse, the reason he got fired.

After a moment of awkward silence, Eldra nodded. "We'll consider this option, but for now, let us move on to other proceedings." She turned her attention to Sear. "Our lead scientific researcher, Vive Lise is here." Her eyes fell on Markarian. "And the Vanguard liaison, Rhe Cordes."

Sear and Markarian's eyes lit up as the two aforementioned natares were led into the room by Dathan.

Caldera couldn't help smiling as the pairs immediately started chatting, fluidly exchanging ideas and hypotheses—throwing out theories and possible rule changes, all to make the Vanguard and technological advancements better for Bersama. She slumped in her chair, as if hundreds of pounds of weight were on her shoulders, unable to actively listen to any of it.

Aloriea's fingers were flying over her holopad, dutifully taking notes on everything that was said.

"You gonna make it?" Rennick asked, leaning in close from the chair beside her.

"Barely."

He smiled. "I'll be sure to nudge you if you start drifting off," he chuckled.

"Like old times?" she whispered, letting a genuine smile break across her face.

"Nothing like a Vanguard Captain and First Officer meeting to put you to sleep," he winked.

"Queen Caldera," the unfamiliar voice of the Vanguard liaison named Rhe said. "Do you agree with Sir Ales assessment?"

Caldera pursed her lips, having not heard a word they had said. She met Markarian's frantic green eyes and smiled. "Absolutely."

THE MEETING LASTED LONGER THAN Caldera wanted, and by the time they were shown to their rooms by a quiet palace worker—down the long windowed hallways and past the areas that she and Rennick had run down all those months ago while escaping assassination—she was all but ready to pass out.

"Here you are, Your Majesty," the worker said, before scurrying away.

Caldera and Rennick opened the door to a large, round room with a wall completely made up of curtainless windows overlooking the ocean. Both moons were high in the sky, casting a silver, rippling glow across the floor and pearlescent sheets of the circular bed as if they were underwater.

Sitting down heavily on the plush bed, Caldera let her gaze linger out to the water. The same things she had felt before, when she was fearing for her life in a tiny alcove off the main hallway, arose once more. She didn't know what it was about the ocean that brought up feelings of insignificance.

Maybe its vastness? Its apparent emptiness? The unknown of what lies beneath?

"How can a place be so beautiful but so bleak at the same time?" she muttered, closing her eyes and rubbing them vigorously.

Rennick sat next to her, rubbing her back. "That's something I don't think we'll ever know the answer to."

Caldera's throat knotted as the events of everything that she had done, everything that she had talked her friends into doing, slammed over her like waves crashing against the breakers of a cliff. *And what have my actions gotten us? Attacked, mistrusted, and under investigation.* Her eyes clouded as she fought back a waterfall of tears.

"Have you ever wondered if there's no order to anything?... If it's just chaos all the way down?"

"What makes you say that?"

"It's like devastating events are unfolding despite my best efforts to prevent them."

"Callie," Rennick said, gripping her shoulder. "I know it's rough right now, but I promise you, there's order in this world..." His tired eyes locked onto hers. "And if anyone is going to find it, it'll be you." He nudged her playfully. "I believe that wholeheartedly."

A weak smile spread across her face as she leaned her head back and tried to let his words fill her with confidence.

CHAPTER 12

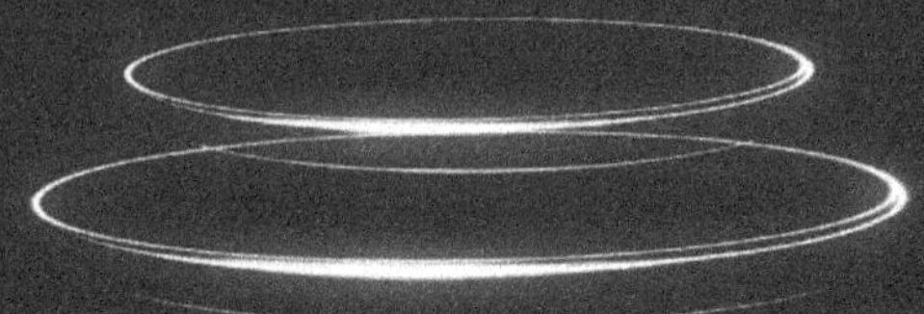

Is it just me, or were they acting... weird?" Caldera asked, running a hand through her hair and heavily sitting on the plush couch of the shuttle as it lifted off the landing pad one day later, finally able to voice her opinion.

"They certainly were a little more reserved than normal," Aloriea muttered, a look of distress glinting across her face, "but Eldra and Fenry usually are."

Caldera bit the inside of her cheek. "Something's not right... I know it."

"They seemed okay to me," Markarian said with a stretch.

"That's because you've never met them before," Caldera huffed.

He yawned. "Well, they *did* kick us out pretty early this morning."

"They did not kick us out," Sear corrected, pointing to the ten-day itinerary on his holopad. "We were only supposed to be there for two days and one night... They were very accommodating," he added. "I cannot believe that they let me consult with their top scientists uninterrupted." He turned to Markarian. "And you were lucky enough to speak with their Vanguard liaison personally."

Markarian shrugged. "That's why we're here. I'm not surprised."

"All I am saying is that I believe you may be judging the queens too harshly, Callie."

"Maybe you're right..."

"I, for one, can't get over how beautiful the Mirstone palace is," Aloriea said, steering the conversation away from the unexpected awkwardness of the past days, and looking longingly out the window. "No matter how many times I come here, I never get used to it."

Caldera smiled, all too happy to take the bait, following Aloriea's gaze out the window. White crested waves broke against sharp craggy cliffs and the water stretched out for miles, until it met the horizon. "You're right, it is. The sunset over the ocean last night was insane."

"I think we should focus on our next stop," Rennick interjected, snapping them back. "Ruler Jasik is expecting us at the Venzor palace in less than four hours."

"Maybe they'll tell me if there's something going on with the queens," Caldera muttered, pulling her knees up to her chest and leaning her head against the window, letting her thoughts wander.

Desrin said she and the other leaders would always be my allies, but... She closed her heavy eyes, letting the paralysis of sleep take over her body.

THE HOURS PASSED AS SLOWLY as the scenery changed—switching gradually from bright blue oceans, green grass, and craggy, unexplored cliffs marred by deep blue swells and white breakers, to flat deserts, scrub lands, and desolate stretches of sand. Arid expanses of land were interspersed with solitary patches of inhabited industry that made up most of the population of

Sector Three, Sedrolla, with nothing connecting them save for a web of roads that looked like they had not been maintained for an uncounted number of years.

From Caldera's position, looking out the window after she had reawakened, it appeared as if sand had been blown over patches of the road system, making it seem disconnected and destroyed. "This place looks…"

"Ill-maintained?" Sear questioned, peering out the window next to her.

"Exactly."

"That's because it is," Aloriea replied, crossing and uncrossing her legs. "Sedrolla's sector is set up in a sort of pod system. The inhabitants live in the industrialized places and the whole area is surrounded by desert with a main road connecting each pod."

"So, depending on how they're connected, there's only one or two ways in and out?" Caldera asked, raising an eyebrow.

Aloriea leaned forward on her elbow. "For the most part. As a reptile-derived species, the setup is to ensure each citizen is getting the dry air and adequate sunlight that they need for survival. It's also why we don't see more saurians in other sectors."

"It seems like the downside is that each 'pod' is almost, if not completely, cut off from each other," Markarian said, crossing his arms. "I don't even see many transports flying around."

Aloriea nodded. "That's what makes Sedrolla such a difficult place to govern. Instead of one big sector, it's like trying to manage the needs of fifty small ones, all requiring vastly different things. It's almost impossible to keep up with every little part of this area."

Caldera bit her lip. If there was a sector leader that she wanted to help the most, it was Jasik. They overcame their fear of their ruling councilmember to become one of her first allies, and she'd never forget that. "How much longer until we hit the capital?"

"We'll be in Venzor in twenty minutes, and the palace in around thirty." Rennick replaced his holopad in the inside pocket of his jacket and rubbed the area above his knee, where the metal and skin met.

Caldera pressed her forehead against the window as a large inhabited pod came into view. *That's gotta be it.*

Within less than thirty minutes, they were touching down on the large concrete landing pad closest to the palace, amid the vast desert. The shuttle ramp descended and the hot, dry air that filled her throat made Caldera gasp for breath despite herself, making her immediately thankful she had taken Aloriea's advice and wore the most breathable material she could find.

Aloriea coughed, covering her mouth as they all stepped off the ramp into the beating, unrelenting sun. "It's not something you'll get used to in the short time we're here."

"At least we're all allowed to wear shorts," Markarian quipped, slapping Rennick on the shoulder.

Taking as deep a breath as she dared, Caldera raised her hand to cover her eyes and led the way to the saurian guard waiting for them at the edge of the cracked landing pad.

The guard, dressed in a black suit with a brown-obsidian colored, encircled crown embroidered on their right breast pocket, placed a hand over their heart and bowed. Their sage-green skin shimmered in the sun and the scales around their neck and forehead vibrated as they absorbed the heat. "Greetings, Queen Caldera and court."

Caldera mimicked the motion. "Greetings—"

"I go by Lady Lec Roas. I am the head of the palace guard and Ruler Jasik's right hand."

"So, you're Jasik's bodyguard?"

"If that helps you understand." She squeezed her fist closed, blinking green, elliptical eyes around at the group behind Caldera, the black slits of her pupils so thin, they were hardly noticeable. "Please, follow me."

Caldera nodded, glancing around her through the glare. Between the high-rise buildings and relatively scarce population of Venzor, she could see wind-worn rock formations reaching toward the sky out in the distant, uninhabited desert.

She shivered. The memory of the rock monster from the ex-oplanet, and the rhetorical questions that had plagued her since, rushed to the forefront of her mind as phantom wind and debris whipped across her face as the group continued walking.

Her breath became shallow as she zoned in on the distant building that was the palace, letting her thoughts twist and spin inside her head.

I almost died that day... Ren and I both... What if we had? What if Vandren had gotten what he wanted—

"Callie?" Rennick's voice pulled her back to reality.

They were stopped in front of the large palace doors.

What... We were at least a half-mile away just a second ago. How long was I lost in thought? She shook her head, forcing the unexplained time-loss away and stepped forward.

"Please, place your hands on the scanner," Lec said, her tongue flicking in and out of her mouth as she motioned to the wall at her side with sharp nails.

One by one, they all pressed their hands to the device, the scanner lighting up green after each approved bio-scan.

Lec's mouth curved into a snake-like smile. "Very good," she said, turning and placing her hand on the door scanner to let them in.

The doors opened directly into the palace's great hall. The walls were made of red brick, only breaking to allow for the occasional window-like aperture, and reaching up to a completely rounded, glass ceiling that let in streaks of bright daylight. A wooden table sat before them surrounded by stiff chairs. Behind the table, square arches opened directly to staircases which led into the rest of the palace's numerous levels.

Shoes clunked against the hard cement floor as the group prodded forward, contrasting harshly with the soft, instrumental background music of plucked-string instruments, chimes, and hand-drums emanating from hidden speakers in the walls.

Caldera tried to control her breathing as it came out in shallow gasps. It was like they had walked into an oven. She swallowed hard as her mouth became dry and sweat immediately began pouring down her back.

"Aloriea?" she muttered, glancing behind her as she was hit with a blast of cool air.

"Welcome my friendss," Jasik said in their thick accent, appearing from behind the square arch wearing tan trousers and a flowing, patterned garment that came to rest right above their knees. A simple black, twisted metal band was wrapped around their head. "I apologize for not being in the room when you arrived, but our air conditioning unit sseemed to be in dissrepair, requiring my attention."

"I was beginning to wonder if you had received my request that it be in use for our visit," Aloriea said, fanning herself and taking a step out from behind Caldera.

Caldera wiped the perspiration from her forehead. "Yes, thank you for attending to that," she added, finally catching her breath and letting the calming *tings* and *plucks* of the atmospheric music soothe her.

They nodded, adjusting their modest crown. "I am well aware that the other sspeciess cannot withsstand heat like we do." They motioned for the group to sit, their wide sleeves billowing. "It wass no isssue. Even *I* am feeling the heat today."

They all took their seats, flinching at the warmth from the furniture that hadn't cooled down yet.

"Sshall we begin?" Jasik asked, lacing their fingers together as they slid into their seat at the head of the table.

"Of course," Caldera replied, shifting until her body adjusted to the temperature of the chair. "I assume you want to discuss what we should do about Area 51?"

"As it iss a new revelation, I do, yess."

Caldera nodded slowly. "Let me ask you a question first."

The group all fixed their eyes on her.

Jasik raised a curious brow, silently imploring her to continue.

"Why are we doing this? If the other sector leaders are concerned about the possible threat of Area 51 and don't want to travel…" She bit the inside of her cheek before forcing herself to continue. "Then why aren't we video calling like we used to when the Council was in control?"

Jasik tilted their head, resting it in the crook of their thumb and forefinger while tapping their other hand against the table-top. "I like you Caldera, and I owe you a lot, but… it iss not my place alone to—"

"Jasik, please," Caldera interrupted, abruptly leaning forward. Her arm seared against the hot tabletop as she did so, she ignored it, unflinching. "I know the other sector leaders don't trust me right now, but… I want to trust them, and I *do* trust you." She paused, never breaking eye contact with Jasik. "Answer my question."

Silence filled the room as a look of apprehension crossed Jasik's face. The waning heat of the palace seemed to settle on Caldera's body, weighing her down and causing her shoulders to droop as she waited for a response. The seconds ticked by at a snail's pace.

Jasik glanced up at the glass ceiling as if asking the universe what they should do, before returning their attention to each of Caldera's friends before their eyes landed back on her.

Finally, they nodded, as if coming to a decision within themselves. "I'm really ssticking my neck out for you here… Rissking my own sstanding amongsst the leaderss." They sighed, lacing their fingers together. "Damn it…"

Caldera's brows rose at the sudden, uncharacteristic, curse from Jasik.

"Very well. I will tell you the true purposse of your trip."

A small, relieved smile spread across Caldera's face as she exhaled. "Thank you."

"By telling you thiss, I'm bassically going behind the backss of the other ssector leaderss, sso lissten clossely, asss I will not repeat mysself."

Caldera glanced at Aloriea, who shrugged. Clear confusion was present on every one of her friends' faces and she knew she shared the same expression. Her heart beat rapidly in her chest, and her body temperature involuntarily rose as she locked eyes with Jasik.

They exhaled sharply. "Although we are your alliess, as you asstutely sstated earlier, mosst of the ssector leaderss don't trusst you, and what little good faith you've sslowly accrued hass quickly dissipated with the appearance of Area 51 and the revelation that you withheld information from uss..."

"S-so what is this?" Caldera stammered, trying everything in her power to keep her voice steady and calm as incredulity rose in her chest. "A way to get us away from the palace?"

She clutched the edge of her chair, forcing herself to stay seated. Images of the combined forces of the other sector leaders storming her palace and taking Mei and John away shot through her mind like a plasma bolt. Her frantic gaze landed on Markarian. Judging by his horrified expression, he'd come to the same conclusion.

Jasik held up their hands, patting the air, seeming to read her mind. "It'ss a way to ssee if you're being deceptive. Thiss iss bassically an interrogation where we 'interview' you sseparately to ssee if your sstory changess from persson to persson. It iss unorthodox, I admit, and a group meeting would make more ssense, but thiss way we are free to come to our own conclusionss about you without the presssure of all the ssector leaderss being over our sshoulders."

You've gotta be fucking kidding me. Caldera exhaled sharply. She had barely heard them over the blood rushing to her ears. "What if you all come to the conclusion—the untrue conclusion I might add—that you *can't* trust me?"

"Then we'll enact the new policy that we voted into effect as ssoon as the councilmemberss were out of the picture... We'll vote you out."

Caldera blanched. *They're trying to use my idea against me...* Despite the situation, she couldn't help but take a little pride in the realization that they were acting on a regulation that she suggested, and got voted into policy, even though it meant she could possibly lose her position.

Her friends' mouths were agape. No one spoke for a while, letting the seriousness of the situation sink into every pore of the palace and its surrounding people. Even the palace workers seemed rigid.

"You think we're hiding more information about Area 51?" Aloriea's voice was sharp and clear, cutting through the thick tension of the room.

"Sseeing how you are reacting, I have come to the conclussion that you are not." Jasik smiled sharp teeth at Caldera. "You are not practiced at hiding your true intent, Your Majessty. You are an open book."

Caldera's shoulders tensed. "Granting Mei and John freedom wasn't a ruse? No one is going to attack my palace and kill them?"

Jasik blinked, surprise flitting across their scaled face. "Of coursse not."

She slumped back against the chair, exhaling sharply. All her muscles ached down to the bone.

They leaned forward, placing a hand on Caldera's shoulder and causing her to involuntarily flinch. "We are not the Council. We will not attack you or unjusstly take from you."

"Just lie to me?"

Jasik sat back in their chair. "If we were to announce a formal invesstigation, everything about you would become public knowledge. Not just your passt, but that of your family and friendss... Everything you've done and everything you ever thought about doing. Nothing would be overlooked.

"There would be nothing left of privacy for any of you." They paused, exhaling sharply and glancing at the stunned faces around the table. "You freed us ssector leaderss from bondss that we were too afraid to break on our own. In order to honor what you did for us, we all agreed thiss wass the better option."

Caldera's inner core cracked; her soul was torn between the generosity and audacity of her fellow rulers. Her hand trembled, a constant tremor that she couldn't control. She gripped it with her other hand, but it didn't stop.

"If there is nothing else you'd wish to enlighten us on," Aloriea said, leaning forward, her controlled political air on full display, "then I suggest we move on. Deception or not, we're here for a reason."

Jasik nodded, motioning at their palace staff to bring out the planned refreshments. "I agree. Let uss continue."

CHAPTER 13

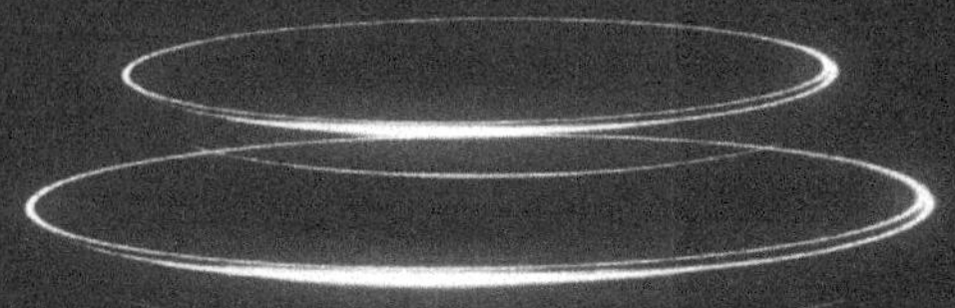

I ssee where you're coming from," Jasik said again, "but I cannot ssacrifice my galactic ssatellite sscanners to monitor for portal openingss on Berssama. Don't forget we're sstill working under the assumption that there are other inhabitable planets in thiss galaxy."

There most likely aren't, though. Caldera thought, stifling a yawn and poking at what remained of her uneaten, dried, flavored rice cakes and fresh fruit, forcing herself not to continually consume the delicious snacks—the attendants had already replaced her plate once. The meeting was lasting longer than she had hoped, and her last-ditch effort to try and prepare for Area 51's inevitable return was not going the way she wanted.

"Please reconsider," she tried, for what had to be the fourth time.

"I cannot," Jasik replied. "I'm ssorry."

Her mind whirled, finally accepting their answer. "Will you at least let me know of any *private* reports of portal openings happen in your sector?"

Jasik tilted their head to the side. "I can do that. Jusst know that you do not have authority to act on the information."

Caldera nodded, downing the last of her sparkling water. "I understand. I can reciprocate if there are any reports from Tellis."

"I would appreciate that," Jasik said, patting their forehead with long, sharp fingers. "I believe it iss well passt meeting time." They stood, prompting Caldera and her friends to follow suit and the palace staff, who were patiently lining the walls, to emerge and take the plates and cups.

Caldera picked one more mini rice cake off her plate and popped it into her mouth before her plate was taken away. The flavor of tomato and basil exploded in her mouth, and she had to force herself not to chase after the attendants and demand more.

"You are dissmissed," they continued, reaching a hand out toward Caldera.

She grabbed it, squeezing with just enough force to let them know that she could push herself to discuss policies longer if need be.

"As alwayss, it wass nice sseeing you, Your Majessty," Jasik said, stepping away from the table and swiftly disappearing behind a square arch.

Lec quickly herded the group through the other arch and away from the Venzor palace's great hall. Small apertures were cut into the stone, letting her see tiny glimpses of the desolate and windswept desert outside. Sand that had been picked up by the harsh wind was tinkling against the glass as they walked. It was the only noise they could hear, the thick brick walls effectively isolating any noise from other areas. As they continued through the palace, the hallway of the structure inclined sharply upward as if the engineers didn't know what stairs were, or were instructed not to build them—as saurians preferred to slither and slink when they walked anyway.

By the time Caldera was escorted to her quarters for the night, her body pleaded for rest—a dull, aching sensation coursing through every inch of her anatomy.

"I'm gonna chat with Markarian for a quick minute," Rennick said, hooking a thumb farther down the hall.

"Okay, I'm going to lay down," Caldera replied, waving goodnight to the rest of her friends. Without another moment's hesitation, she threw her door open and all but collapsed on the surprisingly plush bed.

Rolling onto her back, she stared up at the red-brick ceiling, laser-focusing on each microscopic crack, at a loss for words. Her brain scrambled, the information she had received from Jasik twisting and bashing against the inside of her skull—fighting for dominance.

"I understand your concern for the Earthlings. We can't patrol the entire planet, even with our combined efforts. Make a deal. Area 51." The sector specific concerns were thrown in as an afterthought. Begging to be acknowledged despite the larger issues. *"Vanguard scuttlings have marginally decreased. Funds for the S.W.S. and T.E.R.A. have been allocated and increased. A recent uptick in disappearances have been reported."*

Her mind shifted to Oron Tyse—the head of the justice department at the thought of disappearances. *He said something about that at the Summit Conference—is this a pattern?*

She tried to force herself into an upright position but her body was utterly incapable of moving. She felt nothing. She was frozen in time with her arms outstretched, waiting for the universe to implode in on her, and staring at the ceiling. Everything began to slowly fade. She closed her eyes, not to sleep, but to drift.

A sharp knock sounded at the door, followed by Rennick's voice.

"Callie?"

She didn't open her eyes or respond; his voice was too far away. Her chest slowly rose and fell in a strangely rhythmic way, clashing with her erratic heartbeat. *Maybe I'll stay like this...*

A shift in the air hit her skin, signaling the door had opened and closed. She was being gently pulled into a sitting position. Her feet hit the floor as a hand rested on the back of her neck supporting her head.

"Open your eyes."

I can't. No, that's not right. I don't want to.

Too much had happened in her short, twenty-eight-year-old life, and she wasn't sure she could take on anymore heartbreak. Her mind shifted to a topic she hadn't thought about in months—her parents.

Why did they have to go?... Why did they have to leave me?... Why do I have to shoulder this burden that should be theirs to carry!

"Callie, I know you can hear me. I need you to open your eyes."

His voice was soft and low. Calm. It rushed over her like a wave, snapping her out of the first flickers of resentment she'd ever felt about her parents.

She took a deep breath, forcing her cinder-block lids to rise.

Rennick smiled at her wearily as concern clouded his eyes. "Can you see me?"

"Yes," she rasped, as if her voice hadn't been used in years.

"What else can you see?"

Her eyes slid over the cozy room. "A wooden writing desk. A woven rug. A window."

"What's out there?"

"Sand dunes. The setting sun."

He nodded. "Good. What do you hear?"

Caldera blinked, furrowing her brows. Focusing. The shuffle of feet from the higher levels hit her ears first. "People walking. Air blowing through the vents." Her gaze shifted back to the unopenable window. Gusts of wind sent granules of sand spraying against the glass. "Tapping."

"One more."

She pursed her lips. "My heart."

Rennick nodded. "What can you smell?"

Caldera raised an eyebrow, starting to come back—to feel like herself again. "What are you doing? What is this?"

He smiled, sliding his hand down her neck to rest on her shoulder. "Humor me."

Caldera inhaled deeply. "It's musky—probably because this place is made entirely from brick." She inhaled again, a tentative, almost apprehensive, smile breaking across her face. "And mint—probably from you."

He caressed her cheek with his thumb, tucking stray hairs behind her ear. "Feel any better?"

Caldera nodded, leaning into his touch. "Surprisingly, yes. What was that?"

"It's a grounding technique. My brother used to have severe panic attacks when we were younger, and this always seemed to snap him out of it."

"I don't think I was having a panic attack."

"No, but you weren't yourself. It was like,"—he bit his lip and reached for her hand, squeezing it—"you were gone."

Leaning forward, she wrapped her arms around his neck, her fingers getting tangled in his hair. "Thank you," she whispered in his ear. "You always know how to bring me back."

Rennick tightened the embrace, pressing his face into the crook of her neck. "We'll get through this. I promise."

Caldera leaned back and nodded. "I trust you." She closed her eyes, taking a deep breath, letting renewed perseverance run through her body. "I'm not looking forward to going to Sector Four tomorrow. Desrin's a bitch."

Rennick shook his head, running a hand through his hair. "Now you're starting to sound like yourself again." He stood, stretching. "We'll deal with her tomorrow. State your case and know that we all have your back."

Caldera nodded, patting the bed beside her. "I hope you don't think we're actually sleeping in separate rooms."

He chuckled. "Jasik was nice enough to arrange quarters for all of us..." He tapped his chin sarcastically, grinning. "But it never crossed my mind."

CHAPTER 14

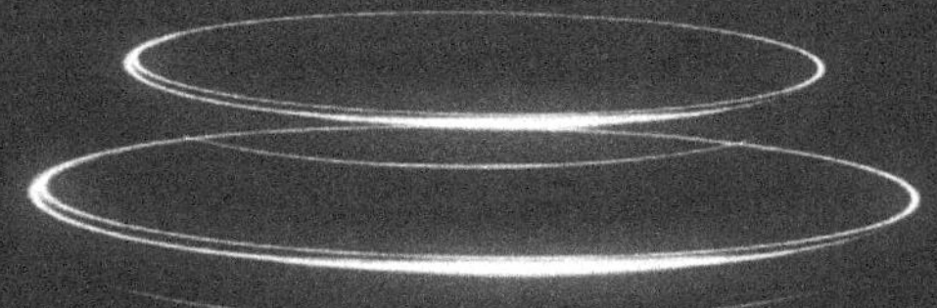

ector Four, Aelmead," Aloriea read from the dossier as the nameless pilot escorted them through the skies. "If we're looking for weapon upgrades, this is the place."

"I'm looking for their Vanguard to stop scuttling ships they deem to be in their territory," Markarian grated, folding his arms across his suited chest and peering out the window as deserts and sand wastes gave way to murky swamps and wetlands. "Didn't the leaders enact a law where that shit can't happen anymore?"

"Yeah, we did," Caldera replied. Irritation that rules weren't being followed pricked at the back of her neck, making her hair stand on end.

"Then I'm going to have a long, possibly violent, talk with their Vanguard liaison."

"No you aren't," Aloriea snapped from her spot on the overstuffed couch, glaring across the spacious shuttle at him.

"Did I say violent? I meant extremely civilized."

"Desrin says she sent out an order," Caldera replied, cutting into the conversation and frantically flipping through her correspondence on her holopad, bouncing her leg up and down in the chair she was sitting at as outrage rose in her chest. "Did she lie to me?"

Aloriea shook her head. "No, but getting akars to work together with anyone is taxing enough—"

"Oh, we know," Markarian interrupted, winking at Aloriea.

Caldera covered her mouth to muffle her chuckle as Aloriea pursed her lips.

"We're a very *independent* species," Aloriea replied, settling abruptly back into the cushion of the seat.

"This is neither here nor there," Sear said, his one good ear twitching. "We need to get Queen Desrin back on your side, Callie." He tapped a claw on the table across from her. "It is the only way to ensure we do not fall behind scientifically."

"Always about the science with you," Markarian muttered, continuing to look out the window of the spacious personal shuttle transport. "How about focusing on the fact that Callie could potentially get kicked out of office?"

"Of course that is something that I am worried about... but when you are in charge of advancing technology for an entire sector, maybe then you will understand my side of things," Sear snarled, his curled lip exposing fanged canines.

"I'm 'in charge' of people getting blown up in space!" Markarian snapped, his booted feet, which were previously resting on the tabletop, hitting the shuttlecraft floor with a *thunk*.

"Okay, everyone calm down," Rennick interjected, speaking for the first time and standing from the chair he was stiffly sitting in across the room, the bottom of his unbuttoned suit jacket waving with the motion. "We're all stressed out but arguing with each other about it isn't going to help."

Caldera exhaled sharply. "He's right. We need to work together. Remember what we can accomplish when we do that?"

The area fell silent as her friends let the weight of her words sink in. An incessant, albeit dull, beeping from the cockpit hit her ears, usually being drowned out by constant conversation.

Markarian propped his elbows on his knees, leaning forward. "No offense, Cal, but I don't think a pep-talk is gonna work this time."

"That wasn't a pep-talk. That was a fact." Caldera bit her lip. "We're still reeling from the Council being exposed and arrested, not to mention everything that happened in the year leading up to it..." She stood and walked across the room, sitting next to Markarian, flicking her gaze between him and Sear. "I know how you feel—like you're grasping at straws—trying to do anything and everything to help your people, and always coming up short, right?"

They both nodded.

"And I know I put you both in this position, but..." She paused, faltering, unsure if she should continue. "But I'm not going to apologize for it. I know you'll figure it out and I'll be by your side every step of the way."

Rennick nodded. "We all will."

"Don't worry, I'll be there to let you know when you've stepped on anyone's political toes, so to speak." Aloriea smiled, her metal horn catching a ray of sunlight.

Markarian huffed sarcastically. "You're all so damn frustrating sometimes."

"I do not think blind optimism is the best way to go about this," Sear added, the black of his pupils becoming a thin vertical sliver, letting the gold of his irises gleam in the light.

Caldera let a grin spread across her face. "Why not?" She pushed herself into a standing position and walked to the large picture window that Markarian was staring out of as swaths of wild forest passed by in a flash. "That's all we've ever had, anyway."

THE SWAMPLANDS OF PENKITH, THE capital of Sector Four, surrounded them as they got off the shuttle. Contrasting harshly with the almost unbearable dry heat of Venzor, the air was thick with tepid humidity. The smell of water-logged tree trunks smashed into her senses, making her cover her nose as the ramp descended.

Aloriea took a deep breath and they all stepped off the shuttle, her long strides uninhibited by the high-waisted, black pencil skirt that hugged her knees. "Ahh, this takes me back," she muttered, stretching long arms over her head.

"Takes you back to what?" Markarian coughed, waving gnats away from his face. "A bug infested sauna?"

Caldera laughed, rolling up the sleeves of her blazer and swishing the flying insects away from her pants. "Are you meeting up with your sisters and mother while you're here?" she asked Aloriea.

"That's the plan. I'll head over to the Vanguard headquarters here with Markarian and meet up with Neira and Therasia. I think Mom is supposed to meet us there too, but..."

Caldera and Rennick glanced at each other.

"What's wrong?" Rennick asked, placing a hand on Aloriea's shoulder.

"I am," Sear interjected, his clawed feet clicking against the concrete landing as he strode off the shuttle ramp and approached the group.

Caldera raised an eyebrow.

"That's not true." Aloriea sighed, wrapping her arms around herself the way she did when she was uncomfortable. "I... I haven't seen or really talked to my mom in a while. Years. And now I'm coming home with a prosthetic horn and matan partner..." She grew quiet, the unsaid words sitting heavily in the air.

Sear furrowed his brow and stared out into the distance, looking particularly troubled.

"I'm so sorry," Caldera replied, taking Aloriea's hand and squeezing it before doing the same with Sear's clawed one.

Rennick and Markarian nodded, offering reassuring smiles and shoulder pats.

"We'll always be here for you both," Caldera said, turning around just as Penkith's palace representative approached.

A black-suited akar towered over them as he came to a stop in front of the group, his long horns bent back, pointing straight behind him. Auburn eyes glared down a sharp-pointed nose. "Queen Caldera and court, I presume?" he asked, flipping lengthy copper-colored hair over his shoulder with a thin, russet, reddish-brown-colored hand, revealing a ruby-red encircled crown embroidered on his suit.

"That is correct," Caldera replied, reaching out her hand.

He didn't take it.

"My name's Panos, Queen Desrin's bodyguard. She is awaiting your arrival in the great hall. Follow me."

They walked in silence the rest of the way. Tall trees, with moss hanging heavy on their branches, and roots soaked in an unknown amount of water, lined the private walkway that led directly to the palace on both sides.

Caldera gazed back into the mysterious tangle of the wetlands as they walked in silence, its darkness dominating despite the rays of sunlight that periodically broke through the mess of leaves, shining down on the brown water. Insects buzzed and flyers cawed as they approached the palace. The doors swung open after the initial handprint scan, causing the vines crawling up the facade to tremble.

Desrin sat at the head of the table in the great hall talking with another pale-skinned akar with short-cropped brown hair, and gray eyes. Two barely noticeable bumps protruded from above her forehead, indicating her horns never grew in.

The queen glanced over at the precession but made no attempt to get up. She wore a white cardigan that buttoned in the middle with a red jumpsuit underneath. The crown that sat atop her head was a golden circlet with an inlaid ruby jewel at the pinnacle.

Panos led them to their seats, directing Caldera to sit adjacent to Desrin.

Much to Caldera's dismay, the only thing waiting for them at the long table were drinks of a dark green color; no food was available to snack on during the proceedings. Her stomach rumbled as she eyed the thicker consistency of the beverage in front of her.

I hope this juice is filling...

With a gentle wave of her hand, the akar Desrin was talking to took a few steps back to stand behind her as if to wait for her next command, bowing her head as she did so.

"Caldera," Desrin said, her red eyes glaring across the table at her.

"Your Majesty," Caldera replied, her sarcastic tone on full display as she took a sip of the mystery liquid. To her surprise, the taste that flooded her mouth was a mix of apple, mango, and pineapple juice.

Desrin almost smirked.

"Let's cut to the chase, shall we?"

"I actually have something to ask you," Caldera replied, setting the glass on the table and glancing over at her friends. She could almost feel Rennick tensing from the spot he was standing in behind her.

Desrin looked amused, her light blonde hair falling over her shoulder as she leaned her cheek on her closed fist. "Well?"

"Why did you tell the people from Area 51 that Mei and John died?"

"Why does it matter?"

"Because you've been reprimanded and I'm under an informal investigation."

Desrin scoffed, laying her hands on the tabletop. If she was surprised that Caldera knew she was being investigated, she didn't show it. "I've already told you. It's because they were trying to disregard what we had already set in motion."

"Okay... but what does that have to do with Mei and John?"

Desrin tapped her nail-bitten fingers on the table. "You've made the Earthlings our problem. And I will not allow an Earth organization to appear out of nowhere and dictate what we do with them."

"They're not objects. We can't, and shouldn't, 'dictate' them."

"That remains to be seen."

Caldera blinked, furrowing her brow and looking over at Aloriea for support before she said something she'd regret.

"Forgive me, Queen Desrin," Aloriea said, clearing her throat and directing the conversation, as if she were a moderator, " but you *have* been the one that has been pushing for 'the Earthlings' to go back to Earth. If you think differently now..." She intentionally trailed off, motioning for Desrin to continue the conversation.

Desrin shrugged. "If Area 51 had taken them, they'd be dead. That much is clear. Honestly, you should be thanking me." She snapped her fingers. "Panos, please show Sirs Arcaro and Ales to Vanguard headquarters. Sir Arcaro should be led to the scientific research and development wing, while Sir Ales should be shown to the Vanguard Overseer."

"Actually," Aloriea interjected, "I was hoping to accompany Sir Arcaro to Vanguard headquarters as well. I have business there."

"You don't think you should stay and advise your queen?"

"It's okay," Caldera interrupted, before Aloriea could respond. "This was previously discussed and approved."

Desrin scoffed, clearly not approving of the unorthodox way the meeting was heading. "Very well. Panos?"

Caldera's eyes flicked to her friends, involuntary nervousness clutching her chest the way it always did when everyone was about to split up.

Desrin sighed, as if reading her mind. "Make sure someone from security is escorting them at all times."

Panos nodded, motioning for Sear, Markarian, and Aloriea to follow him. They patted Caldera on the shoulder as they passed, promising to meet up with her later as their guide walked out the door, not looking back.

"You've got this," Aloriea whispered in her ear before following the procession out the door.

"You sent away your bodyguard?" Caldera asked, glancing behind her at Rennick, who was still standing behind her. "He's a treat by the way," she said, sarcasm dripping from her voice. "Can't seem to get him to shut up."

An uncharacteristically mischievous smile broke across Desrin's lips. "He's... stoic, the way I like my subordinates." She leaned forward. "Having a 'bodyguard' was a luxury I never wanted anyway."

Caldera returned the expression, channeling Aloriea and spotting her opening. "What *do* you want?"

Desrin raised a curious eyebrow. "I want to know that I can fully trust my fellow sector leaders and I need them to know that I am not someone they can talk over, ignore, or bribe... Not anymore." Her red eyes gleamed as she continued, clenching her hands into fists. "I survived under Councilmember Thael's rule by doing things such as that.

"He was ruthless. One step out of line, and my body would have been in the swamp outside before nightfall and no amount of *bodyguards* would've changed that... But you..." Her eyes bore into Caldera, trying to burn her from the inside out. "You came along and overthrew the entire political hierarchy without a thought for your own safety."

Is she... jealous?

"Desrin..." Caldera muttered.

"Councilmember Vandren did nothing—*said nothing*—to you! He let you do whatever you wanted without so much as a threat! And I want to know why."

Caldera's mind flashed to Rennick, beaten, bloody, lying in a ditch almost dead.

"That's not true!" She pressed her palm flat against the table, leaning closer to Desrin. "He threatened everyone I ever cared about and he was close to winning." She swallowed hard. "Vandren played mind games. That's how he liked to toy with people... but there's a simple reason why he didn't succeed."

"And what's that?"

"He underestimated me."

Desrin blew out an exasperated breath, unclenching her shaking hands. "My cowardice through all of that sickens me."

Caldera blanched. "I don't think you're a coward," she said, shaking her head vehemently and taking Desrin's trembling hands in her own. To her surprise, the queen didn't pull away. "Survival is...hard. Tough decisions had to be made, and you all were in power long before I was..."

She glanced at Rennick again, whose gaze was fixed on the interaction.

"I can't even imagine what you had to do, what you all had to do, just see the light of the next morning." Taking a deep breath, she released Desrin's hands. "I admire you for being here today."

Desrin furrowed her brow as long pale hair fell into her face, confusion mixed with surprise seeming to dance behind her eyes. "That's..."

Caldera raised her eyebrows, expectant.

"That's not what I expected to hear of someone who brought political change to an entire planet overnight."

"I try not to let it go to my head," Caldera replied with a wink.

The strange sound of Desrin's never before heard laughter filled the great hall, echoing off the walls. "So then I'll ask you point-blank. Are you aligned with Area 51?"

"No," Caldera replied, never breaking eye contact. "And I never will be."

Desrin nodded. "Begrudgingly... I believe you." She stood, extending her hand, her change in demeanor apparent. "Consider us allies, true allies, from this point on."

CHAPTER 15

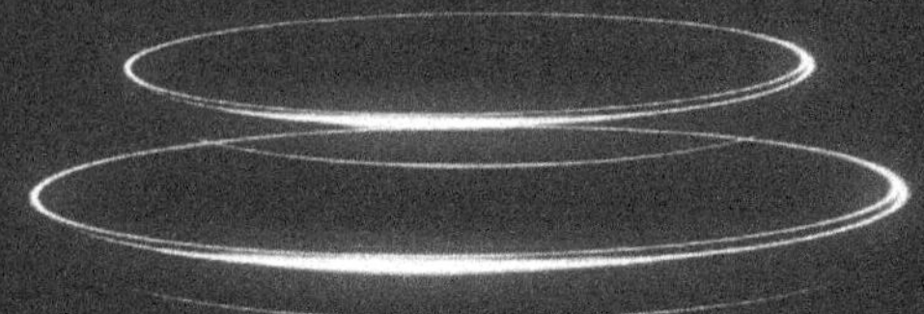

I don't completely trust her, but I'll take what I can get. Caldera grinned, practically jumping to her feet.

"Finally!" She took a deep breath, reining in her thoughts and overexaggerated actions.

Rennick chuckled, his expression and body language visibly softening.

"Well, shall we tell Mokan and Nari the good news?" Desrin asked, snapping her fingers.

A holopad appeared in her hand, handed to her by the brown-haired akar with no horns.

"Thank you, Ivy," Desrin replied.

The woman nodded, silently stepping back to her spot.

Caldera raised an inquisitive brow. "Sure?"

Desrin sighed. "This whole thing was my idea," she said as the holopad attempted to connect with the king and queen of Sector Five.

"I assumed as much."

"Then you should be pleased I'm willing to revoke my initial push to have you investigated."

Caldera crossed her arms, the constant, resonant tremor in her hand gently shaking her elbow.

"Who told you, by the way?" Desrin asked, her attention falling to the still unanswered call.

"Jasik."

"I should've known," Desrin chuckled. "They really are fond of you, aren't they?"

Caldera was about to open her mouth to reply when the holopad in Desrin's hands finally blinked to life.

"At last, Queen Nari," Desrin replied with a short smile. "The call was trying to connect for some time. Why the delay?"

"Apologies, Your Majesty," Nari replied, the irises of her bright blue eyes narrowing. "We are terribly busy." Her cat-like ears twitched back and forth, snow-white fur bristling ever so slightly.

Caldera glanced at Rennick, who had crowded beside her. "What's wrong?" she asked over Desrin's shoulder.

Desrin glared at her but didn't move or interrupt.

"Oh, Queen Caldera... I—"

"It's all right, Nari," Desrin interjected, "she's not aligned with Area 51—that's actually why I was calling." Pausing, she took a deep breath. "Of course, feel free to draw your own conclusions, but since we were closely aligned on this subject..." She let her sentence trail off, encouraging Nari to speak.

Nari blinked, scratching absently behind her ear with an exposed claw. "Very well, if that is your determination—"

"It's the determination of Eldra, Fenry, and Jasik, too," Caldera added, unable to keep herself quiet. A low growl sounded in Nari's throat at being interrupted again. A sound she was more than used to from Sear.

"It's true, the queens and Jasik messaged me mere moments before Caldera arrived," Desrin said, meeting Caldera's eyes. "They stand by her."

Caldera beamed, turning her attention back to Nari. "So... what's wrong?"

"Well, there has been an extreme uptick in disappearances as of late. The people are restless and scared." She paused, taking a deep breath. "Mokan is already at the Ozryn police station getting ready to make a formal statement. That is actually where I am headed as well."

"Jasik mentioned an uptick in civilian disappearances in Sector Four too," Caldera chimed in, her eyes growing wide.

Desrin nodded. "So have Eldra and Fenry." She scrunched her nose. "I have received a few reports, but nothing substantial..."

Could this be what Oron was talking about?... Caldera turned to face Rennick. "Call Saro and Bruna, see if the Tellin palace has received any additional reports from the T.J.S. while we've been away."

"What are you thinking?" Rennick asked, placing a hand on Caldera's shoulder.

"I'm thinking there's more to this than random disappearances," she said, turning back to the conversation between Desrin and Nari.

He nodded, pulling out his holopad and stepping away.

"I don't think we will have the time. This demands our full attention."

"What?" Caldera asked, only hearing part of the conversation.

"Nari was saying that she doesn't think she and Mokan will be able to host you due to these unforeseen circumstances," Desrin said, her red eyes turbulent.

Rennick walked up next to them, replacing the holopad in his pocket. "Saro and Bruna said that there have been a few recent reports to the authorities but nothing too out of the ordinary."

Caldera sighed. "Desrin, if it's all right with you, we'll skip going to Sector Five, stay here for the night, and go back to Tellis tomorrow. I can help, but from home, not from here or there."

Desrin glanced back at Nari, who nodded approvingly. "Very

well, Caldera. This issue is one that will need every sector leader's full cooperation."

"You have it," Caldera said.

"I'm afraid I must go. We will be in touch with you both," Nari said before the screen went dark.

"Okay, then." Desrin placed her holopad on the table. "Ivy will show you to your quarters for the remainder of your stay," she continued, motioning for her assistant to step forward. "I bid you goodnight."

Caldera downed that last of her drink and nodded.

Rennick mimicked her sentiment and they followed Ivy through the archways at the back of the great hall, leaving Desrin, who slumped into a chair, and was instantly surrounded by attendants.

The Penkith palace was more rectangular in structure than Caldera initially realized as they walked down a hallway that seemed to never end. Large picture windows lined the hall separated by ten feet of stone wall before another floor to ceiling window revealed itself, letting her peer out into the wetland environment at intermittent glances.

As they continued to walk, the surrounding swamp gave way to soft ground and thick green trees.

"So... are you two together?" Ivy asked, glancing over her shoulder, effectively breaking the silence.

The sudden, forward question stopped Caldera in her tracks. She raised an eyebrow, smiling over at Rennick. "Yes. Why?"

The woman chuckled. "I only allotted one room for the two of you... As a political advisor, I wondered if that was right to do so." She tapped her chin with a finger. "But I suppose even if you weren't, it would've been all right either way—it has become more dangerous as of late. Staying in the same room regardless would make the most sense. But if you look at it that way people might talk—"

"Wait," Caldera interrupted, shaking her head. "*You're* Desrin's advisor?"

The woman nodded, confusion clouding her eyes. "Why?"

"You seem a little..." Caldera trailed off, glancing up at Rennick for a more tactful way to say meek.

"Reserved," Rennick said.

Ivy blushed. "That's the way Desrin likes her political advisors. Quiet. Always on hand. Ready with an answer at a moment's notice when asked..." She paused, eyes widening. "It's not as demoralizing as it sounds!" She held up her hands, waving them back and forth in front of her. "That sounds bad. It's not what I meant. I actually enjoy it. I—"

"Ivy," Caldera said with a broad smile, interrupting her ramblings. "Everything's okay. Okay?"

Rennick nodded, sharing Caldera's expression. "However you would have set us up would have been perfect." He leaned in like he was about to share a secret. "And don't worry, we won't tell Desrin."

Ivy beamed. "Sorry, I babble when I'm nervous..." She shielded her mouth from the many palace workers that hustled around them. "I never receive affirmation *or* refutation from Her Majesty. It can be very frustrating," she said before continuing to lead them to their quarters.

Caldera and Rennick glanced at each other and shrugged, continuing to follow Ivy down the bustling hallway.

"So... you're not Desrin's first political advisor then?" Caldera asked.

Ivy's shoulders seemed to tense. "No, there have been others..." She let the sentence trail off as they approached a fork in the hallway.

"I see..." Rennick replied, catching Caldera's gaze.

Caldera didn't push for more information as Desrin's words, *'one step out of line and my body would have been in the swamp outside before nightfall',* swirled in her head. *The queen may be harsh, but after what she's been through—abruptly losing people she trusted and most likely cared about—she's just trying to unlearn the years of abuse and threats she suffered at the hands of Councilmember Thael.*

"Here you are," Ivy said, breaking the silence after finally rounding a corner and coming to a stop in front of a large metal door. "The first room in the 'royalty hall' as I like to call it." She giggled to herself as she motioned for Caldera and Rennick to step forward.

The door swished open, revealing a large chamber. One picture adorned the walls, showing the overview of the capital Penkith; it loomed over the chairs encircling a small table that sat atop a furry rug.

A canopy bed with sheer red tulle hanging from its risers and side rails added a soft luster to the area. It sat against the wall, next to screened in doors leading to a sizable patio surrounded by a stone railing that led directly into the forest—the solid glass doors stood open on either side as if waiting to close out the noises of bugs and swamp creatures.

Caldera smiled. *It's nice to be on the first floor for once. I'm sure Ren will appreciate that.*

"Have a peaceful rest," Ivy said, jolting Caldera out of her thoughts. "I'll call Panos to check in on the rest of your court."

"Thank you," Caldera replied. "Please send word to our holopads as soon as you hear back."

"Of course, Your Majesty."

Caldera opened her mouth to resist the formal title, but closed it just as fast, finding to her surprise that it didn't bother her as much anymore. She nodded, closing the door as Ivy pranced away.

"Well that was... strange," Rennick said, settling into a plush chair adjacent to the open patio doors and beginning to remove his boots.

Caldera nodded, sinking onto the edge of the bed. "Yeah... It seems like Desrin is still trying to take the brunt of responsibility off her palace workers' shoulders—like she's still afraid the Council could come in and murder them whenever they wanted."

"I was talking about the disappearances."

"Oh, umm, that too."

Rennick chuckled, walking over to Caldera and pulling her to her feet. "How are you?"

"Better," she said leaning into him, wrapping her arms around his torso and resting her cheek against his chest. "The damn tremor is still there, though. I don't know how to get rid of it."

"Add that to the list of things we have to figure out," he said, resting his chin on the top of her head. "Now that we can head back to Tellis early, we can finally schedule our therapy sessions."

Caldera nodded into his chest. Words escaped her as involuntary heat rushed to her cheeks and her heart pounded unceremoniously against her chest.

There's no shame in getting help. I know that...

"Let's go to sleep. I'm beat."

CHAPTER 16

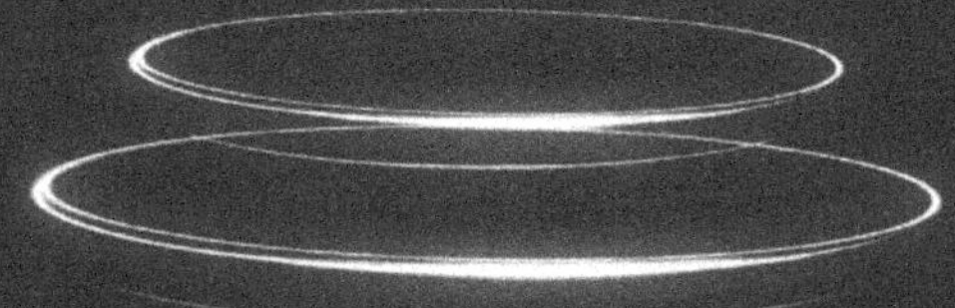

Bright white light pulsed on the inside of her eyelids, forcing Caldera to blink blearily awake. "What—"

The light pulsed again, its sharpness a stark contrast to the pitch darkness of midnight. It came from outside the glass doors leading out to the patio.

Caldera squinted through the sleepiness as it appeared again. *It looks like it's coming from the forested wetland.* She glanced over at Rennick. Even though he had rolled onto his side, she could tell that his chest rose and fell in the deep hypnotic rhythm of sleep—a slow, consistent motion.

The light flashed again.

Biting her lip, she pulled the blankets aside, gently pressing her bare feet against the cold stone, as if the slightest noise would alert whatever it was to her presence. Silently, she made her way to the other side of the bed where Rennick's blaster was laying on the bedside table. Grabbing it out of its holster, she gazed down at Rennick's sleeping face.

She reached for his shoulder to wake him as another flash caught the corner of her eye. Faltering, her hand hovered over him. She shook her head, retracting her reach.

It'll take too long to explain.

Padding back to the patio doors, she opened them as silently as she could as another flash lit up the swampland.

Moonlight danced across her face as she jumped over the short railing that encircled the patio, her bare feet squishing into the damp grass on the other side. *Fuck.* She glanced down at her outfit—a navy blue silk tank top and shorts. *I should've changed out of my pajamas.*

"Or at least put on shoes..." she muttered to herself, brandishing the blaster and making her way through the thick trees toward the flashing light.

Moss-covered trees swayed overhead, periodically obstructing her view of the moons, letting total darkness encroach for brief moments as Caldera prodded her way through the wild wetlands in the general direction of the last flash, the sporadic darkness making her all too aware that she could come across a deep pocket of swamp water, or animal, at any moment.

There was no rhyme or reason to the lights, and they hadn't appeared in some time as her body shook with the breeze, the chill sinking deeper into her skin as her adrenaline waned and her feet continued to get caked with mud. Unknown creatures scuttled across her path, under her feet, or in the treetops, seeming to try their best to scare her back to her room where a warm bed, and Rennick, were waiting for her.

Gritting her teeth, she pushed on as another flash finally came into view around the corner. *I'm getting close.*

A muffled voice met her ears along with yet another quick flash. "This should be enough for now..." it said.

Taking a deep breath, Caldera pressed her back against a thick tree trunk with spiraling roots and readied her blaster.

"...we shouldn't be wasting..."

"Aren't as interesting..."

"...time..."

"...better sectors..."

"Shut up...there's something..."

Only able to catch broken pieces of conversation, Caldera scooted along, her back pressed firmly against the trunk, gripping the blaster with one hand and digging her fingers into the crevasses of the tree with the other. Careful to only step on large, exposed roots as the tree transitioned from solid ground to dark water, she guided herself around the base. Rough bark pulled on her clothes and stray branches caught her hair as she rounded on the source of the flashing lights.

Silhouettes of unidentifiable people standing on what looked like a solid platform, pressed between two trees, met her eyes as anonymous hands suddenly gripped her shoulders, pushing her violently forward.

Catching quick glimpses of more moving bodies, she plummeted toward the water, releasing a single blaster shot before being enveloped in cold blackness.

The sudden icy sensation seared into her exposed skin, making Caldera gasp for breath and causing the inky water to fill her mouth and plunge into her throat; she coughed underwater, involuntarily releasing bubbles of precious air. She opened her eyes only to be met with a stinging sensation and blurry black. Her body trembled as her heart pounded against her chest. Her lungs burned, pleading for air she couldn't readily offer.

She should've been scared. Scared of the lack of light, the lack of air, the unknown creatures that waited in the depths for her... Death. But she wasn't. The sensation—despair, hopelessness—wasn't new, she had lived through it before.

Olivare's hands around her throat flashed across her mind as they so often had over the past few weeks. She blinked, calmly lifting her head as her hair floated around her face, bleary patches of silver light coated the world above her.

The moons, I'm not that far from the surface! Pressing her free hand to her mouth to prevent any more loss of air, and gripping the blaster even tighter at her side, she kicked her legs harder than she ever had, forcing her stunned body to propel upward.

A shift in the current under her feet caught her attention, causing her to look down. A creature that she couldn't recognize, or fully see slithered through the water.

From what she could tell, it had no limbs, only an impossibly long, scaly body narrowing to a sharp point and beady black eyes. The constant *swish* and displacement of the water around her seemed to agree with that analysis as she kicked upward. The creature opened its mouth, rows of teeth on full display. It was after her.

Turning her attention fully back toward the surface, she kicked faster as her legs went numb, firing the blaster indiscriminately at the monster—the weapon continuing to work as the plasma bolt ammunition was protected by an impermeable, sealed chamber—unsure if she was even hitting anything.

White spots floated across her eyes as her vision started to wane. Her lungs burned as the uncontrollable urge to breathe in almost overtook her.

The light of the moons became nearer, but eternal darkness was closing in fast.

I'm not going to make it!

No sooner had the thought crossed her mind, than her head breached the surface.

Hands immediately gripped her arms, pulling her to safety.

The creature snapped angrily, barely missing her feet, before disappearing back into the black swamp.

Caldera coughed, hacking up water from her lungs and gasping for breath. With hair plastered to her face, she lifted the blaster that was still glued to her hand toward where the creature had disappeared and fired a few defiant blasts into the area causing the water to spray up in tiny explosions.

Rennick's voice met her water-clogged ears. "Callie, what the hell is going on?"

She coughed in response as another hand rested on her shoulder. She glanced behind her to see Markarian kneeling next to her, his blaster drawn.

"I told you I'd be able to find her," the unmistakable voice of Desrin said. "I know this area better than anyone."

"Callie, seriously," Rennick said, leaning in close, his voice gruff. "Have you lost your mind? What the fuck are you doing out here by yourself?"

"Yeah, Cal," Markarian added, while continuing to scan the surrounding area. "I gotta agree with Ren here—that was stupid as hell."

Caldera took a few more deep breaths, savoring each one as the air filled and expanded her lungs. "I saw... a light."

"A light?" Desrin scoffed. "You wandered out into dangerous territory because of a light?"

Rennick held up a hand to the queen, never taking his hard, confused eyes off Caldera. "What else?"

"I followed it to this location and there were people I couldn't identify talking about..."

"About what?" Markarian asked, standing.

"I don't know, I only caught snippets of conversation... but they were on a platform over the water."

They all glanced up at the open swampland in front of them. There was nothing there.

"There is not and has not ever been a platform of any kind in this area," Desrin said, crossing her arms and gazing off into the distance, her long ponytail almost swishing the ground.

"I saw it!" Caldera insisted. "Right before I was pushed." She shivered.

"You were pushed?" Rennick asked, shrugging off his jacket and placing it over her shoulders while taking the blaster out of her vice-like grip.

She nodded, her eyes locked with his as he helped her up.

"There's no sign of anyone or anything around here," Markarian said carefully, reholstering his blaster and taking Caldera's other hand while helping Rennick hoist her to her feet.

"Exactly," Desrin said, stepping forward, the soft ground sucking against the boots she wore with each step. "You most likely *fell* in after inadvertently chasing a fireflyer—"

"I didn't fall!" Caldera interrupted as water dripped into her eyes. "And I wasn't chasing a fireflyer, either." She took a deep breath. "I know what I saw... and it wasn't an animal."

"Well, one almost ate you," Desrin quipped, turning on her heel, "and if we don't want that to be our fate as well, we'd better head back to the palace. Leviathans are extremely prevalent in this area. You're lucky you got away... most people don't."

Rennick and Markarian nodded, following Desrin through the woods.

Rubbing her arms to try and counteract the chill that was rapidly settling into her bones, Caldera stared at the empty space between the trees, searching for any abnormalities.

There were none.

"Come on," Rennick said, pausing and reaching out to her.

Caldera tightened the oversized jacket around her shoulders, casting one last glance behind her at the open area of seemingly undisturbed swampland, before taking his outstretched hand.

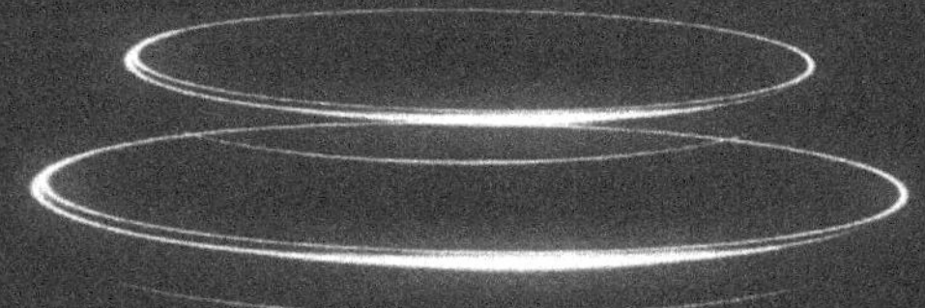

The next morning, the Penkith palace attendants quickly and quietly served Caldera and her crew breakfast as vibrant sunlight glimmered through the oval windows.

In the early morning hours, the great hall bustled, nearly vibrating, with swift activity, contrasting harshly with the desolate atmosphere from the night before.

The clanking of plates and silverware echoed off the walls as Aloriea and Sear savored the sweet breads, sugary yellow juice, and warm, aromatic soup, while Caldera merely picked at her meal despite being ravenous—unable to force herself to take a bite as her stomach rolled over on itself. Gently placing her spoon on the table next to her plate, she saw that Rennick, and surprisingly Markarian, were doing the same thing.

The tension in the air between them was palpable. Even Aloriea and Sear who, at the very least, seemed to be somewhat enjoying themselves, had tight shoulders and shifting eyes.

They were waiting on an explanation. Her explanation.

With an audible sigh, Caldera reluctantly recapped everything to Sear and Aloriea while Rennick, Markarian, and Desrin sat silent at the table in the great hall. Panos and Ivy kept a watchful eye around the room, quickly shooing away any palace worker who let curiosity get the better of them and got too close.

"Thank the universe they found you in time," Aloriea said in a controlled tone, her eyes blazing.

Sear nodded, patting her clenched fist and turning to Desrin. "How did you find her?" he asked. "Why were you involved at all?"

"I may have been born into the role of queen, but I was never much of a palace dweller—learning to track was started out of boredom and formed into a legitimate hobby when I realized I could use it as an excuse to leave the grounds." She smiled wistfully, taking a sip of the yellow beverage in front of her. "My father was a big hunter, so it made him proud."

"After I woke up Markarian, we were actually looking for Panos," Rennick added. "But we found Desrin instead."

"And it's a good thing you did," she interjected. "Panos doesn't know this land like I do. Caldera would have surely died while you three would've been wandering around in the dark, more lost than even she was."

"Oh, please," Markarian said, waving a hand in the air and popping a small piece of bread into his mouth. "Once we heard the shot she fired, we would've made it."

Caldera bit the inside of her cheek glancing from Rennick to Markarian, who looked like he was trying to convince himself more than anything.

"I wouldn't have died," Caldera insisted, trying to keep her voice steady. "I was firing my blaster into that thing... and would've killed it eventually."

Desrin sighed. "That, we will never know."

"We can't thank you enough, Your Majesty," Aloriea said, standing, "but we should really be going."

Desrin nodded, waving them away.

"Before we do, I have something to say," Caldera said, leaning forward so her friends couldn't hear. "I think this has something to do with Area 51, and I'd like you to consider allocating some of your galactic satellites to be used for the purpose of tracking, and alerting you, when a wormhole is opened," she whispered.

"This again," Desrin said, blinking skeptical eyes at her. "On what grounds do you think it was them?"

"I have no proof, just a feeling."

"That's absurd—"

"Is it?" Caldera moved closer until her face was inches away from Desrin's. "If you can think of a better explanation..."

"What does your court think about that assumption?"

"I-I don't want to unduly worry them."

"It's not wise to keep secrets, especially from the people closest to you."

"Let me worry about them," Caldera said, never breaking eye contact. "You said you were never really a palace dweller. Well, what do your instincts tell you is going on?" she whispered, leaning back.

Desrin sighed, lowering her gaze and letting silence fill the empty space around her. After a few moments, she snapped to attention. "They're telling me you're onto something... Very well, I'll see what I can do about repurposing a few satellites, but there won't be very many."

Caldera grinned. "Thank you, Your Majesty," she said, standing and making her way toward the palace doors with the rest of her friends.

As Caldera passed, Desrin grabbed her wrist. "If anything comes of these... these mysterious lights, let me know," she said, releasing her. "I'll do the same for you."

Caldera nodded. "I'll fill in the other sector leaders, too."

"I'd wait until you have actual proof, lest they think you've gone completely mad."

"I..." Caldera let her sentence trail off.

She's right... I just regained their trust, and this'll make me look crazy.

"I will."

THE SHUTTLE LANDED ON THE Tellin palace roof with a *clunk*, jolting Caldera out of her nap. "We're home?" *That was a long trip.* She sighed, stretching her back and arms. "Aloriea, did you do what I asked?"

"Of course I did. I'm actually proficient at my job, in case you forgot," Aloriea snapped.

Caldera blanched, taken aback by her progressively antagonistic attitude since leaving Sector Four. "I never said you weren't..."

"Saro, Bruna, Grey, and Sylvie are gathering reports from all across the sectors pertaining to the mysterious lights you claim to have seen," Aloriea continued, ignoring her.

"I *did* see them."

"Fine, but I don't know what you expect to find."

"The sudden uptick in disappearances, along with this mysterious light, is too much of a coincidence," Caldera replied, biting her lip as the group walked down the ramp onto the roof of the Tellin palace. A rush of relief at being home passed through her body. *I should tell them now.* "I have to see if they correspond to each other because... I think this has something to do with Area 51."

Aloriea, Rennick, Markarian, and Sear nervously looked at each other, just as Mei and John burst through the rooftop door, followed by Sylvie.

John embraced Markarian as Mei skidded to a stop in front of Caldera.

"How was the trip?" Mei asked, clasping her hands together and nearly bouncing up and down.

Caldera couldn't help but smile at the hyperactive girl in front of her, always bursting at the seams with barely contained excitement. "It was eight days too long," she laughed. "I'm glad to be back."

"Ugh, you're so vague!"

"How did the Vanguard recruitment test go over?" Caldera asked, placing a hand on Mei's shoulder. "Are you in?"

Mei beamed, glancing over her shoulder at the red-haired girl behind her. "I'm in!"

Caldera chuckled. "That's great! Congratulations."

"I'm the lowest rank," Mei rolled her eyes, although the grin never left her face. "I didn't qualify to skip ahead, so I'm stuck at VHQ until I do. I think the only reason they passed me is because they're so shorthanded. I was barely able to compete with you tellins—you're just so much... better."

"I think you're exaggerating, but it's okay. You'll work your way up in no time."

"I can't believe I'm not allowed to go into space—you have to tell me more stories about it!" Mei complained, before running back to Sylvie and disappearing down the staircase.

"Mei, you're due back in thirty minutes!" John called, rushing after her, holopad in hand.

Caldera motioned for Rennick, Aloriea, Sear, and Markarian to follow her down the steps.

Saro met them at the bottom, a holopad tucked under his arm, which he handed to Caldera promptly. "I've gathered all the reports we could find about 'mysterious lights' together on this," he pointed to the holopad. "What's this about?"

"I think—"

"It's none of your concern at the moment," Aloriea interjected.

Caldera furrowed her brow up at her friend. "Okay... Thank you, Saro, you can head back to your post."

Saro's face fell as he nodded and marched away.

"What was that?" Caldera asked, nudging Aloriea and leading her friends through the busy hallways—past palace staff and toward the back courtyard.

"I agree, that seemed a little harsh," Sear added, padding along with Markarian and Rennick behind them.

"Harsh?" Aloriea scoffed as the doors opened to the newly

renovated back courtyard. "Have you all forgotten what he did?"

"No..." Rennick replied, making his way to the front of the procession. "But he also wasn't *really* involved—"

"You are so naive, Ren," Aloriea snapped as they came to stop in front of the Vault's entrance.

"Aloriea," Caldera said, tilting her head to the side, activating the scanner stone and scanning her hand as the stairs appeared and descended beside them. "What's gotten into you?"

"Yeah," Markarian added, scanning his hand for approval for entry next. "Why drop the 'regal persona' you're always trying to keep up on now?"

She took a deep breath and scanned her hand, her eyes narrowing. "We shouldn't trust him. That's all I'm saying."

Rennick scanned his hand and punched Markarian's arm.

"In all fairness," Sear said, his handprint lighting up the device, "he was tried, like everyone else who was involved, and it was deemed that he was an inconsequential third party."

"He's aware of his part in what happened," Caldera added, crossing her arms. "And I think he deserves a second chance."

Aloriea shook her head and started to descend the stairs. "Like I said before, just because someone's sorry, doesn't make what they did retroactively okay."

Markarian and Rennick followed silently behind her.

Caldera grabbed Sear's arm as he was about to begin his descent. "What the fuck was that about?" she whispered, looking up into his golden eyes. "She's been on edge since leaving Aelmead."

"She is having a hard time accepting Saro—"

"I know that, but this is on a whole other level."

Sear sighed. "Look, we, all of us, have not really gotten to talk since the sector leaders have officially been in power..."

Caldera swallowed hard. It *had* been weeks, if not months, since she sat down with her friends and relaxed. There was no time lately—there was always something going on, demanding her attention. Demanding Aloriea's attention, Rennick's, Markarian's, Sear's. A shiver ran down her spine, making her heart skip a beat and tightening her chest.

Are we growing apart?

"What are you saying?" she could barely force the words out for fear of the response.

"I am saying that we have all been, let us say, out of sync, with each other lately. Maybe you should ask her about what happened in Penkith."

That's right, she visited her mom and sisters.

"Why can't you tell me?"

Sear shook his head. "It is not my place." He took another step down before stopping abruptly and turning. "I must visit the Vanguard headquarters," he said, ascending the steps and pushing past her.

"Wha—why?" Caldera asked, furrowing her brow in confusion.

"I have a device in my lab there that will help us pinpoint the precise location of the lights relative to where they appeared, so we can travel to that spot."

"Like the portal technology that helped us get to Earth?"

He snapped his clawed fingers and nodded sharply. "It is a modification of a modification." A low snarl escaped his throat. "I may not be able to figure out how to maintain a stable portal across *galaxies*, but I have all but perfected planetary teleportation!"

"How did I not know this?"

"When we were visiting the other sectors, I went to their Vanguard headquarters and collaborated with their top scientists, helping me to perfect what I already had mostly finished," he continued. "I have to get to my lab and add the finishing touches."

"Sear, that's great!" Caldera beamed, ignoring his inherent narcissism. Her smile instantly faded as the revelation proved Sear's point; they were all out of sync. "Okay, hurry back," she said, starting to descend down the stairs, "and take one of the guards with you! Saro, Bruna, Grey, Sylvie, I don't care—just take one of them."

"Sure," he said with a wave, ears twitching. "Perhaps when I return, we could all catch up?"

His suggestion stopped Caldera in her tracks. She always had to force him to go anywhere with her, Rennick, and Markarian in the past. Even if he did end up having a good time, he was never one for 'casually hanging out'. And he certainly never suggested it.

He must feel like we really are losing touch.

"Absolutely," she finally replied, trying unsuccessfully to hide her surprise and letting a mischievous smile spread across her face. "How about we all go out for a beer?"

"Very well. I am thinking I will only be gone thirty minutes—an hour, tops." He waved once more before turning back toward the palace.

Caldera mimicked the motion before starting her descent into the Vault.

CHAPTER 18

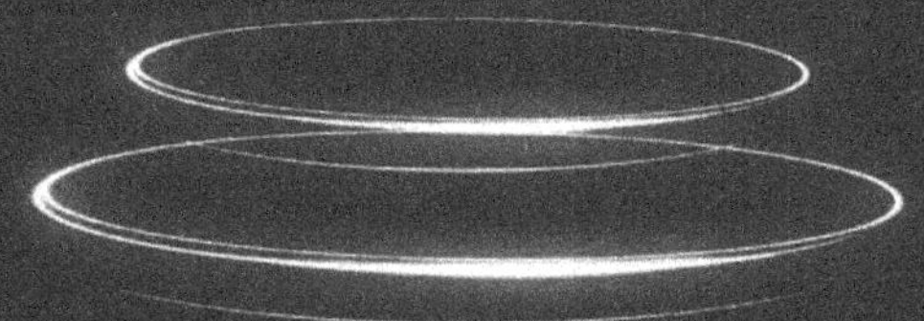

When Caldera got to the bottom of the stairs and stepped into the Vault, her friends had already set up a system and were pouring through reports of recent disappearances.

"A lot of these are actually verified," Markarian said from the computer system, flicking his wrist toward Aloriea.

"Just keep them coming," Aloriea replied, her voice gruff, "and I'll keep organizing them by sector."

Markarian lifted his gaze away from the screen as Caldera walked in. "What took you so long?"

"Where's Sear?" Aloriea added from the table, where she was sorting through the verified reports from Markarian and sending them to the floating screen in front of Rennick.

"He's going to get something from his lab at the Vanguard headquarters."

"What is it?" Rennick asked, as he stared at the names floating in front of him.

"A device that can teleport us anywhere on the planet."

They all looked up from their work stations simultaneously.

"Yeah," Caldera said into the silence. "Let's find something worthwhile enough to test it on," she continued, taking a seat next to Aloriea as Rennick and Markarina went back to their tasks. "All right, grumpy. Talk. What's going on with you?"

Aloriea didn't look up, continuing to flick through the reports floating in front of her face. "What do you mean?"

"You know what I mean..." Caldera clicked her fingers across the tabletop, continuing once Aloriea didn't respond. "You're constantly going in on Saro, who's only trying to do his job, you've been extremely on edge since leaving Penkith, and now you're starting to take it out on us. Or, *me*, really."

Aloriea's shoulders tensed.

"Okay, forget the Saro thing." Caldera lowered her voice and shifted the conversation. "What happened in Sector Four?"

"I'm a grown woman. I don't need to be babied like this."

"True... but I'm your friend. Maybe I can help."

Aloriea closed her eyes, laying her palms flat on the table. A beat of silence passed between them before she opened her eyes again, glancing sidelong at Caldera. "My sisters want me to move back to Penkith to help take care of my mother."

Caldera sucked in a staggering breath. "Your mom's sick?" she asked, unable to even wrap her head around the other part of what Aloriea had said.

"She is. It's a degenerative musculoskeletal disease, so it's been going on for a while."

"Are you..." Caldera started, letting her sentence trail off as her chest tightened. She glanced over her shoulder to see if Rennick or Markarian had overheard them.

Either they hadn't or they were pretending not to, both laser-focusing on their tasks.

"Before you start freaking out," Aloriea interjected, lowering her voice even more and patting the air in front of her. "I'm not leaving."

"Really?"

"Well, besides my mother looking at me like I'm some kind of imposter since this," she pointed at her prosthetic horn, "and completely not approving of Sear for, I want to say, 'ignorant' reasons, the branch of the Aelmead Social Welfare System that focuses on helping the elderly with in-home treatments is adequate." She placed one hand over the other, one finger rubbing the top of her knuckles. "If my sisters need help, they can get it from there."

"Aloriea, this is a big decision. Do you want to think about it a little more?" Caldera replied, gritting her teeth and wishing she could leave well-enough alone. *Why am I trying to talk her out of this?*

"No."

"But it's your mom..."

Aloriea bit her lip, before turning to completely face Caldera. "Not everyone has a good relationship with their parents, Callie." A fire burned behind her brown eyes as she spoke. "And honestly, I think that's okay... My mother is my mother, and our relationship is what it is... but all of that is moot. The point I'm trying to make is that I *can't* help my sisters or her by moving there. I belong here."

She said it so matter-of-factly that it forced Caldera to relax. She blew out a breath, letting a soft chuckle escape her lips. "Is it selfish to say that I'm relieved?"

"Depends," Aloriea replied, tapping her chin. "Are you relieved because you'd miss me, or my knowledge about politics?"

"You," Caldera replied immediately, a wide, white smile brimming across her face. "Definitely you."

"Then I'd say you're a good friend. For what it's worth, I'm sorry for the way I've been acting. I can't promise my mood will improve overnight, though."

Caldera chuckled. "It's okay, we're all under an insane amount of stress right now."

"That's an understatement." Another wave of more comfortable silence fell between them as Aloriea turned her attention back to the reports that were still filing in. She cleared her throat. "Anyway, let's get back to it, shall we?"

Caldera sighed, letting the gravity of their conversation sink in for a brief moment. Taking a deep breath, she stood up from her chair and walked over to Rennick. "What're you doing?"

"I'm narrowing down which disappearance reports coincided with reports of mysterious lights," he said, smiling over at her. "Wanna help?"

She nodded, taking her place beside him and started sifting through the incidents.

A soft smile slowly spread across her face as they worked and she nestled her body against Rennick, letting the background sounds of computer *whirs* and rhythmic beeping soothe her into a comfortable familiarity.

Time seemed to pass quickly, the reports burning into Caldera's eyes.

My brother is missing. He was supposed to show up to dinner and never arrived.

I haven't heard from my mom in a week. I went to her house and she wasn't there.

My sister...

My cousin...

My dad...

My uncle...

My friend...

The reports were all from different sectors and featured people of all species, races, and ages, but they essentially reported the same thing: person x was missing without explanation.

Caldera rubbed her temples as Rennick flicked another missing persons report in front of her that corresponded to another report of mysterious flashing lights. "How many are we up to?"

Rennick sighed, running a hand through his hair. "About one hundred and sixty altogether, with Sectors Two and Three having the most and Sector One with the least."

"That many..." she muttered, the number striking through her heart. "Then I think we should start our investigation in

Sector Two, work through the reports, interview any eye witnesses—"

"Callie," Aloriea interrupted. "What are you talking about?
We can't do that...we honestly shouldn't even be doing *this*. The
other leaders made it pretty clear that they don't want you poking around in their sectors' business."

"She might be right, Cal. They could hold you in contempt—
not to mention arrest us. Maybe we should end it here and report
what we found to Oron, or at least the proper authorities," Markarian said, standing up from his chair and stretching. "There's
enough circumstantial evidence to do that, at least."

She opened her mouth to reply, but Rennick put a hand on
her shoulder. "Why don't we send the information pertaining to
the different sectors over to their leaders and let them decide how
to handle it?" He took a deep breath. "And we can look into the
reports from our own sector," he said, looking from Markarian
to Aloriea and nodding almost imperceptibly, as if silently pleading with them to agree to the compromise.

"Sounds like a plan," Markarian replied, rubbing the back of
his head.

"Fine," Aloriea said after a moment of silence.

They turned to Caldera, waiting for her response. "All
right..." she said, slumping her shoulders. "That does seem like
the right thing to do." She furrowed her brow. "How many reports are from Tellis?"

Rennick paused, glancing away. "Twenty."

Caldera's eyes widened. "Twenty! That's only ten percent of
the disappearances. We'd hardly be helping anybody."

"You'd be helping the people of our sector, so that's something," Aloriea replied. "But send the information to the other
leaders and request that they let us be involved if you really want
to," she continued, leaning forward. "Even though Jasik already
told you no."

"I will," Caldera said with a nod. "With Sear's device..."
She trailed off, distracted by her own words, frantically looking
around the room.

I'm overreacting. It's only been... She glanced down at her watch *Five hours!*

Trepidation set in—a small prickle at the base of her neck making way for wave after wave of uneasiness.

"Callie?" Rennick asked, concern flooding his features. "What's wrong?"

"Where is Sear?"

The group looked around as if noticing his absence for the first time.

"I—" Aloriea abruptly rose from her chair. "I'm not sure."

"It hasn't been that long since we've been down here, has it?" Markarian asked.

Caldera took a deep, shaky breath, breaking out into a cold sweat. "Five hours. It's been five hours."

How did I not notice he wasn't here?

"Five..." Markarian whispered.

"He definitely should've been back by now," Caldera continued, the words fumbling over each other as they left her mouth. "He said he'd only be an hour max!"

"Hey," Rennick said, touching her arm, "maybe he got caught up talking to one of his scientist buddies."

"Or maybe he went back to his quarters," Markarian added.

Caldera shook her head vehemently. "No, no. He said that we should all go somewhere after he got back."

"That doesn't sound like him," Aloriea said, tilting her head to the side.

Caldera inhaled sharply. "He thought we might need a break," she insisted, meeting each of their eyes. "Come on, let's get out of here!"

They hurried out of the Vault, closing and locking it behind them as the stairs disappeared.

"Follow us," Caldera commanded as the group rushed by Grey and Sylvie, who were diligently guarding the back courtyard doors.

Rushing through the palace, the group came to a stop at the

front entrance, coming face to face with a confused looking Saro and Bruna.

"Your Majesty, what's—"

"Where is Sear?" Caldera said, cutting Bruna off.

"We don't understand, Your Majesty," Bruna said, glancing at Saro.

Caldera straightened, biting down her frustration and turning her attention to all the guards. "Who went with him to Vanguard headquarters?"

Grey and Sylvie shook their heads.

"None of us," Bruna replied, her tone stark and decisive.

Caldera blinked. "Damn it, I told him to take one of you! Has he come back?"

Bruna squared her dark shoulders. "He didn't mention any such request, and no, he has not."

"We did offer to accompany him," Saro added, flicking his gaze away from Aloriea and letting it land on Caldera, "but he declined."

"You aren't supposed to let him, or any of us, *decline*," Caldera replied through gritted teeth, as heat began radiating throughout her body.

Saro gulped. "I—"

"As mere employees of the palace security team, we cannot deny a command from a member of the royal court," Bruna said, taking a small step forward, her brown eyes serene as she delivered the information. "He wished to take his personal transport instead of the palace designated one, and we could not legally stop him from doing so."

Without replying, Caldera turned away from the guards, looking to Aloriea for confirmation.

She let out a soft sigh. "It's true. Members of a royal court hold almost as much power as a sector leader."

"Son of a bitch. That stubborn ass..." Caldera muttered, pulling out her communicator, tapping Sears name with her finger, and pressing the device to her ear.

The canned ringing echoed in her ears, once, twice, three times, as the two devices attempted to connect. After the fourth alert, the rings stopped and Sear's pre-recorded voice met her ears.

"This is Sear Arcaro. Please leave your name, communicator contact, and a brief message and I will be sure to reply as soon as I am able."

"He didn't answer," Caldera said, biting her lip and gripping the communicator tighter in her hand. She pressed it to the base of her chin and closed her eyes, contemplating what to do next. "All right," she said, "let's head to Vanguard headquarters... maybe we'll intercept him."

Even as the words left her mouth, an overwhelming sense of dread twisted her stomach into an impenetrable knot.

To Caldera's surprise, there was no snappy retort from Markarian, no argument from Aloriea, and no gentle caution from Rennick; they simply nodded in simultaneous agreement and started walking toward the entrance, ordering Saro to bring the transport around.

He's okay. I'm overreacting. He's okay. I'm overreacting. Caldera repeated the words over and over in her head as she descended down the marble steps of the palace entryway, the chill of the night air cutting into her skin and rustling her hair. The constant tremor that plagued her once steady hands was back in full force as she stepped onto the paved drive. The lit-up fountain bubbled its indifference as the transport appeared in front of them a few moments later.

Caldera, Rennick, Aloriea, and Markarian piled into the back, nervously looking out the windows, not wanting to break the fragile silence. Saro whipped the transport around the circle drive and in minutes they were off, flying through the night sky toward the Vanguard.

Lacing her fingers together, Caldera shoved her hands into her lap, the lights of Astrum flying by at what seemed like light speed. Visions of her old ship crossed her mind in a way they hadn't in what seemed like forever, but although the memories held a special place in her heart, she didn't long to live them anymore.

She didn't want to be on a ship hurtling through endless space...
but she didn't want the burden of having everything solely land
on her shoulders either.

Who am I?

They touched down behind the Vanguard headquarters,
with only one other transport in the lot.

Sear's.

CHAPTER 19

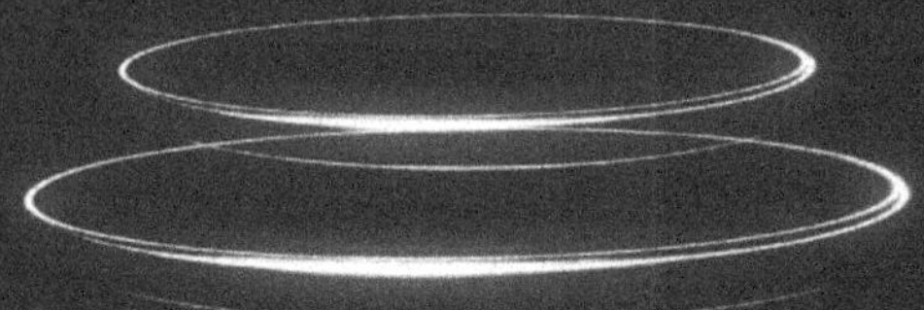

Caldera jumped out before Saro had completely parked the hovering transport, dropping the remaining four feet to the ground and running over to the locked vehicle and peering in the windows.

"Empty." She turned to her friends. "Markarian and Aloriea, you stay out here with Saro and keep trying to get through to Sear on his communicator. Rennick and I will go inside and check out his lab. Hopefully, he'll still be there." Her heart raced.

Maybe if he's still here, that's why he's not answering. Normal communicator signals can't penetrate the walls of the underground laboratories.

Aloriea and Markarian nodded, pulling out their communicators.

Caldera headed to the door, pressing her hand against the door scanner, only unlocking late at night for authorized personnel.

I guess being queen is useful in some instances.

Once it lit up green, Rennick mimicked her action. They ran past security guards who promptly got out of their way, pressing their backs against the wall and placing a closed fist over their chest while bowing and saying *'Your Majesty'*.

She thought she recognized them from when she was a captain. Clenching her jaw, she forced the caustic, irrational comments about how she didn't need to be bowed to, or treated any differently, back down her throat.

Why doesn't anyone understand that?

Rennick ran beside her, silent. The *creak* of his metal prosthetic leg scraped against her ears as they rounded corners and sprinted down hallways.

When was the last time he had that serviced? She swallowed hard as they came to a stop in front of the check-in desk for the labs department.

"Name and section code?" a light, tired sounding voice said.

Caldera and Rennick didn't answer right away, catching their breath, bent over, hands on their knees.

"Name plea—oh my universe! Your Majesty! I can't believe I'm actually meeting you again."

"Again?" Caldera blinked over at the spindly, black-haired person behind the desk. A hint of familiarity tugged at her mind. "Do I... know you?"

The person beamed, a crooked, sweet smile and shook their head. "No, not officially, but you... you changed my life. I mean... *I* changed my life, but you were kinda the catalyst."

Caldera glanced at Rennick, who shrugged, rubbing the connection between his skin and metal knee, shaggy hair flopping in his face to cover his eyes.

"It doesn't surprise me that you don't remember, or even recognize me, though," the person continued, tucking a strand of straight, shoulder-length hair behind their ear. "You uhh... you helped me out when I was going through a really tough time." They fidgeted with their thin fingers, glancing away, dark eyes clouding. "I want to say that... the reform to the S.W.S. you implemented really made a difference." They grinned again. "It helped me get back on my feet."

The social welfare system? That was one of the first things I changed. Caldera furrowed her brow, trying to process the situation, and desperately trying to figure out how she knew this person. The air filled with awkward silence. "I'm glad I could help, but—"

"We need you to check to see if someone by the name of Sear Arcaro signed into the lower labs earlier today," Rennick finished, leaning against the desk.

The person snapped to attention. "Of course. He's one of your court members, yes?"

Caldera nodded. "That's right. He hasn't returned to the palace and we're...worried about him."

They tapped the holoscreen in front of them, bathing their pale face in blue light as it activated. "Okay, let's see..."

Seconds inched along as Caldera bounced her foot up and down, anxiously tapping the fingers of one hand along the desktop, and chewing a nail on the other.

The person's finger flicked upward, moved to the right and flicked upward again, indicating that they were scrolling through multiple lists. They stopped after a few minutes, pressing their palms against the table. "I'm sorry, it looks like he didn't sign in today."

Caldera's breath froze in her throat. Everything Sear had ever done for her, everything he helped her with, and the way, despite coming off brash and egotistical, he had never forsaken their friendship, rushed into her mind like a dam that had broken open. She turned to Rennick, grabbing his arm to steady herself.

"Where is he?"

Rennick pulled her close, steadying her wavering body. "We'll keep looking, let's check his lab."

She took a deep breath, regaining her composure and taking a step back. Turning to the confused face of the desk-worker, an idea formed in her mind. "Do you have access to the security tapes?"

"For the entirety of the Vanguard?"

"Yes."

"I'm not really supposed to look at them, but I can get you into the office."

Caldera faced Rennick. "You head to his lab, I'll go to security and see if he's on any of the recorded footage there. His transport's here, so we know he at least made it to the building."

Rennick nodded, squeezing her shoulder before heading to the elevators that dropped down to the lower-labs, while Caldera followed the familiar person behind the desk, through a back door, and down a short hallway.

"Here," the person said, swiping a keycard and scanning their handprint at the same time. "It's double protected because everything recorded in Vanguard headquarters is funneled through here, and this late at night, the guards usually prefer to walk the grounds instead of being stuffed in this room, so you won't have to explain why you want to see this footage." They winked playfully.

"And you're sure you haven't seen Sear today?" Caldera couldn't help asking, tilting her head to the side.

"I have not." They shook their head. "Sir Arcaro doesn't come here that much, to be honest. I see Markarian—err—Sir Ales, much more often. He reviews this footage bi-weekly."

Without waiting for a response, they stepped out of the room.

Caldera's head spun; she really had no idea what her friends were up to. Not since she promoted them all to members of her court without asking—tasking them with immense amounts of responsibility. Guilt exploded in her chest.

"Tha-thank you," she stammered, "umm—"

"Zee," they replied, their face etched with kindness. They took another step back, just enough for Caldera to close the door between them and pointed to the left hand side of the room. "Those are the security recordings for the labs, and those," they pointed to the middle bank of holoscreens, " are the recordings of the parking area."

"Thank you, Zee," Caldera replied, gripping their hand in a quick shake, still not quite sure how she knew them, and closing herself into the small room.

Once alone, she turned to the monitors, going for the parking area screens first. *Might as well start from when he got here.* She pressed a button, and the screens blinked to life. Typing in the approximate hour she was looking for, she pressed play.

After a few minutes of fast-forwarding and switching to different views, she saw Sear's transport touch down into his designated space and he emerged from the driver's side door.

"Okay, there you are—" The communicator chimed at her side, making her jump. "Ren, what did you find?" she asked, bringing it to her ear and pausing the footage.

"That device Sear was talking about," Rennick's voice answered. "It's still here. I mean, I'm assuming this is the thing he was telling you about. It's locked up…"

Caldera furrowed her brow, resuming the playback on the holoscreen. "Meet me in the security room, I've got someth—"

The words were ripped out of her throat as a blazing flash enveloped her vision, making her squint and hold a hand up to her eyes. It was quick, bright, and made the footage completely unreadable. The communicator slipped out of her hand, tumbling to the hard linoleum floor with a *clank*.

Caldera sat in silence as the light faded on the recording. Rennick's frantic voice continued to call out—muffling into the background until she couldn't hear him at all. Time seemed to slow and distort as the blank screen stared back at her.

Sear was gone.

A single thought swirled in her head.

Olivare was right… I can't protect my friends.

CHAPTER 20

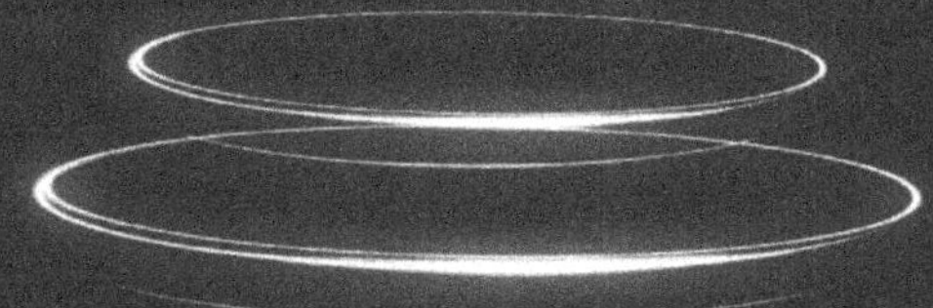

Caldera busted through the door of the security office and past a confused Zee, her legs shaking with such intensity they were barely able to hold her up. She leaned heavily on the desk, not wanting to believe what she had seen.

Zee's voice was far away as they spoke. "Are you okay, Your Majesty?"

Caldera couldn't respond, she could only push herself forward, one leaden leg in front of the other. *It's happening again. Another person I care about is gone. They could be dead.*

She heard Rennick's voice calling for her. "Callie!"

"What happened to her?" he asked, although the question wasn't directed at her.

"I don't know," Zee said. "She—she ran out of the office like that."

A hand was gripping her arm. She didn't turn around; she was doing everything she could not to collapse.

Rennick's face appeared in front of her. "Callie, what happened?"

"They..." she tried. Her voice was thin, less than a whisper. "They took him..."

"Sear? Who took him?"

Caldera's chest heaved as she sucked in breath after breath, her cheeks stained with tear trails. "*They* did!"

A look of understanding washed over his features. His gaze drifted over her shoulder. "Watch her," he said to Zee, and ran into the security office.

Caldera glanced over her shoulder and waited. Her pounding heart never slowed in its acceleration.

After a few minutes, Rennick reemerged, his face pale. "We have to tell the others," he said, meeting her eyes. A device she didn't recognize was clutched in his hand. "We have to find him."

We have to get him back.

The single thought ignited a fire in her chest, and a wave of pure energy coursed through her body. Her eyes instantly dried and she dug her nails into her palms.

"Come on!" she said, making a beeline down the hall and to the door, taking a split second to call a 'thank you' over her shoulder at Zee. The look of confusion never left their face as they lifted a hand to wave.

Rennick followed beside her, his face a solemn mask, his grip never loosening on the device he held in his clenched fist.

They ran out of the Vanguard headquarters and over to the palace transport at full speed, throwing themselves into the vehicle where Markarian and Aloriea were waiting.

"Whoa, what's going on?" Markarian asked, as Caldera and Rennick collapsed onto their seats, slamming the doors behind them.

"What did you find out?" Aloriea added, looking around, her brown eyes wide. "Where's Sear?"

"He—" Caldera faltered, out of breath. "He's—"

"Callie, what's going on?" Aloriea insisted, her voice rising in pitch.

"They took Sear," she finally managed between breaths. "The people from Area 51."

"What?" Markarian said, shock and disbelief coating the word.

"Are you sure?" Aloriea gasped as her hand shot up to cover her mouth.

Rennick nodded solemnly. "We both saw it…"

"Then we have to go!" Aloriea cried as uncontrolled tears streamed down her face.

"Go where?" Rennick uttered, taking a deep, shuddering breath and running a hand through his hair, gripping Sear's device that he stole from his lab tighter in his hand.

She grabbed his arm, squeezing. "Earth. Area 51!"

Markarian nodded vehemently. "We have to act!"

Caldera stared at her frantic friends, her mind swirling in the wake of yet another devastating tragedy. *They're not making sense…They're acting reckless. They're acting like… like me…*

"And we will…" she said, cutting through their squabbling for a brief moment, "but it won't do Sear any good if we jump into something without thinking about it first."

"You're advocating for reason," Aloriea snapped, turning and wiping her glittering cheeks. "That's a first!"

"Hey," Rennick said, holding up his hands. "Calm down—"

"No! What happened to shoot first, ask questions later?"

Caldera clapped her hands together once, the echo reverberating throughout the air. "That line of thinking made me a killer." Her expression softened as Aloriea's distressed gaze fell. "All I'm saying is that we need to go about this logically…like Sear would." She plucked the device out of Rennick's hand and looked it over before tucking it away into her jacket pocket. "We'll go back to the palace and figure things out from there."

THE TRANSPORT RIDE BACK WAS clogged with shell-shocked silence that only continued as they made their way back through the front doors of the palace.

The events of the last three hours replayed in Caldera's mind on a repetitive, mind-numbing loop as the group stumbled through the halls, past the questioning gaze of Bruna, and back to Caldera's quarters.

Her friends distributed themselves at her table, on the edge of the bed, or leaned against the wall, looking distantly out the glass doors into the night. No one spoke.

Caldera *couldn't* speak.

What can I say? She eyed each of her friends, their downcast and averted gazes a mix between sorrow and hollow emptiness—a look that she knew, and understood, all too well.

"Well... what do we do now?" Aloriea whispered, wrapping her arms tightly around herself, her voice so hushed it was almost inaudible.

"What would Sear do?" Markarian muttered, his shoulders slumping.

Rennick put a hand on his shoulder. "He'd tell us to start at the beginning."

Caldera nodded, inhaling deeply through her nose and releasing the breath out through her mouth, letting the stillness of the room level out her frenzied emotions. "We need to find out if this really is Area 51, and I mean with one-hundred percent certainty. There can be no doubt."

Aloriea raised a brow, brown eyes red and puffy. "And why is that?"

Caldera met her eyes, a rapid fire igniting inside her chest. "Because I am going to come down on whoever did this with a vengeance."

Tentative smiles spread across her friends' faces.

"How can we know for sure?" Rennick asked.

"I think we need to call in some experts," Caldera replied, her gaze landing on Markarian.

He grinned. "One blond-haired cutie and his gremlin of a little sister, coming up," he replied, walking to the door and disappearing into the hallway.

"Mei and John?" Aloriea asked. "What do you think they'll know?"

"They lived close to where Area 51 is located on Earth," Rennick replied.

"They, or at least, Mei, knows everything a civilian can know about that place," Caldera added. "She seems to have some kind of obsession with it—"

"I like to call it *passion*," Mei interjected, stepping into the room, hands on her hips, followed by John and Markarian. "What d'ya want to know?"

"Everything you can tell us about the facility itself," Caldera replied, motioning for her friends to gather around the table. "Forget the conspiracies," she continued. "I want facts."

Mei sighed dramatically, pulling her legs up to her chest. "You'll want to talk to my brother then."

The group turned to John.

"Well, I—there's not really much to tell if you want to ignore the conspiracies surrounding it. It's technically an Air Force base."

"What's an Air Force?" Aloriea asked, furrowing her brow.

"It's a branch of the military."

"But Area 51's existence within that branch was unconfirmed for years," Mei added, picking at a paint stain on her jean-covered knee. "Information about what 'actually' goes on there was only recently released to the public around ten years ago."

Aloriea nodded, gripping her chin with her thumb and forefinger. A dark shadow seemed to pass over her face as the overhead light glinted off her metal horn.

"What does the Earthen public think they do?" Caldera asked, knowing full well that it was at least used by the Council, behind the scenes, as a landing point—a connection—from Bersama to Earth.

John shrugged, the sleeves of his loose-fitting shirt fluttering against his arms. "It's a flight testing facility..." He tilted his head to the side. "What's going on?"

The group glanced at each other.

"We think Sear was,"—Caldera paused, swallowing hard and forcing herself to continue—"taken by them and we need to know exactly what Area 51 does so we can get him back."

Mei and John blinked disbelieving eyes at her.

"Sear..." Mei whispered, her shoulders tensing.

Caldera patted her shoulder; she had been so wrapped up in the world of budding politics that she hadn't realized how close Mei and John had gotten to all of them since their first meeting almost six months ago.

"What can we do?" Mei asked, glancing around the spacious quarters as if an answer would pop out of thin air.

Caldera leaned forward, her elbows pressing against the glass-topped table. "Tell us everything you know about that place."

John nodded, sitting across from her and taking a deep breath. "Okay, from what has been declassified, it's known that Area 51 is an unregulated government facility—"

"There are basically no rules there," Mei interrupted.

"—and the people who work there aren't government agents, but rather civilian scientists," John continued, quieting her.

"But it's a military operation?" Markarian questioned.

"That doesn't make sense," Rennick agreed. "There would need to be some form of rules, right?"

John nodded. "That's what it's perceived as on the surface—the Air Force *uses* it as a flight testing facility and all that—but, what's actually come to light is that the scientists there have been trying to reverse engineer UFOs, among other things not yet disclosed to the public."

"Unidentified flying objects," Mei elaborated, glancing at each of them.

Caldera nodded, the confused look she knew she and her friends wore dissipating. "How many people work there?"

"Hundreds? Thousands? Maybe less than fifty. The exact amount is unknown."

Aloriea scoffed, crossing her arms. "So possibly 'thousands' of people are fine with kidnapping?"

"It's honestly possible some of them don't even know what's going on. The scientists are prohibited from communicating with anyone else in the outside world."

Aloriea shook her head, her expression hard as stone, but didn't respond, leaning against the wall and turning her attention to the growing night.

"So, it's not a monolith—the different sections are compartmentalized within the organization itself..." Caldera muttered, her mind racing as she pieced the details together in her frenzied brain. "Who were the three people who made contact with us?"

"At the sector leader meeting?" Markarian asked.

Caldera nodded, turning to Rennick and Aloriea. "What were their names?"

"Evie, Dominic, and Barrett," Rennick replied.

"And who knows who they were talking to on the other end of their communicator?" Aloriea added in a monotone voice.

"They could be the ones actually running Area 51," John said, a troubled expression flashing across his face. "Since no one knows who they really are."

Uneasy silence filled the room as the group stewed over the information.

"It's looking more and more like they *are* the ones responsible," Markarian said, tapping a finger against his leg.

"Obviously," Aloriea muttered, still not looking at the group.

"What're our next steps?" Rennick asked no one in particular. "We have the background of the facility now, and while it seems extremely suspicious, it doesn't tell us if they really are abducting people or not."

Caldera closed her eyes as her mind raced. The only thing she could think of was the portal opening; its gaping maw of swirling reds and metallics. The icy coldness. The loss of vision. The feeling of simultaneously knowing everything and nothing at the same time. How others would have to live those experiences. The destruction an opening left in its wake.

Her eyes shot open as her hand instinctively reached for Sear's device that was still resting, forgotten, in her pocket. "I have an idea."

THE SUN'S RAYS BEAT DOWN on Caldera's exposed shoulders the next day as she and her friends sat on top of the wall surrounding the back courtyard of the palace—their new designated meeting spot. She had proposed it as an alternative to meeting in the Vault, since they had to log their every action when down there.

"You're sure about this?" Markarian asked, looking around at the group.

Caldera nodded, pointing to the device that was sitting in the middle of them on the stone walkway. "Sear was going to get this when he disappeared. It's a teleportation device that he had been collaborating on with scientists from the other sectors.

"Since this is untested tech, everything's being documented, so we'll have to work fast—as soon as we activate it, the other head scientists from the other sectors will be alerted, meaning, so will the leaders."

"Okay..." Aloriea said, crossing her arms. "What are we going to do with it"

"We'll use it to visit the disappearance sites in Tellis, talk to any witnesses, and scan the area for any wormhole residue that's still in the atmosphere—like I did when... Ren disappeared," Caldera said, before turning to Markarian. "You'll have to log into the Vanguard coordinate system for this to work."

"But you said Sear was going to put some finishing touches on it... and he never got there," Aloriea said, pulling her knees up to her chest.

"I still think it's mostly done." Caldera bit her lip. "Knowing Sear, whatever 'finishing touches' he wanted to add were most likely him being a perfectionist."

"You think any residual residue from the portal openings will still be in the spots corresponding to the disappearances?" Markarian asked, shifting the conversation back around and raising an eyebrow.

"It should," Rennick replied, pulling up the data from his disappearance over a year ago on his holopad, which was connected to the palace security cameras. "Look."

He brought up the area scanner that faced the back courtyard.

"This is the same place where the wormhole that pulled me in opened, and if we scan it today..." He pressed a button on the screen, activating the scanner. A 3D model of the area appeared in the air in front of them, faint red and yellow lines crisscrossed the diagram.

"It's negligible, but it's there," Aloriea replied, the colors reflecting off her brown eyes.

Rennick nodded. "And this is the conference room—the last place the people from Area 51 have been seen." He pressed another button and the scanners read the room. Bright yellows and reds appeared on the screen. "And that was obviously much more recent. Only about a month ago now, right?"

"A little less, actually," Aloriea said.

Caldera's stomach involuntarily twisted. She pushed the sensation away, wishing she wouldn't have had to cancel her therapy appointments indefinitely.

There's no time for that... Not anymore. She shook her head, letting a shiver run down her spine at the thought of Rennick's disappearance and the proof that it had actually happened, despite all her attempts to block it from her mind, stared her in the face.

"See," she said, her tone forceful, trying to push past her unresolved issues. "Signs of the initial opening are still there even after all this time. This is going to work."

CHAPTER 21

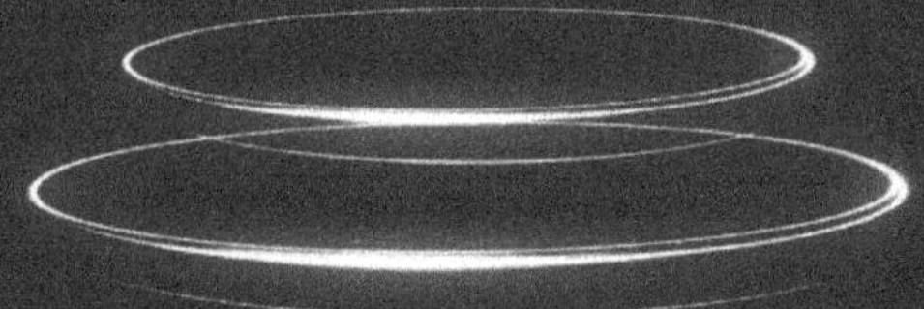

"Callie!" Saro's voice called from below them, sounding out of breath. "Are you up there?"

"There's nothing stopping you from walking up the steps, Saro," Caldera replied, shooting a questioning look at her friends before getting to her feet and leaning over the edge.

"Right..." he said, placing a foot on the bottom step. "Wait—is Aloriea—?"

Caldera glanced over her shoulder at her judgemental friend with a look of disapproval.

Aloriea glared back, but said nothing.

"Don't let her scare you," Caldera said, turning back to Saro and waving him up the steps. "Come on."

Saro rushed to the top and faced the semi circle of Rennick, Markarian, and Aloriea while Caldera stood in front of him.

"What is it?" she asked.

"There's been a development."

"Of what kind?" Aloriea questioned, seeming more curious than hostile.

"Area 51—umm, Evie—the one in charge. She's made contact again," he replied in a breathless rush.

Caldera's eyes widened and then she was running past him down the steps before she could respond, her friends rushing after her. She slowed her pace, letting Saro catch up. "Where and when?"

"Just now. Apparently she contacted Queens Eldra and Fenry through a pre-recorded message." He took a breath as they burst through the doors into the palace. "The queens have tapped the message through to every sector leader to watch, and they're all on the holoscreen waiting for you in the conference room."

"What does it say?"

"I wouldn't know… but based on the urgency of them wanting the security team to find you—"

"It must be pretty important," Caldera finished, as they approached the conference room doors.

What are they up to? Are they officially declaring an invasion?

Caldera, Rennick, Markarian, and Aloriea burst through the conference room doors where the other sector leaders were waiting on the large, split-holoscreen on the far wall for her.

The pre-recorded video from Area 51 was already queued up and waiting on another split-screen, designed to be played at the same time. Their spokesperson, Evie, sat behind a large wooden desk that was waxed to a persistent glimmer. The plants hanging behind her were vibrant—the leaves and vines of the greenery displaying that she likely took careful care of them.

"Saro," Caldera said, placing a hand on his shoulder, "guard this door. I don't want any surprises."

Like another unannounced visit.

"Yes, Your Majesty." Saro bowed stiffly, his eyes on the holoscreen behind her, before quickly disappearing and closing the doors behind him.

"Queen Caldera… and entourage," Desrin said, her eyes shifting from each of Caldera's friends to the next.

"We weren't expecting your full crew to be in tow," Eldra said, as if finishing Desrin's thought process.

Caldera narrowed her eyes. "Well... they are. So, if you don't mind—"

"What we are saying is that it would be better if they were not," Mokan interrupted, his green eyes gleaming. "For their sake."

Fenry nodded. "You've proven time and time again that you're an 'unorthodox' leader, but—"

"But nothing," Caldera quipped, glancing from her friends back up to the holoscreen, and holding up her hand to stop the second queen of Sector Two from continuing to ramble. "I may hold the title of 'Queen' but I'm not above them. What I know, they know." She smirked. "So you might as well get on with it."

Eldra sighed solemnly. "If you insist..."

"We were trying to help," Fenry scoffed. "Remember that."

The paused face of Evie sprung to life at the press of the button. Her short red hair shifted with movement and her voice started out garbled—static filled, the product of jumping a signal through a wormhole, before evening out.

"Hello, leaders of Bersama. I hope this message finds you well." She paused to grin into the camera. "We at Area 51 are reaching out to see if you would possibly reconsider your involvement with us."

Another smile.

"I understand that Queen Caldera can be quite convincing in her reasoning for disliking us, but I assure you... her claims are only partially justified." Evie's gaze fell, as if she were looking down on the recipients—somehow landing right on Caldera.

Caldera's skin crawled as goosebumps shot up her arms.

"I'm afraid that if you won't work with us, drastic measures will have to be taken." Evie tilted her head ever so slightly to the right. "Moreso than they already have been, anyway—but that's a conversation for another time." She leaned forward, lacing her thin fingers together, her brown eyes hard. "Earth and Bersama will be completely divided. Starting now."

Caldera's breath was coming in short, shallow gasps.

"What does this mean? Well, it means that without coming to an agreement, Bersaman *aliens* will no longer have access to Earth. No food. No water. No resources. Nothing."

She's trying to blackmail us.

"You may think you're self-sustaining, but you aren't. You may think you won't need us, but you will. And you may think you have nothing to lose, but you do," Evie continued, holding up a black tie with an embroidered 'S' at the bottom between her thumb and forefinger.

Caldera's blood ran cold. "Sear!" She couldn't hold it in; his name had left her mouth before she could stop it. She took a step forward, as if in doing so she would be able to respond to the message.

Aloriea's hands were clamped over her mouth, while Rennick and Markarian stood there in stunned silence.

As if on cue, Evie dropped the garment, letting it float down to the tabletop. "We await your decision. Use the encrypted signal relay in this message to directly contact us back," she said, her voice calculated—methodic. "And I would seriously reconsider letting Queen Caldera make any future decisions regarding this matter. After all... she's compromised."

The video faded to a solid black, with Evie's last words still ringing in Caldera's ears.

"Now you are up to date on the situation," Mokan said, wasting no time, his dark black fur bristling. "We must decide what our next course of action should be."

Caldera couldn't speak; blood rushed to her ears, and she barely heard him.

"What options do we have, exactly?" Fenry asked. "Our conservation efforts aren't producing the results like we hoped—at least, not in Natioh."

Eldra exhaled sharply. "It's true, despite our best efforts, Sector Two's resources are dwindling at an alarming rate."

"My people are alsso barely sscraping by," Jasik added, their lips curling over sharp teeth.

Nari trilled under her breath, white fur bristling. "I am afraid that if things keep going in the direction they are, Sector Five will no longer be able to export Muléan goods."

"But Muléus is the most lush sector on Bersama!" Caldera stated, her voice wavering.

"This is true," Mokan replied, his black ears twitching back and forth, "but we have already had to put one stipend on exported goods just so we have enough for our own people. If we have to put another on, there would almost be no benefit to anyone."

"The prices would simply be too high," Nari added, glancing to her side. "Please excuse me, our advisor needs something." In one quick motion she disappeared from sight.

Caldera's breathing quickened. "I recently refinanced our environmental restoration agency—T.E.R.A.—surely that would help," she tried, frantically grasping for anything that could stop where the conversation was headed. "We can get through this on our own."

"And we will continue to try and work together to accomplissh that, but Callie... There'ss ssadly only one alternative at thiss point..." Jasik said, their tongue flicking in and out of their mouth.

No...

"Yes," Desrin agreed, as if reading her mind. "We must work with them."

"We can't," Caldera said, clenching her hands into tight fists. Aloriea's gaze snapped in her direction.

"You're still holding out?" Desrin questioned, raising a genuinely curious eyebrow. "Even considering that they have a member of your court?"

"That's precisely *why* I am..." Caldera said, mustering all her courage to continue—to push past the preconceived notion that all she was capable of was brute force, and the bias that since she wasn't raised within the royal hierarchy, that she wasn't cut out to make tough, rational, decisions.

Don't worry Sear, we'll get you back somehow, I swear!

Caldera clenched her fists even tighter. "They think that they're infallible right now—that we can be bullied into submission, but give me a little time," she pleaded. "We have Sear's transporter device he was working on to facilitate teleportation throughout Bersama.

"They're clearly the ones abducting people, that much is obvious now... Let us investigate to see if we can find out how they're doing it, and we may be able to exploit them!"

The other leaders looked down at her from their respective screens, a range of curiosity and doubt playing across their individual faces.

"Wait... You have a teleportation device in your possession?" Desrin asked, her expression clouding.

Caldera nodded, clenching her fists. "Sear, and the scientists he was working with, almost had it perfected."

"That doesn't mean you can use it!"

"I need it! *We* need it..."

"I don't know..." Eldra mused, biting her lip, the twin white-dotted lines that ran down either side of her cheeks glimmering.

"I need a little more time," Caldera pressed, never breaking eye contact. "I'll document everything—you can send reps to monitor me—I don't care. Let me do this... Please."

To Caldera's surprise, Desrin's hard red eyes softened. "Okay. I'll back you on this, but I'll be sending Ivy to keep an eye on you throughout the process."

The nod from Eldra was so subtle that she almost missed it. "Unfortunately, we cannot spare a representative."

"Neither can I," Jasik said.

Mokan glanced away from the screen for a moment. "My queen informs me that all of our representatives are working with the authorities on the disappearances, so we cannot spare a person either."

"One should suffice," Desrin replied confidently. "Ivy's very trustworthy."

"Very well, then," Eldra said, squaring her shoulders. "Shall we say two weeks?"

A chorus of voices replied, *"Agreed"* in unison.

"That's all we'll need," Caldera said, clasping her hands behind her back in an attempt to stop her body from shaking.

"All in favor, say aye," Eldra continued, motioning for the vote to begin.

A chorus of ayes rang out into the conference room, and Caldera couldn't help but smile at the support.

"Two weeks." Eldra sternly reiterated. "Otherwise, to stop the kidnappings, we'll have no choice but to take Area 51's offer. Keep us updated on your progress."

"I will," Caldera promised as the leaders all disconnected and the holoscreen went dark.

CHAPTER 22

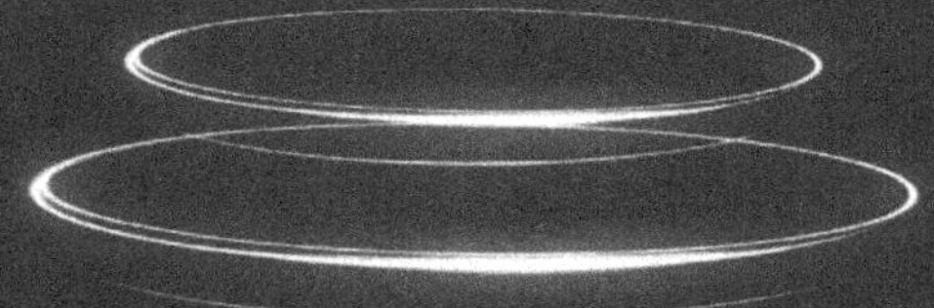

oments after the conference call ended, Caldera ushered her friends down into the Vault, where they all sat around the faux wood table, tapping their fingers and racking their brains for the next move.

"All right…" Aloriea mused, pacing back and forth with a furrowed brow. She turned her attention to the device sitting on the table. "How does *that* work?"

"I have no idea."

"Of course not."

Caldera blinked. She hadn't heard that short tone for a while. She glanced from Rennick to Markarian, who were both sharing her confused expression. "Aloriea…What is going on?"

Indignation raged behind her friend's eyes, making her lean back despite herself.

I haven't seen her this angry since I first came here.

"How can you ask me that? Sear is gone!" Aloriea snapped, slamming her hand down on the table. "You lobbied for more time to investigate disappearances instead of taking Area 51's offer, this stupid device is all that's left of Sear, and nobody even knows how to use the damn thing!"

"Aloriea," Rennick said, holding up his hands, "we'll figure it out—"

"We're all acting like we're going to rescue him, but what if… we don't?"

Markarian placed a hand on her shoulder. "This'll work, Lor—"

Aloriea pushed his hand away and turned on Caldera. "Sear never should have been by himself!"

Caldera lurched like she'd been slapped. "You—you think this is *my* fault?" Sorrow quickly made way for fire as heat rose to her face. "That is bullshit, Aloriea, and you fucking know it!"

She trembled, unable to contain her raw emotions. Tear trails streamed freely down her cheeks.

"I already blame myself enough for what's happened. I don't need you to do it for me."

Aloriea shook her head, clenching her hands into fists. "I'm not. I'm not blaming you—That's not what I meant—I—" Her chest heaved as she stumbled backward, covering her face with her hand.

Rennick hustled to her side, catching her by the elbow before she crashed to the floor. "It's okay," he whispered, gently guiding her to a chair. "You'll be okay." His eyes were sad as he turned to Caldera.

Caldera's chest rose and fell in quick succession as she tried to gain control of her ragged breathing. Standing, she took a step forward, then another. She walked until she was in front of the sobbing Aloriea and knelt in front of her, taking her violently shaking hands in hers.

Rennick and Markarian crowded on either side. Rennick placed a hand on Caldera's shoulder while Markarian rested his on Aloriea's.

"Remember what we promised?" Caldera breathed, squeezing Aloriea's hands. "After we stopped the Council?"

She sniffed. "That we wouldn't let ourselves end up like that."

Caldera nodded.

"That we wouldn't let ourselves fall into endless despair," Markarian continued, squeezing her shoulder.

"We'd be each other's ladders," Rennick said.

"And no matter what happens, we'll help each other out of those dark places before we're consumed," Caldera finished. She took a breath. "Listen, we're all in over our heads, even you, Aloriea, but I know exactly what you're going through," she said, never breaking eye contact. "Not many people can say that to their friend. So you need to believe me," she said, standing and snatching the device off the table. "We *are* going to get him back."

Aloriea blinked red puffy eyes up at Caldera, not moving from her seat. "Okay, Callie... Lead the way."

AFTER COMPLETELY TRANSFERRING SEAR'S NOTES from his lab at Vanguard headquarters to the Vault computer system, and after countless hours of sifting through the record, as well as consulting with other sectors lead scientists—under the watch of the corresponding sector leader, Caldera—with Rennick, Aloriea, and Markarian's help—finally figured out how the device, which they were tentatively calling the S.G.T.—*Sear's Geocode Transporter*, worked. It worked much like she predicted; first, connect it to the planet-wide coordinate system, managed through the Vanguard, and second, target-lock onto the desired location for teleportation.

"All right," Markarian said as he finished typing in the coordinates. "We're locked onto the first location and your round trip is set." He whisked his hair into a messy bun. "I still can't believe everyday teleportation is real."

"It *kind of* is," Aloriea countered, unhooking the S.G.T. device from the computer system. "It's still in its prototype stages—hence why you have to enter the primary and secondary locations all at once. Otherwise, you won't be able to use it to get home. Not to mention, as of right now, it's also sector locked, so we can't go anywhere but places in Tellis. Those were the things that Sear probably needed to put 'finishing touches' on."

"Good thing we don't want to go anywhere but Tellis right now," Caldera said with a nod, snatching it out of Aloriea's hand.

It looked like any other random geocode device given to every Vanguard member as a standard tool to keep in their arsenal—a handheld black and yellow box with a touch screen protected by a thin layer of thermoplastic to prevent cracks. The only difference being the small chamber made of borosilicate glass that was filled with liquified artificial painite, and a clasp integrated onto the S.G.T. itself so it could easily be clipped to a belt loop.

She couldn't help but smile. *With all the sectors working together, we made a stable, upgraded version of the portal bracelets that'll be available to everyone—putting the painite to good use in a way that helped Bersama, and didn't affect Earth.*

It was a small step, but it was the start of something bigger. Vindication coursed through her. *I knew we could make it without relying on stolen resources.*

"I'll go first," Rennick said, breaking her out of her thoughts and reaching out his hand. "These devices were designed for personal use, so it has to be calculated to one specific person—"

"Meaning two people can't use it at the same time," Markarian finished, placing his hands on his hips. "Ahh, so that's why it's asking for a thumbprint. I knew there'd be a catch."

Caldera flinched, holding the S.G.T. closer to her chest. The thought of watching Rennick go through another portal-esque structure, even if it were controlled, made her body break out into a cold sweat. She shook her head, remembering the plan.

His face softened as if he read her mind. "It'll be okay. I'll call you as soon as I get through, and the palace shuttle can take you to the location."

"No, you don't understand," she said, running a hand down his arm as the rush of reflexive fear subsided. "We'll each have our own devices."

Rennick raised an eyebrow. "I thought Sear only made one."

"He did," a familiar voice said from behind them.

They turned around to see Desrin descending the final steps of the Vault, followed by Panos and Ivy.

Panos's blaster was drawn as he stepped in front of Desrin into the open area, prompting Rennick and Markarian to draw their weapons.

"So *this* is what your family's been hiding for years?" Desrin asked, gazing around the room, her red eyes gleaming, long, braided hair draped over her shoulder. She patted the air and Panos reholstered his blaster.

Caldera nodded at Rennick and Markarian, who mimicked his action.

"You really shouldn't leave it open like this," Desrin continued.

"You really shouldn't be down here," Aloriea said, flicking hard eyes at the intruders.

"I wouldn't be if this place were properly guarded."

Caldera narrowed her eyes. "It was—wait... it *was*. What did you say to Grey and Sylvie?"

Desrin flashed a sharp smile her way, her black horns seeming to glow under the fluorescent light. "Nothing. I suppose people are... intimidated by me."

"We knew you were coming and yet you still insist on making an entrance?" Aloriea snapped.

"I'm here to help," Desrin said, turning her gaze to Caldera. "Right?"

She sighed. "It is what we agreed upon... Do you have the other device?"

Desrin motioned for Ivy to step forward. "Of course. I would've preferred to send a messenger, but since this technology isn't released to the public yet, I can't risk it falling into the wrong hands."

Ivy presented Caldera with a small metallic box from the satchel she had draped over her shoulder. "Here you are, Your Majesty." She held the box out to her but her mystified, gray eyes were searching the surrounding area.

"Thank you," Caldera said, opening the lid to see an almost identical device as the one they already had, the only difference being that instead of gold-colored trim around the edges, it was red.

"Like yours, that's also a prototype," Desrin said, tapping Ivy on the shoulder to get her attention. The lithe woman jumped as if she had previously been in a trance, and hustled back behind the queen. "So the same rules of use apply."

"Of course," Caldera replied, nodding again.

"Hold on," Markarian began, furrowing his brow. "You're giving this to us?"

"Think of it as a gift to help your fleeting cause," Desrin said, waving a hand in the air. "Sector Four specializes in creating weaponry, and while this is no weapon, it's still in the same vein, so to speak. It's essentially of no consequence."

"Meaning?" Rennick asked, resting his palm on the butt of his blaster.

"Meaning we've already made more than one," Desrin replied. "Consider this..." she paused, tapping her chin with a long finger, "a preliminary field test."

"You're all right with us potentially dying?" Caldera questioned.

"Of course not. I don't expect anything to go wrong. I trust fully in our scientific team, just as you do in yours."

"This is out of the goodness of your heart then?" Markarian replied sarcastically.

"Oh no, I wouldn't say that." Desrin chuckled. "This was the deal that Queen Caldera and I struck. She keeps me informed and I'll do the same for her." She held up her left hand, palm directed at the ceiling. "She helps me,"—she held up her right—"and I help her." She clapped her hands together. "Give and take."

Aloriea scoffed, shaking her head and wrapping her arms around herself.

"We'll most likely end up needing more," Caldera found herself saying, her eyes never leaving Desrin.

"You're asking for *another* favor?"

"Like you said," Caldera retorted. "It's of no consequence, right? Our lead scientist is... gone and we need to get help from other sources."

Desrin smirked, tilting her head to the side. "How many?"

"One for each of us, plus an extra."

"Hmm. I'll think about it," she replied, with a wave of her hand. "On that note, I'm afraid I must depart, but I'm leaving you in the hands of my more than capable advisor," she continued, motioning to Ivy before turning to Panos. "Come on, let's get out of here. We've spent enough time in this muggy air."

She turned, bodyguard in tow, and started back up the steps, before glancing over her shoulder, her hard demeanor dropping for an instant.

"I expect a full report on what you find, and for what it's worth... I hope it's your friend."

Caldera's chest ached as Desrin and Panos disappeared up the steps, the weight of the situation settling heavily on her chest.

"And... they're gone," Markarian said, breaking the silence and walking over to the steps to glance up the staircase into the bright, mid-afternoon sun.

"I shouldn't be surprised that you made a deal with another sector leader without consulting me first," Aloriea muttered, settling into a chair.

"That's only partly true," Ivy offered, eyes bright. "Back when you were visiting our sector is when the initial deal was struck about sharing knowledge, but as far as me being here—"

"Ivy," Caldera cut in, interrupting the akar's rambling.

"Yes?"

"She understands."

Redness flushed across Ivy's face. "Right."

"I'm just glad it worked out," Caldera said, walking over to the computer system, plugging in the device.

Markarian quickly entered the round-trip coordinates into it and handed it back to her. "Okay, scan your prints," he said, looking from Caldera to Rennick.

They obeyed, simultaneously pressing their thumbs to the devices.

Markarian pressed a button on the computer screen. "All right, you're all synced up." He flicked his wrist toward the holoscreen and two 3D images, one of a map of Astrum, and one of body functions, linked to Caldera and Rennick each, appeared in the air floating between the four of them.

"You two'll monitor our location and wellbeing from here?" Caldera asked, hooking the red S.G.T. to her belt loop.

"Tracking you every step of the way, obviously," Markarian said, a small smile breaking across his face.

"What should I do?" Ivy cut in.

Caldera met each of her friends' eyes. "Why don't you go read the journals over there?" she replied with a shrug.

Ivy beamed. "I'd be happy to!"

Caldera blew out an exasperated breath as the woman—who was essentially there to be a snitch—bounded across the room to the ceiling-high shelves of notebooks and dove into reading.

"Are you sure about this?" Aloriea asked, taking a step closer to her. "What makes you think people won't recognize you?"

"We'll be in disguise," Caldera replied with a shrug.

"Fabric hoods and street clothes does not a disguise make."

"They'll be fine, Lor," Markarian said. "The first reported Tellin abduction was in a particularly desolate part of Astrum."

Aloriea shook her head and sighed. "Make sure to keep your wrap-around on. The teleportation devices don't monitor health."

Caldera glanced down at her wrist and forearm, seeing the wrap-around monitoring device was still securely in place; one of the things she couldn't let go from her time in the Vanguard. It was too comforting to give up.

"No problem," Rennick replied, adjusting his as well.

"Okay," Caldera said, hovering her finger over the teleportation device's screen. Her body shook, and the realization that her and Rennick were essentially guinea pigs for never before tested technology pounded full-force against her brain.

"Three," Rennick began, reaching out his hand to her.

"Two," Caldera continued, lacing their fingers together.

"One," they both said in unison, pushing the buttons at the same time and disappearing from the Vault with a *blink*.

CHAPTER 23

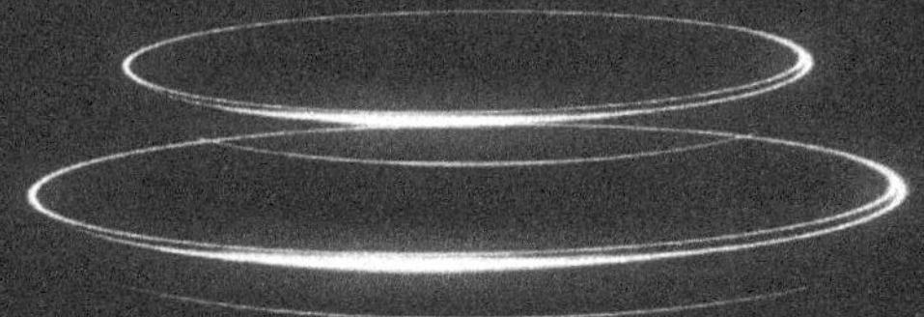

*I*t worked!

Caldera gasped, shocked there was no sensation from using the S.G.T. and shielding her eyes against the onslaught of the bright sun.

She glanced down at her empty hand before taking in her surroundings as the white dots encapsulating her vision slowly diminished. Seconds before, she was in the Vault, but now she stood in an empty alleyway behind one of the most industrialized parts of Astrum.

"Ren?"

"I'm here," he called from behind her.

She turned and he lifted his hand in a small wave.

"I guess it's good that Markarian entered coordinates that were next to each other instead of the exact same spot—otherwise we would've ended up on top of each other," he said, rubbing his eyes.

Caldera lifted a brow and smirked, holding in a chuckle.

He opened one eye and grinned. "Not like that."

Re-lacing their fingers, she leaned forward, kissing him on the cheek. "Maybe later," she said, dropping his hand, lifting the hood over her head, and taking a step back to survey the surrounding area. Even though it was the middle of the day, it appeared no one had seen them.

The desolate alley they had arrived in was tucked away behind an industrial park housing shuttle and personal transport part factories for the Vanguard as well as other private companies, storage facilities, and supply hubs for transportable goods to and from the capital. The multiple bars lining the nearly empty street in front of them sat dark, their neon signs and plasma displays waiting patiently for nightfall, when they'd bathe the world around them in an array of vivid colors, beckoning tired workers inside with the promise of a cold beer and relaxing night.

Caldera closed her eyes, letting the fond memories of blue, pink, and purple flashing neon lights and her friends' laughter thump rhythmically against the inside of her eyelids. "This is the site of the first disappearance?" she asked, taking a deep breath and opening her eyes.

"The report states it's up the road a ways," Rennick replied, pulling the hood he was wearing up over his head. He took out his holopad, beginning to scan the area. "And I'm not getting any traces of portal activity this far back."

"Is the person who reported it available to talk?"

"They declined. It says here that they 'simply can't relive the experience'. If you would have told them that you were the queen, and not some random reporter—"

"No," Caldera said, as they reached the sidewalk. "I'm not going to force someone to talk to me. Especially with what they've gone through..." Sympathy coursed through her. "We have the official police report to go off of, and that's enough."

Rennick nodded solemnly, instructing her to turn right. "There's a hint of substance that way."

Leaning over the holopad, a faint yellow blur met her eyes. The mass of color spread out, seeming to form a loose line, leading away from the alley they had come out of.

"Why is it in the form of a path?"

"It probably just seems like it is," Rennick replied. "With the way the buildings are placed here, for the residue to spread out, it would have to 'maneuver' around the physical surroundings."

They walked in front of a bar called The Triangle, turned down another alley and were met with bright yellow and red readings across the holopad.

"This is obviously it," Caldera said, biting her lip. The alley was much the same as the last one; empty trash cans were waiting to be filled, and levitating fire escapes hovered overhead for the bars that also housed their owners and other tenants. There was no sign that anyone had been abducted, no sign of a mysterious disappearing platform, and no sign of Area 51.

The readings don't lie. A portal opened and closed here, taking an innocent person with it.

A voice called from behind them. "Hey! What're you two doin' back there? Do y'all need help?"

Caldera and Rennick instinctively tightened the hoods around their faces.

"We're fine," Rennick called over his shoulder, but the man continued walking toward them.

"Great... I don't need rumors spreading about the queen and her bodyguard being spotted in random, unoccupied alleys," Caldera muttered, stepping closer to Rennick. "Aloriea will kill me if she has to clean up that mess... and rub it in my face."

"Let me do the talking. We can't use the S.G.T.s and go back to the palace. That'll add a false disappearance report into the mix."

"Not to mention, scare the shit out of this guy."

"Exactly, and my face isn't nearly as recognizable as yours."

She nodded, pressing her back against his as the stranger approached.

"You youngins shouldn't be out here," a grizzly voice said. "This be where an abduction took place."

"We know," Rennick said with a confirming nod. "That's actually why we're here. We're, uhh, reporters."

"Both of ya?"

"She's... shy," Rennick said, rubbing the back of his head. "Do you know anything about this particular disappearance?" His shoulder shifted against Caldera's back as if he was holding the holopad out for the man to talk into.

"Ya seem familiar—"

"I've heard that before. Must have common features. Anyway... you were saying?"

"Nothin' of substance, I'm afraid. I had just got in from my shift at the shuttle factory—takin' over for the day manager.

"The only thing I can say for sure is that the poor woman who survived the attack ran into my bar screamin' 'bout bright lights and a platform that appeared out of nowhere. I went with her to check, but I didn't see anythin'."

Caldera's eyes widened. *I knew it!*

"A platform? That wasn't in the police report?"

"Probably left it out. Who'd believe 'em even if they didn't?"

"And nobody else corroborated, or even repeated, this person's 'crazy' story?"

"It was a quiet night, so's not a lot of patrons... and I don't like spreadin' rumors."

"Do you own this place?"

"Sure do."

"Well, if you hear anything else, please let us know."

Caldera bit her nail, thoughts swirling in her head. *So there is a platform... but why do they need it? Unless they've found a way to contain and transfer a small area without it destabilizing?*

If they've done that, then they could bring a small group here each time, as opposed to one person... This 'platform' might be some sort of mass-group teleportation system...

Unable to resist any longer, she peeked around her hood and Rennick's back to try and catch a glimpse of the person who was talking. He sounded like an old factory hand, born and raised in the manufacturing industry.

His dark eyes met hers. "Vega?"

Caldera's body froze, air instantly gone from her lungs as her stomach somersaulted and twisted into a tight knot. She took a step back, gasping for breath and catching Rennick's open-mouth expression.

"No..." she finally managed between rapid heartbeats. "That was my mother's name."

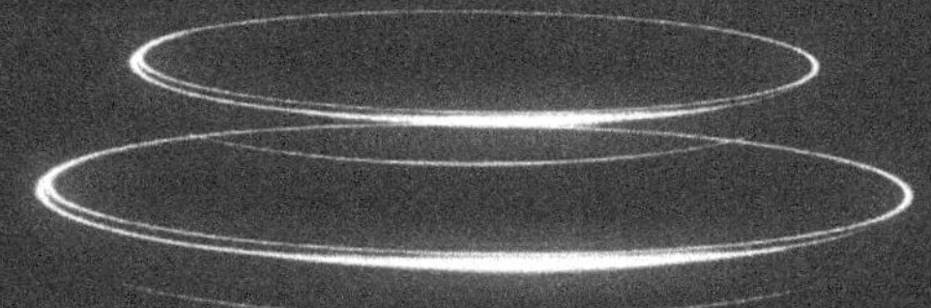

CHAPTER 24

Y ou be Vega's daughter?" the man mused. His eyes widened as he got a better look at her. "You—you be the queen!"

"Why did you think I was my mother?" Caldera demanded, taking a step forward and ignoring his surprised sentiment. "*How* could you think that?"

"A slip of the tongue," the old man said, blinking bespectacled eyes at her, and holding up shaky hands as if he were cowering—even though he towered over both of them at over six feet tall. Wearing a tucked in button up shirt, deep-blue jeans, and silver-dust covered boots, it looked like he'd just gotten off work. "I'm sorry. Y-you look so much like her, is all."

Caldera swallowed hard. It was as if a knife was being thrust into her heart over and over again.

"She and my father have been dead for thirteen years! Why would you think—" She stopped, furrowing her brow. "Wait... How do you—*did you*—know my mom?"

"I knew both your parents. Vega and Reed."

My mom and dad. Caldera glanced at Rennick. His eyes were filled with the same curiosity that hers must have held. "How?"

"I've been 'round here all my life, Your Majesty, runnin' my bar and workin' in the factory," he replied, a soft, deep-wrinkled grin spreading across his face. "They would frequent my bar when they were youngins like yourself—regulars, they were." He tucked his hands in his jean pockets and rocked from heel to toe. His short white hair shifted with the movement. "Sometimes they'd come by later in life too—never stayed as long, though."

Caldera shook her head, trying to recall her previous objective, but she couldn't help but continue the line of questioning in an effort to gain some new level of understanding them. "Do you know why?"

"Besides having a child?" The old man laughed, rough and authentic. He took off his glasses and rubbed his eyes. "I heard 'em whisperin' 'bout something right before..." He trailed off, scratching the back of his head and shifting his gaze to the ground as if unsure he should continue.

"Before their deaths?" Rennick offered, never taking his eyes off Caldera.

The old man nodded, replacing his spectacles.

"What was it?" Caldera commanded as the hood slipped completely off her head and settled around her shoulders.

"'Twas somethin' I'd never heard before or since, which is probably why I can remember it so clearly." He took a deep breath, his shoulders rising and falling heavily. "They said that they were 'bout to be late for a meetin' with some 'Area 51'."

Caldera was sure the world had stopped rotating. "Area 51..." Rennick's hands were on her arms, gripping her elbows and holding her upright.

"You're sure about this?" he asked, gripping her forearms tighter. "You're *absolutely* sure?"

"I may be old, boy, but I ain't losin' my mind." The old man tilted his head to the side. "You're lookin' pale, Your Majesty. Would ya' like to come in and have some water?"

Caldera weakly shook her head, unable to speak. *My parents were in talks with Area 51. Did they know about the Council's plan then? They had to.* Bile swirled in her stomach, rising rapidly into her throat. *Then did they know they were royalty? Quill assumed they didn't.* The acrid mass continued to ascend into her mouth. *The Council—Vandren—couldn't have known about them, could they?... What the fuck is going on?*

Her body went limp in Rennick's arms as vomit projected out of her mouth and onto the ground. She continued to hack as he gently lowered her to the ground and held back her hair. She placed her palms flat against the cool concrete, locking her arms into place so she didn't fall into the growing pile.

A chill rocketed up her arms, making her want to press her fiery cheek to a clean piece of ground and close her eyes instead of continuing to hold up her weak body. Her nose and throat burned as the last contents of her stomach were expelled.

"Get us the fuck out of here," Caldera spat, wiping her mouth.

Rennick nodded, helping her to her feet and wrapping an arm around her shoulder. "Sir, please..." He paused, glancing around the area.

It was still unoccupied.

"I won't say a word, lad," the old man replied. "Like I said before, I don't like spreadin' rumors."

Caldera turned her head to face him, her body shaking. His dark eyes were kind. Concerned. Truthful. She nodded her thanks before wrapping her arms around Rennick's torso and leaning against his chest. Closing her eyes, she readied herself to push the button on the teleportation device.

"Thank you," Rennick said, mimicking her action. "Would you, uhh, mind turning around?"

The old man must've obeyed because Rennick whispered in her ear, "Now."

Without hesitation, Caldera pressed the button, leaving the old man, the alley, and her vomit behind.

WATER PATTERED AGAINST CALDERA'S SKIN as she stood in the shower, wet hair plastered to her face, neck, and back, the steaming hot temperature bringing her no comfort.

It had been a full day since she and Rennick had talked to the old man—whose name she didn't even bother to ask—in the alley, and Markarian and Aloriea had been pestering her non-stop ever since.

Rennick had gone over what was said, but that only made them more anxious. She knew they were worried given her history, but she didn't want to talk about it.

Sear, her parents, the continuing string of disappearances. It was all too much. What right did she have to burden her friends even more? And she didn't want to admit to herself—let alone them—what she had to do next. She hadn't even told Rennick yet.

I need to talk to him... I need to talk to Vandren.

Caldera shuddered; the thought of him made rage pump through her body, and those emotions were mixed into her feelings about her parents. She punched the wall, letting out a high-pitched shriek as pain soared up her arm.

Rennick appeared in her vision, blurry through the rivulets of water that slid down the glass shower encasement. "Hey! What happened?"

She squeezed her wrist, the pain already subsiding. *Not broken... again. Good.* "Nothing."

"Callie—"

"Give me a second, okay?" A sigh met her ears as the door opened and closed again. *It may not be fair...but I have to tell them. I need them.*

Turning the water off with a wave of her hand and wringing the excess water out of her hair, she quickly dried off and changed. Letting her hair air-dry and leaving wet spots on her shoulders, she opened the door to a familiar sight—her friends gathered around her quarters, waiting.

Mei immediately jumped out of her seat, ran up, and hugged her, pinning her arms down to her sides. "I left VHQ as soon as I could after all my daily tasks were completed... I'm sorry about your parents! What're you gonna do?"

Caldera blinked, looking over Mei's shoulder at the wide eyes of the rest of her friends.

"Mei," John snapped, walking over and tugging his sister off of her. "That's not—"

Caldera shook her head. "Actually, I appreciate the bluntness... It'll make this next part easier."

They all met her eyes eagerly.

"I have to talk to Vandren."

The room erupted in a storm of questions and protests, but she wasn't looking at where they were coming from—Rennick, Aloriea, or Markarian. She held her attention on Mei and John, who were sitting quietly at the table in front of the empty fireplace, their conflicted expressions snapping around the room.

Caldera took a deep breath and sat in front of them, effectively quieting her other friends' outbursts. "What do you two think I should do?"

"What?" John asked, shaking his head. "Why would you ask—"

"You're asking for their opinion?" Aloriea snapped, motioning toward the table. "No offense you two, but... why?"

"I gotta agree with Lor on this one, Cal," Markarian said, squeezing John's shoulder. "They... don't know the full situation."

Rennick nodded. "We've filled them in, but they've only lived a *part* of it."

"Exactly," Caldera whispered. "I already know you all are against the idea, but they don't know Vandren or the remaining councilmembers personally... They're practically unbiased."

"Sear would say, simply by knowing stories about the situation makes them biased," Markarian muttered.

"That's why I said practically."

"I think you should go wring all the answers ya' can out of

him," Mei said, crossing her arms, dark eyes narrowing and black hair cascading over her shoulders.

"And what are we doing about getting Sear back?" Aloriea asked, ignoring Mei. "Is going to see Vandren furthering that cause or is it for you to find out more about your parents? Because, look, I don't want to be a bitch, but one is a little more pressing than the other."

Caldera exhaled sharply, meeting Aloriea's distraught gaze. "It's about getting answers."

Standing, she walked over to the balcony doors and swung them open. Fresh air blasted into the room, blowing her hair out behind her as Astrum shimmered in the distance.

The metallic buildings and flying transports reflected the setting sun, making them seem to glitter in pinks and purples. She absently reached out toward the city for a brief moment before dropping her arm back to her side.

"Area 51, Sear, the disappearances, my parents—they're all tied up in this now... So, like it or not, the next step to getting what we want is through Vandren."

CHAPTER 25

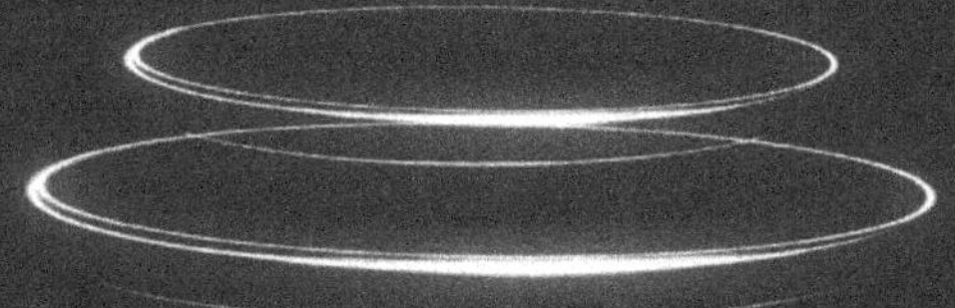

One day turned into two, then three and four as Caldera waited for clearance to visit Arlune—Bersama's second moon and home to the prison compound holding the most dangerous criminals the planet had ever seen. People responsible for murder, assault, kidnapping, and other heinous acts she couldn't even allow herself to think about.

That's where Vandren, and the other surviving councilmembers, were living out the rest of their days. Not even the sector leaders had a free pass to go there.

With each passing day, her anxiety grew. The timeframe the other sector leaders had given her was dwindling.

On the fifth day, she was finally approved. With caveats.

"Queen Caldera Jin Keane cannot go into the holding area by herself. She cannot go into former Councilmember Vandren's cell. She cannot get within twenty feet of former Councilmember Vandren... What the hell is this?" Caldera said, sliding the prison-issued holopad holding her letter of acceptance across the table at Aloriea.

They were sitting in her quarters with the balcony doors pulled open to let in the light breeze of the early afternoon.

"Stipulations, because of your... let's say, 'history' with Vandren."

"What? They think I'm going to try and kill him?"

"Exactly right," Aloriea said with a sharp nod.

Caldera pursed her lips. "Astute observation on their part..."

"You should count yourself lucky they even allowed you in at all."

Caldera pinched the bridge of her nose, wishing Rennick and Markarian were there to share in her irritation. They were escorting John to his first day on the job at T.E.R.A. She sighed, trying to find the silver lining in the situation.

At least he finally decided what he wanted to do—much to Mei and Markarian's delight.

"What else does it say?" she asked, forcing her mind to focus.

Aloriea scanned the document. "'No weapons of any kind, breaking the rules will result in immediate detainment'... Oh no..."

"What?"

"This last one. It says, 'In an attempt to eliminate potential collusion to do harm to the imprisoned persons, the accompanying party cannot have had any involvement in Queen Caldera Jin Keane's actions regarding the events of the past year'."

"What the hell does that mean?"

"It means that you have to have someone go with you, but it can't be Ren, Markarian, or even me."

Caldera's eyes widened as she jumped out of the chair. "What the fuck!" She paced back and forth, her mind racing. "What about Saro?"

A flash of raw anger darted across Aloriea's face before she settled into her regular solemn expression. "No."

"Grey or Sylvie?"

"They helped get Mei and John out of the palace. So, no."

"Fuck," Caldera said, throwing her hands up. "Who are we left with then?"

TWO HOURS LATER, CALDERA WAS strapped into a shuttlecraft, ascending into space with Bruna by her side. The long lost but familiar push and pull of thrust, the weightlessness of null-g, and the gentle pulling of her body against the safety straps tugged at her memories as they broke through the atmosphere and floated in place.

Bruna deftly pressed a button on the console to restore gravity, plummeting them back into their seats with a *thunk*. "Are you all right, Your Majesty?" she asked over her shoulder.

"Never been better," Caldera replied, unstrapping herself and rubbing her tailbone. "You know, you could've gradually restored gravity."

"Hmm. Interesting. I apologize for not knowing the nuances. I have never been to space."

"What?"

"I've had training, of course—it's required of all palace guards in case of emergency, but I've never felt the need to come out here personally."

Never felt the need... Caldera balked at the information she was receiving. "You were never even curious about what's out here, at the very least?"

Bruna shook her hairless head, walking to the large window and pressing her dark hand against the triple-paned silicate glass. "There's already too much for me to worry about on our planet. I cannot afford to waste time with curiosity."

Okay, we have absolutely nothing in common. Caldera exhaled sharply. "So, all those weeks ago... what you said before... about mending your legacy... about your father?"

"Yes. That's why I can't afford to be curious about what's out here, and don't get me wrong, it is fascinating, but what he did... It can't be forgiven. Not by me, anyway."

"What was it?" Caldera asked, letting her curiosity get the better of her.

"He was a coward—a coward who took his own life in disgrace, while dragging our family name through the mud in the process, leaving my mother and I to pick up the broken pieces he left behind."

Bruna's biting words pierced through the flight deck, eviscerating any semblance of empathy that Caldera could have given her. She had experienced the deaths of loved ones before, but never like that.

Caldera's breath caught in her throat. She wanted to object to the ideology that because someone took their own life, they were therefore a coward, but she didn't know Bruna, or her father, or their family dynamic. Sympathy was all she could offer—what she *wanted* to offer, but she found she couldn't speak.

"Do you know why I agreed to come work at the Tellin palace instead of continuing my fast track toward the militia special forces?" Bruna asked, effectively breaking the silence.

"No," Caldera said, shaking her head and realizing she'd never asked. "Saro said he knew you from the academy, and you were friends with his brother."

"I did, but that's not why." She slumped her shoulders and turned around to face Caldera, her gaze never wavering. "Your actions match your promises."

Caldera nodded slowly but said nothing, letting Bruna elaborate on her own.

"You said you were going to revamp the welfare system and you did. You said you were going to give T.E.R.A. the ability to pass stricter conservation laws, and you did."

"All I've ever wanted is to help the people of Bersama..."

"Exactly. My point is, you are someone I can follow, Your Majesty. Our planet is teetering on the edge of destruction, and I want to help protect it before it's too late." Bruna paused, walking toward her. "That means I'm going to help protect you. You're my means of repairing the Ward name."

Caldera met her dark eyes. "Thank you. For believing in what I'm doing."

"Thank you for caring about something other than yourself."

She let a small smile quirk up the corner of her lip. "You're welcome."

THE REST OF THE THREE-HOUR trip was spent in awkward silence, with Bruna diligently pacing back and forth across the flight deck as if she were on patrol, while Caldera focused on her video call.

"It's just us now," Rennick was saying after Aloriea and Markarian made their exits. His image stared back at her, crystal-clear through the holopad. "How are you really holding up?"

"Fine. I wish you were with me, though…" Caldera replied, biting her nail. "My ass still hurts from that stunt she pulled earlier," she continued, glancing over the holopad to make sure Bruna wasn't listening.

Rennick laughed. "I wish I was there too, but listen, despite having no actual space travel experience, you're in good hands. From what Saro's told me, Bruna's all about the job." He paused, his eyes filled with nervous energy as he fidgeted with his hands. "She'll protect you if you need it," he said, sounding like he was trying to convince himself more-so than her.

Caldera offered him a small, reassuring smile. "I won't."

"We're here," Bruna said, stalking toward her.

Caldera nodded, turning her attention back to Rennick's face. "I have to go. I promise I won't do anything… reckless," she said with a smirk. "I love you."

"Love you too. And I'm holding you to that," Rennick replied, mimicking her expression and cutting the feed.

She pushed herself away from the table, taking a deep breath and meeting Bruna's patient but ready stare. "Let's go."

They quickly drifted through the shuttle, to the lift elevator. After the shuttle had cycled through, and the landing area had been replenished with breathable air, they stepped off the ramp to find themselves enclosed in a transparent and airtight tunnel leading to the entrance of the prison.

Caldera glanced behind her at the shuttle sitting at rest on the circular concrete landing pad, the airlocked opening in the ceiling that it had descended down from was closed tight.

Stars glimmered overhead and the desolate, crater-pocked landscape of Arlune stretched out endlessly on either side to the horizon with Bersama sitting thousands of miles away—a small green and blue ball floating in an endless vacuum—as they walked the short distance to another airlocked door.

"Grant request?" a voice barked at them through a speaker-scanner on the wall.

Bruna plugged the holopad that held the letter of admittal on it into the device. It lit up green and disappeared through an opening that appeared in the wall behind it.

"Scan your hands, please," the voice said after a few moments.

Caldera went first, then Bruna. The pad lit up green for both of them.

"Head of palace security Bruna Ward and Queen Caldera Keane. Enter," the voice said, as the doors *whooshed* open in front of them.

They were met by a small, stocky man wearing a combat exo-suit, complete with a blaster-resistant chest plate. He stared up at them and down at himself, noticing Caldera's surprised expression. "Every single one of these pieces of shit would do anything to get out. We have to protect ourselves."

"They don't have anywhere to go," Caldera found herself saying, glancing over her shoulder as the doors closed behind them.

Even if they got through security and broke the tunnel, an airless void is all that would be waiting for them.

"They don't care," the man said, as if reading her mind. "Some would say suffocating in the vacuum of space is better than going on living here."

"Are they not treated well?" Caldera blinked, surprised by her own question.

Why the fuck did I ask that? They're murderers, etcetera... Who cares? This isn't the time to get political.

The man tilted his head to the side and nodded slowly as if not sure what to make of her. "They're treated fine..." He glanced down at his holopad that confirmed their identities, skepticism in his eyes. "You *are* Queen Caldera Keane, right? The woman who exposed a century of corruption and discovered a new planet?"

She blew out a breath and ran a hand through her hair. "Yep. Can we get on with this?"

The man nodded. "Of course. Any weapons on you? I can check them here and they'll be available to you again once you're finished."

Bruna shook her head. "No. Per the instructions, none were brought."

"Then follow me."

They passed through two arching metal bars that beeped unpleasantly when the man walked through but were silent for Caldera and Bruna. Caldera was sure it was a scanner to check for body mods and hidden weapons—a second fail-safe in case the pre-approved visitors had initially lied to the guard.

The man led them through gray blocks of cells, the front doors of which were not transparent, or even had a window. "So they don't disturb the visitors that pass by, or each other," he said, glancing back at Caldera.

"How do you know if they're still... alive?"

"We monitor them through cameras embedded in the ceilings."

"Got it..."

They were led to a lift at the end of the hall. The man motioned for them to get on and he followed, pressing his hand against a scanner pad on the inside and typing in a set of numbers.

"Where are we going?" Caldera asked as the elevator slowly dropped.

"Generally, this place is made up of twenty-four floors, each housing about eighty-four inmates, totaling just over two-thousand prisoners," he said. "We're going to the twenty-fifth floor. Solitary."

"That's where the councilmembers are?"

"Among a few others who would be immediately killed if they were in the general pop."

"General admittance isn't allowed, then?"

"That's why it took so long for your clearance to go through," the man continued as the doors slid open. "Civilians are not allowed down here under any circumstances—even if they're family."

"You were checking to make sure Vandren and I weren't related?"

"We're very thorough."

"Councilmembers don't have family," Bruna offered, squaring her shoulders and stepping off the lift.

"So they say," the man replied, ushering Caldera off the elevator and following behind her. "It's the last door on the left. There's an X on the floor; that's where you can stand so as not to break the twenty-foot rule. I'll unlock the outer door and wait for you by the lift. If you need anything, holler."

He guided them down the hall, did what he said, and stepped away, leaving Caldera and Bruna alone with Vandren, only separated from each other by a pane of tempered glass.

"Hello again, Your Majesty."

CHAPTER 26

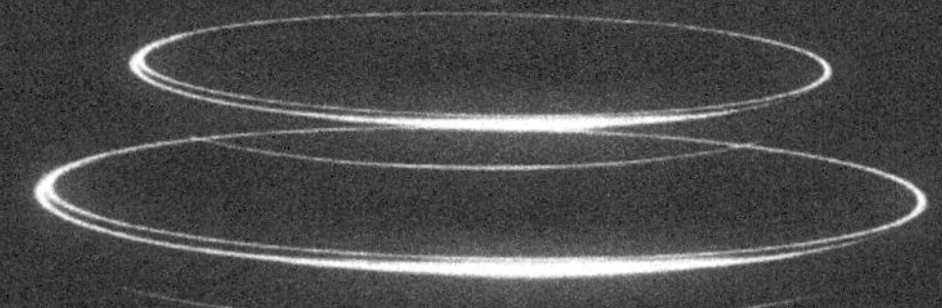

aldera swallowed hard, shifting her weight over the X she stood on, a shiver running down her spine at the sight of him. His hair had turned completely white, matching his prison jumpsuit, and the wrinkles around his gray eyes seemed even deeper-set than she remembered.

"Vandren," she croaked breathlessly, forcing his name out of her mouth.

"Why the sudden response to my invitations?" he asked, sauntering up to the glass.

His voice was smooth. Controlled. Manipulative. It wormed its way into her brain, making her want to cover her ears.

Caldera glanced at Bruna standing behind her, close enough to intervene if something were to happen. She silently made her peace with the woman—basically a stranger—hearing everything that was about to transpire.

"A situation has come up, and I need answers."

"Situation? Such as?"

"That's none of your concern."

"Dear, if you want answers, I need the context first."

Caldera bit the inside of her cheek, forcing herself not to approach the glass—keeping the twenty-foot rule intact... barely. "I need to know about Area 51. Two months ago, three of their representatives appeared in my conference room with portal technology and ever since, there has been an increasing number of disappearances... including Sear's," she said. Every word she spoke to him twisted her insides like two opposing hands wringing out a towel.

He tapped his forefinger against his chin. "What a tragedy... Although, I am surprised they went after a member of your court. Bold."

"No. Stupid," Caldera corrected, clenching her hands into fists. "I need you to tell me everything you know about them. What they're capable of... and what they have to do with my parents."

His brows rose. "Your parents?"

Caldera's heart ricocheted against her ribs. "I-I came across some information that leads me to believe they were," she stumbled through the sentence, inhaling sharply, "working with Area 51. So... they were working *for* you."

She was barely able to speak the words, finding herself looking for comfort from Rennick, only to find Bruna's emotionless stare.

Vandren was quiet for a while, his attention focused on the small one foot by one foot window at the very top of his cell—the holoscreen behind it projected a fake night sky, presumably there so the inmates wouldn't go crazy from isolation.

After a few moments, he clucked his tongue, as if making a final decision. "What was done to Vega and Reed was a tragedy I never wanted."

Caldera blinked, taken aback. "Did you know about them?" she mumbled. "Did they know about themselves?"

He nodded slowly, meeting her eyes. "A secret like the one Quill and Reed's father tried to keep... could never be fully concealed." A look of what could have been regret passed over his face. "I found out eventually. And by extension, so did the rest of us."

"Then why wait to kill them?" Caldera asked, tears stinging her eyes threatening to pour down her cheeks at the slightest blink.

"They were brilliant. A skilled weapons specialist and an advanced environmentalist. We needed them to further our goals, so a deal was struck."

"What kind of deal?"

"The most basic of kinds," he said with a shrug. "If they continued to work for us and keep their heritage secret, then we wouldn't kill them... or their daughter."

Tears flowed freely down Caldera's cheeks, but she didn't care. There were no airs that she could be bothered to put on in front of Vandren. She didn't care enough about him for that. She didn't care about him at all. "What changed?"

"They did." Vandren smoothed his hair back and locked his eyes with hers. "Don't worry, they were never 'in the loop' with what we were really planning. Your precious memories of them are safe. But they found out, and that's when they changed their minds."

Caldera wiped her eyes. "They threatened to expose you?"

Vandren nodded. "They said they were going to go to Quill, to tell him who they were and what they found." He shook his head. "I never wanted to end their lives, but they left us no choice."

He's being very forthcoming with information... What does he want? She pursed her lips before squaring her shoulders in determination. *Let's push it further.*

"What about me?" Caldera asked. Her voice rose with a mix of pent up rage and sorrow, but she couldn't control it. "My parents died when I was sixteen. Why didn't you kill me then?"

Sighing, Vandren tilted his head back and looked at her from the corner of his eye. "Not only would that have raised suspicions,

I thought, and in turn convinced the other councilmembers, that since you were not only a child, but also never privy to your lineage, you wouldn't cause a problem to us.

Why's he so forthcoming? He definitely wants something...

"I also assumed Quill would simply accept that he had no family and not look into that further, eventually making you aware of who you were."

"It sounds like you don't know us—my family—very well..."

"Obviously. Regardless, I'm not *fond* of getting blood on my hands." He bowed his head. "A lot of wrong assumptions on my part. All leading to this." He lifted his arms as if to present the white-walled cell to her. "And to answer your earlier question, Area 51 is capable of quite a lot. It would be foolish to underestimate them simply because they're located on Earth."

Caldera's mind swirled into a tornado of raging thoughts, long dormant emotions, and explanations that she hadn't even realized she'd wanted. "Why are you telling me all of this?"

"Is it so hard to believe that I've changed?"

"Yes. I don't buy that for a second."

He smirked, gray eyes shining. "Believe what you want, but I've reflected on my actions... and I'm not necessarily proud of them. The whole reason I've been trying to get you here is to help."

She squeezed her eyes shut, reminding herself of who she was talking to—of the real purpose of this visit. "Fine. How do I get into the facility?" she asked, clenching her teeth and forcing down the growing lump in her throat and stomach.

"Planning a rescue mission in futility?"

"I'm getting my friend back and putting a stop to Area 51's plans," she replied, balling her hands into fists again. "You've been helpful up until this point. Why stop now?" The rhetorical question hung on her lips as she and Vandren locked eyes.

He clucked his tongue again, and Caldera could have sworn she saw something in his expression—a glimmer that finally reached his eyes—as if something had been reignited in him. In one swift motion, he slammed his hand onto the edge of a small desk that was placed in the corner of the cell, leaving an open gash that ran down his forefinger. He didn't make a sound.

She couldn't hold in a gasp, raising a hand to her mouth, but she quickly quieted herself when he shushed her, forcing herself not to step forward out of curiosity and break the twenty foot rule.

Vandren walked over to the pristine wall and began running his damaged finger over it. "If you want to know how to get into Area 51..." Blood dripped down the wall as he made line after line, leaving a crude drawing and a string of numbers in his wake. "You'll need more to work with than guesses." He glanced toward the ceiling. "I'd act quickly if I were you. They'll be coming for me soon."

Caldera faced Bruna, who was miraculously still maintaining her composure, even though the faint swirl of unease lingered in her eyes. "You have your holopad?"

She nodded.

"Take a picture. Hurry."

Bruna complied with a motion that was so quick Caldera couldn't be sure she had captured what was on the wall accurately, but it would have to do.

Caldera stared at Vandren, his hand still dripping blood, staining the pant-leg of his white uniform as he pressed it against him. "Th..." She paused, unable to believe what she was about to say to him. "Thank you."

The smile that formed across his face, although genuine, held a malicious bite. "Of course, Your Majesty... But now, you must do me a favor."

And there it is. She scoffed. "Oh really?"

He nodded as if completely unaware of his situation. As if he were still in control. "It's nothing complicated, and actually for your own good. I don't like helping people for no reason, and if you don't heed my words, you, and all your friends you've been trying so desperately to protect, will surely die. Along with everyone else on both planets."

"What is it?"

"Simply put, the Phoenix will rise."

"Time's up," the guard called, motioning for them to return to the elevator. He pressed his finger to his ear, eyes widening as the doors opened. "You two, over here. Now!"

Caldera nodded at Bruna and the two hurried down the hallway, passing two uniformed prison nurses that had stepped off the lift and rushed past them. She glanced over her shoulder right before he was out of sight.

Vandren waved a bloody hand at her. "Come back any time, Your Majesty."

CHAPTER 27

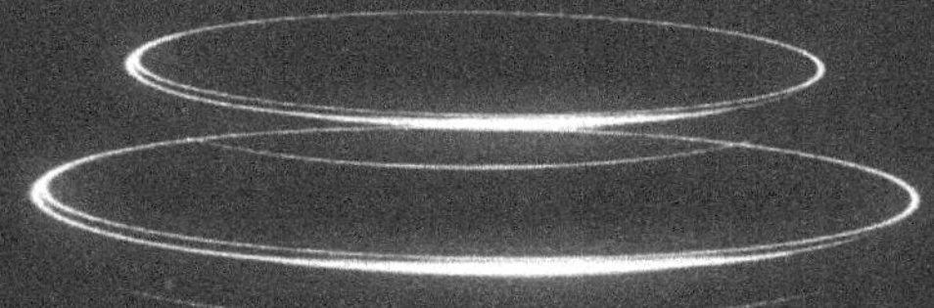

Caldera sat on top of a merlon attached to the surrounding wall lining the back courtyard of the palace, knees pulled up to her chest.

A gentle breeze blew through her hair and warm sunlight dappled her skin as she gazed down at the lush garden below her, eyes trailing along the red-brick footpaths and trees, lingering on the various gardeners and the fountain spitting water before moving on to Grey and Sylvie, who were standing diligently at their posts. Multicolored flowers wobbled back and forth as if they were waving.

Closing her eyes, she took a deep breath as her friends continued to incessantly argue beside her.

"This is what it's come to?" Aloriea cried. "Taking the word of that madman?"

Caldera winced. The more days that passed and the closer the deadline became, the more Aloriea seemed like she was losing herself. She turned to face her friends, pulling out her holopad and glancing down at the image Bruna had transferred to her.

"What other options do we have?" She darted her eyes from Rennick, to Markarian, to Aloriea. "Hmm?"

"I don't know, Cal, from what you said happened, it kinda seems like Vandren has lost his mind," Markarian replied, pacing up and down the wall-walk. "Talking about Phoenixes and debts and bullshit."

Rennick nodded. "A crudely drawn map and coordinates written in blood don't exactly bode well for the success of this mission," he said, reaching up to take the holopad out of her hands and lifting the image off the screen to float in the air between them.

Caldera jumped down, the 3D image reflecting in her eyes. "We've done more with less."

"Yes, but that was *us*," Aloriea said, pressing a hand against her chest, "*our* research. We weren't potentially going to trust information given to us by some psychopath that almost eradicated an entire planet full of people!"

Markarian snapped his fingers and pointed at Aloriea. "She has a point."

"I'm not saying I trust him. I don't. But we're pretty limited on options, and time, right now."

"Look at this," Rennick interjected, still squinting at the image.

Caldera walked a few steps to stand beside him. He had the image zoomed in and as enhanced as it could be, which, for the blurry picture, was not a lot. "What is it?"

"There." He pointed to a bloody fingerprint in the middle of what looked like a rough sketch of a small room. "What is that?"

"A mistake?" Markarian asked, tilting his head to the side and leaning forward. "Can't imagine blood is a very cooperative medium."

Caldera shook her head, remembering Vandren's swift, sure movements. The glint in his eyes. His words swirled in her head. *'I don't like helping people for no reason'.* "It's deliberate. Everything he does is." She zoomed the image out, searching for any other potential mistakes. There were none. Reaching out, she touched the floating image. It shimmered, distorting the picture even more. "I bet those coordinates are to this specific spot. This is where he's telling us to portal into."

"There has to be another way..." Aloriea muttered, as a rush of warm air blew through her hair and tangled in her horns. Her body shook. "We can't... trust him."

The words sounded so desperate, so dire. They made Caldera want to pull her friend into a hug and keep her there until the sun set and she expelled all the tears she had been holding in since Sear's abduction. But there wasn't time for that.

"We *don't* trust him," Caldera said again, taking a step forward and gripping Aloriea's shoulders, "but what he said about Area 51 is true. They're dangerous, and we can't waste any more time. Not if we want to get Sear back before... before it's too late."

"It's a trap! I know it's a trap." She pushed away from Caldera and walked to the newly-built steps. "We won't do Sear any good if we're dead."

Caldera, Markarian, and Rennick leaned over the concrete banister lining the wall walkway between the protruding merlons to watch her descent.

"What're you going to do?" Caldera called after her as the growing wind whipped through the trees.

Aloriea stepped onto the grass and looked up at them. "I'm going to get in contact with the other sector leaders. Eldra specifically said to keep them updated—and surely one of them will have another option." Her metal horn glinted in the sunlight as she stomped into the palace.

Caldera faced Rennick and Markarian, pressing her back against the merlon and sliding down it until she was sitting. She pulled a knee up to her chest and stretched her other leg out in front of her, leaning her head back against the wall. "Okay... We've just taken about a thousand steps back."

"What do you mean?" Rennick asked, sitting beside her.

"Aloriea... She clearly doesn't trust my judgment."

Markarian took a seat opposite her, bumping his boot against hers. "Has she ever?"

Caldera chuckled. "For the most part... Begrudgingly."

"She wants to get another opinion. Who cares?"

"That's not the part I care about. She's wasting time we don't have."

"She's scared, Callie," Rennick said, resting a hand on her shoulder.

"I know she is. I know exactly what she's feeling, which is honestly why she should be listening to me right now."

"I think we should see what the other leaders have to say. When it's all said and done, Aloriea's right. If we portal directly into an enemy facility with no plan and no idea where we'll even end up and get shot on sight... there won't be anyone left to save Sear."

They all fell silent, letting the sounds of rustling leaves and the cawing of distant flyers fill the space.

"Okay," Caldera finally said with a sharp nod, standing. "But we're not entertaining this idea for long." She helped Rennick and Markarian to their feet. "We simply can't afford to. In the end, we'll most likely end up doing things my way."

THE NEXT FOUR DAYS WERE a blur of conference calls, filing reports, and attempting to bring all the sector leaders up to speed on what exactly was going on—trying to get them all on the same page. It was not going well.

They all had their own opinions on what should be done. Eldra, Fenry, and Jasik wanted to attempt contact again, while Mokan and Nari remained firmly neutral in their opinions— undecided.

Desrin surprisingly agreed with Caldera in that they should act as quickly as possible, also providing her with the extra S.G.T. devices that were previously requested, but was not on her side about the proposed raid.

No one was on her side for that.

Much to Caldera's disdain but ultimate approval, Ivy was still hanging around the Vault, helping to sort through the records to try and find anything pertaining to Area 51.

"You know," Ivy said, flipping through a particularly worn journal, "even though the only reason I'm here is to essentially keep tabs on you, and to make sure you're logging all the appropriate information, *and* so you don't go through with your 'attack' on Area 51, I really enjoy helping out." She beamed, tucking a strand of short brown hair behind her ear. "Thank you."

"Thank Desrin..." Caldera sighed, putting down her own book and staring up at the Vault's ceiling, Ivy's incessant giddiness grinding against every nerve in her body, like it had ever since she arrived over a week ago. "Even if you were interested in the contents, you're still here essentially against your will... Why you're so chipper about this situation is beyond me," she muttered, walking over to the wall of seemingly endless information and grabbing another book off the shelf. "But I guess I'm glad you're enjoying yourself."

"I like to learn new things," Ivy replied with a shrug as she turned another page.

Caldera eyed Rennick, who was sitting at the computer. He blinked knowing eyes back at her. They had found nothing so far to make it safer for them, but the deadline the sector leaders had given her ended in three more days—three more days and they were going to make a deal with Area 51. The raid she and her friends had planned *was* going to happen. Whether the other sector leaders agreed with her methods or not.

Aloriea was becoming especially desperate, even going as far to rescind her statement that they should formulate an actual plan of attack in favor of wanting to jump full force into a rescue mission as things became more and more dire.

Caldera bit her lip; the more she thought about it, the more it made sense to wait for a concrete plan, but that didn't mean she wasn't having a hard time controlling her own impulses to leap without looking.

Aloriea's voice, along with the clicking of her heels against metal, met Caldera's ears before she physically saw her.

"Markarian is helping secure a direct line of communication, using the signal frequency that the representatives from Area 51 gave us, based out of the combined Vanguard headquarters and Eldra, Fenry, and Jasik sent out a formal request for another meeting," she said, bounding down the Vault steps, her voice tight.

Caldera furrowed her brow. "Good. If they think we're ready to finally strike a deal, the more we'll get out of them."

"And what do you think that will accomplish? They've already threatened us," Aloriea scoffed, walking up next to Caldera.

"It'll give us more overall information."

"Three days. Then you, Ren, and Markarian are going in and getting Sear regardless," Aloriea whispered, leaning in close so Ivy wouldn't hear. "That was the deal, and this plan of yours isn't working."

"You're the one who said we needed to go about this logically," Caldera hissed, unsuccessfully trying to mute her irritation. "It was your plan!"

Aloriea clenched her jaw. "Yeah. We tried that, and it's not working."

"I'm not gonna let you risk Sear's life because you're too impatient!"

"*I'm* not going to let you risk his life because you're too reluctant."

Caldera took a deep breath, meeting Aloriea's eyes, knowing it must have been hard for her to admit she was wrong.

Aloriea scoffed, her eyes hard and hollow. She turned, walking over to the drawer next to the computer system and rummaging around inside.

Caldera shook her head, rubbing out the crease that had appeared in the center of her forehead.

"Hey," Rennick interrupted, standing. "I think maybe we all need some fresh air." His eyes darted from Caldera and Aloriea to Ivy, who was still engrossed in the journal she was reading and acting as if she hadn't heard a thing.

"I agree." Caldera replied, her mind swirling. *Me, too reluctant?* That was something she'd definitely never been called before. The three started walking to the stairs that led up to the back courtyard. "Ivy, come on," she called over her shoulder when their guest didn't follow.

Ivy's gray eyes lifted off the page, locking with hers in a way that was eerily familiar—they seemed hard and cold, not at all belonging to the bubbly, talkative person they had grown accustomed to.

The hair on the back of Caldera's neck and arms stood on end as she repressed a shiver. *What the hell...*

The command must have sunk in, because the woman's gaze and demeanor changed instantly, the light returning to her features in less than a second.

"Oh. Sorry. I was... lost in thought, I suppose." She closed her eyes and smiled.

Caldera blinked. "It's all right, but you can't be down here by yourself." The unsettling sensation was gone before it had even completely registered, though it still left a bad taste in her mouth.

Ivy nodded, deftly turning to the next page without looking down, and resting her finger in the center crease between pages as she looked for a bookmark. "Right, let me just..." She trailed off, glancing down at the journal again and sinking back into her seat.

"What?" Caldera asked, walking over and looking over her shoulder.

"I think I've found something you can use."

Aloriea and Rennick ran over and huddled around them.

"Let me see," Caldera said, leaning down closer. The image that met her eyes spanned across two pages.

The lines were sharper, more precise, and the sections were labeled, but the bones of the image itself were strikingly familiar and the scrawling 'A51' at the top of the pages left no doubt in her mind.

Her eyes widened and she pulled out her holopad, pulling up Vandren's bloody, hand-drawn map. They essentially matched. She sucked in a breath. "It's a blueprint of the facility."

A wide grin spread across Aloriea's entire face. Motioning for them to follow her up the stairs, she all but ran up into the sunlight, the group following close behind. "We have it," she muttered as they reached the top of the steps.

Caldera stepped in front of her, deftly pressing her hand against the scanner stone, causing the stairs to retreat into the ground. "I know what you're thinking," she said, flicking her eyes over to Ivy, whose curious attention was on the memorial bench for Quill, "but we shouldn't blindly act on this information."

Her leg bounced up and down as she quickly tapped her foot on the red-brick path, frustration roiling in her chest, but not from Aloriea. From herself.

I agree with her. We should move. But if we act too soon, it could cost Sear his life. It could cost all of us our lives...

"We have everything we need. What else is there to do?"

"How do we even know it's accurate? Tell me and I'll go along with you."

"We... don't but—" She cut herself off, hands trembling.

"Aloriea—"

"Callie, this is ridiculous! When something bad happens to *you*, you're allowed to go catatonic for as long as you damn well please, jump through portals, and be generally unreasonable, but me?" She shook her head. "No, if I act out the norm then suddenly there's a huge problem? Suddenly we 'have to think things through'. Suddenly it's, 'let's wait and see'."

"Aloriea! What the hell is going on with you?"

"I'm tired of everyone's double standards! My grief matters just as much as yours!" She turned on her heel as tears marred her cheeks, and ran into the palace.

Caldera's chest rose and fell in quick succession as her friend disappeared from sight. *Son of a bitch!* She caught Rennick and Markarian's gaze, and immediately started after her.

"Your Majesty," Ivy interrupted, stepping into their path. "Queen Desrin has informed me that Queens Eldra, Fenry, and Ruler Jasik made contact with the Area 51 representatives," she said, holding up her communicator. "Queen Desrin and Their

Majesties Mokan and Nari are on their way to Sector Two right now and request we head that way immediately."

Caldera stopped dead in her tracks, causing Rennick and Markarian to bump into her back, completely forgetting that Ivy was even still there to witness the breakdown of not just political order, but a friendship as well.

The men's expressions ranged from curiosity to irritation at the interference as Caldera glanced over her shoulder at them. She nodded slowly, waving Grey and Sylvie over. "We... can meet you there... Grey, Sylvie, ready the shuttle and tell the pilot to drop Ivy off at the Mirstone palace and come back to get us."

The siblings furrowed their brows in a mirror of confusion before nodding sharply and running off.

Ivy's face mimicked a startled expression. "Your Majesty, I don't think—"

"We have unfinished business here," Caldera said, cutting her off. *We have to get Aloriea under control.*

"Very well," Ivy replied, closing her eyes and bowing slightly before locking eyes with her. "But I'm going to have to tell my queen about the blueprint right away. Even if you're not there."

Caldera tilted her head to the side, never taking her eyes off Ivy. It was a simple statement of an inevitable fact, but the way her tone dipped low and how her body was snapped to attention—hands clasped behind her back and gray eyes staring down at her—Caldera found herself waiting for an ultimatum.

There's something... Familiar about her...

She shook her head. "Of course."

"Although, I don't have to right away."

"What are you saying?" Rennick chimed in, crossing his arms, hazel eyes narrow.

"Nothing!" Ivy replied, holding up her hands in mock surrender and her voice taking on a cheery tone. "I was only saying that I didn't have to tell her right away is all..." She looked down at the grass almost bashfully. "If you had some other plans..."

"That's very... *nice* of you," he said, stepping forward, "but we wouldn't want to get you in trouble."

"You should definitely tell Desrin about what you found," Markarian added, glancing over to Caldera. "We could probably even expedite the process of having to explain everything if that were the case..."

"Yeah," Caldera replied. "In fact, I'll send her the blueprints right now, to share with the rest of the sector leaders," she said, taking out her holopad and sending Desrin the image, along with a quick message explaining everything.

When she looked up, Ivy was staring down at her, lips quirked into what seemed like a forced smile.

"Thank you... That will... save me time."

Caldera forced a chuckle. "Why don't you go find one of the palace guards? They can escort you to the shuttle. We'll meet you in Mirstone."

Ivy nodded, the mask of geniality reappearing full-force across her face. "Thank you, I will!" She turned, bounding away through the back courtyard and disappearing through the palace door.

Caldera exhaled sharply. "You guys saw that right?"

The two answered simultaneously, "Yes."

CALDERA, RENNICK, AND MARKARIAN RACED up the steps to the hall that housed their living quarters as the shuttle took off from the rooftop, carrying Ivy away to Sector Two.

"There's something off about that woman," Markarian muttered as they made their way up the second flight of steps.

"We can't worry about that right now," Caldera breathed as they stepped onto the third floor landing where the quarters for the royal court resided. "We need to find Aloriea."

"You think she's okay?" Rennick asked as they stepped through the looming arch of the hallway that housed their quarters and stopped in front of Aloriea's door.

Caldera took a deep breath. "I wouldn't be... I *wasn't*."

She lightly rapped her knuckles against the metal, waiting for an answer.

Silence was the only thing that responded.

"Aloriea, open the door," Caldera called, knocking again more forcefully. The stark realization of role reversal smashed into her stomach like a wave. *How long did I lock my friends out of my life when I thought Ren was dead? One straight week? Two?*

Markarian stepped forward, pounding his fist against the door as hard as he could. "Come on, Lor. Let us in."

Rennick nudged him out of the way. "Aloriea, listen—" His voice cut off as his eyes fell to the floor, body going rigid. "Callie..."

Her name came out in an almost inaudible whisper and she followed his gaze.

Caldera froze. Time seemed to stand still as her heart thundered against her chest—the only sound she could hear was the blood pounding in her ears. Heaviness, followed by an icy, empty, chill settled into her core as she tried to wrap her head around what she was seeing.

No... The drawer she was digging through in the Vault... It must've been the one that had—

A red and black swirling mist filtered out from under the doorway.

A portal had opened.

CHAPTER 28

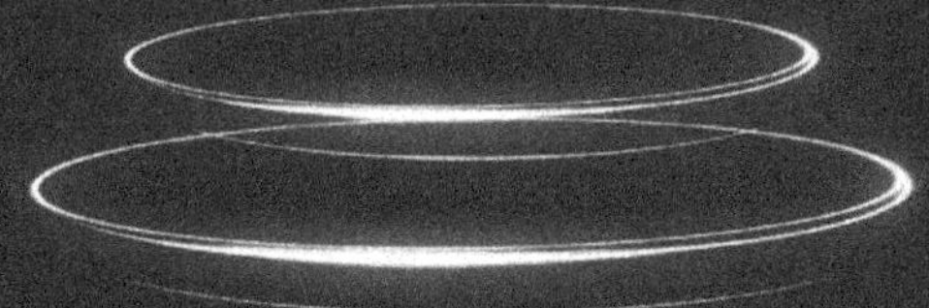

"We have to get this fucking door open. Now!" Caldera screamed as time jolted forward. Without a moment's hesitation, she rammed her shoulder into the door. The impact caused her to stagger back and sent a jolt of pain down her arm.

"We can't get in this way," Markarian yelled, grabbing Caldera's arm and jerking her back just as she was about to try again. "These doors are solid. Why do you think I climbed through your balcony window?"

Caldera and Rennick locked eyes, a look of synchronicity passing between them.

"Come on," Rennick said. Taking Caldera's hand in his, he led them to the nearest hallway window. "Like old times?" He shrugged, unholstering his blaster and aiming it at the window.

Caldera barely waited for the plasma bolt to leave the barrel and the glass to shatter before she was already cleaning away the debris with her elbow, cutting into her exposed skin. She flinched, gripping her elbow with her opposite hand. "Fuck!"

"Callie!" Rennick called, running up to her.

"It's fine, but..." She glanced down at her tan, flowing pants, exposed midriff and white, sleeveless tank top. "I don't think I'm dressed properly to be climbing out the window this time." She shook her head. "The wind will blow me to the ground."

Markarian put a hand on Caldera's shoulder, gently pushing her into Rennick's hold. "I'll go. Wait by the door and I'll let you in." Without another word, he slipped out of the window and started making his way around the outside of the palace to Aloriea's balcony.

Caldera let Rennick lead her to Aloriea's door again, her mind twisted—eyes playing tricks on her—thinking she was still seeing the red, swirling tendrils of portal residue. Her hands began to shake uncontrollably, the unresolved tremor coming back in full force—coursing through her whole body.

"Callie," Rennick said, his voice seeming impossibly far away. "You need to listen to me. Wherever Aloriea's gone... we can get her back." His voice strained on the last words.

'Wherever' she's gone? We all know where she's gone. But Caldera knew Rennick didn't want to admit it. And neither did she.

It seemed that the intelligent and always rational Aloriea was gone.

Caldera gripped her elbow as blood continued to drip through her fingers, as if that was the only thing tethering her to reality. She shivered, unable to speak.

"Here," Rennick said, gingerly taking her elbow in his hand and examining the cut. "It's not too bad, all things considered." He loosened the tie from his neck, lifted it over his head, and began wrapping it around her arm.

She flinched as he pulled it taught, tying the excess ends into tight double-knots.

"Sorry."

"It's fine..."

Rennick placed a hand under her chin, lifting her gaze to his. "We will get her back. We'll get them both."

Caldera swallowed hard as footsteps met her ears, rushing up the staircase.

"Callie?" Sylvie called, coming into view with Grey only a few steps behind, both their blasters at the ready. "Are you okay?"

They reached the top of the steps, scanning the area with their weapons. Their black suits were crisp and clean and their green-eyed expressions more serious than Caldera had ever seen them.

"I'm fine. Put those away."

They obliged immediately, holstering their blasters, but continuing to skeptically look around the area.

"We saw that a window was broken when we did our hourly scan of the palace openings and entryways," Grey said, pulling his holopad out of his pants pocket and flicking through the reports, lifting the assessment off the screen to float above the device.

The image that floated in front of her face was a simple schematic of the outside of the palace, showing all the windows and doors in a 3D-model fashion—every way a person could try and break in. The window in question was highlighted red and next to it was a brief summary of the fastest way to get to said disturbance for the responding guards.

Caldera gripped her elbow, hoping it wasn't bleeding through the fabric Rennick had wrapped around it. *That explains why Grey and Sylvie are here and not Saro and Bruna. This window is closer to the back courtyard.*

"Everything's okay—" she started as the guard's eyes drifted to the shattered window behind her.

"What happened?" Grey asked, his voice curious as he walked past Caldera and Rennick and over to the opening. His black shoes crunched over the glass that was strewn across the floor.

"Don't worry about it," Rennick said, taking a step toward Grey. "We're all right, nobody's broken in."

"I'm the one that did it," Caldera added, placing her hands on her hips. "I'll call and have it fixed later."

"We can do that," Sylvie replied, her fingers flying over her holopad screen. "Done!" Her brows furrowed, as if she had just processed Caldera's words. "Wait, did you say *you* did it?"

Grey ran a hand through his red hair as he turned to face them, his freckled face an amalgamation of confusion. "But... why?"

Caldera sighed, glancing over at Aloriea's door that was still shut tight. *This isn't something that I should put on them. They'll only want to help, and they can't. I don't even know the full scope of what's going on yet.*

"Like Ren said, don't worry about it."

The siblings shared a look before silently making their way toward the staircase.

Grey hesitated at the top step, his hand clutching the railing, expression hard as if he wasn't sure if he wanted to speak. He stood up straight. "You know, if you don't trust us, then why are we even here?"

"Grey!" Sylvie said, her tone halfway between scolding and resignation. She took a deep breath. "Actually, I kinda agree..."

Caldera blinked, the way they were acting was unorthodox, different—she had only ever seen a bubbly Sylvie and a stoic Grey.

I mean, Grey might be a little more hostile since he's trying to quit smoking, but Sylvie?

"I do trust you."

"Then we'd appreciate it if you acted like it," Grey replied, fully committing to the confrontation. "We get that we're young, and not the most experienced guards here, but I think we've made it pretty clear that we'll follow you to the end."

"You saved my life, Callie..." Sylvie added, smiling softly. "In more ways than one." She fidgeted with her hands, wringing them together as her red braid fell over shoulder. "You gave me," —she glanced at Grey—"us, newfound purpose."

"It's true," Grey said, turning and crossing his arms over his thick chest. "Yes, at first I was following you because you saved my sister's life from that psychopath Olivare... but you have to know by now that our planetary views line up with yours." He blew out a breath. "We want to help Bersama. That's why we joined the Vanguard, that's why we helped you in the first place, and that's why we're here now."

Sylvie nodded emphatically. "Exactly."

Tense silence fell over the area as Caldera, Rennick, Grey, and Sylvie stared at one another.

A light breeze rushed in from the busted window, bringing on it the sweet smell of flowers and fresh air. It blew against Caldera's back, whisking hair across her face. Her chest heaved.

How long have they felt this way? She set her jaw, not wanting to face the fact that she wasn't treating her guards, people that had done so much for her in the face of uncertainty, with as much respect as she should be just because they were younger; or because she was trying to protect them in some way.

The realization stung.

"I'm sorry," Caldera said, rubbing her arm. "I promise I'll fill you in on everything as soon as I get a handle on it myself. Okay?" Rennick patted her back, looking over his shoulder at the still closed door behind them. No more than five minutes had passed since the siblings had shown up, but it felt like an eternity.

Grey and Sylvie nodded.

"We'll hold you to that," Grey said, motioning for Sylvie to follow him back down the steps.

"They're good kids," Rennick said, as the brother-sister security duo disappeared. He leaned against the wall next to Aloriea's door.

Caldera nodded. "They really are."

"Markarian should be here any second now."

Tears welled in Caldera's eyes but didn't fall, her mind instantly flipping back to the situation at hand. Another piece of her soul shattered. Sear had been missing for one week Bersaman time, and that meant two Earthen, and if Aloriea had portaled into a well populated area...

"They're dead, Ren! There's no way they're still alive."

Caldera's hand shot up to cover her mouth as if that simple act could retract everything—her spoken words, thoughts, feelings—but it couldn't. *Failure!*

Everything was boiling over. *Weak!* She wrapped her arms around Rennick, digging her fingers into his back and pressing her cheek against his chest, squeezing her eyes shut. Her body shook with such intensity that she thought she would fall, but Rennick's arms were around her, tighter than she was sure they'd ever been, but that wasn't helping either.

Olivare was right! There was so much sorrow, rage, defeat; every emotion she ever manifested was trying to push its way to dominance from the deep crevices of her mind, churning inside her body like a writhing storm.

She blinked, a forced realization taking over. *There's only one thing I can do now.* It was as if someone else, someone who wasn't Caldera Keane, was in control. *I have to destroy Area 51. They've taken their last victim.* Taking a deep breath, she quieted the desperate calls within her, realizing that no tears had actually fallen.

She took another breath, and although the emotions were still there, they were no longer fighting for her attention. She was completely empty save for a singular thought.

Kill.

CHAPTER 29

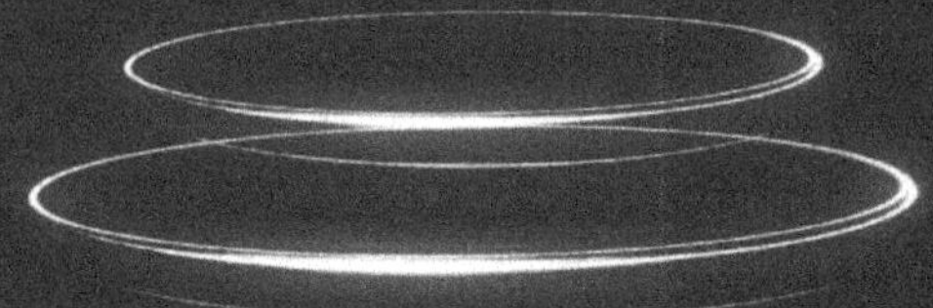

Caldera gently pushed away from Rennick, meeting his gaze, a dull, constant ache echoing through her body. "Ren, are you with me?"

He tucked a stray hair behind her ear. "Always."

"What if I told you we had to do something…" She swallowed hard, searching for the word. "Horrible."

"Like what?"

Aloriea's door finally whisked open.

"She's not here," Markarian said, still holding his blaster, an unconcealed panic floating across his features. "She really did…"

Caldera didn't want to tell them her plan—what she had to do. She didn't want to tell Rennick. There was nothing she wanted more than to leave him in the dark, to have him follow her blindly into this disaster along with Markarian. Her bottom lip quivered as she contemplated and she bit down on it, her mind made up.

"I'm going to dismantle Area 51… I won't hesitate to kill

them, and knowing what we know... there'll most likely be no survivors," she said, meeting their eyes, unflinching.

There was a pause. Rennick and Markarian glanced at each other, a look passing between them—sharing in a decision that she wasn't privy to.

Markarian holstered his blaster, pulled out his communicator, relocked Aloriea's room, and started making his way to the staircase. "All right, let's go."

"Where are we going?" Caldera asked, as Rennick followed behind. "And who are you calling?"

"The Vault, John, and Mei."

Confusion must have crossed her face, because Markarian went on.

"We need people on this side to monitor us while we're over there." He paused before starting down the steps. "Plus, we'll have the added bonus of Earth knowledge. If we have questions, someone will know the answers." He looked down at his communicator. "They're meeting us at the Vault entrance."

Caldera nodded and started to follow him when Rennick grabbed her arm.

"Callie, I'm with you... And I know I can't stop you... but I also know you're not a murderer—even if you like to think you are. There's a possibility that there are innocent people in that facility—"

"Aside from the kidnapped inhabitants of our planet," she said, cutting him off and jerking her arm away from his hold to continue her descent, "no, there's not."

He ran down a few steps to stand in front of her. "This isn't you." He started to reach for her again but caught himself, as if thinking better of it.

She tried to move around him to follow Markarian, but Rennick sidestepped, blocking her.

"There's also a possibility that Sear and Aloriea are still alive."

"So what if they are? Does that really change anything about what Area 51 has done?" She crossed her arms, letting her voice drop. "Or what they deserve?"

"Either way, Sear and Aloriea wouldn't want you—*us*—killing people in their name, that's for damn sure," Rennick replied, his brows furrowed. "Think about what you're doing."

Caldera shook her head. "My mind is made up. Come with me or don't."

He opened his mouth to respond when Saro and Bruna ran up the steps—palace issued holopads in hand.

"What happened?" Saro asked, tapping the screen as they came to stop in front of Markarian. "The sensors say a window was broken."

Caldera and Rennick quickly ran the rest of the way down the steps.

"It's taken care of," Rennick said, holding up his hands. "Grey and Sylvie were already on the scene."

Saro scoffed. "Those damn kids need to get better at communication."

"This is certainly not the first time they've failed to fill us in on a situation," Bruna agreed.

"What happened?" Saro asked, his blue and brown eyes flicking up the steps before landing on Caldera.

"We had to get into Aloriea's room," Caldera replied, taking a step in front of Markarian.

"For what purpose?" Bruna asked, lifting a brow and tapping something onto her holopad screen.

Another choice. I made the decision to keep Grey and Sylvie in the dark... And I'm not going back on that now, even with my more trusted guards.

"She wasn't answering and we wanted to make sure she was okay..." She eyed Saro and Bruna, one a former lackey for Vandren, and the other almost a complete stranger. "Which... she is. She's fine. Please relay that to Grey and Sylvie, too."

Bruna nodded, tapping one last time on her holopad before replacing it in her jacket pocket. "Right away, Your Majesty." She nodded sharply before turning on her heel and walking away.

Saro remained, staring at them with his multi-colored eyes. "Are you... sure everything's okay?"

A twinge passed through Caldera's chest. Saro regretted everything that had to do with former councilmember Vandren, resulting in his twin brother's death. He had worked hard to get in her and her friends good-graces, even demoting himself from head of palace security and finding Bruna to take his place—working under someone less qualified, all to prove himself trustworthy. He deserved honesty, but she couldn't give it to him. The less he knew, the better.

Caldera nodded, ushering Rennick and Markarian past her. "Everything's fine," she said, pausing as she walked by him. "Keep your eyes open, and we'll be indisposed until further notice. Do you... *understand*?"

Saro calmly met her eyes, a look of unspoken comprehension settling into his features. "You might want to call the sector leaders back and let them know you won't be making it to the meeting then," he said, without any further questions.

Her eyes widened. "Shit." Grabbing her holopad out of her pocket, she started toward the back courtyard and the Vault. "Saro," she said, catching his attention as he began to walk away. "Thank you."

A sad smile spread across his face. "Of course, Callie."

She reached the back doors and made her way past Grey and Sylvie, who had retaken their post. They nodded, staying silent.

Caldera motioned for Rennick, Markarian, Mei, and John to go into the Vault without her. After they complied, she walked over to the wrought-iron bench and sat down. With a sigh, she pressed the call button on her communicator, holding it out in front of her and waiting for the faces of the sector leaders to fill the screen so she could lift their images into the air.

"We've been waiting for you to arrive," Desrin said, forgoing all formalities, her voice echoing through the speakers. "What's the holdup?"

"Indeed," Eldra added, a weary smile breaking across her face making the blue skin around her eyes crinkle. "The message you sent us is rather... interesting."

"That iss an undersstatement," Jasik said. "You have found a blueprint to the facility that you believe iss holding the combined kidnapped inhabitantss of our planet?" They paused, leaning forward, tongue flicking in and out of their mouth. "Sso, I believe I sspeak for everyone when I assk, what do you plan on doing with that information?"

"Well..."

This is it. I can either tell them the truth and receive pushback and possible detainment. Or lie, losing their trust forever... but if Sear and Aloriea really are alive there isn't any time to waste.

Caldera's heart pounded against her ribcage, the two options weighing heavily on her chest. She'd do anything to get her friends back, if that was still even an option, but how would she function as a queen going forward with no allies? What would the fate of Tellis be if they were essentially cut off from aid in the future? A cold sweat formed on her neck and down her back as she contemplated her options while being met with the floating, expectant faces of the sector leaders. *What should I do?* Time seemed to slow as Aloriea's past teachings sparked an idea. She could almost hear her friend's voice in her head.

When in doubt, don't lie. Omit. Omissions to the truth are easier to justify than outright lying.

"I—I think you should still contact Area 51 today... but I won't be there."

A cacophony of objections and questions met her ears.

"What!"

"You what?"

"—won't be here?"

"Prepossterouss."

"Why?"

She couldn't make out who said what, but it didn't matter. "I'm sorry... report what they say and send it to me. I'll explain everything as soon as possible."

With a deep breath she disconnected the call and, most likely, herself, from her political allies.

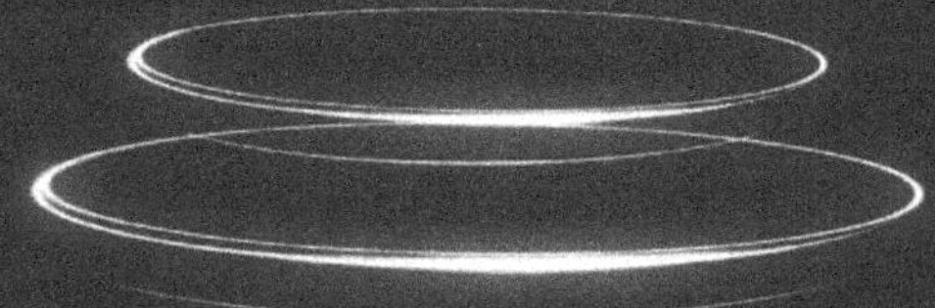

CHAPTER 30

"Ready?" Caldera asked as she walked into the Vault.

"Ready for what?" Mei's black hair was pulled tightly behind her head in a ponytail and whisked from side to side as she spoke.

John placed a hand on Markarian's shoulder. "What's going on?"

"We're doing what we should have done in the beginning, when we first went to Earth," Caldera said, walking over to a drawer attached to the computer desk and rummaging around inside. "We're infiltrating Area 51."

Their jaws dropped.

"You can't be serious..." John muttered, his hand finding Markarian's.

Caldera didn't respond. Neither did Rennick or Markarian. Mei stayed silent, studying their every action.

After a few moments, Caldera pulled out her old exosuit and blaster she had kept from her time in the Vanguard—the very outfit from her first bout on Earth—even though she wasn't supposed to. It had been cleaned and repaired, almost begging for another mission.

"Oh, she's serious," Mei finally said, crossing her arms. "What happened?"

"Sear's gone... and so is Aloriea," Caldera replied coldly, not looking up and beginning to slip the exosuit on over her clothes. "Along with a good chunk of the population... They're not taking anyone else."

"They took Aloriea too?" John said, panic in his voice.

"She went after Sear," Markarian replied, squeezing his hand tight before letting go. "And we're going after her."

"She most likely portaled herself into capture," Rennick added, typing into the computer system.

"Okay..." Mei muttered, walking up behind him. "But how are you going to follow her? How did she portal over there, anyway?"

"With this," Caldera answered, tying the exosuit arms around her waist, not wanting to get fully suited up yet, leaving the legs baggy and holding up a portal bracelet that she had retrieved from the drawer. "She used the other one we still had."

"Why didn't she use an S.G.T. device?"

"They weren't set up or connected yet," Markarian replied.

Mei's eyes widened, pointing to the old portal bracelet. "Weren't those confiscated?"

"They were supposed to be surrendered," Markarian said, leaning on the desk next to Rennick.

"But you didn't... obviously," John replied, crossing his arms.

"We gave most of them up."

Caldera met Rennick and Markarian's gazes. "We decided to save two...one for each of you." She took a deep breath. "Just in case."

"In case?" Mei asked, as her face turned red.

Involuntary silence filled the room. Caldera's mouth was dry as she tried to come up with an explanation that would make their actions make sense to the two Earthlings.

"In case of what?" Mei said again, her voice continuing to raise.

"You were going to force us to go back?" John whispered, turning a heartbroken eye toward Markarian. "We helped you, trusted you, and you were going to make us go back?"

"No," Markarian said, taking a small step forward and shaking his head. "No. It's not like that."

"Bullshit!" Mei yelled, grabbing John's arm and pulling him away and toward the steps. "Were you planning that the whole time? Were you planning to send us back after you got bored? When you got sick of your little 'pets'?"

"Hey!" Caldera snapped, releasing some of her own anger. "That's fucked up! We never thought of you that way and you know it!"

"Okay fine, we—we accept that," John said, his blue eyes watery, "but to never even talk to us about this plan of yours…"

Mei's eyes were all fire. The chances of talking her down were dwindling with each passing second. "You want us to help you now? No fucking way," she said, continuing toward the steps.

Caldera cut her off, stepping in front of her and putting an outstretched hand on her shoulder. "Stop. We were only going to make you go back to Earth if the sector leaders didn't rule in your favor. Wouldn't you rather be free on Earth than a prisoner here?"

John clenched his hands into fists. "A lot has happened against our will, and we've been making the best of it, and don't get me wrong, we don't *want* to go back to Earth, but this decision, we should've been a part of it—don't you think we were owed that?"

Mei lowered her gaze to the floor, becoming surprisingly calm. "Plus, being separated from the people you care about is a prison in and of itself, isn't it?"

John's eyes fell on Markarian. They were angry and sad. "You, at least, should have talked to me about this."

Markarian ran a hand through his hair, genuinely looking like he didn't know what to say. "John, I—I'm sorry—"

John blinked tearful eyes, shaking his head and turning away.

Caldera's mind raced to the aftermath of Rennick's disappearance, when she thought he was dead, to the revelation about her parents, and to how her stomach twisted into a jumbled knot that would never fully untangle now in the midst of Sear and Aloriea's absence.

Five months had passed since she officially took charge of Sector One, post councilmembers. And it felt like a lifetime.

She wasn't in a physical prison, but she was in a mental one.

Taking a step forward, she placed a hand on John's shoulder, embracing him as he turned around. "I'm sorry. You should always have a choice," she whispered, releasing him and taking a step back. "But we can't turn back time, or change the decisions that were made... So, are you going to help us take down Area 51?"

John's expression softened and he looked over at his sister, still avoiding Markarian.

They eventually nodded in unison.

"Yes, we'll help you," Mei said, a sharp grin spreading across her face. "And I know exactly how to do it."

HOURS PASSED AS CALDERA SAT at the table in the Vault, tapping her fingers against the faux wood surface and waiting for Mei and John to return from Vanguard headquarters.

Rennick sat next to her, studying the blueprints of Area 51 intently—no doubt committing every turn, hallway, and room to memory—like he used to with the flight dossiers they would receive before Vanguard exploration missions.

She leaned over periodically to get the gist, more concerned about how they were going to pull it off.

Markarian steadily typed away at the computer, readying the system for their departure and using the new technology developed by Vanguard scientists to link the Bersamin-Earth Coordinate System to the old portal bracelet, to create a portal that could send multiple people through at a time. His shoulders were tense.

"This upgraded geocode coordinate system you allowed Deimi to put in place is really saving our asses right now," he said, leaning back in his seat as he pressed another key. "But there are two downsides. One," he said, holding up a finger. "Even though, thanks to Desrin, we'll each have personal S.G.T. devices that are synced up to our individual bodies, this B.E.C.S. device is the *only* 'multi-person' portal we'll have. So, we've gotta be careful with it."

"How does it work?" Caldera asked, tilting her head to the side and eyeing the modified device.

"You press this button on the side and it links the two coordinates together, creating a stable, or *semi*-stable, thirty-six-inch wide by eighty-inch high portal that can be closed at any time."

"Holy shit..."

"I know, and it hasn't been tested yet, either. The technology exists, but this 'device' is, for lack of a better term, a hack-job."

Caldera sighed, rubbing her forehead. "That seems to be our M.O."

"What's the second downside?" Rennick asked, bringing the conversation back around.

"Only part of the coordinates Vandren gave you match up with what we found in the blueprint."

Caldera scowled, shaking her head, thankful to the head of the Tellin Vanguard, Deimi Auris, for not only helping to successfully stabilize the wormhole technology and creating the improved coordinate system that allowed users to only need partial coordinates—that was also constantly connected to Earth's satellites—but allowing Markarian to have unbridled access to it.

"Vandren's still trying to trick us..."

"That's what I'm not sure of. The Bersamin-Earth Coordinate System seems to be fairly accurate; when it was first being tested, people from Bersama portaled exactly to where the coordinates said it would be on Earth. But it's also comprehensive—"

"Meaning B.E.C.S. won't work if you put in coordinates that don't exist," Rennick finished, looking up from the blueprints for the first time. "What are you saying?"

"We *can* portal using Vandren's full coordinates, just not using B.E.C.S. It's not that they're necessarily made up—"

"They're undiscovered," Caldera said, snapping her fingers. She furrowed her brow, gripping her chin. "What the fuck is that facility hiding..." Her eyes widened as another thought took over her mind. "What coordinates did Aloriea use?"

Markarian bit his lip. "I traced the residual signal to the Area 51 facility, but I can't get a lock on her from there... I think she used the full set."

Caldera shuddered. The portal bracelets that she and her friends created were unrefined. They could, and would, take someone to any coordinate they typed in, charted or not. But B.E.C.S. wasn't like that—as a safety precaution, it wouldn't allow people to travel to unverified locations.

She shook her head, forcing herself to focus. "What do we know?"

"If we were to use the partial coordinates, that we know for a fact will take us to a place that exists, we'll end up in this small, closet-like area," Rennick answered, sliding the blueprints closer to her and pointing to a small square shape on the paper. "I'm not sure exactly what it's used for, but it's labeled 'storage'."

"And B.E.C.S. will get us there without making a scene," Markarian added. "No destruction from arrival or departure, or flashes of light."

Caldera nodded, her mind racing. "And what do we *assume*?"

"Aloriea most definitely made a scene when she arrived," Markarian said, crossing his arms and dropping his gaze. "She was probably instantly detained."

"We can also assume that, if Vandren is telling the truth, these coordinates lead to a secret underground space within the Area 51 facility," Rennick added, returning his full attention to the blueprints. "With how coordinates are created, that area would be below this room."

"So the 'storage space' closet is the entrance," Caldera muttered, an idea slowly forming in her head.

"Presumably," Rennick quickly replied.

The room fell silent for a long while as the three contemplated. Caldera's heartbeat was steady, the way it always was when she was planning her next move.

There's really only two choices. Portal directly into the unknown area, with the old portal bracelets, causing a scene and most likely resulting in immediate capture. Or—

"We're back!" Mei called, jumping down the last three steps into the Vault, a backpack slung over her shoulder. The contents *clinked* as her feet connected with the cement floor.

"Careful!" John replied, reflexively reaching out a concerned hand and sucking in a sharp breath.

Caldera raised an eyebrow. "What did you bring us?"

Mei grinned, unshouldered her pack, and sat it on the table, unzipping it.

Caldera, Rennick, and Markarian leaned forward, their eyes widening respectively.

"Bombs," Rennick said, raising his brows.

"And grenades," Mei added, placing her hands on her hips.

John leaned one arm on the table. "A lot of them."

"That's my guy!" Markarian said, wrapping his arms around John and giving him a tight squeeze. "This'll do the trick for sure!"

"Tsk," John muttered, lightly pushing him away. "I'm still mad at you, remember?"

"How many times do I have to apologize?"

"A lot more."

"How were you able to get these? Aren't you a desk worker?" Caldera asked, ignoring their conversation and turning to Mei, furrowing her brow.

"It's amazing what you can do when you make friends," Mei replied, blowing out a breath. "Zee showed me where the weapons were stored, and I may have stolen their keycard when they weren't looking..."

"That's a serious offense—"

"Yeah, well, maybe you were right... The Vanguard might not be for me, especially since I'll never be able to go into space..." Mei said, sheepishly looking down at her feet.

"What? Why—"

"According to the doctor that did my evaluation, 'my earthen body won't be able to handle the g's it takes to leave the atmosphere'."

"Mei, I'm sorry..."

"It's whatever. Art really is my true passion..." she said, although her voice sounded hurt. "So, *anyway*, I figured I might as well go out with a bang... What do 'ya think?" she asked, disposition immediately changing and determination beaming from behind her eyes.

"To avoid arrest, I think we should never speak of this again..." Caldera sighed, hanging her head and letting a sly grin spread across her face. "But mostly, I think we're in business."

CHAPTER 31

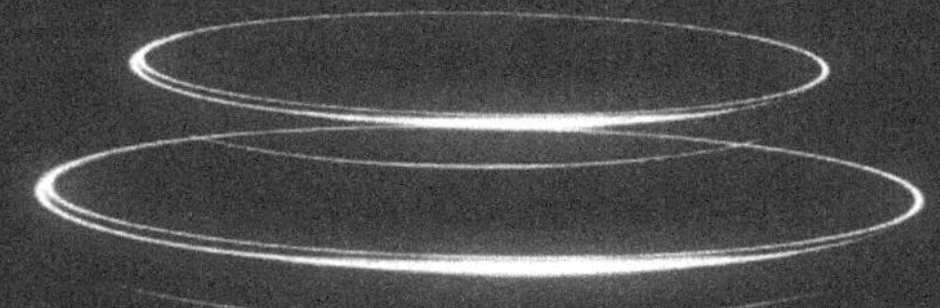

Caldera slipped the exosuit on the rest of the way, attached her personal S.G.T. device to her suit, and shouldered the pack of explosives that Mei had brought. "All right, everyone clear on the plan?"

"Crystal," Markarian said, hitting the button on his suit causing it to form-fit to his body. "We're using the B.E.C.S. to *all* portal into that 'storage closet' thing at the same time—"

"To hopefully find the entrance to the underground facility from there," Rennick finished, mimicking Markarian's actions with his own suit.

"And we're your contacts on this side," Mei added with a chuckle, nudging John's arm before spinning around in the computer chair.

John scoffed, clamping down on her shoulders—effectively stopping her circular rotation. "This isn't fun, it's dangerous." He sighed, his gaze flicking from Markarian to Caldera. "We're taking this seriously, I promise."

"I *am* being serious!" Mei said, rolling her eyes.

"We'll be monitoring the B.E.C.S. portal and the individual S.G.T. devices," John reiterated, ignoring his sister. "But what do we do with this one?" he asked, pointing to another S.G.T. device sitting dormant on the tabletop.

"There's something wrong with it. It won't connect to the network," Markarian said, blowing out an exasperated breath. "And without a certain genius here to fix it, it doesn't work. So we don't have any extras."

Caldera's mind raced at the thought of two rookies operating what was essentially their only communication and transportation back to Bersama.

"I need you to lift off..."

"I can't—I don't know how..."

A cold sweat broke out on her neck at the remembrance of the poorly trained crew she used to command and the failed directive that almost cost her, and Rennick, their lives.

She shook her head. *Over a year has passed, but a memory like that could still come so quickly to the forefront of my brain?*

She gritted her teeth and forced a smile across her face. "Markarian, why don't you go over the operating system with them again?"

He nodded, nestling close to John—who seemed to have mostly forgiven him, considering the circumstances—and started pointing at buttons and screens.

Caldera took a few steps away as he began his explanation for the twentieth time, lowering the pack from her shoulder to the ground—the contents as heavy as her heart—and taking a deep breath, leaned heavily against the table.

"Are you okay?" Rennick asked, stepping in front of her.

A concerned look settled across his face, and Caldera flinched at how familiar that was becoming. "I'm fine, " she said, reaching up to cup his face in her hand.

He leaned into her hold. "How many times have you successfully lied to me?"

"Successfully? None, I believe."

"Right... So, why don't you tell me the truth?"

She caressed his cheek with her thumb and absently tucked hair behind his ear before dropping her hand. "I... I've never..."

She sighed, biting her lip as frantic, jumbled thoughts pushed their way forward, and she struggled with how to phrase them. Rennick reached out, rubbing her arm, silently, patiently encouraging her to continue.

"You know how on Vanguard missions, I knew... I *knew* that we'd come out on top?"

"I remember you *thinking* and believing that so relentlessly that it became a fact in your mind."

"Exactly. Failure was never an option."

He chuckled. "Okay, go on..."

Caldera grabbed his hand, squeezing as hard as she could. Gripping it like a lifeline. Her heart pounded with the urge to indiscriminately destroy everything in her path—everyone at that facility—but the newfound, rational, part of her hesitated. No longer willing to blindly leap without looking.

"I don't think I can overcome what's thrown at me anymore." She glanced over her shoulder at Markarian, Mei, and John and lowered her voice, hating, *resenting*, every word that left her mouth. "This isn't going to work..."

She had thought those words before but never dared to utter them outloud lest they become true. *But they are true... Maybe they always were.*

"Callie," Rennick said, taking a step closer, his grip never loosening. "Whether you believed it or not, failure was *always* an option, and sometimes, from an objective standpoint, we did fail, but you always spun the situation in a way that made it work in our favor." He smiled, tilting her chin upward with his free hand. "That's your gift."

"It's shit."

"Maybe." He shrugged, the smile never leaving his face as he pulled her into a tight hug. "But it's something we can work with."

Caldera rested against Rennick's chest, letting his heartbeat echo in her ears. She matched her breaths with the rhythmic rise and fall of his chest and focused on the soft material of his shirt against her cheek. Her head cleared, and a smile broke across her face. "Then let's work with it," she whispered.

"These two are as trained as they're gonna get," Markarian said from behind them.

"All right." Caldera swallowed hard, and met Rennick's eyes before turning her attention back to Markarian, Mei, and John. Her chest swelled with fire and purpose that reached every extremity of her body. "Here's the plan. We teleport into the storage closet area that leads down into the bowels of Area 51. From there it's search and destroy. Search for Sear, Aloriea, and the kidnapped inhabitants. Destroy everything and everyone that gets in our way."

"We should probably expect heavy resistance," Rennick added, holstering his blaster.

Markarian mimicked his actions. "Way ahead of you."

Rennick tilted his head to the side. "Even so, that doesn't mean we should go on a murder spree."

Caldera stayed silent, unwilling to admit he was right. *We may not win, but neither will they. That's something I can make sure of.*

"Okay," she said, taking a step forward and attaching the Bersaman-Earth Connection System device to her exosuit. "Here we go."

CHAPTER 32

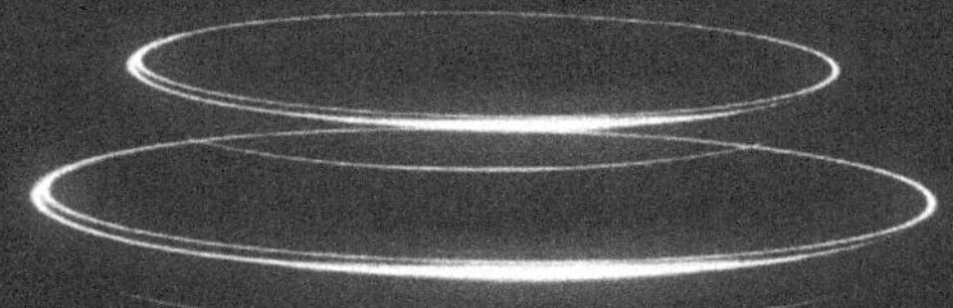

The icy sensation was gone before it could even be registered. There was no pulling of her body in infinite directions. No nausea or discombobulation. There wasn't even any light. There was only The Vault and then a closet-like area with storage shelves lining the walls and various products haphazardly strewn across the ledges as if they were only there for show.

The area was small. Smaller than small, and Caldera jolted against Markarian as she caught her breath, his large frame taking up most of the space, causing a bottle full of sloshing liquid to tumble to the ground and the handle of a tall broom to smack against her head.

Rennick grabbed both of their arms to try and steady them but all he did was kick the loose container into her shin as Markarian's head bumped against the ceiling.

They all grabbed the shelves next to them, remaining as still as possible while holding their breaths and regaining their balance. There was barely enough room to shift around after they oriented themselves.

Footsteps approached, drawing nearer to their location.

Caldera bit her lip, sucking in her breath and slowly unholstering her blaster, glancing down at the settings. *Set to kill. Good.* A pang of regret stabbed through the back of her mind at the thought before quickly dissipating.

"I know I heard something," the voice said, gruff and quizzical.

Another voice responded from farther away. "No you didn't. We're the only one's patrolling this area tonight..." There was a pause. "Unless... it's the 'aliens' *ooooo.*"

Caldera froze, locking eyes with Rennick and Markarian, who also had their blasters out. *Aliens. That's what Earth-people call us.* Her mind raced, wondering how fast she and her friends could take them out as a shadow came into view, stretching under the door.

Will we be fast enough to stop them from calling for backup? What if there's more around that aren't talking? She gripped the butt of the blaster tighter, readying herself for the confrontation.

The unidentified voice was overcome with raucous laughter.

"Fuck off, Phelps," the first voice replied, their tone shaky. The shadow stepped away from the door. "You've been readin' too many conspiracies again. Aliens don't exist."

Caldera blanched, Rennick's words plowing through her brain, into her conscience. *There might be innocent people in that facility.* She met his eyes as the footsteps became quieter and quieter until they could no longer be heard. She motioned for them to holster their blasters.

"Okay, that was ridiculous," she said, her voice a barely audible whisper.

"This space is too damn small," Markarian replied, matching her tone.

Rennick nodded. "Much smaller than the specs indicated."

Caldera pressed her finger against her ear where the small communications earpiece that connected them with Mei and

John sat. "All clear. You two are on standby until we need you."

"Roger that," Mei replied through the device that was interlinked between her, John, and the three.

"Make sure you let us know what you need," John added before the line went silent.

"All right," Rennick muttered, turning around as much as he could in the cramped space, effectively elbowing Caldera in the chest, and pressing his palms against the door. "How do we get down?"

Caldera took a deep breath and aimed her blaster at the floor. "It's simple... We *go down*." Her finger pressed gently against the trigger, about to pull it.

Markarian flattened himself against the wall as much as he could, but didn't try to stop her.

"Wait," Rennick said, grabbing her wrist. "It might not be as simple as that!" He let her go and lowered his voice even more. "We have the element of surprise. Let's not waste it."

"Then what do you suggest we do?"

"The same thing we did when we were searching for The Vault. Look for a hidden panel."

"That sounds like a pretty good idea, Cal," Markarian said, scratching the scar on the side of his head. "I'm all for blowing shit up, but—"

She exhaled sharply. "Fine, but I need room. You two guard the door while I search."

They nodded, redrawing their blasters. Rennick grabbed the door handle and nodded to Markarian, who nodded back. He twisted the handle, and nothing happened.

"What?" Rennick muttered, trying again to no avail. "It's locked?"

"From the outside?" Markarian asked, gently nudging Rennick out of the way to try the handle for himself. It was the same outcome.

"Satisfied?" Rennick quipped, holstering his blaster yet again.

Markarian tried one more, unsuccessful, time to turn the handle. "Why though?"

Caldera's stomach sank. "It's not to keep the people who work here out... It's to keep whatever—*whoever*— they have locked up down there in..." The contents of her bowels roiled. "If they somehow managed to escape—to get this far..." She couldn't finish her sentence. The thought pounded against her chest and head like an off-beat drum; to have the hope of escape only for it to be ripped away at the last second, to be dragged back down to the depths of whatever torment surely awaited them. Her stomach lurched, mouth filling with saliva, and she had to swallow hard to keep herself from vomiting.

Without a word, she began to fling the useless supplies and appliances out of her way—not caring if she made noise, or if she was inadvertently hitting Rennick or Markarian— searching for any break in the wall or floor—anything to get her closer to finding Aloriea, and holding on to what little hope she had of finding Sear.

This room is so small, there has to be something. She clawed past the patched-together shelves, seemingly there only for the sole-purpose of making the area look like storage space. *There has to be something.* She pressed her cheek against the exposed area of the wall at the back of the closet, tapping her knuckles against it. *There has to be—*

Her knuckle hit a hollow patch. She caught her breath, tracing the square with her finger. It looked no different than any other tiled square that made up the rooms walls and floor but it was hollow in a way she recognized.

"Here," she muttered, as Rennick and Markarian crowded behind her, peering over her shoulders. Pressing hard against one side of the square, the unit flipped over, revealing a panel with a small screen and keyboard attachment.

"No scanner," Markarian said, placing his hands in his pockets and leaning his chin on Caldera's shoulder to study the device.

"That's probably a good thing," Rennick said, tapping the screen with his exosuit-covered hand, causing it to blink to life. "We wouldn't be able to get in if it were..."

"But we also don't know the passcode…" Caldera finished, blowing out a breath. "Damn it."

"We could go back to Plan A and try blasting it?" Markarian offered, resting his hand on the butt of his holstered blaster.

Rennick shook his head. "We don't know if that'll work. It could completely lock us out. Not to mention draw unwanted attention to our position." He studied the wall panel. "It looks like it's a fourteen-character code."

"That could be anything!" Markarian replied, his voice raising.

"We could ask Mei and John to go through the A51 journal again."

"That'll take too long."

"We've come too far… There has to be something…" Caldera whispered, squeezing her eyes shut as thoughts rushed in and out of her brain. *What can we do? What options do we have? We wouldn't even have known about this area if it wasn't for…* "Vandren."

"What?" Rennick asked, placing a hand on Caldera's shoulder.

"Vandren…" Caldera muttered, "he—" She shook her head, taking a deep breath. *What did he say…*

I don't like helping people for no reason—heed my words or you and your friends will surely die—

Caldera's eyes shot open. "The Phoenix will rise," she said, repeating his words.

"Callie," Rennick said, his voice low, "what does that mean?"

She raised her hands to the keyboard. "I don't know," she whispered. Her fingers trembled as she typed *'PHOENIX RISING'* into the keypad.

The wall didn't make a sound as it opened in a single fluid motion next to the wall device, revealing an elevator larger than the room they were currently all squeezed into. The three silently clambered inside and Caldera pressed the only available button.

Down.

CHAPTER 33

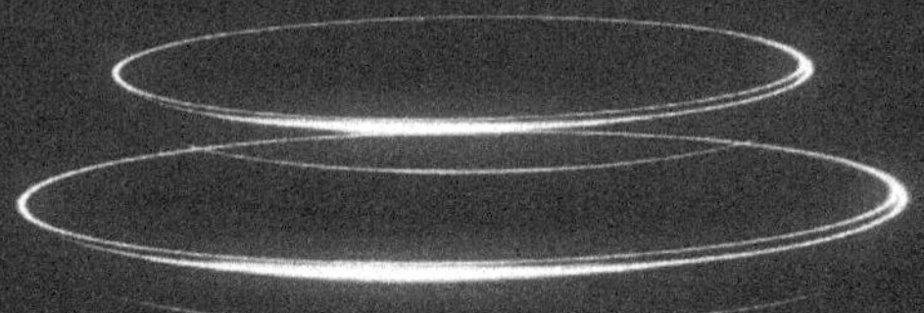

The elevator dropped, and continued to drop second upon second, minute upon minute. They were going far underground, farther than Caldera thought.

With each passing moment her heart rose higher in her throat until she was sure she'd choke on it. Swallowing past the growing lump, she looked around at her surroundings. An idea popped into her head as her eyes caught a familiar sight.

"Let's get up there," she said, pointing to the elevator hatch in the ceiling.

Markarian furrowed his brow, following her gesture. "Why?"

"This elevator's entrance is probably guarded," Rennick replied, grinning at Caldera while lacing his fingers together to make a cradle for her to step into and getting into a squatting position under the latch.

Her heart pounded with long-dormant exhilaration as she opened the door to the top of the elevator and climbed up as the lift continued to descend. It had been so long since she and

Rennick had worked together on a mission, and her body was hungry for it.

Markarian helped Rennick on top of the elevator and proceeded to jump up himself with little help as the lift slowed down.

Caldera felt eyes on her and turned to see Rennick and Markarian staring. Waiting. Her heart fluttered before beginning to settle into a steadier rhythm as she realized they were waiting for her orders. She was their captain again.

The elevator came to a complete stop, and Caldera raised a flat hand over her head before pointing down the still open hatch.

Rennick and Markarian nodded at the non-verbal communication for 'cover me,' and unholstered their blasters.

The doors slid open and a man in a slate blue camo uniform walked inside. "What the f—"

Caldera swung herself down from the open hatch, kicking the man hard in the chest, knocking him off balance and causing him to fall backward onto the floor just outside the elevator. She landed with a *thunk* on top of him, ripping the Earth-gun out of his hands and tossing it to the side before he had time to take a breath while jamming her own weapon under his chin. A *clunk* sounded behind her as Rennick and Markarian dropped to the floor.

Rennick ran up beside her pressing the barrel of his own blaster to the man's head as Markarian knelt on her other side, surveying the area with his weapon at the ready, poised and prepared to shoot if necessary.

"Don't make a fucking sound," Caldera hissed, clamping a hand over the uniformed man's mouth as he tried to shout. She pushed down harder on his chest with her knee. "You will only nod 'yes' or 'no' in response to my questions unless I say otherwise. You see this?" She lifted her blaster from his jaw and waved it in front of his dark green eyes. "This'll end your miserable life. Do you understand?"

"I'd listen to her if I were you," Markarian added, scooting closer.

Rennick flicked his eyes in her direction but said nothing, keeping his blaster pressed against the man's temple.

The man nodded and Caldera slowly removed her hand taking a deep breath. "Is this Area 51?"

He blinked.

"Speak!"

"Above us is. *This* place has no name." The man gulped. "It's off the books... most of the airmen upstairs don't even know about it."

Airmen? Caldera shook her head at the Earth term; she didn't care if the facility upstairs was technically disconnected or not, they were still compliant. They had to be.

A whole underground laboratory couldn't exist, literally, under another facility's nose without *someone* knowing about it.

That's not my problem right now...

"We're looking for two people. First, a woman," she continued, "with horns. Have you seen her?"

"There's more than one of those here," the man said, his voice growing steadier. "You'll need to be more specific."

Caldera's breath caught in her throat. *The kidnapped inhabitants of Sector Four...*

She flicked her eyes toward Rennick, knowing if she continued with the line of questioning the man would be dead before they got any real answers.

She pressed her blaster harder against her captive's throat.

"She's tall, dark-skinned, and...would've appeared out of nowhere," Rennick said, taking over, his brows furrowed, a look of barely contained distress creasing his forehead.

"If she wasn't instantly detained, she would've most likely been aimlessly wandering the halls or rooms," Markarian added.

Caldera stared into the man's hard eyes when he didn't respond. "She would've been looking for someone named Sear... and so are we. That's the other person we're after."

A long moment passed in silence as the man studied Caldera, Rennick, and Markarian as if seeing them clearly for the first time. Although they had the same physical attributes, unless the man was particularly short, they towered over him in both height and build.

"I don't know where they are... but Evie had one of the subjects brought to her office a while ago," he said before pausing. "You're aliens aren't you?"

Caldera scoffed, glancing from Rennick to Markarian, her stomach roiling at the term 'subject'. "I prefer the phrase *extra-terrestrial*," she said, leaning in even closer to the man's face as her ponytail slipped over her shoulder. "And I didn't say you could ask questions."

She nodded at Rennick before standing, leaving him to decide what he wanted to do with the captive. Taking a deep breath, she took in her surroundings for the first time as a blaster shot went off behind her.

"He'll be out for hours, maybe more," Rennick said, pulling the unconscious man into the elevator. "Markarian, help me lift him up into the elevator hatch; hopefully that'll buy us more time before he's found."

Caldera reluctantly turned her blaster to *stun* instead of *kill*. She glanced at Markarian to see he was doing the same.

"You're too nice," he muttered as he helped Rennick with his request.

"I'm not killing someone in cold blood."

"Well, they are! You heard what the man said—using words like 'those', and 'subjects'."

"Stop," Caldera said, stepping between Markarian and Rennick and holding up her hands as they reclosed the elevator latch, locking the unconscious man above them. "I left the decision to Ren for how we were going to handle these people moving forward. The precedent has been set." She lowered her palm to Rennick's chest. "We'll respect your decision."

He gently placed his hand over hers. "Thank you."

Caldera nodded, stepping back into the hallway and glancing up one side and down the other. There were no signs indicating which way they should go and no sound of people bustling around. Just plain light gray walls and a white tiled floor that curved around in a loose semi-circle in both directions, like a snake eating its own tail.

Looks like it's a fifty-fifty shot.

"You heard him. We have to get to Evie's office. Let's try heading right first," she said, pointing down the hall. "Ren, you take point. Markarian, you're behind me at my six."

Rennick and Markarian nodded and got into position.

The three moved swiftly down the long, curved, windowless hallway. Something nagged at Caldera's mind. *Where are all the people? The guards? The scientists? The captives? Anyone.*

Markarian moved up closer to her while still scoping the area behind them. "Why did you leave the decision up to him?" he whispered in her ear, jolting her out of her trance.

"Because out of the three of us, he's the only one capable of making rational decisions right now."

"So, you wanted to kill that man too?"

"Without hesitation," she said, meeting his green eyes. "I want to kill them all."

"He's most likely going to try and evacuate the facility before we set the bombs off."

Caldera adjusted the pack on her shoulder and let out a sigh. "I know. The best we can hope for is that the Earth government will make these people pay for their crimes."

"Against people and species they don't even know exist?" Markarian clenched his jaw, his grip on his blaster tightening. "I don't know, Cal... That sounds like a long shot. Not to mention, they might retaliate against *us*... We're trying to destroy their facility after all. They might think we're acting on behalf of Ber-sama."

Caldera didn't respond, motioning for Markarian to resume his post behind her. *He's right... If we let them go, how are these people going to be brought to justice for what they've done?*

A few more minutes passed in silence before they came to an area where the hallway opened with the words 'Holding Cells' engraved in large letters over a large metal door.

Rennick stopped short, before they would be in view of any potential cameras in the entryway, and pressed his body against the curved wall. He held up a balled fist and pointed two fingers ahead, indicating for them to stop, follow his movement, and draw their attention forward.

They followed suit, peering over his shoulder.

Caldera squinted, examining the area in front of her.

A red triangle was plastered on the wall next to the set of doors with a symbol she didn't recognize in the middle of it and the words 'Decontamination Area Ahead' underneath.

The doors themselves were lined down the middle with black and yellow stripes. There was a scanner at the top of the doorway with a red light fixture next to it that was currently sitting dark, telling her the doors that slid together to meet in the middle were automated—opening automatically to let people in, closing and locking until the process was complete, and then releasing the newly neutralized person into the chamber on the other side.

"Okay," Markarian said, breaking the silence, "what's the plan? This chamber has to be where they're keeping the imprisoned inhabitants of our planet."

Caldera pursed her lips, furrowing her brow in contemplation. "Well, we're armed and unfamiliar to everyone who works here—which, from what I can tell so far, is an extremely limited number of people, and we'll be walking into an unknown number of hostiles... I don't think we have the luxury of *not* coming out shooting."

Rennick was nodding next to her. "I agree, we need to subdue the enemies in this chamber as quickly as possible, release our people and send them back to Bersama."

Caldera beamed. "Spoken like a true leader."

He raised an eyebrow.

"What? Did you think I'd be ruling by myself forever?"

A soft smile spread across Rennick's face. "As I've always said, I'm with you."

"Yeah, yeah, you two are the cutest," Markarian said, playfully rolling his eyes and lifting his blaster, "but can we get on with it?"

"Of course *Kari*, give me a second," Caldera replied, winking at Markarian and pressing a finger against her ear. "Hey? You two still there?"

"At your service!" Mei's excited voice said, echoing through the ear-piece.

"What can we do for you?" John added.

"Has B.E.C.S pinpointed and calculated our coordinates yet?"

"It's finishing up compiling the data now," John replied.

"Good, lock onto us once it does," she said, glancing from Rennick to Markarian. "Get Doctor Celestin Vareis over there and make some room; the Vault's about to fill up."

"Really?" Mei exclaimed.

"That's right," Markarian said, pressing a finger against his own earpiece. "The rescue operation is about to start."

"We'll keep you updated," Rennick added, "but for now we have to put you on standby again."

"The hostages are coming home..." Caldera said, conviction coating every word and filling her entire body.

The three slowly walked up to the decontamination doors, which slid apart in one fluid motion, welcoming them into the unknown darkness beyond.

Rennick and Markarian stood on either side of her, and nodded. They were ready.

Caldera nodded back, throwing a sharp grin Rennick's way before lifting her own blaster. "On my count," she said, taking the lead. "Three. Two. One. Go!"

CHAPTER 34

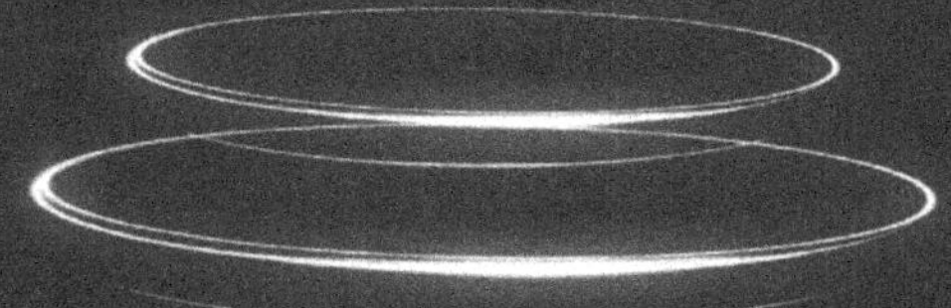

The three stepped into the dark room, causing the doors to slide shut behind them with a *shick* and usher in an overhead fluorescent light.

Caldera shielded her eyes from the sudden brightness before being overtaken with a loud rush of air that hissed against her ears and blew hair across her face. The smell of antiseptic was thick around them, causing her to wheeze and gasp despite herself. Rennick and Markarian also had their hands over their nose and mouths trying to contain their coughs and regulate their breathing.

The rush of artificial wind stopped as a wall of red light descended in a parallel, downward motion from the walls on both sides, hitting her body—instantly causing it to tingle.

Lasers? This is how they're decontaminating themselves? Her mind raced to self preservation, but there was nowhere to go— nowhere to hide in the large empty room. She could only stand there and let herself, and two of the people she cared about most in the universe, get irradiated.

The lasers moved up and down and side to side, successfully covering every inch of their bodies from front to back. Caldera set her jaw, all too aware that with every pass of the decontamination process, more of her cells were dying.

Doctor Vareis is going to be overloaded with radiation cases if the captives had to continually go through one of these machines.

With the fourth pass, the lasers turned a bright green, apparently satisfied with their cleanliness.

"Just so we're clear," Rennick said, readying his blaster, "we're all in agreement about not killing the opposition?"

"Crystal," Markarian replied, stepping up next to him. "Although, I don't know how we're going to evacuate them before we blow the facility..."

"Not evacuating is the last-ditch option," Rennick pressed.

Caldera nodded silently and stepped forward, waiting for the inner doors to open to the chamber beyond, checking and double checking to make sure her blaster was set to stun. *Okay, Ren, we'll try it your way.* Her heart and blood raced, beating in unison—faster and faster—like a drum in her ears as the doors finally opened.

Caldera shot first at the closest person, a young bespectacled man in a white lab coat, and ran for cover behind a metal desk directly in front of her as he dropped to the ground.

Rennick was next to her, firing to the right, while Markarian was on her other side, firing to the left.

Yells and screams of confusion met Caldera's ears as well as general commotion—the knocking over of chairs, clicking of shoes against the tiled floor, and heavy breathing of sudden and unexpected exertion. Peeking over the desk, she blasted another white-coated person, dropping them unconscious to the ground.

"I'm counting fifteen total," she said, lowering herself back down and raising her voice over the growing chaos.

"That's what I had too," Rennick replied, his chest rapidly rising and falling as he shot blindly over the top of their cover.

"Same," Markarian said, releasing another plasma blot from

his blaster. "These people all look like scientists. I don't think they're armed."

"This'll go quick, then," Caldera muttered, trusting Markarian's judgment and standing up, completely revealing herself to the enemy and dropping two more people. The remaining scientists were frantically trying to make their way to another decontamination chamber on the other side of the room.

Caldera, Rennick, and Markarian broke apart, zig-zagging around desks with computers running through indiscriminate tests on their flat screens, and scattered papers strewn across the top—much of which were on the floor, all the while blasting at anyone they saw.

A dimly illuminated hallway on the far side of the room caught her attention, causing her to miss the last shot, the blast hitting right above the person's shoulder, letting a single, gray-haired scientist escape through the second decontamination chamber.

"Fuck!" Caldera holstered her blaster, stepping over an unconscious woman and surveying the aftermath of the brief encounter.

The large room had fallen eerily quiet, allowing her to completely take in her surroundings. They were standing in what seemed to be a bullpen of metal desks while images of the outside world cycled across the walls and ceiling from either a built-in screen or hidden projector.

There was nothing else in the surrounding area besides the hallway and the two decontamination chambers on either side of the room.

"How long have these people been down here to need reminders of what's above them?" Markarian asked, beginning to gather all the unconscious scientists together.

"Who knows?" Caldera muttered, walking toward the entrance of the hallway. "Ren, you're with me. Markarian, keep doing what you're doing—secure them to the desks or something for now."

"You got it, boss," Markarian said, walking toward the far decontamination chamber doors, where most of the scientists were lying.

The entryway loomed tall over her as Caldera and Rennick approached. The closer they got, the clearer they could see a greenish-blue light undulating—waving—from deep within around a small curve, like water shimmering off the walls of what looked like cells. Wordlessly, they started down the hall, their blasters ready.

Turning the corner, Caldera's blood ran cold; her arm fell, hanging limp at her side, blaster useless in her frozen, horrified state.

The right and left hand walls were lined floor to ceiling with plexiglass and inside were the kidnapped inhabitants of Sector Two. The group was mixed with inhabitants of every kind and gender, even children. They sat on small islands of rock that were sprinkled throughout the specialized cell, while the water that took up most of the area broke in tiny waves against the islets and the glass, hitting the inhabitants' feet or bare legs. They were unclothed, their blue, teal, and indigo bodies huddled together in groups for warmth with their knees pulled to their chests to try and give themselves a sliver of privacy.

Some, she could tell, had fresh scars on their legs, arms, and chests, and some had parts or all of the gills on their neck removed.

Caldera's chest tightened so much that she had to gasp for air at the atrocities she was witnessing and that were surrounding her, knowing it was only the beginning. Pressing her trembling hand against the glass, she attempted to speak.

"Why..." The words tangled in her throat as tears ran down her face. She pounded her fist against the glass, causing a loud echo to bounce off the wall and getting the attention of every captive inside. "Why would they do this?" she screamed, to no one in particular, pounding both fists against the glass now. "Those bastards!"

The captured natares tilted their heads to the side; some of their eyes lighting up with recognition.

"Callie," Rennick said, his voice wavering, attempting to get her attention. "Callie!" he said again, grabbing her arm when she continued to pound on the glass. "We're going to get them out. Okay? We're going to." He took a deep breath. "Let me deal with this here and you go on."

Caldera met his eyes; they were red, like he was trying to keep himself from crying. She nodded, viciously wiping her tear stained cheeks.

"There have to be around fifty captives in each of these," she said, motioning all around her, "but according to the reports from Sector Two, they have disappearances in the upper hundreds."

"There have to be more holding tanks," Rennick said, taking her shoulders in his hands.

"Or they're..." she began, but couldn't bring herself to finish the sentence.

"I'll find out, and if there are more, I'll find them. I promise..."

"I'll go break the locks on every regular holding cell that's in this sick fucking place," Caldera said, steeling herself for what lay ahead.

Rennick squeezed her shoulders, giving her a quick kiss on the forehead. "Go!"

She nodded, turning and running to the next section of holding cells.

THE NEXT SECTION HELD NO less horrors. Akars with their horns removed, saurians with scales missing. Even tellins were covered in black and blue bruises. Inhabitants from all sectors were locked away. Nobody was off limits.

Swallowing the bile in her throat, Caldera approached the first cell holding two terrified matans. They hissed, cowering in the corners of their prison, their cat-like ears pressed back against their heads.

"It's okay," she began, holding up her hands. "My name is

Caldera Keane, I'm the Queen of Tellis, and I'm here to set you free."

They blinked, their ears slowly lifting. "Queen Caldera?" one questioned, their voice deep and tired as he walked up and gripped the bars. His brown fur was singed in spots along his arms as if he had been burned. "What are you doing here?"

"The only thing you need to know is that I'm getting you out," she said, lifting her blaster to the cell lock. "Get back!"

He obeyed, retreating to the other matan and turning away from the door.

Caldera shot the lock until the metal melted enough for her to kick the door in. "Come on, hurry," she said, waving them forward.

The two gingerly stepped out into the open, shivering and looking worse for wear. Patches of fur were missing, and cuts and bruises adorned much of the open skin.

Caldera steeled herself at the sight, wishing more than anything that she had a blanket to give them to help cover up their bare bodies.

"What now?" the female matan asked, the dullness in her icy blue eyes getting a little brighter. She scratched her arm and a clump of silver fur floated to the ground.

"Follow this hall all the way down, to the office space, or whatever that central hub is," Caldera said, pointing in the direction she came from. "A member of my court, Markarian Ales, is there. Meet up with him and he'll send you home."

"What about the scientists?"

"They're taken care of. Now go!"

The female matan took a step forward and in one swift motion, bent down and wrapped her arms around Caldera. "I do not know why or how you are here," she whispered, "but thank you... thank you..."

Caldera squeezed as hard as she could before pulling away, leaving her exosuit covered in fur. *She's really sick. A matan should not be shedding like this.*

A ball formed in the pit of her stomach as she wiped the tears from the matan's cheeks. "There's a doctor on the other side. Please get checked out when you get back."

The two nodded and sprinted down the hall as fast as they could muster.

Caldera pressed a finger to her ear as she watched them disappear from sight. "Markarian? I don't know where Ren's at with freeing the natares, but I'm freeing the captives from the regular cells and they're starting to come your way."

"Copy that. I'm ready. All scientists are secure."

"I've found the hatch to let the natares out without flooding the area," Rennick replied, answering Caldera's earlier question. "They'll also be coming your way, Kari."

"Got it, I'll send 'em as they come. You got that, Mei? John?"

"Roger!" the siblings both said in unison.

"We'll monitor each group as it gets here," John said. "Hopefully none need immediate medical attention since Dr. Vareis isn't here yet.

"But she's on her way," Mei added.

"Just be prepared, all of you," Caldera added as she continued down the hall. "What's happened here... What these people have gone through..." she let her sentence trail off, and no one requested clarification.

She continued on, freeing everyone from each cell she passed, her heart breaking a little more each time. The more she witnessed, the more she realized what the people of her planet had to endure, and the more she began to lose hope about finding her friends alive.

Finally, the hall came to a deadend, there were only two cells left before she would be forced to turn around and head back. With a deep, shuddering breath she walked up to the first one, repeating her spiel.

"My name is Queen Caldera Keane and..." She stopped when she saw who was inside. "You're... a human, aren't you?"

The man sitting on the edge of a hard-looking cot tilted his head to the side, wavy strawberry-blond hair swaying against the tops of his ears with the motion. "I'd ask you the same thing, but you're clearly not. What are ya, like over six feet tall?"

Caldera scoffed. "Maybe on your planet."

Walking up to the bars, he wrapped his hands around the cylindrical steel. The sleeves of his orange jumpsuit were tied around his waist, and the plain black t-shirt he wore was crumpled, like it had seldom been washed. "How'd you get here, or even find this place?" he asked, glancing up and down at Caldera with his blue eyes. "You clearly aren't a prisoner that escaped... and did you say you were a queen?"

"I don't think you're in a position to be questioning me," Caldera snapped, glaring down at the earth-man. "I, on the other hand, would like some answers."

"Fair enough," the man replied with a shrug, returning to the edge of his cot. "Ask away. I've got nothing better to do."

Caldera furrowed her eyebrows at the man's nonchalance. "Why are you in this cell?"

"Curiosity paired with a classic case of 'wrong place, wrong time'. Pure and simple."

"*Really?* They made you a prisoner because of curiosity?"

He laughed, almost jovially. "Area 51 isn't an organization you get 'curious' about and then go on with your day. Especially when you get as close as I did, or see what I saw."

Caldera gritted her teeth, biting down the urge to fire back at him with a smart aleck remark, when she noticed the healed over scars running down the man's neck and arms. *He was tortured too... Maybe not for a while, but still...*

"How long have you been here?"

"Hard to say," he said with a sigh. "One year maybe? More or less."

Caldera pursed her lips. "Well, you want out?"

"I thought you'd never ask."

She glanced behind her. "Who's over there, in that last cell?"

"I don't know, one of the cat-people. We talk sometimes, but he mostly sleeps. They take him a lot—"

Without hesitation, Caldera turned and headed for the cell behind her.

"Hey. Hey! Where are you going?" he shouted, running up to the bars again.

"The people of my planet come first."

The man sighed, leaning heavily against the bars, but didn't protest further.

Caldera approached the cell to see an indistinct form laying on the cot in their cell, the darkness obscuring her vision. "Hey, wake up. Wake up! I'm here to help."

The shape stirred but didn't make any move to stand.

She tilted her head to the side and taking a deep breath, started to recite her spiel while squinting through the dimness. "My name's Caldera Keane, I'm the Queen of—"

"Callie?"

Her words froze at the familiar voice as the shape slowly rose to their feet. Tears were streaming down her face before the name choked out of her mouth. "Sear!"

CHAPTER 35

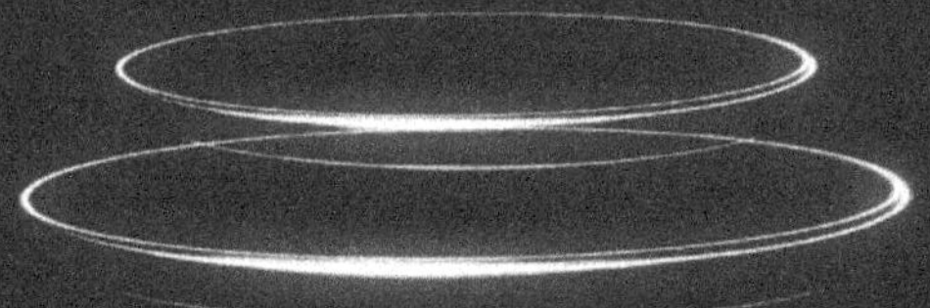

Caldera reached through the bars as Sear limped up to her, taking his outstretched hand in hers.

"You're alive," was all she could say as she gripped his hand as tight as she could. Her knees began to tremble, having a hard time holding her up. The guilt of allowing herself to think he was dead hammered against her heart. "Sear—"

Her eyes met his before trailing down to his hands that she was so desperately holding on to. They were haphazardly bandaged up to the wrists and little specks of dried blood had leaked through the gauze of each covered fingertip.

A horrific realization stuck through her body like a lightning bolt.

He had been apart of the torture, too.

It didn't matter that they had kidnapped him purposefully to try and leverage him against her. He was just a 'thing' to them, a 'subject' to be studied, and if she hadn't infiltrated Area 51—even if she had complied without question to their demands—they never would have given him back.

She released his hand and quickly shot the lock of the cell door.

He stumbled out and before she could stop herself, she was wrapping arms around his torso and squeezing as tightly as she could.

"Callie," Sear said, quickly returning her hug and flinching, before taking her shoulder and gently pushing her away. "I am beyond ecstatic to see you, but not only am I in copious amounts of pain, this is quite awkward as I am... umm, unclothed."

Caldera blinked; she hadn't noticed. All she cared about was that her friend was alive. She set her jaw, looking around. "You. What's your name?" she asked, turning back to the human prisoner.

"Bailey."

"Okay, Bailey. Pants. Now."

"It's a *jumpsuit*, and no way."

"I'll leave you in there if you don't hand it over."

Bailey scoffed, glaring at her through the dimness as he stepped out of the garment and threw it through the bars at her.

"What am I supposed to do?" he asked, standing there in only a t-shirt and covering himself.

"You have a blanket, unlike everyone else in here," Caldera said, handing the outfit to Sear, and walking over to Bailey's cell, aiming at the lock. "Wrap it around your waist and get out of the way."

She fired three quick shots and stepped back. The ripping of cloth caught Caldera's ears as Bailey busted through the cell door, clutching the blanket that was now tightly tied around his waist.

She turned to see Sear biting the pant legs off roughly at the knee so they would fit over his bare legs and tying the arms around his thin waist to keep the orange suit from sliding down. Her heart lurched at the fact that he no longer had his claws.

"Can I assume that Ren and Markarian are here?" Sear asked, his emaciated form limping forward.

Caldera rushed to his side, slinging his arm over her shoulder and wrapping her arm around his waist to steady him. "They're here." She pressed a finger to her ear with her free hand. "Ren, Markarian..." she paused, unsure why she was hesitating.

The shock of seeing so many people of our planet bruised, battered, and near death must be taking a toll on them. What would seeing Sear like that do? She took a deep breath, forcing the urge to protect her friend's remaining morality, knowing that once they saw him, everything would be out the window—especially for Markarian.

They'll have to see him eventually. "I have Sear. He's alive!"

The cheers and yells of celebration hit her ears, but she didn't respond to any of it as she helped Sear back down the long hallway toward the central hub area.

"What should I do?" Bailey asked, stepping in front of her.

"I don't care," Caldera said, brushing past him, her full attention on balancing Sear against her. "Just go."

"Go where?" he said, stepping in front of her again and laying a hand on her shoulder to stop her, successfully shoving her and Sear a step backward. "How the hell am I supposed to get out of this place?"

Caldera unholstered her blaster, smacked his hand away with it, and shoved the barrel in his face.

"Listen to me very carefully. I don't care what you do. I don't care where you go. And if you ever touch me again, I'll blow your fucking brains out. Now get out of my way."

"Callie. I do not think that is completely necessary," Sear said, his voice weak. "Bailey has been a prisoner here longer than I have—"

"Much longer, Scraps," Bailey interrupted.

"It's *Sear*," Caldera snapped, glaring at him.

"I know, I know, it's a little nickname I gave him. He was fighting tooth and nail against these people until they took his claws—"

"Shut the fuck up!" Caldera released a shaky breath, not ready to hear the truth about what Sear had to go through, or *unwilling* to hear it.

"Okay, I see how it is," Bailey said, still trailing next to them. "But since you don't care—and seem pretty capable—I think I'll stick around."

Caldera scoffed, placing a hand on Sear's chest to steady him as he flinched and stumbled forward. The outline of his ribs met her hands as she righted him. "Fine, then make yourself useful," she muttered, forcing the frustrated tears that constantly threatened to overflow back into her tear ducts. "I have one more question."

"Shoot."

"What the *fuck* are these people doing down here?"

They turned the corner around the empty water tanks that used to hold the imprisoned natares. It was only a short jot to the hub area where Rennick and Markarian were helping inhabitants get back home.

Bailey pursed his lips and looked down at his hands.

"Are you going to try and tell me you don't know?"

"No. I do…"

"Then spit it out. Now. I need to know why they did this to my people!"

Bailey sighed. "They needed them to further Earth's own tech—as quickly as possible," he replied, his voice low.

Caldera slowed her and Sear to a stop, staring Bailey in his blue eyes. "What does that have to do with us?"

He took a deep breath, his shoulders rising and falling in a quick jerky motion. "The reptilians are extremely durable—thick skin, hard scales. The cat-people are inhumanly strong, and the sirens can breathe underwater." Bailey paused, running a hand through his hair. "Even your kind, the ones that look like humans, can heal faster than anyone from our species… And those kinds of enhancements sell."

Enhancements?

"Sell?" Caldera's voice shook as her head spun from the misnomers of what he was calling the species of people from Bersama, barely able to wrap her head around what he was saying.

"That is correct, Callie," Sear said, gripping her shoulder and leaning heavily against her. "This place... This Area 51 is trying to facilitate genetic enhancements to sell to the governments of Earth who want to start a world war. That is its purpose."

"*Another* world war." Bailey corrected. "The third one, to be specific."

"How do you know that?" Caldera said, looking up at Sear.

"We have talked occasionally, Bailey and I."

"It's not hard to wheedle answers out of people when they think you're going to die underground," Bailey added with a shrug.

Caldera swallowed hard past the growing lump in her throat. *Two world wars already with a third on its way? That's... That's...* "Evil," she whispered, her whole body shaking.

Bailey nodded. "And Area 51 would be the facility that would get rich from it all, selling their 'enhancements' to the highest bidders and their soldiers, while keeping themselves in a position of power."

"Just another reason to blow this place to shit," Caldera muttered, finally able to force her feet to walk forward the rest of the way into the central hub of the chamber again.

Rennick and Markarian ran forward, abandoning their posts, their eyes widening when they saw Sear.

"Holy shit," Rennick whispered, his voice trembling as he took Sear's arm in his hand, slowly placing it around his shoulder, relieving Caldera and helping him into a chair.

"Those fuckers," Markarian said, unholstering his blaster and shooting a computer screen out of frustration, causing the captives that were waiting to go through the transportation portal-link to flinch in fear. "Fuck!" he shouted, continuing to fire his blaster at random objects. "Fuck!"

"Markarian!" Caldera yelled, grabbing his shoulder with one hand and his wrist that held the blaster with the other. "Markarian, stop! You need to calm down."

"Our friend is sitting there half-dead and you're telling me to calm down?"

"Hey!" Rennick said, taking a step forward and grabbing Markarian's other wrist. "This isn't about us right now," he hissed, releasing Markarian's wrist as he jerked it away.

"It's about them," Caldera finished, pointing to the shivering, terrified captives in front of her. "We can't break down right now... Not when we have a job to do."

Markarian's chest heaved but he stopped his tirade, slowly reholstering his blaster. "I'm... sorry," he muttered, clenching his jaw and rubbing his forehead. He took a few more deep breaths before his eyes landed on Bailey. "Who's that?"

"A human they had locked up," Caldera replied, walking over to the pack of explosives and quickly filling them in on everything Bailey had told her. "Markarian, you keep helping the inhabitants get back to Bersama. Ren... Bailey, you're helping me set the explosives... And then we'll find Aloriea."

Sear sucked in a breath. "Aloriea is here?"

Caldera winced, walking over to him. "She is." She bit her lip. *What should I—I won't lie to him. I can't.* "She teleported here without us because... she was looking for you."

Sear clenched his bandaged hands. "This cannot be... Not her..."

"We're gonna find her, I promise," Caldera said, kneeling in front of him. "She wasn't in the holding cells, and we teleported here right after her, so it's probable that Evie has her in her office."

"Or she's in a different chamber..." Bailey crossed his arms. "You know the one, dontcha Scraps?"

Sear tensed so visibly that Caldera thought he might snap in half. The vertical slits of his eyes dilated and his ear fell flat against his head as a seemingly involuntary snarl escaped his lips, revealing sharp canines.

"What other chamber?" she asked, searching his distraught face and forcing herself not to take an instinctual step back.

He shook his head, unable to speak, sweat beading on his forehead.

"The Interrogation and Experimentation Chamber," Bailey replied, his voice low. "I've been taken there, and I'm sure they all have too," he said, motioning toward the Bersaman inhabitants. "So, *along* with the Technology and Development Chamber—which, judging from your confused expressions, I assume you haven't been to yet—and Evie's office, you're looking at three possibilities."

He paused, his eyes landing on the bag of explosives. "Which brings me to my next point. You're gonna need a whole lot more of those if you want to completely destroy this place... I assume that's what you're doing here."

Caldera's body shook with rage; the injustices were mounting, threatening to never end, washing over her in wave after concrete wave and not only that, she had completely underestimated the scope of the facility. Taking a shaky breath, she lifted a trembling finger to her ear.

"Mei. John. We need more bombs... We need help," she said, just as the lights went out and a red glow, followed by the steady wail of sirens, filled the chamber.

CHAPTER 36

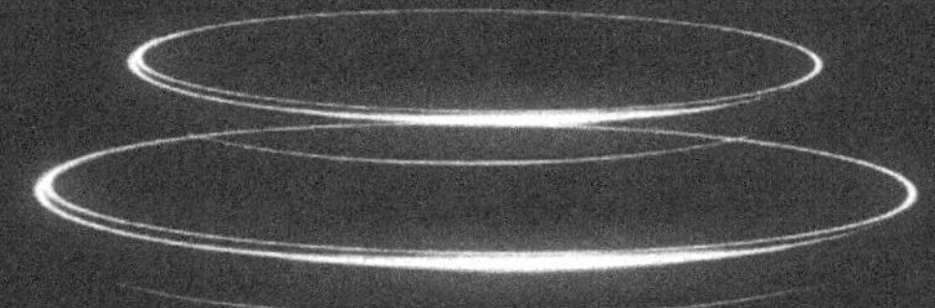

"W e must've triggered silent alarms from destroying the holding cells!" Rennick yelled over the noise, crouching down behind a desk.

"And now the whole damn facility knows we're here!" Markarian added, scanning the area.

The rhythmic wail of blaring sirens continued to fill Caldera's ears as she snapped into a combat-ready position, followed closely by Rennick and Markarian. "Hurry, get the rest of the inhabitants home!" she shouted over the noise.

Markarian nodded and ushered the remaining prisoners through the portal-link using the B.E.C.S. device.

"Hello, Your Majesty," Evie's voice boomed over hidden speakers. "I see you've been busy—destroying my property and releasing my prisoners. No matter. We can always get more."

Caldera clenched her jaw, gripping her blaster tighter and fighting the urge to scream as Evie's voice continued to talk.

"I want you to know I understand it would be a waste to try and capture you. I'm well aware that you can leave at any point..."

She chuckled. "But we both know you won't," she continued, her voice low as if she was sharing a secret. "We still have something that you want... Or should I say, *someone*."

Caldera's body shook so intensely that she couldn't hold her blaster steady.

"And despite what I tell them, Barrett and Dominic really want to kill you—especially since you didn't drown or get eaten when Dom pushed you into that swamp. All I have to say now is good luck."

So Dominic was the one who almost killed me in Penkith... Rage flowed freely through her being, eradicating every other emotion.

Rennick ran over to Caldera, crouching next to her. "This is bad."

"No shit, but even if we *had* Aloriea, we couldn't leave."

"Why not?" Sear asked, straining to sit up in his seat.

"Because we're trying to blow this place sky high," Markarian answered, placing a hand on Sear's shoulder.

"But as Bailey pointed out," Caldera said, glaring at the Earth-man, "we don't have enough explosives to do that."

Sear furrowed his brows. "How were you planning to accomplish that without a delayed relay charge?"

The three stared blankly at him.

His frown deepened. "The explosives need to be on delay so they can be detonated from a distance. Or put more simply, once you are far away from the demolition site!"

Caldera swallowed hard. "This all happened very quickly, okay? I didn't think about it."

"None of us did," Rennick added, rubbing the back of his head.

Caldera gritted her teeth. "Mei, how's getting help coming along?"

"We anticipated this! Give me a second."

Sear took a shaky breath. "Hand me that Earth-holopad," he said, pointing to a computer desk with a black square resting on top. "Using the signal device that is already built into the explosives, I can rig a delayed charge that will be shared between this cluster, but I suggest having that already set up for the subsequent charges before coming here."

"This is called a tablet, buddy," Bailey said, snatching the device off the table before Caldera could get to it. "And I have a proposition for you."

"I thought I made it pretty clear that I have no problem shooting you," Caldera snapped, reaching out her hand for the tablet.

"What's the proposition?" Markarian asked, crossing his arms.

"Take me with you."

"Oh no," Caldera said, shaking her head. "We're not taking any more Earth people onto Bersama."

"Any more? You mean... The Miller kids... *You* have them?"

"You know Mei and John?"

The decontamination chamber door in front of them exploded inward, causing everyone to gasp and fall to the floor before Bailey could answer.

"Mark! Are you okay?" John's frantic voice blared through the earpiece, causing Caldera to flinch.

"I'm fine!" Markarian's voice responded. "Just stay focused over there!"

"Well, where is everyone?" a deep, familiar voice sounded once the *boom* of the explosion and scraping metal had cleared the air.

"Dominic. Shit!" Caldera muttered under her breath. She peeked over the desk to see the stocky man stepping out of the mangled doorway, which was now a large metal gash in the wall, followed by a dozen camo-wearing soldiers. "Damn it, where is my fucking backup?" she said, pressing a finger to her ear as multiple footsteps echoed throughout the room.

"Here," a voice said from behind them, followed by a quick round of blaster shots that dropped three of Dominic's soldiers.

Caldera looked up to see a dark figure bounding over the computer desk to drop in front of her as gunfire sounded throughout the room. "Bruna!"

More blaster fire caught her attention as a person rolled into view, firing a quick shot before taking cover behind the desk as well.

Caldera couldn't hold back a smile. "Saro."

"The others are on their way," Bruna said, firing quick rounds over the desk.

"What others?"

"Grey and Sylvie. They're acquiring more explosives as requested," Saro replied, releasing his finger from his ear.

"Sorry," Mei's voice chimed through Caldera's earpiece. "That's all we could do."

"The other sector leaders may have sent over more S.G.T. devices for Bruna, Saro, Grey, and Sylvie— after much begging— but they won't get directly involved until you explain to them what's going on," John added.

"Well," Caldera said, as a chunk of the desk-top blew off above her, showering her hair with metal shavings. "I don't really have time for that right now."

"That's what *I* said," Mei replied, her voice tight.

"We need to get to the other chambers and clear them so when Grey and Sylvie arrive with more bombs they can be set without issue," Caldera said, grabbing the current bag of explosives and shoving them into Sear's arms and grabbing Bailey by the collar of his shirt. "You two are gonna get these ones linked," she continued.

Bailey held the tablet tighter to his chest. "If you're not letting me go with you then what the hell's in this for me?"

"How about your freedom? Unless you'd prefer to be stuck down here for the rest of your life."

He pursed his lips, contemplation shading his face. "Fine."

Turning away and without thinking, Caldera shot suppressing fire blindly over the desk before turning to Bruna. "Do you think you can set the bombs all throughout this chamber once they're linked and the soldiers disposed of?"

"That will be a non-issue," Bruna replied, without looking away from the firefight.

Caldera nodded, turning her attention to Saro and placing their only portal-link device in his hand. "Protect Sear. That's all I need you to do, okay?"

Saro nodded. "Of course."

"And as soon as he's finished setting up the delayed relay, send him back to Bersama through B.E.C.S. Be careful with it; it's the only one we have."

"Understood."

Sear grabbed Caldera's arm as she crawled toward Rennick and Markarian, stopping her in place. "Callie, no. You need me here."

Caldera sighed, letting a small smile break across her face amid the chaos. "No I don't... and neither does Aloriea." She took his bandaged hand in hers and tried to drown out the yells and blasts of the ongoing fight. "I know you want to help, but you're severely malnourished, injured, and everything else under the sun... You need to go back to Bersama."

She paused, patting the top of his hand as an idea sprouted into her mind. "But since I know you won't be able to sit idly by and do nothing, the best way you can help Aloriea is by creating a personal S.G.T. device that's specifically linked to her—we already have one, but it's broken. Fix it.

"And the best way you can help the rest of us is by linking the additional explosives that Sylvie and Grey are getting to a delayed relay. Once you're done, send everything back to us through the portal-link. Safely under the scrutiny of Doctor Vareis."

He opened his mouth to respond before closing it seconds later and sighing, a look of understanding shaping his features. "Very well."

She squeezed his shoulder before making her way to Rennick and Markarian, who were still fending off Dominic's troops.

"Ready?" Rennick asked, pressing his back against the desk as she approached.

"Ready."

"Markarian?"

"Let's do it!"

Rennick nodded sharply. "We're heading back out the decontamination chamber that we used to enter this place. Countdown in three—"

Caldera readied herself to sprint toward the only other exit out of the chamber, her fingers tightening around her blaster.

"Two—"

Her body surged with exhilaration at their unspoken bond, and at the thought that the team she had missed so fiercely was still working despite being more split up than ever this past year.

"One!"

"Rush!" she said, jolting to her feet and bounding over a desk.

Shots filled the area as she focused all her energy on running. Blasts from indiscriminate weapons blew chunks of metal and computer parts into the air all around her and she continued to push forward, trusting that Rennick and Markarian were close by. Another blast hit the tiled floor right next to her foot, sending a shockwave up her leg, but she didn't slow down as her heart pounded against her ribcage, nearing her target.

Just a little closer. I'm almost there. I'm almost—

A hot, stinging sensation gripped her arm, jerking her sideways and causing her to let go of her blaster, sending it clattering across the floor and out of sight.

She gasped, catching herself and falling to her knees as a wave of hot burning pain coursed through her entire being, emanating from her bicep, as if a large needle was slowly being pushed into her skin. Clambering behind a desk for cover, her other hand instinctively raised to clamp over the injury without her brain having to tell it to perform the action.

Letting out an involuntary scream from deep within her

throat, Caldera glanced over at the blood that was pooling between her fingers, surging from the fresh gunshot wound.

"Callie!"

Before she could catch her breath, Rennick was next to her, tying a piece of his mangled shirt around her arm as Markarian continued forward, opening the decontamination chamber doors.

Rennick gazed into her eyes with such intensity that she had to gasp for air.

"You're gonna be okay," he said, wrapping the shirt once more around her arm.

His voice was stern, as if he was commanding her to be alright. Caldera only nodded, unable to look away.

He took a deep, shuddering breath, compounded concern shining in his eyes. "This is gonna hurt," he said as he simultaneously pulled the makeshift wrap as tightly as he could.

Caldera screamed. Involuntary tears stung her eyes and freely rolled down her cheeks as Rennick continued to tighten the wrap. *Why is this hurting so much?*

The simple question popped into her head before she could push it away as the realization dawned on her. She had never been shot before. Attacked by a rock monster, yes. Caught in an explosion causing her cheek to be sliced open, yes. But never *shot*.

She used to be a Vanguard explorer after all, and while danger was assumed, it wasn't a certainty, or even expected most of the time.

She slumped against Rennick's chest, fighting off the blackness that began to surround the outside of her vision. The sensations were almost unbearable—the searing pain, the sudden numbness, the unrelenting pressure—it was worse than she ever could've imagined.

"Come on," Markarian called, waving them forward while offering cover fire. "Hurry the fuck up!"

She threw her good arm over Rennick's shoulder, leaving the injured one dangling at her side and dripping blood, and tried to stand. Her knees shook, barely able to hold her up.

"Hold on," Rennick whispered, scooping her into his arms and sprinting the rest of the way to the decontamination chamber.

The doors whisked closed behind them, automatically starting the sterilization process.

After the initial rush of air and blast of antiseptic, the lasers reappeared, giving them enough time to recuperate.

Caldera took a few shaky breaths, clutching on to Rennick's shoulder as if he were the only thing keeping her tethered to reality. He stood still, his arms wrapped around her—cradling her body against his, his fingers from one hand dug into her back, while the other gripped her knee. He showed no signs of letting her down.

"Let me have a look, Cal," Markarian said, as the lasers made their second pass over their bodies. His voice was uncharacteristically cold and calculating—his face a stoic mask. He was clearly trying hard to hide what he was truly feeling.

Caldera lifted her numb arm toward him. *At least the pain has subsided.*

He gingerly pulled the wrapping away to look at the wound. "Passed through clean," he said carefully, replacing the makeshift bandage. "You're gonna be fine. The bleeding has already stopped." He gripped her hand, a mixture of fear and relief drifting behind his eyes.

Her head swam. *This is Markarian? Giving me advice?* "Good..." she said, her voice weak.

Markarian nodded sharply before turning and walking to the door, readying his blaster at the entrance as the lasers began their third and final cycle before releasing them from their radioactive prison.

Caldera looked up at Rennick, his face glowing in the red light. "Ren..." she whispered, reaching up and cupping his face, her hand covered in now dried blood. Her blood.

Rennick covered her hand with his, pressing it firmly against his cheek. "You need to go back," he said, his voice stern and his body shaking. "Markarian and I can handle things here."

"No... the mission—"

"You're *my* mission, Callie, and I can't keep going here until I know you're safe... Losing you would mean losing everything to me."

She stared into his eyes. The concern, care, and love she found there was so powerful she couldn't help but nod, for once unable to protest. "Okay... I trust you."

"Mei, John," Rennick said, already pressing his finger to his ear, "Callie's coming back. She's wounded."

"Umm..." Mei started, her tone uncharacteristically monotone. "That's a problem..."

"What is it?" Caldera asked, finding her voice.

"You left the B.E.C.S. mechanism with Saro right?"

"Yes."

"Well, your personal S.G.T. device... is broken."

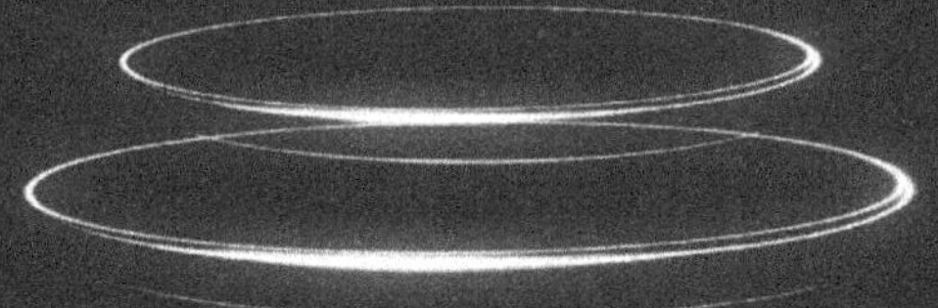

"Y**ou're fucking kidding me!"** Rennick snarled, removing his earpiece and throwing it to the ground, shattering it into tiny pieces. His grip tightened around her, body shaking.

Caldera sucked in a surprised breath as she unhooked her S.G.T. from her exo-suit. It was indeed broken; the screen flashed white, blinking the words 'connection lost' in her face.

It must've broken when I fell.

She wriggled herself out of Rennick's arms, setting unsteady feet on the ground as the final decontamination cycle finished up. "Ren, look at me," she said, gripping his arms. "This may be the worst situation we've ever been in."

"Callie, actually talking sense? I think she's lost too much blood," Markarian said, walking over to them. "She's delirious."

Caldera exhaled sharply, ignoring him. "It's true... But when has that ever stopped us?" She swallowed hard, the pain in her arm a low, constant *throb*. "This past year has been... difficult and we're facing the consequences of our actions every day, but we've never given up. So please, for the love of the fucking universe, let's not start now... Because I'm not gonna stop. Not until things are set right." She took a deep breath, her body and mind finally accepting the past and knowing what she wanted for the future. "*That's* who I am."

Rennick and Markarian glanced at each other before a wry laugh escaped both their lips.

Markarian ran a hand through his bunned hair. "Here, you'll need a blaster," he said, handing Caldera his weapon.

"What about you?"

"I've been taking Krav Maga lessons from John," he replied, stretching his neck. "Let's see if I've learned anything."

Caldera's eyes met Rennick's.

"We can't go back to get the B.E.C.S. device... I know that, but that doesn't mean I have to like it," Rennick said, his features hard as stone.

Caldera nodded slowly, taking a step toward him. "Ren, do yourself a favor and try to embrace the positives of the situation."

"Which are?"

"No matter what happens, this facility is going up in flames," she said, holding up a hand and clenching it into a fist.

"You're impossible," he said, tucking a loose strand of hair behind her ear.

"Would you have me any other way?"

He smirked. "Wouldn't dream of it."

The decontamination door slid open and the three readied themselves for another altercation, but the hallway was suspiciously empty.

"Bailey said this place is designed like a big circle," Caldera said, stepping into the fluorescent light of the hall and making her way down it, staunchly ignoring the fact that her entire arm from the bicep down and half of her exo-suit were plastered with blood. "As long as Bruna and Saro hold Dominic and his team off, and we work clockwise through each chamber, we should avoid the most dangerous confrontations."

"Unless Barrett is coming to cut us off," Rennick added, keeping pace beside her.

"And I'm willing to bet he is," Markarian said from behind them. "Dominic saw us escape and probably alerted him."

"Then we'll have to work fast," Caldera replied, forcing herself to pick up her pace. "Before they can make it around to cut us off."

They ran past the elevator they had come down on and didn't stop until they were at the entrance of another chamber. The words 'Technology and Development' were engraved over the decontamination chamber doors and the three sighed simultaneously as they stepped inside, activating the harmful rays.

After the decontamination process, the doors opened to an eerily vacant area that looked like it had been evacuated in a hurry. The words 'Network Reboot', followed by a string of letters and numbers blinked across every black computer terminal on every disarrayed desk and error messages flashed on the giant, wall-mounted screens.

Broken glass from beakers and other ruined science equipment crunched under Caldera's boots as she, Rennick, and Markarian advanced into the room.

"It's almost the same as the holding cell chamber," Markarian whispered, as if raising his voice would somehow cause soldiers to appear out of nowhere and attack them.

"Except instead of plain computer desks, they're lab desks," Rennick replied, his eyes darting from side to side, trying to clear the room as fast as possible.

Caldera stopped walking, taking in the area for herself. The desks were all clumped together like they were in a science class.

"I'm no computer expert, but it looks like the individual computers are connected to these larger screens," Rennick said, pointing to the flat black rectangles hanging from the ceiling.

"Probably so when a scientist team discovers something, they put it up there for everyone to see and work off of," Markarian scoffed.

So no one has the privacy to work on something that isn't sanctioned by Evie... "Speaking of," Caldera said, pointing to one of the large screens that was still operational. "Look!"

Rennick and Markarian followed her finger to see a 3D rendering of a platform slowly rotating in a circle on the screen. Labels detailed each part of the blueprint of the mechanism.

"That's what I saw in the Penkith swamp," Caldera said. "Right before I was pushed into the water."

Rennick squinted up at the words on the screen, reading the labels out loud. "'Soldiers here—ten total per platform. Storage cells—five total per platform—one specimen each. Toroidal propellers—underneath for hovering purposes'."

Caldera tried, and failed, to hold in a visceral gag at the word 'specimen'. "We were right," she muttered. "That's how they've been abducting so many inhabitants at once."

"And apparently there's more than one of these platform things too," Markarian added. "They could send as many of these out as they're able, at the same time, to completely different sectors."

All three of their faces fell as the pieces of the puzzle continued to fall into place.

Caldera grimaced. *These people are going to pay... How could this get any worse?* Those thoughts were running through her head when she caught sight of a completely enclosed and windowed laboratory within the area.

"John, are Grey and Sylvie back yet?" Markarian asked into his earpiece. "We're ready to start setting bombs."

Caldera tilted her head and made her way over to the sealed off lab space, ignoring them and taking the communication device out of her ear as it crackled to life with John's response. Peering into the area, she saw not only a lab table like the others on one side of the room, but a bed and other basic amenities as well. "What is this?" she whispered, walking over to the entrance door.

It was locked from the outside. Furrowing her brows, Caldera shot the lock, disabling it. Rennick and Markarian said something she didn't hear as she stepped into the isolated room.

The desk was neat and tidy, as was everything else. Caldera walked over to the computer screen—it wasn't wiped, and she pressed the spacebar, awakening the screen from its sleep. A blank bar blinked in her face requesting a password.

"Fuck—"

"Hey, Grey and Sylvie are waiting for instructions. What is this?" Rennick asked, walking up to Caldera.

She shrugged. "My thoughts exactly."

He glanced around the room. "No luck with the computer?"

"I can't hack it, and Sear better be back on Bersama by now."

"He is. Grey and Sylvie are here with the B.E.C.S. device, but since it's the only one, that means Saro, Bruna, and... the human—"

"Bailey."

"—are trapped until they meet up with us again."

"Saro and Bruna could leave him behind. They have S.G.T. devices after all."

"Do you think they would though?"

She shook her head. "We need to act quickly—"

A male voice came from behind them. "You don't need to hack it. We'll unlock it for you."

"In exchange for your help," a female voice added.

Caldera and Rennick whirled, blasters drawn, ready to shoot down any opposition.

The sight that met Caldera's eyes froze her body in a way she never expected.

She *expected* to feel something—anything. Surprise. Horror. Relief. Happiness. Anything. But there was nothing.

She felt nothing. Even the pain in her arm had completely gone away. She was empty as words she hadn't spoken in over a decade escaped her lips.

"Mom? Dad?"

THE TWO STRANGERS STARED AT Caldera, seeming not to comprehend the words that had left her mouth. The woman's platinum-white hair was pulled into a tight bun on the top of her head and the man blinked dark blue eyes in her direction. A thick metal apparatus adorned each of their necks.

The woman grabbed the man's arm, covering her mouth as if to hold in a gasp, eyes widening. "*You're* the one that's causing all this chaos?"

They both took a step forward, and Caldera instinctively took a step back, knocking into the desk behind her.

"Sta-stay back," Rennick said, holding out his hand to them as if he were trying to block their movement. He turned toward Caldera. "Callie... talk to me."

"This isn't real..." Caldera whispered, unable to take her eyes off the people in front of her. "You're," her voice caught, "dead."

The woman released the man's arm and clasped her hands in front of her, gaze falling to the floor. "We have been, for a long time, ever since we were forced to come here..." Her tinny voice tapered off with a gasp as tears filled her eyes.

The man ran a hand through his graying black hair. "There's nothing we can say. No excuse that will fix anything," he said, his voice deep, blue eyes shining. "I'm sorry, CJ."

Caldera Jin Keane. CJ. The only person who's ever used that nickname was... Dad.

Caldera gripped the desk-top behind her until her fingernails dug into the metal and placed her other hand over her face, closing her eyes against the rush of tears, futilely trying to contain them.

The pain was coming back, in her body, her arm, her mind—everywhere—racking her very being.

Her parents had been gone for so long, and the pain of their passing had been buried so deep and deliberately ignored, she wondered if the tears would ever stop.

Arms awkwardly wrapped around her in a way that was distantly familiar—trying to comfort her as if she were still a child. Opening her eyes, Caldera stared up into the faces in front of her. Their eyes were red and puffy with tear trails staining their cheeks. Soft smiles broke across their faces, and she didn't have to see herself to know she looked exactly the same.

"Cal," Markarian's voice started, jolting her back to the current reality, before cutting off. "Who are these people?"

Caldera sniffed, wiping her eyes and cheeks. "Vega and Reed. My parents."

"Holy shit…"

"I know," she said, taking a step toward Rennick and hugging him tightly, desperate for his comfort. After a few seconds she took a shaky breath, eyeing her parents, still not believing they were there. "Let's go."

The pair looked at each other and then back to Caldera before her father spoke. "We can't leave this chamber."

"This room was built for us," Vega said. "We live here."

It was like her heart was being ripped out all over again. "Why can't you leave?"

"These," Reed said, pointing to the metal apparatus around his neck.

Rennick took a step forward. "What are they?"

"A means to make sure we never even think about escaping," Reed replied.

"It will automatically kill us," Vega added in a soft voice.

Caldera's heartbeat ricocheted off her ribs. "We have to get them off. We could… shoot them off."

"No. No, we're not," Rennick said, patting his hands in the air toward the wide eyes of Reed and Vega. "Don't worry, Mr. and Mrs. Keane, we aren't going to *shoot* them off."

"Then what?" Caldera snapped. "We don't have time for this."

"If you've been living here, you can log in to this computer, right?" Markarian asked, turning to Reed.

"Of course, and I said I would."

"Then how about we call in some backup?" he continued, holding up the B.E.C.S. portal-link.

SEAR'S NEWLY BANDAGED FINGERS TAPPED away on the keyboard, crowded by Reed and Vega, as Rennick and Markarian kept watch at the door and Caldera impatiently tapped her foot.

It had only taken seconds for Markarian to contact Mei and John and to have them send Sear back to Earth, but the time they were wasting in the chamber continued to eat at her.

Over an hour had passed. Grey and Sylvie had finished placing the bombs and were waiting at the far decontamination doors for further instructions.

"We need to get to the last chamber," Caldera said, unable to hold it in any longer.

"If you must go, then go," Sear said over his shoulder, his fingers never slowing down.

"I'm not leaving until my parents are free and you're back on Bersama!" Caldera snapped, clenching her jaw.

"Then try to be patient. The system of Area 51 is complicated, and I want to make sure I am hacking into the correct program."

"This is true mastery of a computer system," Reed said. "Amazing."

"*This* is nothing," Markarian countered from the doorway. "You're looking at the creator of portal tech."

"One of *many*. It was a group effort—"

"Focus," Caldera said, trying to keep her voice low and controlled.

Her parents blinked over at her as if surprised by her outburst.

She sighed and ushered them away from Sear's back. Swallowing hard, she forced herself to ask the question that had been pounding against the inside of her mind from the moment she saw them. "Why are you here?"

Reed blew out a breath. "In essence, we were betrayed."

"By who?"

"Vandren," Vega replied.

Searing heat coursed through Caldera's body. "How, and why, were you working with him in the first place?"

"We're a weapons specialist and an environmentalist," Vega answered. "When the councilmember representing Tellis approached us and asked for our skillset... we thought we were helping Bersama."

"By teaming up with Area 51? By stealing resources from another planet? Or were you making weapons for them to help the proposed *invasion* of Earth?" Words were spilling out before she could stop or moderate them.

My parents were helping these people. They were helping to destroy Bersama...

"No!" Vega said, placing a hand on Caldera's arm, which she jerked away. "I thought I was hired to help create sustainable avenues for Tellis and the other sectors to explore, and that Reed was hired so he could create better weapons and tools for the Vanguard explorers to use when they were out in the galaxy searching for other planets."

"And when we found out about what they were really planning... Well, that's how we ended up here," Reed continued.

"But he... Vandren..." Caldera shook her head. "He said you were dead..." Her eyes widened. "No... he didn't." *He never outright said, 'your parents are dead'. I said that, and he never corrected me. That bastard!* "He said your lives were ended."

Reed nodded solemnly. "They were."

"You've been helping these psychopaths?"

"We—"

"Did you know they've been kidnapping and murdering inhabitants of Bersama? Did you know they've been experimenting on them?"

"Caldera—"

"These people are trying to start a war on their *own planet,* and you're helping them!"

"We didn't have a choice!"

"No. Don't give me that bullshit! You're complacent. There's always a choice!" Caldera yelled, unable to contain even a fraction of her rage. "It's just the right one didn't have a favorable outcome for you... So you ignored it."

"You'd rather us die?"

"I thought you *were* dead!" Caldera screamed. "I'd rather you have done what's right!"

The familiar sound of Sear snapping his fingers—or, at least trying to—met Caldera's ears, as well as a click resounding from her parents' necks.

"Mr. and Mrs. Keane, you may remove your shackles."

Her parents tore off the metal collars that were around their necks, revealing years of scar tissue, and threw the devices on the ground.

"Markarian, get my parents out of here," Caldera said, her voice low.

He nodded, wordlessly ushering them forward and activating the portal-link. The two disappeared, sent back to a home they would most likely barely recognize.

"Okay, genius," Markarian said, turning to Sear, "your turn again."

Sear patted Caldera's shoulder before stepping forward. "You know, they really were in danger, Callie. The substances contained in those collars were sodium thiopental, pancuronium bromide, and potassium chloride."

Caldera let out a dry chuckle. "What?"

"They are chemicals used in lethal injections."

"They still knew what was going on here... Th-they should be held accountable."

"Perhaps, but being scared of death is not a crime, and neither is wanting to protect the ones you love," Sear continued, turning toward Markarian and taking the portal-link. "All I am saying is they may not be as cowardly as you are beginning—or *wanting*—to believe."

Caldera absently rubbed her arm as Sear disappeared. She knew he was right, she shouldn't be so hard on them—they're her parents and they're alive. They were trying to survive within the circumstances they were dealt, she knew that, but the pain was too much.

Once I get a chance to talk to them... Then maybe...

"You okay?" Rennick asked, walking up and pulling her into his chest.

"I will be."

"Come on, we still have another chamber to prep," Markarian said, waving them toward where Grey and Sylvie were waiting.

CHAPTER 38

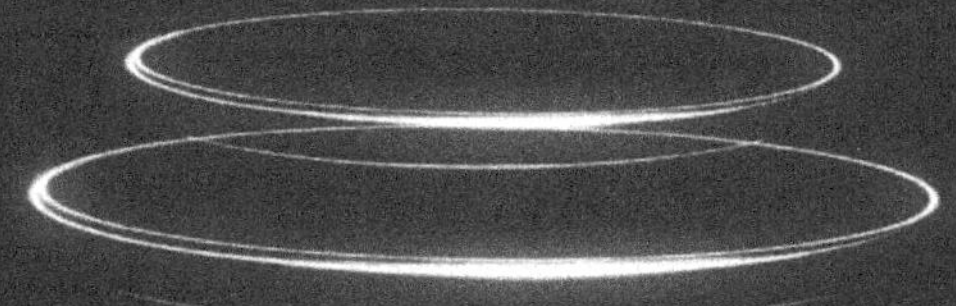

The group raced down the next hallway with Markarian, Grey, and Sylvie in the lead. Caldera trailed behind, her mind swirling like a tornado, her blaster all but glued to her white-knuckled hand as she forced herself to keep pace with them.

The fact that there was still no sign of resistance tugged at her thoughts as she defiantly kept her gaze straight ahead, avoiding Rennick's cautious and numerous glances, as if she were one step, one lung, one breath away from crumbling into dust.

Within minutes, they arrived at the last chamber, the wording above the door reading 'Interrogation and Experimentation'.

"This is it," Caldera said, her stomach turning as she and the group stepped into the all-to-familiar decontamination chamber.

After the cycle, the doors opened to a blast and constant gun fire.

There's the resistance. Damn it! Caldera's mind swirled as Rennick, Grey, and Sylvie returned fire. Her arm ached with phantom pain as she joined the firefight.

"Hit!" Sylvie called out, taking the opportunity to duck through the open doors and into the room.

"Follow her!" Caldera commanded, pointing to Rennick and Grey. "We have to push forward!"

They did as she said, and she found herself hiding behind yet another desk as the gunfire ceased.

"Caldera Keane," Barrett's voice called over the dead air. "It sure took you long enough to get here."

"I was a little preoccupied," she replied, peeking over the desk, taking advantage of the stillness, and dropping two more soldiers with quick blaster shots.

She was unable to see where Barrett himself was hiding, but recognized that it seemed like there were only about seven soldiers with him.

"Ahh yes, very unfortunate. Your life, that is... Too bad it's about to get a lot worse." He clapped his hands together, the sound echoing off the walls. "Find them. Kill them. And bring them to me. In that order."

A myriad of voices chanted in response. "Yes sir!"

"Split!" Caldera commanded, as the shootout commenced.

The group broke apart, scattering in all different directions. They were faster, much faster, and stronger than the Earth soldiers, despite them having automatic weapons.

Caldera's mind flashed to what Bailey had said about Area 51 wanting to enhance the people of Earth, and she could see why.

She weaved her way around desks, popping up behind a soldier whose focus was on Rennick and shooting him in the back. Her injured arm throbbed as she dove to the ground, avoiding a mass of bullets, and crawled forward.

The coolness of the tiled floor seeped into the skin of her exposed injured arm while the exosuit protected the rest of her body against the chill.

The smell of antiseptic hit her nose, reminding her of one of her many bouts in Astrum's hospital as the commotion above her continued. Mysterious brown and black stains met her eyes, unable to be scrubbed away, as she continued inching across the floor. Knowing what chamber she was in, she didn't want to let herself think about what they could be.

Reaching her target, she swiped another soldier's legs out from underneath him just as he noticed her, causing his gun to fire into the air as he landed on his back. Caldera rose, instantaneously jumping over his disoriented body and shooting him as she did so. Moving on to another assailant, she let out a shriek as she tackled them to the ground, grabbing their uniform, and unceremoniously blasting them under their chin.

Markarian's voice boomed through the room as he rushed forward, avoiding gunfire and grabbing the arm of a soldier, redirecting their weapon, and flipping them over his back. "Clear!"

The noise of the fight died down. No more weapons were being fired.

Caldera took a deep, shuddering breath, glancing behind her at the wake of bodies she had left. Another pang surged through her body at the thought that her blaster was only set to stun.

"Where's Barrett?" she asked, gingerly getting to her feet and surveying the surrounding area.

"We lost sight of him and he escaped," Markarian replied, walking over to her. "There must be a secret door or passage into this chamber."

Her blood began to boil. "Fuck! We could have used him as…" Her sentence trailed off as she finally processed the full view of the horrors in the chamber.

The outer walls were lined with pods that were barely big enough to stand in, with a temperature control device on the outside. It appeared whoever was observing the victims could change the severity one way or another. She closed her eyes, instantly wondering how many Bersamans had been frozen to death or suffered fatal heat-stroke in those very capsules. Bile began to rise in her throat again, but she pushed it down.

Multiple metal beds were bolted into the floor with sharp, three-pronged arms ending in sharp needle-points dangling above them in another corner, while numerous gurneys littered the room. Small tables covered in various tools—archaic medical equipment—stood beside each one.

Caldera tentatively walked up to a gurney that no doubt had once held a struggling, scared inhabitant of Bersama, and couldn't hold in a gasp when she saw that the straps were stained with blood. "Let's burn this place to the fucking ground," she whispered, clenching her hands into fists. "Come on!"

After tying up the unconscious bodies of the soldiers and gathering their discarded weapons into a pile, the next ten minutes were filled with furious work to set the explosives; the group eager to move on to Evie's office and confront her. Mournful silence filled the space as no one spoke to each other, using it as a moment of silence for all the victims the chamber had taken.

It was all that they could do until the explosives went off and freed not only Bersama, but Earth as well, from the plague of Area 51.

The only glimmer of hope Caldera held on to was that at least they didn't find Aloriea in that chamber—but it didn't mean she hadn't been there. "Only one more place to go," she said, as the group gathered by the far decontamination chamber doors. "Grey, let's get going." She took a few steps toward him, waving her hand in a 'hurry up' motion.

"Just one more second... Done!"

Grey stood up from his crouched position to face her after setting the last bomb and was immediately shot in the head.

CHAPTER 39

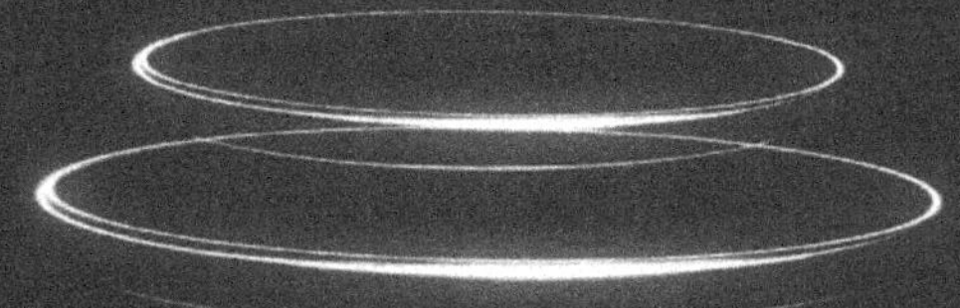

Blood sprayed across Caldera's face. Time seemed to slow as she processed what had happened before being dragged to the ground by Rennick.

Sylvie screamed and rushed forward, firing her blaster indiscriminately toward the reappeared Barrett.

"Sylvie, wait!" Caldera pleaded, reaching her hand out toward the frantic woman and trying not to look at Grey.

"Go!" she commanded, grabbing her brother's lifeless body and dragging it behind cover with her in futility. "Fucking go!"

"Come on!" Markarian yelled as the doors opened.

Rennick dragged Caldera into the chamber as Sylvie successfully got a hit on Barrett that looked like it would eventually bleed out, but it was in vain. She looked on in horror as Sylvie was gunned down as the door cycled closed.

As soon as the doors opened, Caldera ran. Her stomach was turning over on itself, threatening to empty its contents at any second as the scene of what she had witnessed played over and over in her mind. She gritted her teeth, forcing the rapidly rising bile down her aching throat. The mission was almost over; all they had to do was get to Evie's office, find Aloriea, and set the remainder of the bombs.

She didn't have time to wallow in sorrow, or regret—sorrow for the loss of two young people that had died prematurely under her watch, and regret for not getting to know them better while they were alive.

Her arms and legs pumped, lungs burning as she tore down the hallway, completely unwilling to confront what had happened, as if she could forget simply by running fast enough.

As Caldera began to round the corner, Rennick and Markarian grabbed each of her arms, jerking her back just in time to avoid being gunned down herself, pressing her against the wall as a storm of bullets battered its edge. She yelped, jerking her injured arm away from Markarian's clutches to see that it had started bleeding again.

"Damn it," she huffed, her chest rising and falling rapidly as she tried to catch her breath.

"We need to come up with a plan," Markarian said, pressing his back against the wall beside her.

Rennick followed suit, glancing down at his blaster. "I'm out of plasma bolts; we haven't been able to refill our blasters since we've been here."

Caldera's eyes widened, and she looked down at her own weapon. *Four, maybe five shots left.* Closing her eyes, she leaned her head back against the wall.

"What can we do?" Markarian continued. "There's way too many of them.

Caldera exhaled slowly, the events of the past few hours beginning to play over in her head as she opened her eyes. "This is what we do," she said, deftly reaching into the pack of explosives, pulling one out, and disconnecting it from the relay chain.

She pressed the button down on the top of the bomb, waited three seconds and threw it as hard as she could around the corner toward the gunfire.

"Ignition," she whispered, covering her ears as the bomb detonated.

The explosion shook the hallway, causing debris to rain down from the ceiling and her ears to ring in a high-pitched *trill*. Rennick and Markarian were saying something, but she couldn't hear them, the disorientation completely taking over her body, causing it to go numb. The gritty, fine powder of exploded concrete floated into her nose and coated her shoulders and hair, making her sneeze, followed by the smell of copper blood.

"Callie!" Rennick's words finally got through, snapping her out of her trance and back to reality. "Let's go."

Caldera took the lead as the only one of her group to have a working weapon. Through the dust, they stepped over bloodied bodies, severed limbs and viscera, and various Earth guns, but she was empty—no—she was *glad* they were suffering the same way she was. The realization startled her, but she pushed forward, coming across someone who was somehow still alive. She blasted them.

They coughed as the dust grew thicker.

"Damn. This must be where the detonation originated," Markarian said, waving his hand in the air.

They continued walking until Caldera almost tripped over something. She looked down to see a lifeless body, their head half crushed from fallen concrete.

"Oh fuck," Markarian muttered, covering his mouth.

"Come on," Rennick whispered, guiding them both forward.

Good riddance. Caldera spat as they continued on.

"Look," Rennick said, running forward. "This is it, the elevator that leads up to Evie's office."

A voice called from further down the other side of the hallway. "Ren, is that you?"

"Saro?"

"And Bailey," another voice called.

"You made it," Caldera replied, waiting for them to emerge from the dust cloud. "Did you set the explosives?"

"Yes..." Saro said, as he and Bailey—who was wearing camo

pants he must have taken off a soldier—stepped into sight. "We were barely able to, though. That area was huge."

"You didn't run," Caldera stated, facing Bailey.

"Where would I go?"

"You could've joined them."

"I'd rather join you."

Caldera rolled her eyes, her heart sinking as she realized who was missing. "Where's Bruna?" she asked, forcing the words out of her mouth even though she knew the answer.

"She... didn't make it," Bailey replied, his grief sounding genuine.

Saro hung his head, taking a step forward. "She said..." He paused, his voice catching. "She said she hoped she could tell her father that she 'mended their legacy.'"

Caldera gasped, raising a hand to cover her mouth as tears stung her eyes, threatening to overflow. Guilt bashed against the inside of her chest, wave after wave of remorse coursing through her body. *I hadn't been there... If I had, then maybe—*

She stopped her quickly derailing train of thought. *Self-condemnation isn't going to change anything. It won't honor those who gave their lives for this, it certainly won't help the people I have left, and it won't stop Area 51.*

Setting her jaw, Caldera took a deep breath, locking eyes with Saro. "I hope she knows that she did."

Saro nodded, trying to force a small smile, but failing. "Grey and Sylvie?" he asked, finding his voice.

Markarian and Rennick shook their heads, lowering their gazes to the floor.

Caldera clenched her jaw and attempted to wipe Grey's now dried blood off her face with the cuff of her exo-suit sleeve. "We have to get Aloriea. Now, before it's too late. I'm not losing someone else." She turned her attention to Saro. "You stay down here and guard the elevator entrance, just in case."

He nodded deftly, readying his weapon.

The rest of the group nodded and clambered onto the elevator. It rose four floors, still below the main facility of Area 51, and opened to a beautiful room covered in lush green potted plants, with a 3D image of Earth floating in the middle.

A large, polished, wooden desk sat pressed against one wall and behind that was Evie. Sitting next to her, with a gun to her head, was Aloriea.

"Aloriea!" Caldera couldn't stop herself from calling out to her friend.

Aloriea didn't respond; her head was lowered and her shoulders shook. She was crying.

Caldera sucked in a breath, realizing what was also behind the desk, surrounding Evie and Aloriea. Monitors—five in total. Four had recorded what had been going on in each of the chambers and hallways, real-time, and showed the brutal aftermath—and one that was replaying the events of the past six hours.

Evie sucked in a breath, a grotesque grin spreading across her face as she leaned forward. "You're right on time. You may have saved some test subjects, but after successfully killing all my subordinates, I was showing your friend who you really are."

"A savior to the Bersaman people?" Caldera snapped, careful to keep her voice from wavering.

"A murderer," Evie retorted, waving a dismissive hand in the air. "Behind all that bravado and exhausting set of principles, you're no different than us—when it comes down to it, you'll do anything to further your goals."

"I'll do anything to stop you," Caldera agreed, balling one hand into a fist while raising the blaster toward Evie with her other, "but she knows who I really am. The only person here who doesn't, is you."

Evie chuckled, pressing the barrel of her gun against Aloriea's head. "See," she whispered, raising one red manicured hand up and angling it on one side of her mouth toward Aloriea, as if she were sharing a secret. "I told you this is what she'd do. Kill first, ask questions later."

"We'll get you out of this, Lor," Markarian called, his fists balled so tightly that his arms were shaking.

"You might," Evie said, snapping the fingers of her free hand and pointing to Markarian before switching her attention to Caldera. "But that all depends on the queen."

Caldera lowered her blaster immediately.

"Good," Evie said, sporting a wicked smile.

"What the fuck do you want?"

"I want what I'm owed. I want what that *bastard* Vandren promised," she snapped, losing her composure for a brief moment before she returned to a calm and collected demeanor.

"Which is what?"

"Earth. Or, a part of it anyway. I'm not greedy, especially now that my colleagues are dead."

Caldera scoffed. "I can't help you with that. I'm a ruler of Bersama."

Evie waved a nonchalant hand in the air, sighing deeply as if she were annoyed that she had to explain herself. "Yes, but you can help me get technology that will cement my place on this miserable planet."

"You're nuts!" Bailey called out.

"Excuse me, I was talking to the queen," Evie said, her smile growing more dastardly. "Though, are you sure you don't want to switch sides? I could always use someone like you beside me," she continued, eyeing him up and down as if he were an object.

Bailey fidgeted with the Earth weapon he held before lowering it uncomfortably to his side, eyes darting back and forth.

"Hey!" Caldera yelled, successfully snapping Evie's attention back to her. "I thought *we* were talking," she said, stepping forward. " Fine... let's make a deal."

"Callie," Rennick said, taking her arm. "Don't do this."

"Ren," she whispered, turning completely to face him. "Are you with me?"

A soft smile spread across his face, which he quickly hid, running his hand down her arm before releasing his grip. "Always."

"Well?" Evie questioned, tapping long nails across the tabletop.

"Let Aloriea go, and we can negotiate."

"Make your entourage disappear," she countered, waving behind Caldera in a shooing motion.

"Fine." Caldera turned to her friends. "You heard her."

Nobody moved.

Caldera eyed Rennick and Markarian. "Go," she said, motioning with her eyes toward the elevator. *Please let them get the hint. Reappear at the bottom and ride back up with Saro. I'll distract her until then.*

Markarian raised his eyebrows, nodding subtly. "Okay," he said, pulling out the portal-link and activating it. He locked eyes with Rennick and Bailey. "Come on."

One by one, they disappeared through their personalized portals, and Bailey through the B.E.C.S. device, leaving Caldera and Aloriea alone with Evie.

"All right," Caldera snapped, realizing that Aloriea, at least for the moment, had no way of getting back to Bersama—just like her. "Let her go."

Evie smiled, laying the gun down on the table and motioning for Aloriea to stand.

Aloriea sprinted over to Caldera and wrapped her arms around her. "I'm so sorry," she sobbed. "I never should have come here alone. I wanted to find Sear so badly that I... I'm so sorry—everything you went through, I—"

"Aloriea," Caldera whispered, rubbing her friends back. "It's okay," she said, squeezing Aloriea's hands before turning back to Evie. "Now, stand over there until we can get you home. Please."

Aloriea's body shook as she exhaled, meeting Caldera's eyes. Her resolve seemed to harden as she nodded, stepping to the side and out of the way, pressing her back against the wall.

"See, I can keep my word," Evie said, interlacing her fingers, she was turned away from the monitors that were still active, her focus completely on Caldera. "Now it's just me and you."

Caldera couldn't hold in a laugh as she saw her friends ascending the elevator on the monitor behind Evie's distracted head. "I wouldn't say that."

As if on cue, the elevator doors opened again and Rennick, Markarian, and Saro ran out—they still didn't have blasters, but it didn't matter. She had one shot left.

Caldera raised the blaster once again at the same time as Evie was lifting her gun, never standing from her seat.

"It seems we have a stalemate then."

"Seems so."

Rennick, Markarian, and Saro quickly set the rest of the explosives around Evie's office as the two women pointed their weapons at each other.

Neither said a word.

"Done," Rennick said.

"If you do this, you'll be killing all the innocent people up above," Evie snarled.

Caldera hesitated. Rennick's words rang in her head again. *There might be innocent people in that facility.* Before, when she was consumed by anger, she hadn't cared who got in the way, as long as the facility got destroyed.

Thinking clearly, more than anything, she didn't want to admit that Evie was right... but she was.

Swallowing hard, Caldera squared her shoulders. *We're down to our last-ditch effort.*

She was calm.

She was being rational.

And she was facing what she was about to do head-on.

"There's no other way."

A flash of silence passed between them as their eyes met.

"So be it," Evie whispered, leaping to her feet, pressing her foot against the desk, and pushing it forward as hard as she could in a flash.

It rammed into Caldera's legs, causing her to fall to the floor and the last blaster shot to go off, hitting one of the bombs and damaging the signal relay. They all turned red, beginning to count down.

CHAPTER 40

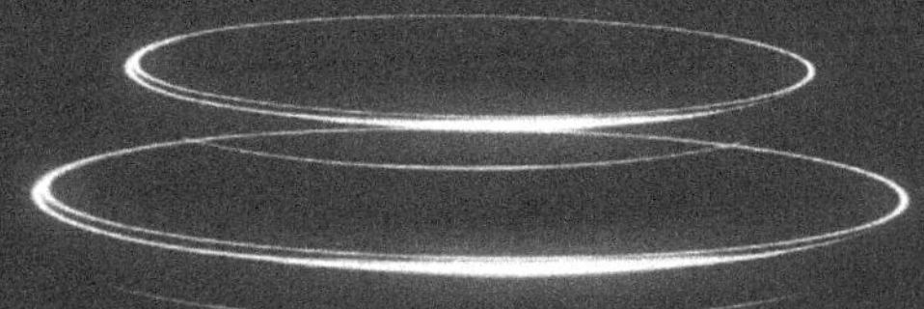

"*Five,*" the robotic voice of the signal relay chimed.

Time slowed. She was on her knees, watching the last few seconds of her life in the universe play out before her.

Rennick lunged toward the bomb, but tumbled to the ground before he could reach it. "My prosthetic leg! Fuck! I can't move it!" He continued to claw at the ground inching himself forward.

He won't get to it in time. For a moment, everything was still, and Caldera could completely assess the situation.

The mission was botched.

She was going to die.

Rennick was going to die.

Markarian was going to die.

Aloriea was going to die.

Her breath was so shallow that she could barely breathe, not wanting to accept the facts of the situation. *What's so different about this time... I've accepted it once before—or, no...I guess I hadn't, not really.* When she destroyed the portal that the councilmembers had made, there had been a part of her that selfishly assumed she would live—that she would still be able to save everyone.

"Four."

But there was nothing to be done. Nothing that *could* be done. She had tried everything in her power to save her friends, her people, her planet, even Earth; and the only thing she accomplished in doing so was destroying this facility, along with passing minor laws on Bersama that, in the end, most likely wouldn't amount to anything.

I can't die! I have so much left to do. The thought struck her with such force that the remaining air her lungs were desperately holding onto was knocked out of her. Caldera gasped, switching her focus to Rennick while Markarian went after Evie—who was trying to escape in a hidden elevator behind her desk.

Dropping down next to Rennick, who was gripping his knee, she helped him into a sitting position.

"Three."

Fleeting thoughts swirled around in her head. Pushing away the failure of trying to rule a sector, she had accepted that, and landed on the one person she wished she would have spared in the beginning. Rennick.

He had a family—his younger brother, who had recently graduated university and had joined the workforce. Willix, who had already been through the pain of losing his only sibling once, would be forced to relive that experience, but it would be real. She was depriving another person of someone they could rely on. Someone they cared about.

Caldera's breath staggered in her throat, and she squeezed her eyes shut.

She was a scourge to the one person who had always been by her side. She was stealing him away from his family... She was stealing him away from his *life.*

And for what? Because I loved him? I'm selfish... Reckless.

She blinked. That was the crux of it.

She *was* reckless. Reckless with her dreams. Reckless with her goals. Reckless with her love. She was trying to get better—to think before acting, but that hadn't changed.

Maybe it never would.

"Two."

I accept that, but I've done some things right...haven't I? Caldera's eyes shot open. *'Being reckless in-and-of itself doesn't have to be a bad thing.'* Rennick's past words blasted through her self-loathing. *'Think about it like this. Forget the general definition, it's not about that. It's about how you use it... Callie, whether you realize it or not, because of your reckless tenacity, you've already done great things for Bersama. For everyone. I hope one day you'll realize that.'* She wiped tear-stained cheeks and stared at the man she loved. *Okay... Maybe he's right...*

Caldera wrapped her arms around Rennick's torso and closed her eyes, her fingers digging into his back, accepting whatever was to come. "I love you, Ren. I always have, and I always will."

He squeezed her tight. "I love you too, Callie."

"On—"

Saro scrambled to the bomb and pressed down on the button, stopping the countdown with less than a second left.

Caldera and Rennick let out a simultaneous strangled gasp as Evie wriggled out of Markarian's reach and bounced away toward the elevator only to be met with a chair to the face courtesy of Aloriea, who had run along the perimeter of the room to cut her off.

"Take that, you bitch," Aloriea snarled, her brown eyes fiery.

Evie gasped for air on the floor as Markarian crouched next to her to hold her in place.

The whole struggle was over in five seconds.

"Holy shit, Lor," Markarian said as Aloriea dropped the chair, surprise coating every feature of his face.

"What? Are you going to make me stand trial on Bersama?" Evie spat, struggling in Markarian's grip again.

Caldera stood up, her legs shaking, built up adrenaline coursing through her body. "I don't think so," she muttered, walking over to a monitor and ripping the cords out of the wall.

She bent down and tied Evie's hands behind her back, fastening her to the overturned table. "You're going down with this ship."

"Wait. Wait!" Evie begged, wriggling an arm free and holding it up to Caldera. "I have information—information you need."

"You're pathetic," Aloriea grated, stalking forward.

Caldera held up a hand. "What could you possibly have that I would want?" she retorted.

"Project Phoenix. I know what it is, and more importantly *who* it is."

"Phoenix is a person?"

Evie nodded. "You won't figure it out without me... So, what do you say, do we have a deal? You take me back to Bersama, and I'll tell you? Otherwise, you're all doomed."

Caldera looked at each of her friends, their expressions telling her everything she needed to know. "We'll take our chances," she said, slamming her elbow against the side of the woman's head and knocking her out.

She turned to Markarian and Aloriea, giving them a quick hug each. "Go back to Bersama."

He furrowed his brows, looking like he wanted to say something.

"Come on," she said, forcing a chuckle. "Are you really gonna fight me over this? We've done that before and... you lost."

Markarian let out a broken laugh. "I get it, Cal," he said, placing a hand on her shoulder. "Come home soon, okay?" He turned to Aloriea, handing her a brand new, personalized, S.G.T. device. "I grabbed it from Sear in the brief minute we went back; he fixed it. Let's get you home."

"I'd like that," she muttered, pressing her finger to the screen to successfully link her body's specific signature to the device, and rubbing her arms as if she were cold. Her somber, exhausted eyes met Caldera. "Thank you, Callie. For everything..."

Caldera pulled her into another hug. "Don't thank me Aloriea... Just take care of yourself." She pulled away and turned back toward Markarian. "Take Ren with you. His leg is busted, and it needs servicing."

"Sure thing," he said, taking a step toward Rennick where he still sat on the floor.

Rennick held up a hand. "Don't even think about it."

Markarian chuckled. "And you think *she's* impossible?" he said, hooking a thumb at Caldera. He shook his head when Rennick didn't respond. "Both of you better come back," he said, tossing Rennick the B.E.C.S. portal-link he retrieved from Bailey and activating his personal S.G.T. device while helping Aloriea with her own.

They both waved as they simultaneously disappeared.

Without a word, Caldera walked over to Saro. "Switch places with me."

Rennick's eyes widened. "Callie!"

Saro shook his head. "I can't do that."

"Saro, that's an order."

"And one that I cannot abide!" He lowered his head. "Callie, this isn't about me. It's not even about this place... It's about Bersama and Earth finally interacting. We've been divided for too long. No more stealing, no more secret facilities. Just, everything out in the open," he said, meeting her blue eyes with his multi-colored ones. "But I'm not the one that can make that happen." He smiled, wiping blood from his split lip. "That's you."

Her eyes filled with tears. "But Saro..."

"It's okay," he said, forcing a laugh. "I'll be with my brother soon."

She whimpered. "I can't let you do this..."

Saro looked past her. "Ren?"

"Callie... he's right," Rennick said, crawling next to them and holding out the portal-link. "Bersama and Earth need to be connected eventually. Once we're back, we can make a plan for that to happen."

She shook her head, helping him to his feet, Saro's words ringing in her ears. "No. If we're doing this, it's going to be now."

"What do you mean?"

Caldera turned toward the elevator that Evie was trying to escape through moments earlier.

"We're making Bersama known to Earth. Tonight." She glanced over at Saro once more as she placed Rennick's arm over her shoulder, steadying him. "Thank you... for everything."

He smiled, readjusting so his back was leaning against the wall, legs spread out in front of him with the explosive in his lap. "It was a pleasure, Your Majesty," he said with a wink. Using his free hand, he tapped his ear. "Let me know when you reach the top."

Caldera nodded, wiping tears from her eyes as she and Rennick hobbled onto the elevator and went up.

After what felt like hours, the elevator opened out into the desert with the Area 51 facility behind them. It was night but the single moon of Earth shone so brightly they could see with no issue.

Caldera gripped Rennicks arm so tightly she thought she might break it, but he didn't flinch, only reciprocated with a death-grip squeeze of his own on her shoulder. Swallowing hard, she pressed a shaky finger to her ear, talking to Saro, Mei, John, and whoever else was listening.

"Blow it."

Within seconds, the ground shook wildly underneath their feet and the entire facility began sinking into the ground.

Caldera held onto Rennick to help him run as well as he could with only one usable leg. A few paces away, the ground they were standing on began to wave, threatening to suck them under.

Hobbling over to a large boulder outside of the explosion radius, they clambered to its peak and watched from a distance as fire flew up from underneath the ground, along with the disorganization of the disoriented armed soldiers that tried in futility to save the decimated facility.

"Hey!" a stern voice called, finally noticing them and pointing a flashlight toward where they were seated, hand-in-hand, on the boulder. "Freeze!" the voice yelled while calling for backup.

The *sting* of radio squeals hit Caldera's ears and soon a group of uniformed soldiers were running toward them.

"Well," Rennick said, tightening his grip on her hand. "This is it."

Caldera nodded. "It is..."

"You think they'll take a look at your arm and my leg?"

"After what we've seen, do we really want them to?" She paused. "You can go if you want," she said, sarcasm coating each word. "Your S.G.T. is still viable."

Rennick smiled, unhooking the device from his exo-suit and carefully looking it over before tossing it over his shoulder into darkness. "Never."

The soldiers got closer and closer, continuing to yell that the 'unidentified people' were going to be detained until 'Section X' arrived, and something about a 'Project Bluebook', but Caldera and Rennick didn't move.

"You know, we still have the Bersaman-Earth portal-link," Rennick said, turning the multi-person portal device over in his hand. "We *could* still escape."

"No." Caldera replied, shaking her head. "We need to make contact. Consider that our... insurance policy, if things start going too far south."

They both breathed in deeply.

Leaning back on her palms, Caldera tipped her head upward, letting the chill of the desert night sink into her skin and observing the twinkling of the star-studded Earthen sky.

How in the world am I going to explain this to the other sector leaders? She almost laughed at the absurdity of it all, how, even in this moment she was still thinking about politics. *Maybe I really have changed...*

Absent-mindedly, she found her thoughts wandering to Vandren. *We couldn't have done this without his knowledge, but what was his plan?* A large flier—a bird—cawed overhead, and the dewy smell of the boulder they were sitting on wafted up to her nose. *What did he get out of all this? And who is Phoenix?...*

The unanswered questions gnawed at her.

"So," Rennick sighed, breaking the silence and briefly leaning back on his hands before beginning to mess with his metal leg. "What should we tell them?"

"The truth," Caldera said, leaning forward and resting her elbows on her knees, eyes gleaming in the light of the moon as the strangers approached. "That we come in peace."

ABBY R. LAUGHLIN

is a science fiction adventure author and an ERA at a veterinary clinic. The Cosmic Principle, the first in the Nexus Series, is her debut novel. Future projects include books two and three of the same series, as well as a prequel and two companion novels set in the same universe. Abby is currently living her life in the Midwest with her cats, lizard, and husband.

W W W . A B B Y R L A U G H L I N . C O M